SURVIVAL

Species Imperative #1

JULIE E. CZERNEDA

DAW BOOKS, INC.

DONALD A. WOLLHEIM, FOUNDER

375 Hudson Street, New York, NY 10014

ELIZABETH R. WOLLHEIM

SHEILA E. GILBERT

PUBLISHERS

For Roger . . .
Because.

- Acknowledgments -

My first hardcover release. An awe-inspiring, spine-tingling, totally wonderful event—for me, at least. Thank you, Sheila Gilbert, for moving my work up to the next, albeit scary, level. Isn't it gorgeous? All due to the creative talents of Luis Royo (wow), G-Force Design, and all those at DAW.

I take great care with my facts. While some places are fictitious, and this story is an extrapolation into an imagined future, I've done my utmost to reflect what is known now, from shorelines to eye sockets. My thanks to the following individuals for letting me pick their brains: Erin Kinney, Kaila Krayewski, staff of Nahanni River Adventures, and Dr. Isaac Szpindel. Any factual errors in this book are mine. (If I've forgotten anyone who helped answer my endless questions, you may smack me with a salmon.)

The final version of this book I owe to the insightful comments of my editor, Sheila Gilbert, as well as those of colleagues who kindly read it in first draft. Thank you, Doranna Durgin, Kristen Britain, Nalo Hopkinson, Jack McDevitt, and Jana Paniccia, for wanting more.

There are real people whose names appear in this story, each for good reason: Professor Jabulani Sithole, as a gift from my Jennifer, who values what she learned from you so highly. John Ward and Lee Fyock, from me to thee, gentlemen, for your friendship and support.

My sincere thanks to those wonderful folks of www.sff.net,

who've created such a welcoming, enthusiastic community for writers and readers alike. Hounds and IPU? Get ready to wait again! Heh heh.

Last, and never least, thanks to my family for taking for granted I could do this, which meant, of course, that I could. Hugs to all. Thank you, Scott, for listening to my plot. And thanks for "Mac," Jennifer.

- Table of Contents -

How do we know

why we act

as we do?

The root causation

of civilization

eludes me.

*(Earliest recorded wall inscription,
Progenitors' Chamber, Haven.)*

- Portent -

THE DROP glistened, green and heavy, as it coalesced at the leaf's tip. The drop trembled, then tumbled. It fell into the calm water of the pond below, sending a ring of ripples outward, its green diffusing until invisible. Mute.

Another fell. Then another. Within moments, there were drops forming and flowing to the tips of thousands of leaves, each drop falling free in turn, the sum etching the pond's surface, staining its clarity an ominous turquoise. Released from their burden, the leaves stirred the air as they sprang upward, only to be bent again under more of the green liquid. Below, the pond blurred and grew, consuming its banks.

Yet more fell.

The leaves themselves began to blur, their sharp edges washing away, the softer tissues dissolving with each new drop until skeleton veins rattled with the beat of false green.

More.

Ferns lining the pond's edge rotted as the floodwater reached their base, fronds having no time to curl into death as they toppled and sank. The trees themselves began to blur, their bark no match for this new and hungry rain, their branches weakening first where the green drops collected in fork and crook, so they cracked and fell, landing with a splash.

The drops continued for hours.

Until all that remained was a green lake, cupped by lifeless stone.

Then the mouths began to drink.

1

MEETINGS AND MISSION

"**M**Y MONEY'S on the plant."

The antique clay pot on the windowsill ignored Mac's comment, preoccupied with containing the immense aloe that folded its lower thick leaves over the pot's rim like grasping fingers and burst roots from beneath so the combination tilted in its saucer. There weren't cracks . . . yet. But the plant would win. Time, toughness, and a single-minded refusal to accept barriers to its growth. Mac approved.

Not that she *had time on her side.*

Her "pot" was this waiting room, her discomfort in it undoubtedly a pleasure to the man whose offices filled the remaining two-thirds of this floor. Mac was convinced those who ran the Wilderness Trusts shared a disdain for those who required roofs and meetings, begrudging any budget toward such things—even for their own staff. This building was shabby, the neighborhood matched, and the floor space was probably donated. The waiting room? Bland, square, and furnished to test the resolve of anyone waiting. The carpet gave off a stifling aroma, a combination of stale body and damp fiber. The only window had been frosted for no imaginable reason except to prevent gazing at anything but the imprisoned aloe on its sill. The reader on the side table? Never worked. There was a framed piece of art on the wall not occupied by window or closed, forbidding door. As this was an aerial view of a dense forest, with the words: "Leave Me Alone!" blazoned in threatening yellow across the center, Mac's eyes automatically avoided it.

Dr. Mackenzie Connor, just "Mac" to anyone she cared about, avoided the mainland's cities, including this one, just as automatically. Her preferred environment was at the ocean's edge, where the tallest structures were snow-covered peaks. It wasn't hard to confine her excursions to the halls and labs of academia, with the occasional foray into shopping or visits with her dad. At one time, she'd even been able to avoid entanglement in the many layers of bureaucracy and politics that governed Earth and her solar system. During elections, Mac would ask Kammie, who was as political as they came, which representatives were most likely to keep or raise funding levels for their work and would vote accordingly. It kept her life simple.

Until Mac encountered the politics of the Trusts. One Trust in particular. The one whose Oversight Committee consisted solely of the man sitting on the other side of that door.

Mac glared at it, well aware that Charles Mudge III knew to the second how long he could make her wait before she'd throw something.

There was an Oversight Committee for each of the Wilderness Trusts beading the western coast of the Pacific, from the Bering Strait to Tierra del Fuego. Their mandate, like such Trusts elsewhere on Earth, was identical and straightforward: keep the Anthropogenic Perturbation Free Zones, Classes One through Fifteen, exactly that: off-limits to Humans or Human activity.

As an evolutionary biologist, Mac approved. To become a Trust, these fortunate patches of nature had to have been undisturbed for a minimum of two hundred years—some perhaps for the extent of Human history. They were standards against which to compare restoration and preservation efforts elsewhere, not to mention a source of biodiversity for the rest of the planet. Earth had come a long way since relieving her Human population pressure by moving much of it, and her heavy industry, offworld. She had a long way left to go, and the rules protecting the Trusts were part of that journey.

Unfortunately, as senior coadministrator of Norcoast Salmon

Research Facility, located just offshore of the Wilderness Trust that encompassed the shoreline and forested hills surrounding Castle Inlet, Mac found herself in the unexpected position of asking for those rules to be, if not broken, then seriously bent.

Mac sighed and went back to the room's only chair, the seat's padding warm from the last time she'd sat on it. She liked rules. They helped people behave in a reasonable manner, most of the time. Unfortunately, other living things tended to run rampant over rules, blurring boundaries and refusing to conveniently exist in isolation. Case in point: Castle Inlet. Norcoast's mandate—her mandate—from Earthgov was to conduct ongoing studies of the metapopulations of local salmonide species, a valued Human food source as well as a crucial portion of the energy and nutrient web of the area. Fine, but that meant more than counting fish in the ocean and waterways. Salmon were essential to the surrounding forest and its life, their bodies carrying nutrients from the ocean depths to land. The forest organisms, in turn, were essential to the vigor and health of the waterways the salmon needed in order to reproduce. Researchers at Norcoast thus required access to the land as well as water. Earthgov, through the Office of Biological Affairs, had readily granted Norcoast's scientists that access.

Legally, that should have been it. However, a clause in the Wilderness Trust charter granted each Oversight Committee the power to ban any specific encroachment it deemed detrimental to the life therein. Which put Mac in this same chair, watching the aloe fight its pot, twice each year. Once to deliver, in person, the details of all research proposals for the coming field season, complete with Norcoast's planned precautions to avoid any anthropogenic interference with the Trust lands.

Once a year, in other words, to beg permission to continue their life's work from Charles Mudge III.

As if that wasn't demeaning enough, Mac was also required to report, in person, any and all slips in those precautions, no matter how minor, that may have occurred during the course of the field season, these to be included in the Oversight Committee's annual catalog of outside, undue influence.

Once a year, in other words, to grovel and confess their sins to Charles Mudge III.

Today's meeting would be one of the former: begging. Mac winced. Regardless of having plenty of practice, she wasn't good at it. Arm wrestling, verbal or otherwise, was more her style.

It had only been an hour and thirteen minutes since she'd arrived. Too soon to be pacing and scowling, though Mac admitted to temptation. To keep still, she pulled out her imp—a tougher-than-standard version of the ubiquitous Interactive Mobile Platform carried by almost everyone on or off Earth—from the ridiculous little sack she'd been forced to carry. No pockets. She laid the stubby black wand on her left palm and tapped her code against its side with a finger of the other hand. In answer, a miniature version of her office workscreen appeared in midair, hovering at the exact distance from her eyes that she preferred.

Just as Mac was about to review the access request she knew by heart, she glanced at the black, unblinking vidbot hovering at the ceiling. Pursing her lips, she disengaged the 'screen and put the imp away.

Privacy wasn't an option on the mainland.

Not that she'd anything to hide, Mac assured herself. *It was the principle of the thing.*

Time. Time. Time. She folded her hands to resist the urge to fiddle with her hair. It was, unusually, tucked up and tidy. As was she, dressed in her mainland business suit and borrowed shoes. There'd been the expected startled looks from those at Base when she'd left this morning. Dr. Connor, professor and friend to an ever-changing group of grad students every summer—when not investigating the evolutionary impact of diversity within migratory populations—typically went about her business in clothing with useful pockets, her hip-length hair in a braid knotted into a loose pseudo-pretzel, and her feet bare or in waterproof boots with decent tread.

A fashion statement, she wasn't, even now. Mac had reluctantly taken her father's advice after graduating, investing in The Suit for those all-important tenure interviews. Ironically, she'd landed her first choice without it: Norcoast, where she'd been a student herself.

Which made The Suit a decade and a half out-of-date. *If she waited long enough*, Mac thought pragmatically, *its short jacket and pleated pants would come back in style.* The dark blue weave was, in her estimation, timeless, if a trifle warm for this time of year.

The dress shoes were Kammie's, Mac's not having survived being worn through waves and sand one memorable night. Dr. Kammie Noyo was the other coadministrator at Norcoast and loaned her favorite shoes with the clear expectation that Mac wouldn't mess up the applications of Kammie's own lab and students. Mac squinted down her legs and flexed one ankle, wondering who in their right mind would design footwear to topple the wearer down the first set of stairs she might encounter.

But it would be worth the shoes and Suit. Worth the wait. Worth whatever it took. *It had better be,* Mac amended, time crawling over her skin. This meeting was unusual and an alteration in routine never sat well with Mudge. She'd been here, as always, midwinter to confirm his permission—however grudging—for this field season's projects. However, thanks to Emily's—Dr. Emily Mamani's—recent accomplishments in the Sargasso Sea, Mac had seen an opportunity to move her own work up by three years, maybe more. With that motivation, she'd chanced Mudge's temper and scrambled to get the changed request to him by spring, hoping for permission before the early fall salmon runs—her target—approached the continental shelf. But with the damnable timing of bureaucracy in general, suspicious timing from an organization and individual that surely understood that much of the natural world it was supposed to protect from Human interference, she was in this waiting room when she should have been calibrating sensors at Field Station Six.

The salmon were coming.

And Emily was late. Emily, who could charm a clearance from Earth customs, let alone a curmudgeon who called himself a committee.

Mac scowled at the empty room. Emily, her coresearcher and friend, was never late for the start of their field season. The first time *would* have to be this one, when so much was at stake.

The plant caught her attention and Mac transferred her scowl to its pot, willing the aloe to grow faster and shatter the damn thing. She contemplated helping it along by tossing pot and plant at the door. *Satisfying, if hardly beneficial to her own cause.*

With impeccable timing, the door in question abruptly opened wide enough to let a slice of face and one pale eye peer into the room. "Dr. Connor," said a voice with clear disapproval. "You're still here."

"Yes, I am," Mac confirmed. "You'd think I had nothing else to do but wait, wouldn't you?"

"The office is about to close for the day. I suggest you come back tomorrow."

The thin smile stretching Mac's lips was the one which gave inadequately prepared students nightmares, but all she said was: "You're new here, aren't you?"

The opening remained a slit, as though the person on the other side, older and female by the voice, preferred a barrier between herself and imagined hordes in the waiting room. "I've been here since last fall, Dr. Connor," complete with sniff. "You really should go—"

Mac felt a twinge of remorse. Not at forgetting the woman—she tended to focus on Mudge, not the receptionists who appeared and vanished like shoe styles—but last fall had been the Incident. The Oversight Committee, namely Mudge, had been outraged by the report of a near-attack by a grizzly, an episode he treated, with intolerable smugness, as incited by the grad student in question. He'd claimed the student had grossly interfered with the animal's normal movements through the forest—a serious charge, possibly enough to cancel Norcoast's access.

Upon hearing this, Mac had forced her way past the futile protests of a pimpled young man into Mudge's office, there dumping a bucket of distinctly ripe salmon on his desk. The so-called incitement had been no more than a similarly fragrant sample on its way back to the lab. The bear, needless to say, had willingly followed the scent and student. The Wilderness Trust didn't control the air.

She'd made her point, but Mac hadn't wished to cost someone their job. *Still.* Mudge seemed to have a limitless supply of new staff. She leaned back comfortably and gazed at the eyeball in the door slit. "You can go home, if you like."

The door closed. Mac sighed and raised an eyebrow at the vidbot's lens. "The game's getting old," she told it, in case anyone was watching.

"Norcoast."

"Oversight."

"Counting this—this change of yours, Norcoast, there are three more applications from your facility than last year."

No apologies, no pleasantries. Not even names, as though to Mudge their roles mattered more than their own existence. Mac couldn't disagree.

She ran a finger along the edge of the bare, gleaming white table separating them, gathering her patience around her.

The man with authority to grant or refuse the land-based portion of Norcoast's research was florid in face and manner, with a body determined to stress the midline of his clothing. *How many underestimated him?* Mac wondered. *Their mistake, not hers.* Charles Mudge III's lineage could be traced back to the earliest wave of loggers to settle the Pacific coast and, beyond any doubt, he was obsessed with its forests. Castle Inlet's forests in particular, since it was partly his great grandmother's doing that so many of its slopes had remained pristine enough to qualify for Trust status. Mudge vehemently opposed any Human presence in the Trust.

Mac was here, as she had been each of the past fourteen years— in The Suit—to arrange just that. "I turned down twenty from my staff," she replied calmly. "We understand the restrictions, Oversight. We follow them."

Mudge looked rumpled and aggrieved, not that Mac could recall seeing him otherwise. Now he scowled at her, his round face creased with wear and sun. His cheeks and chin sported the beginnings of a beard, mottled in gray, red, and black despite the brown hue of what hair struggled to cap his shiny head. "You'd better. Castle Inlet gains Class Two rating in fifty-one years, three months, and two days. *If* it survives your scientists. And you know what that means. No exemptions, none. I plan to be there on that day, Norcoast, to see your people ousted permanently."

Mac hid her dismay. The active lifespan of a Human was lengthening with each generation—on Earth, anyway—so it was entirely possible she and Mudge would continue these meetings into the next century. *Sit in that waiting room another hundred times?* For a moment, she seriously considered delegating the job, something she'd never done—even to Emily the charming. Then Mac looked into Mudge's small and anxious eyes, read the determined defensiveness of his hunched shoulders and lowered head, and gave a slow, respectful nod.

"I'll be there," she promised. "Norcoast will be overjoyed to see the Castle Inlet Wilderness Trust reach its four hundredth birthday unspoiled. We aren't at odds on that, Oversight, by any measure. Now, about my application?"

She knew better than to hope for a curt "yes" and an end to waiting. Sure enough, Mudge tugged his own imp from a chest pocket and set an enlarged workscreen between them, one that reached to the ends of the table and almost touched the ceiling. Proposals and precautions formed chains of text in the air, most glowing red and trailing comments like drops of gore. She'd been afraid of this. He'd complain about everything possible all over again, a knight defending the virtue of his forest against the pillages of field research.

Elbows on the table, Mac propped her chin in her hands and plastered an attentive look on her face.

Good odds the aloe plant would escape before she did.

The hired skim deposited Mac on the deserted pier, in time to watch the second-last northbound transport lev rise and bank out over the harbor. The driver was apologetic and willing to take her somewhere else; Mac paid him and sent him away.

She didn't mind this kind of waiting, the kind where the city lights played firefly over the dark waters of the bay, skims darting from building to building in such silence the lapping of waves against the pylons rang in her ears. She took her time walking to the pier's end and discovered a small series of crates there, a couple stacked atop one another. Taking off Kammie's dress shoes with a groan of relief, Mac placed them carefully on a lower crate. She climbed the stack, sat on the topmost, and dangled her bare feet over its edge, admiring the view. She had time, all right. The final t-lev of the night would be late; its driver lingering at each stop so as not to strand anyone.

Meanwhile, the cool sea air held pulses of city heat, scented with late summer flowers. Mac half closed her eyes to puzzle at the scents, letting the tension of her meeting with Mudge escape with every exhalation, feeling her bones melt. Castle Inlet was too far north for plants that couldn't take a little bluster and gale with their winter. *Bluster.* She smiled to herself. Mudge had certainly done enough of that, but even he'd found nothing in her changed request that would impact his precious Trust. *Not for want of trying.* In his own way, he was as tough as the aloe.

Mac's hands strayed to her hair, tugging free the mem-ribbons making it behave. Loose, the stuff drifted down her back and arms until Mac swept it forward over her right shoulder and began to braid, fingers moving in the soothing, familiar pattern.

The meeting hadn't been a disaster. *Chalk one up for diplomacy,* Mac decided proudly. It sounded better than saying she'd managed to keep her temper. They'd had their share of confrontations in the past; times when she and Mudge had shouted at one another until both were hoarse. Once, he'd walked out in a fury. Only once, since Mac had proved herself willing and able to camp in his office for as long as it took. Today? He'd agreed to her request, confirmed all but one of the existing permissions, insisted on onerous but doable increases in their precautions, and been, all in all, reasonable. For Mudge.

Now one of Kammie's grad students would have to travel up the coast to find a new study site. Mac could live with that, being finished with Kammie's shoes for six months. *Flexibility was worth learning,* she grinned to herself. Mac always included one or more projects she knew Mudge wouldn't allow. It let them both get some satisfaction out of the day. She'd been surprised he'd passed it in the first place.

Leaning back on her hands, Mac smiled peacefully at the city outlining itself against the night. *Not a bad meeting at all.*

The voice startled her out of an almost doze, an hour later. "I can't believe you wore that thing again!"

Mac turned awkwardly and too quickly, almost falling off the crate into the bay. "Emily? What the—" Smiling so broadly it hurt her cheeks, she clambered down, her bare feet landing in a puddle of cold seawater. It didn't dim her joy one iota. "About time—"

The glows lining the pier's edge were sufficient to put color to the tall slim woman standing in front of her, touching a gold shimmer from a dress that was most likely the latest rage in Paris, sliding warm tan over the skin, and lifting red along the scarf supporting Emily's left forearm. *A sling?*

"What have you done to yourself?" Mac demanded, drawing back from the relieved hug she'd planned to offer.

"This?" Emily raised her left arm. The scarf fell back to show a flash of white. "Little collision between the edge of a stage, a dance floor, and yours truly."

Mac took Emily's left hand and pulled it gently into the light. "A cast?" she said worriedly, looking up. "A bit archaic, isn't it?"

"I had a reaction to the bone-knitting serum. Just have to heal up the old-fashioned way. Don't worry." The fingers in Mac's hold wriggled themselves free. "Won't slow me down."

"You're late, you know."

"Glad to see you, too, Mac."

Mac grinned. Looking beyond Emily, she could see a trio of skims parked near the entrance to the pier, figures unloading boxes. "That your gear? Is it—is it ready?"

"You find me your salmon run, and I'll tell you who's in it. Name, rank, and DNA sequence."

A shiver of anticipation ran down Mac's spine. "I've such a good feeling about this, Em," she said. "What we'll accomplish—what we'll learn—" Mac stopped, embarrassed by the passion in her voice. "Great to have you back."

Emily stilled—or was it merely a pause in the waves tasting the pier? Mac decided she'd imagined it, for her friend went on briskly: "Before you publish our results, Dr. Connor, mind calling in a t-lev on Norcoast's tab? I'd rather not stand out here all night."

Mac pointed to the nearby crates. "Have a seat. Public transit will be arriving soon enough. While we wait, you can show me the upgrades to your DNA Tracer."

A laugh and a shake of Emily's head greeted her words. "Don't you want to know what I've been up to these last few weeks?"

Mac moved Kammie's shoes so Em could sit without climbing, joining her on the crate. "Nope. Not if it involves ridiculous prices for clothes, seedy bars, or places I've never heard of," she stated firmly. "Or anything about men," she added, to forestall Emily's usual list of adventures. "Salmon, girl. That's why you're back in the Northern Hemisphere." Mac pulled out her imp, chewing her lower lip as she activated the workscreen and hunted for the latest schematic.

The city lights faded behind the radiance of the three-dimensional image floating in front of the pair, its network of wiring and data conduits peeled back to show the innermost workings of the device. Emily reached over and traced a series of components with one finger, turning them blue within the image.

"Happy now?"

"I will be when we know it works in the field," Mac muttered, eyes devouring the modified image. "We'll set up right away."

"After I settle in, you mean."

"Settle?" Mac sputtered. "You're late, remember? We're moving out at dawn. The tents and my gear are already at the field station."

"Kammie's right. You're a damned workaholic," Emily bumped her good shoulder into Mac's. "A day at Base to unpack. Two." The display gleamed in her dark eyes. "Not to mention a chance to look over this year's crop."

Mac bumped her back. "The students are busy. As we'll be. The run won't wait—" She glanced at Emily's injured arm and sighed. "One day. We can run some sims . . ."

"*Muchas gracias,*" Emily said dryly. "I trust you'll let me eat sometime in there?"

Grinning, Mac let the plaintive request be answered by the hum of the approaching t-lev.

No more barriers, she thought with triumph. *No more delays. Nothing but the work.*

Life didn't get much better.

2

SUCCESS AND SURPRISE

"**B**AH! THERE'S no sex in this one either."

The offending book sailed over Mac's head, landed with a bounce, then began slithering down the massive curve of rock. She lunged for it, scraping both knees on wet granite in the process, and somehow managed to hook one finger in the carry-strap before the book sailed off the rock for the river several meters below. Sitting back, she caught her breath before glowering at Em. "At last we have the truth about Dr. Emily Mamani Sarmiento, consummate professional researcher from Venezuela, holder of more academic credentials than I knew existed. She's nothing but a randy teenager in disguise."

"Nice catch."

Mac's lips pressed together, then twitched into a grin. "And she's impossible."

Emily tilted the brim of her rain hood enough to show Mac a raised eyebrow. "What I am is stuck on this rock, reduced to watching you, my dear Dr. Mackenzie Connor, also holder of innumerable awards which don't pay rent, chase lousy books that have no sex in them. Remind me again why I agreed to such suffering."

Mac snorted, busy sorting through their pile of waterproof bags for one to protect the latest of Emily's rejects. Lee would not be pleased to find a member of his novel collection soaked and nonfunctional. *Ah*. There was the one from the sandwiches, consumed hours past. She shook the bag, and book, to remove most of the raindrops, before unzipping the one to shove in the other.

Mac made sure the bag was securely wedged in a crevice before turning her attention back to the river. She tucked her throbbing knees against her chest, and put her chin on a spot that seemed unscraped, her rain cape channeling the warm drizzle into tiny rivulets that converged on her bare feet. She wiggled her toes, playing with the water.

"I don't see why there has to be sex in everything you read," Mac commented absently, her eyes sweeping the heave of dark water below with the patience of experience. She could relax now. They'd delayed at Base for two days, not one, while Emily fussed over her equipment, settled into her quarters, and charmed "her" new students. Mac's anxious complaints hadn't hurried her fellow scientist in the least.

Hard now to complain about Emily's lack of speed, after five days camped with no sign of salmon whatsoever. Em had been insufferably smug the first day; bored and smug the second; simply bored by the third. Mac was rather enjoying her discomfort.

"And I don't see why it has to rain here every hour of the day," that worthy countered predictably. "This is worse than the Amazon."

A bright little head suddenly popped out of the river depths, patterned in bold white and rich chestnut. The Harlequin bobbed for an instant in the midst of the maelstrom, the water's froth seeming to entertain it. Then it dove again, seeking its prey in the rapids. Mac smiled to herself. "The sun was out this morning," she reminded Emily.

"Oh. Was that the sun? Tell my sleeping bag. Which, for your information, barely achieved damp status before we had to haul the gear back into the tents." A rustle of synthrubber as Emily came to sit beside her. *With their hoods and capes, the two of them,* Mac decided, *must look like small yellow tents themselves.*

Emily was quiet for about thirty seconds. "How long before they get here?"

"When we see them—right there." Mac pointed downstream, where the river wrapped itself around the base of a wall of rock and disappeared.

Below their toes, and the generous outcrop of granite beneath them, the Tannu River was over forty meters wide, in its mid-reach already swollen, powerful, and swift as it sped down the west side of the Rocky Mountains to the Pacific Coast. Along its surface, mist competed with the unceasing rain: some tossed where the river did its utmost to dislodge boulders and tumble gravel, some curling up along the eddies where the ice-cold glacial meltwater met the warm, saturated late-August air. The river always won. It had carved the sides of its valley into downward sheets of sheer rock, anchored at their base by the lushness of riparian rain forest, itself a thin line of green stitched to the water's edge by the pale gray of fallen tree trunks. The river's edge was a perilous place to grow.

Yet grow here life did, with a tenacity and determination Mac had long ago taken as personal inspiration. Cloud clung to the forests; the forest clung to any nonvertical surface, lining cliff tops as well as valley floors. Where trees couldn't survive, lichens and mosses latched themselves to rock face and crevice, nourishing the mountain goats who danced along the perpendicular cliffs.

The mountains' own relentless push skyward added force to the river. The river gladly tore at the mountains. Life thrived in the midst of geologic conflict. It was, Mac firmly believed, the most wonderful place on Earth.

And the ideal location for Field Station Six.

"I don't think it will be much longer, Em," she assured her, relenting. "This afternoon, if I'm any judge."

What Emily muttered to that was too low to compete with the river. Its thunder overwhelmed the rustle of leaves in the trees and the beat of rain on their gear. Waterfalls merely underscored its voice, wherever the mountains split to add their outflow from the snow pack and glaciers above.

They'd learned to shout over it. Mac raised her voice: "Pardon?"

"I should have taken Cannings' offer."

Mac turned and stared. "Work with manatees? Whatever for?"

A grin lit the shadow of the rain hood. "At least they copulate."

Mac threw up her hands. "As I said. You're impossible. Entertaining, but impossible."

"I do my best— Look!"

Mac had seen for herself. Both women rose to their feet so quickly they had to grab one another for balance, then push off to run to the consoles attached to the stone. It was a race to pull the protective sheets, Mac winning. Of course, she had two good arms to use. Her eyes locked on the rising glow of the observation screen as it sparkled through the raindrops, the standby flicker of indicators transformed into a psychedelic polka as data roared into the collectors.

"I'm tracking 35—make that 240—make that upward of 5,000," Emily's voice held a hint of excitement, but only a hint. She'd already taken control of the Tracer emitters from the autos, an operation demanding intense concentration as well as quick hands. This was her technology, the latest model to be tested away from her original site in the Sargasso Sea, with its convenient lack of cliff and forest. Emily had insisted on running extra simulations at Base, making adjustments to compensate for any slowing of her left arm by the cast, working to speed up the reaction time of the equipment and herself. A perfectionist in every way.

Mac made sure the incoming feeds were all active, then tore her eyes from the resulting display to look down the river for its source.

The Harlequin was looking, too. The bird stood onshore with a trio of its kind, as if preferring the stone to the unsure safety of the river—or at the very least showing disapproval of this novelty. The Tracer couldn't harm them, but they'd never seen anything like it before. *No one had*, Mac thought with triumph.

The Tracer. It was as if a translucent curtain made of rainbows and fairy dust had begun flowing upstream. It started in the air, three meters above the water surface, a distance Mac's surveys had indicated should be above the tallest of the protruding debris and boulders in the Tannu. It stretched from side to side across the valley; where it met the river's banks fading to a shadow that passed lightly over log, stone, and ducks. Within the roiling water, it was a wall moving ever forward.

On the screens, that wall sectioned the water column down to the gravel bottom. Invisible below the surface, this version of

Emily's device was marked above for the convenience of air breathing observers.

Like curtain rings, a line of tiny aerial 'bots formed the Tracer's top edge, each projecting a portion of the scanning field downward into the river while obeying the directions provided by both proximity sensors and Emily. At the same time, they retrieved the data and beamed it to the equipment under Mac's rain-damp hands.

"Em—"

"I see it." The correction was made before the line reached the upcoming bend in the valley, the curtain swinging more rapidly at its near reach to compensate. "How's it look?"

Mac ran her fingers over the screen, following the patterns shifting and surging across the display, feeling the cool droplets under her skin as if she stroked what they represented. "Better than sex."

"You really need to get out more." But the quip was automatic, Emily as captured by what was happening as Mac. For this was why Emily had picked Mac out of all the biologists eager for her expertise: to be here at this moment, to be part of life as it responded to the imperatives of its nature.

Within the curtain, behind it as far as the river showed itself, dorsal fins sliced the dark water, disappeared, rose again with a muscular heave. Rose-black bodies jostled in the shallows, then vanished before the eye could be sure what it saw. The water roared to the ocean; the first fall run of Chinook up the Tannu raced against it to their destiny.

And at Field Station Six, the leaders of that race had unknowingly activated the Tracer, an ambush undetectable by senses adapted to follow clues from water, light, air, and earth. Through this stretch of the Tannu, while the fish swam oblivious, the Tracer scanned and recorded the genetic code of every individual that passed through its curtain. The codes would be matched in the weeks to come with Mac's survey data from the past twelve years, compared to that from other rivers and other runs, to that of the resulting generation of smolts when they migrated back to the estuaries and ocean. Together, this data would test her hypotheses about the necessity for diversity, of the significance of strayed, hapless newcomers as well as those locked on course to their natal stream.

Mac felt a visceral thrill as she watched the scroll of code schooling in the depths and fighting the current. "How many?" she whispered. "How many of you are strangers; how many kin? What mix will it take for your species to endure another ten millennia? Tell me."

This time, they might.

Having proved her device could be activated by the leaders of the run, then follow to verify those individuals, Emily halted the Tracer at the point Mac had selected during the spring low-water survey, a deep area before the next major rapids upstream turned the water into a mass of gleaming rock and mad foam. The salmon paused there too, as if gathering their strength in its relative calm, but only for a moment, individuals exploding into the air with a powerful twist from head to tail. Dippers, short tailless birds that resembled gray balls on tiny stilts, bobbed up and down on the rocks, seemingly unperturbed by either shimmering curtain or the huge salmon leaping overhead.

Meanwhile, Emily was singing at the top of her lungs as she fine-tuned the Tracer. Something in Quechua, Mac judged, and likely bawdy as could be. She'd have to ask for a translation later, over some celebratory beer.

They were a good match, Mac smiled, grateful for every step of the process that had drawn Dr. Emily Mamani from one ocean and hemisphere to another, to come here and join her at Norcoast. There were never guarantees a scientist's personality would be as welcome as his or her abilities. Being trapped together for a field season brought out the worst in people; Mac had endured the consequences many times before. But Em had not only fit right in, she'd single-handedly turned the facility into a place where Saturday night meant a party about to happen.

To the surprise of everyone else at Norcoast, rowdy, raucous Emily had become the perfect foil to Mac's more reserved approach to life. Within moments of meeting, they'd recognized a kindred passion for the work; within a week, it was as if they'd always known one another. *Perhaps*, Mac admitted to herself, *it was because they were both such complete frauds in public*: herself wary of showing her intensity, Emily disguising hers with jokes and flirtation.

By now, in their third northern field season together, there was no one Mac would rather have share this moment. She hummed along, doing her best to follow the melody. The drumming of rain against hood, cape, and console was her private percussion section.

After a few moments, Mac activated her imp. The imp had a ten-year power supply of its own—and the ability to tap into local supplies, such as those maintained around most cities—but not so the consoles or Tracer. No need to verify the power feed from Norcoast's broadcast generators; it was obviously reaching them, as it would be other researchers in the field and at sea.

What concerned Mac were their results. The 'screen now hovering over the console mirrored the one in her office at Base, winking with tallies that showed the data stream making the return trip as steady, the system flawlessly making and sending copies. *She'd have it all.*

Reassured, Mac let her shoulders relax and rubbed a wet hand over her face, putting the device away. "Ready to anchor it, Em?"

"Not yet. I want to make sure we don't get some lateral drift with that wind. It's not much up here, but there's a funneling effect closer to the surface I have to watch—*ai caramba!*—like that. How's the feed? Still okay?"

Mac gave a quick glance. "Nominal. This looks to be just the initial group. I'll heat some soup while you make sure we're stable. There won't be time for a break later."

"Now this is why I keep telling you we should have brought along that helpful grad student of yours, John. Wonderful cook."

Mac patted her console fondly before heading for the tents nestled against the cliff face. "I hadn't noticed it was his cooking you liked," she tossed over her shoulder. The fact that the good-looking John Ward blushed so abundantly had been a bonus, as far as Em was concerned, likely the reason he'd requested Field Station Four this year. Emily's admiration tended to be outspoken and results-oriented.

"So I like men who are— Mac, get back here! Hurry!"

"What is it? What's wrong?" She returned to her console as quickly as she dared on the rain-slicked stone. "The wind . . . What the hell?" Blinking rapidly, then rubbing her hand over the screen didn't change the wrong-scale image now among the salmon. The display red-flagged its code.

Unknown.

"You get whales up here?" Em asked shakily.

"No, but we get idiots." Mac hadn't felt this infuriated since she'd found someone fishing a headwater lake with explosives, nets, and a truck. She left her console to go as close to the bluff's edge as she dared, then judged the distance. Grabbing a piece of jagged rock, she threw it with all the force she possessed.

Close enough. Bubbles exploded on the surface, startling the ducks into flight. A shape appeared shortly afterward, bouncing up and down in the current. Before it could be swept downstream, a repeller activated to hold it in place, a telltale ring of vibrating water plainly visible. Offended salmon burst from the river in all directions as their lateral line sense reacted to the output from the device, dropping back to scatter into the depths.

Any chance of calling this a natural, undisturbed run was gone. Emily didn't need to be told. Mac watched the Tracer's curtain snap out of existence, Emily's 'bots left hovering above the river as if lost.

Meanwhile, the begoggled head was turning from side to side as if hunting the source of the rock. Mac gritted her teeth and fought the urge to hunt for something else to throw. Something heavier—or at least pointy.

"You've got to be kidding." Emily came to stand beside her. The rain conveniently eased into a light drizzle so they had a clearer view, but the diver floating below still hadn't thought to look up. "How'd that *cabrón* get this far without setting off an alarm?"

Mac thrust her arm downstream, as if her finger could impale what was coming toward them. "Like that." The big skim moved above the water's surface, though close enough that spray from the rapids splashed over its cowling. It was heading for the diver. "Best bring in the 'bots before it bumps into one."

With a growl better suited to one of the grizzlies they'd watched yesterday, Emily went to her console. Mac watched the 'bots break formation, a couple swooping near the diver's head so he—or she—ducked back under for a moment, then they all rose until level with the rock shelf. Like a string of beads, the tiny, and very expensive, devices came to rest at Emily's feet. One-handed, she began tucking them inside her console's locker without another word.

Silence, from Dr. Mamani, was not a good sign.

Feeling herself beginning to shake from head to foot wasn't good either. Mac made herself take slow, steady breaths through her nose, fighting back both disappointment and fury, forcing her heart to calm itself. They might—*might*—be able to salvage something if they could get the river cleared of interlopers before the big runs started to arrive—likely by tonight. She'd have more chance of that if she wasn't throwing more rocks, tempting as it was.

Especially at a skim bearing the insignia of her own research facility, hovering beside the diver. *They'd brought him, all right.* They were already lowering the harness of hooked cables that would connect to one of the high-end commercial dive rigs. Interference from those who knew better was worse than unwitting trespass.

Mac turned away, uninterested in the details of extricating her problem, refusing to speculate and have her blood pressure rise even further toward rock throwing. She spent the next few minutes locking down her console, its screen again mute and empty of code.

She was on her knees, struggling with the cover fasteners on the river side of the device, when a deep hum announced the skim had set down on the ledge. Mac ignored both the arrival and the sound of footsteps that followed, including the unfamiliar voice saying: "Dr. Connor, I presume?"

When she was good and ready, Mac rolled her head to gaze at a pair of soaking wet, though shiny, men's shoes, better suited to an office than lichen-coated, bepuddled granite. Her eyes traveled up a pair of damp beige dress pants, were unsurprised to encounter a suit jacket of the same color and condition topped by a conservative yet fashionable—and damp—cravat, and finally stopped at a face she didn't know.

And didn't care to know. Even through the rain, she could smell a bureaucrat. Sure enough, he had a portable office slung under one arm, doubtless jammed with communication gear and clearances someone, somewhere, thought gave him the right to ruin her observations.

The bureaucrat offered her his hand. Mac stared at the manicured fingers until they curled up and got out of her way.

She rose to her feet, shoving her rain hood to her shoulders, and looked around for someone with answers. *There.* A familiar figure stood beside the skim. Tie McCauley, her stalwart chief of operations and the man who single-handedly kept all Norcoast equipment running through budget-pinching and Pacific storms. Catching her eye on him, he simply raised both arms and let them drop at his sides.

That wasn't good.

Mac found herself forced to look to the bureaucrat after all. Up at the bureaucrat. He was taller than he'd appeared at first glance, despite what seemed a permanent slouch. An ordinary, almost pleasant face, bearing rain-spattered glasses and hair that looked to have been actually in the river, so neither eyes nor hair showed their true color. Drips were running down both sides of his face, which bore an expression that could only be described as anxious.

That expression made Mac swallow what she intended to say, replacing it with a much milder: "Do you realize you've seriously disrupted our work?"

"I know, Dr. Connor. It is Dr. Connor?" At her nod, he continued, "Believe me, we wouldn't have come if it hadn't been so important to the Honorable Delegate—"

A booming voice interrupted. "That would be me, Mackenzie Connor."

Mac's eyes widened as if that could somehow help her mind fit the figure now climbing from the skim into the reality of a field camp in the coastal ranges. He—she assumed it was a he—waved off Tie's offer of assistance. *Just as well,* Mac thought numbly, *since their visitor looked to outmass the chief several times over.*

The diving suit, and distance, had helped disguise the nonhuman. Now, his head free and his body wrapped in what appeared to be bands of brightly colored silk, there was no escaping that she was standing three meters from a Dhryn.

Mac had seen the news report on the t-lev from Vancouver. Dhryn—the only oxy-breathing species within the Interspecies Union to never set foot—or more accurately, pods—on Earth, had sent a representative.

Here?

She licked rain from her lips and recaptured the hair strayed from her braid, pushing it behind one ear. "We're honored," she said at last, after a quick look to Emily, who could only shrug and roll her eyes. The Dhryn finished piling himself out of the skim, which rocked as if in relief, and stood before her.

Xenobiology wasn't something Mac had cared to study—there being more than a lifetime's worth of Earth biology to learn, in her opinion—still, she couldn't help but be intrigued by her first, up-close look at an alien.

The Dhryn seemed a sturdy creature, capable of standing erect in Earth gravity—assuming a 45° angle from stern to head was erect. Mac thought it likely, given the placement of limbs, seven in number, appeared useful in that stance. Three limbs were paired opposite each other. These were jointed similarly to human arms, although movement at those joints suggested a more free turning ball-and-socket arrangement than an elbow, and the musculature implied greater strength. A heavier gravity world, perhaps.

She really should read more.

The seventh limb, originating high and central from the chest, was—perplexing. It appeared to have several more joints, giving it an almost tentaclelike nature. Instead of the trio of grasping fingers at its tip, like the other six arms, the seventh had something more like scissors, with a hard, chitonous material lining the inner surfaces. As if her attention to this limb was impolite, the Dhryn tucked it under one of his other arms, but gave no other sign her inspection was at all unwelcome.

Legs and feet were one and the same, the being balanced on two elephantlike limbs. The limbs appeared to spread at their bases, ever so slightly. Perhaps the bottoms were adhesive.

The body might have been mammalian, what she could see of it past the gaudy bands; hairless, but with a thick, blue-toned skin that had a sheen, as if waxed. There were dark, pitlike ovals scattered over the body's surface. *Glands? Or sense organs,* Mac debated with herself, unwilling to rush to conclusions.

The head sat between narrow shoulders, and bore thick bony ridges that overhung the two large eyes. Their pupils were shaped like figure eights lain on their sides, black and lustrous, embedded within an oval iris of yellow that spread over the rest of what Mac could see of the eye. The nose and ears were also shaped by curved rises of bone beneath the skin, protected and also likely augmented in their function by those shapes. The mouth was unexpectedly small and tidy, with a pair of thin lips coated with what appeared to be pink lipstick. Now that she paid attention, there were signs of colored pigment applied, quite subtly, to accentuate the shape of eyebrow and nose ridges. There were tiny rings embedded along the top of each ear.

Mac found herself disarmed by a giant bearlike being who'd applied makeup to go diving with salmon, and warned herself—again—against drawing any conclusions at all.

"Mackenzie Connor." The creature's low voice made her jump. From the way her skin shivered, it could well be uttering additional tones below her hearing range, possibly infrasound. "I deeply regret if my curiosity has interfered with your research. I had heard of the wonders of diving with the spawning run. It was never my intention to disrupt your fine work."

Reminded, Mac couldn't help but scowl. "I hope you were bagged," she said, eyes flicking to Tie.

That worthy managed to look offended and embarrassed at the same time, protesting: "Hey, Mac. You think I'd let him in without? There was no chemical contamination. The repeller was on auto—to hold him for pickup. The water's pristine."

"It had better be." Mac shuddered to think of the confusion downstream if the dissolved odors of the Tannu River this year contained added Essence of Dhryn.

"I repeat, Mackenzie Connor. I intended no disruption—"

"Intended or not, Mr.— What do I call you?" The bureaucrat leaned forward, as if this was a question he'd like answered as well.

A graceful, if ponderous, tilt of the head. "Having not yet served in *grathnu*, Mackenzie Connor, I regret I can offer only one name for your use. Please do not be offended."

The Dhryn's face conveyed emotion that matched her human interpretation of his words, the edges of both eyes and mouth flexible enough to turn downward as if in regret. Mac felt chilled. *How much was true similarity in thought processes—how much coincidence—and how much the mimicry of an accomplished diplomat?*

"One name's fine," she said warily.

The Dhryn angled his body more upright, spreading six arms in what appeared a ritual gesture. The seventh was now out of sight under the silk bands. "Brymn is all my name."

The ensuing pause was silent except for the background roar of the Tannu, the intermittent patter of raindrops, and Mac's own breathing. The Dhryn didn't move. Finally, Mac slid her eyes to the bureaucrat and frowned meaningfully. *This was his problem.*

The man seemed very careful not to smile. Instead, he took a step closer, to stand beside Mac, and said, spreading out his own arms: "I take the name of Brymn into my keeping. Nikolai Piotr Trojanowski is all my name."

The Dhryn clapped all six hands together and bowed in the bureaucrat's direction. "I take the name Nikolai Piotr Trojanowski into my keeping. A very fine name, sir." The lips parted, revealing a row of small, even, and brilliantly white teeth, each curved like a rose petal. "Most pleasing."

Emily, not one to miss a cue, spoke up. "Emily Mamani Sarmiento is all my name."

Tie pointedly leaned back against the skim. Mac presumed he planned to stay out of this. *Wise man.*

"I have the name Emily Mamani Sarmiento in my keeping," Brymn acknowledged with another hearty multiple clap. "Most impressive. You are very accomplished for one so young."

Emily smiled. Mac wrinkled her nose at her. The clouds were sinking into the treetops and a return to heavier rain was only moments away. *They had no time for this*—but Brymn had turned to her expectantly. She sighed. "Fine. You can call me—" The bureaucrat with the mouthful of names caught her eye and shook his head very slightly, as if he guessed she planned to say "Mac" and be done with it.

Mac weighed her impatience against what was probably informed advice, given the bureaucrat had come with the alien and knew about this ceremonial exchange of names. "Mackenzie—" she hid a wince, "—Winifred Elizabeth Wright Connor is all my name." From the choked sounds coming from Emily, the "Winifred" would soon be all around Base.

"Magnificent!" The Dhryn clapped, then reared almost vertically, its tiny mouth stretching in what looked like a human smile— or a reasonable facsimile. "I most proudly take the name Mackenzie Winifred Elizabeth Wright Connor into my keeping. An honor, as I expected it would be. Please, accept my invitation to dine together this evening. We have much to share with one another."

Mac scrubbed her bare toes against wet granite, just to verify her surroundings. A line of four eagles flew by, barely visible among the clouds, and she wondered what they thought of this intrusion into their world. *She was*, she decided, *quite sure what she thought*.

"Thank you, Mr. Brymn—"

"Brymn."

"Brymn. A kind offer, but I can't leave this field station. Dr. Mamani and I are in the midst of the most important phase of our work. By the end of the month, I should have time to—"

The Dhryn let out a plaintive wail, not loud but certainly piercing. At the same time, he closed his eyes tightly and began rocking back and forth. There seemed little doubt of his suffering.

"Excuse us," Mac told the decidedly inattentive alien. She grabbed the bureaucrat by one arm and hauled him as far away from Brymn as the rock outcrop allowed.

"What the hell is going on here, Mr. Trojanowski?"

"To quote Brymn, I'm most impressed." The corner of his mouth twitched. "Most people have trouble with my name."

"I've heard all I want about names for one day," Mac warned. "What I want is to hear how quickly you're going to get this— this—intruder off my river! And you, too," she added, just to be clear. "We'll be damned fortunate if we can reinstall the Tracer before the rain hits."

"Isn't it raining now?" He glanced upward with almost comic dismay.

"This?" Mac snorted. "Not hardly."

He used a finger to wipe the drops from his glasses; they were immediately replaced. "I'll take your word for it, Dr. Connor. As for leaving—believe me, I'd like nothing better. The IU's going to rake me over the coals as it is. Our distinguished guest is supposed to be attending a state dinner in his honor at the Consulate, not snorkeling with fish in the middle of—" He broke off and looked around as if startled by a sudden thought. "Where are we, anyway?"

Obviously not deep enough in the bush to save her from desk jockeys, Mac thought with disgust. "Where you shouldn't be, Mr. Trojanowski. Just shut him up and take him away." The Dhryn's keening hadn't abated. In fact, Mac thought it had climbed a notch or two in volume.

The bureaucrat hugged his bag to his chest and leaned down to say very quietly, "He doesn't exactly listen to me, Dr. Connor."

Mac narrowed her eyes. "Then he'll listen to me, Mr. Trojanowski. I guarantee it."

His bleated "I wouldn't—" was left behind as Mac walked back to confront the unhappy Dhryn, but the man caught up to her. "Please, Dr. Connor. We can't have an interspecies incident. Brymn is the first of his kind to visit Earth—"

"And I don't care if he's the last." Mac pulled out her imp and used it to poke the Dhryn in the middle of his widest band of rose-colored silk.

Brymn's eyes shot open and his wailing ended in an exaggerated "whhooff" of air leaving his mouth. Before anything else came out, Mac put her hands on her hips and said firmly: "Leave. Now." She put away her imp and hoped it still worked; she went through several a year as it was. "I have work to do and you are interfering."

Without another word, the Dhryn turned and clambered back into the skim. Tie jumped in after him, possibly afraid the creature would take off with the team's vehicle.

Not surprisingly, the bureaucrat was staring at Mac, his mouth working as though unsure what expression would be safe. He did take a cautious step out of range.

As Mac feared, the rain chose the least convenient moment to turn from drizzle to blinding sheets that made it hard to breathe. She tugged her hood over her head and waved impatiently to the sodden figure still hesitating in front of her. Emily was already splashing toward her console. "Goodbye, Mr. Trojanowski."

The fool was digging into his office pouch. As Mac prepared to tell him where he could file his paperwork, she saw what he was pulling out.

It was an envelope, in the unmistakable blue and green reserved for documents pertaining to the safety and security of humanity. Such an envelope must be accepted by any person; refusing such an envelope was treason against the Human species. Its contents were both secret and vital.

Mac had only seen them in movies featuring spies and inter-galactic warfare. She'd half-believed they were nothing more than a handy plot device.

Her hands lifted to accept the envelope, closing over what wasn't rain-coated paper, but instead felt like thin metal, heat-stealing and sharp. Her name suddenly crawled over its surface in mauve-tinted acknowledgment.

Did she imagine a flash of sympathy on Nikolai Trojanowski's face before he turned to join Brymn in the skim?

Mac watched the vehicle lift, then drop to the river's surface, vanishing into the rain. Beneath, dorsal fins sliced the heaving dark-ness of the river and bodies twisted to leap through the foam. The Harlequins landed on the shore, walking in single file to plunge into the river. Left alone, life on the Tannu sought its own rhythm, heedless of Human affairs.

Emily shook her cape as she approached, adding her spray to the deluge. "Well, that broke the boredom . . ." Her voice trailed away as she spotted the envelope. "*Ai.*"

Mac's hands wanted to drop the thing but couldn't. "Lock us down, Dr. Mamani," she ordered, wondering at the steadiness of her own voice. "I expect the other shoe to drop will be— Ah, yes. Base sending a pickup."

On cue, a shape formed itself from rain and mist: the transport lev from Norcoast, angling for a landing that wouldn't crush either tent or console.

"It seems someone thinks we're finished here," Mac said, giving the t-lev a short nod that had nothing to do with agreement.

And everything to do with challenge.

3

ARRIVAL AND ANNOYANCE

ON HER OFFICE wall, Mac had a satellite image of Hecate Strait, its intense blue kept from the Pacific by the lush green arms of the Queen Charlotte Islands, the Haida Gwaii. To the east, the strait tried to sneak its waters into the snow-capped Rockies, wrapping around islands and through inlets like fingers grabbing for a hold, thwarted by the growing bones of a continent. Rivers, like tears of sympathy, leaked through the mountains to join the Strait.

From an eagle's perspective, the midst of the strait might be the center of the Pacific, especially during storm winds. The submerged mountains forming the Queen Charlottes hid their tips below the horizon; the continent was nowhere to be seen. Mariners treated the area with respect. Whales sang here.

But approach the coast and the landscape shot skyward again, as if the ocean waves constantly pushed the rock to heaven and forest anchored cliff to cloud. On clear days, the scale changed again, as the mountain ranges laughed down at forest, cliff, and ocean. Victor and goal in one.

As the eagle flew, the coast was a labyrinth of deep cut channels that bent, fractured, and found one another again. There were hidden coves of water so still the bird's reflection chased it. Along every shore, the bleached remains of giant trees competed with splintered bits of mountain, a rubble reshaped every spring.

Every spring, the Norcoast Salmon Research Facility, or Base, as its staff of scientists, techs, and students preferred to call it, came back to life.

Base floated within the southwest curl of Castle Inlet, a peaceful intrusion of humanity consisting of a half dozen pods, various docks, and landing pads linked by walkways. The pods were domes, their mottled grays, mauves, and browns matched to the exposed rock of the shoreline in the hope they'd resemble tiny islands themselves. It might have worked, if there had been forests of cedar and fir on the flattened roofs instead of aerials, solar collectors, skylights, and the occasional deck chair. Though the practice was discouraged, students tended to hang their laundry from the balconies surrounding each pod, further dispelling the illusion of blending with nature.

The walkways were also employed to dry both wet towels and fish specimens. On those rare occasions when the sun encouraged such effort, they formed the favored spot for people to dry out as well, making it impossible to walk from pod to pod with any speed.

Not that speed was the point. Norcoast's researchers worked by nature's timetable, not their own, and endurance mattered more than haste. As the Coho, Pink, Chinook, and King salmon arrived from the Pacific, feeding on the immense schools of pilchard converging in Hecate Strait, survey crews hovered overhead in aqualevs, sleeping over their monitors, if at all. Those studying the impacts of oceanic predation slept at Base, but only at the whim of orca pod, shark, and seal. Easy to know the predator researchers. Preds were the ones running along the walkways with still-lathered hair or wearing pajamas under their rain gear, a consequence of wearing wrist alarms activated by remotes listening at the entrances to the Sound as well as the various inlets.

A few at Base lived by Human hours, in order to process data from their compatriots with the commercial harvesters. To compensate for that luxury, Harvs wound up cooking for the rest, being more likely to be awake and functional when supplies had to be ordered and received.

They were doubtless all awake now, Mac thought grimly. She'd tucked the envelope from Trojanowski under her clothes, where it molded with unsettling comfort against her skin. There'd been no time or privacy to read its contents. She and Emily had sealed their equipment against weather, bear, and packrat. There'd been the required clarification for the t-lev's crew—namely that Mac had no intention of letting them dismantle and remove Field Station Six, no matter what fool had ordered it. The crew, in turn, wisely professed themselves exceedingly content to remove only the two scientists and their personal gear.

At the very last moment, Mac had remembered to pluck the bag with Lee's book from its soggy crevice.

Now, as the t-lev sank within the arms of the inlet and approached the north landing pad, Mac heard Emily click her tongue against her teeth. "We've company waiting."

"I see." The rain hadn't stopped, so the figures lining the walkway to the pad wore either rain gear or bathing suits. Only one carried an umbrella. "Trojanowski," Mac concluded, pointing down. "Knew he was a tourist."

"Nice butt, though," Emily countered. "Not that you noticed."

Mac snorted. "The day I check out someone like—" She shut her mouth and smiled despite herself. "You are impossible."

"Of course. Now that we have both formed our opinions of the meddlesome Nikolai, what's next?"

The t-lev took its time coming to rest, the pilot knowing exactly the reaction he'd get from onlookers if he so much as rocked the landing pad, let alone dumped anyone in the inlet. Mac leaned back on the bench, gazing at Emily.

They were both filthy as well as barefoot, with streaks of gray mud running from toes to thighs. Em's knees were only muddy; hers were scraped and bloody, like some kid coming in from street hockey. Their rain gear was clean enough; underneath, though, their clothing was, to put it kindly, ripe. Emily's hair was so black as to have blue highlights; she wore it short and snug, a style that not only accentuated the fine lines of her neck and high cheekbones, but also forgave a few days of living in the bush. It really wasn't fair. Mac tried to poke a finger through hers but couldn't reach her scalp. Despite the braid, the stuff had reached the point of feeling like lichen. Tangles were doubtless the least of what rode her head.

"What's next?" Mac repeated, contemplating the disturbing message lying against her stomach and the expectant crowd below. "A shower."

Mac and Emily, backpacks on their shoulders and the rest of their gear to follow when the t-lev was unloaded, disembarked with every intention of simply walking past those waiting. The first person they encountered, the bureaucrat, seemed to grasp that point. He met Mac's warning scowl with no more than a searching look, then stepped aside, holding his umbrella high so she and Emily could pass without having to duck under it. Annoyingly, he was impeccably clean and dry, wearing what had to be the twin of the suit and cravat he'd had on at the field station. His eyes, now visible through clear dry lenses, were hazel; his hair was light brown, thick, and prone to curl. *Doubtless,* Mac thought, *Emily would have something to say about both.*

For her part, she was grateful not to be delayed, more determined than ever to set her own pace regardless of the business at hand. She needed privacy to read the message. Not to mention the fact that she wasn't going to conduct any business whatsoever without a shower. But as easily walk on water as evade the curiosity of grad students. As they pressed closer instead of giving way, Emily thoughtfully let her lead.

As if she could simply push past them all. Mac sighed, taking in the intensity on those young faces, and slowed her pace. Jumping in the water and swimming to the next pod would only encourage them to do the same, probably turning it into a race pitting preds against harvs, with the rest cheering. She'd seen it happen more than once.

Of course, the instant they knew they had her attention, questions began flying from every direction, interspersed with hugs of welcome and offers to carry her bag. Mac returned the hugs as quickly as was polite, held on to her bag, and kept up a running patter of answers. She reassured Cecily and Stanislaus that the other field stations were running as usual, then achieved two full steps before having to stop and tell Roman that no, this didn't mean there would be weekend passes to Prince Rupert or any other shoreline destination with restaurants. A glower and five steps brought her face-to-face with Jeanine Duvois, who looked about to cry.

"What's wrong?" Mac asked involuntarily.

The sudden hush wasn't reassuring.

"I didn't have any choice, Dr. Connor. They made me do it."

"Do what?"

Definitely close to tears. "You won't hold it against me, please? I know my grades aren't the best, but I've been trying—"

"Hold what against you?" Mac demanded.

A hiccup and a wild-eyed glance around for nonexistent help. "I—I helped move the Dhryn into your quarters this morning, Dr. Connor."

"The Honorable Delegate needs a fair amount of space," said an unapologetic and by-now familiar voice in her ear. "Yours were the biggest available, Dr. Connor. I'm sure you understand."

Grad students had a finely honed instinct for when to become invisible, while staying close enough to catch the juicy details. The light slap of seawater against the floats underfoot was suddenly louder than the rain.

Mac gritted her teeth and stared longingly at Pod Three, where her admittedly spacious quarters waited, complete with shower and clean clothes. "What about my things?" she demanded, turning to glare at Trojanowski.

The bureaucrat eased back a step, a move that put him against the railing. "The furnishings are satisfactory," he assured her warily. "Brymn is very accommodating about such things."

"Your personal stuff is piled in the main hall," Jeanine sniffled in Mac's ear. "Beside the spare generator. We didn't have time to do anything more with it."

First Brymn in her *river, the envelope, being summarily dragged back to Base, and now this?* Ignoring Emily's alarmed protest, Mac planted both hands against the dry fabric of Trojanowski's suit and shoved with all her might. The bureaucrat was over the rope rail of the walkway and into the water before he could do more than tighten his grip on his umbrella.

As the students cheered, Mac resumed walking to the pods. No one else got in her way. Emily kept up, making a few strangled noises as if testing her voice.

"What?" Mac growled.

"Think he can swim?"

"Think I care?"

"Point taken." Another few steps. "You realize the poor man probably lost his glasses." Em lifted her cast. "We old-fashioned types are at such disadvantage."

"He had a spare suit. He'll have spare glasses," Mac said, resisting a twinge of remorse. She paused at the intersection of the walkways to Pods Three and Two, then resignedly turned away from "home." "Mind if I borrow your shower?"

"And some clothes, no doubt. I've a nice little number in red that should fit."

The walkway became a ramp, shifting gently underfoot as they climbed in synchrony. There was another splash in the distance. Mac presumed either the bureaucrat was being rescued or her helpful students had tossed him in again. "Base coveralls will do. You were issued three pairs, remember?"

Emily made a sound of disgust. "Fit for scrubbing bilge."

"That could be what I'm doing."

"Not with what you're carrying."

Mac wiped her hand dry on her shorts before slapping it on the entry pad. "We don't know what I'm carrying," she said in a low voice as the door opened. "We don't know anything yet—but I intend to get some answers. And my quarters back."

"No argument here. No offense, but having you for a roomie would seriously cramp my lifestyle."

"Spare me the details, please."

Each pod had two floors above sea level and one below. The submerged space was used for wet labs and as bays for the underwater research equipment and vehicles. The first floor above the surface was divided into dry labs and offices, while the uppermost held residences and lounges.

Pod Six, the newest addition to Norcoast, was the only exception to this plan. Larger and broader than the others, its interior was hollow and flooded, an isolated chunk of ocean protected from the elements. Entire schools of fish could be herded inside, scanned, then released. They'd even housed a lost baby humpback whale until acoustic and DNA samples could locate his mother and aunts.

Pod Two was reserved for visiting researchers, like Emily, so its walls were free of the bulletins, vids, and outright graffiti that adorned the student habitats: Pods Four and Five. Pod One held the fabrication and repair shops, while Pod Three held Norcoast's administration and archives—as well as Mac's year-round home.

Until now. Mac let Emily lead the way up the stairs that ringed the inside of the pod's transparent outer wall. Mac found it perfectly appropriate that the stunning view of inlet, coast, and mountain was opaqued by rain.

"His being here has to be a secret," Emily said, halfway up.

"Brymn's? What makes you say that?"

Emily rapped the wall with her knuckles. "No tiggers mobbing a crowd; I didn't see any vidbots either."

The "tiggers" were the automated warn offs that discouraged kayakers and other adventurers from venturing into Castle Inlet. They looked more like herring gulls than the real thing, which added to the shock effect when they flew over a trespasser's head and began intoning the hefty fines and other penalties for entering a restricted wildlife research zone, or worse, the Wilderness Trust itself. If ignored, a tigger would deposit an adhesive dropping containing a beacon to summon the law. If someone were foolish enough to try and evade the dropping—or shoot at the tigger? Suffice it to say there were other droppings in its arsenal, and a flock was a serious threat.

Vidbots didn't belong here either, though they were a familiar nuisance in cities. The little aerial 'bots were the eyes and ears of reporters—local, planetary, and, for all Mac knew, they reached other worlds as well.

"That doesn't mean it's a secret," she protested, unhappy at the thought of more conspiracy. The envelope was bad enough. "Maybe a Dhryn visiting a salmon research station isn't news, Em."

At the top of the stairs Emily palmed the door open. They passed into a corridor with thick carpet, blissfully soft and dry underfoot. The ceiling was clear, though patterned by now driving sheets of rain. Supplementary lighting glowed along the base of the walls and around each residence door. Norcoast provided superb accommodations for its guest experts, even though they rarely had time to use them before heading into the field. It looked good on the prospectus.

It had looked good to Mac, her master's thesis on St. Lawrence salmon stocks under her belt and her new professor willing to send her west to Norcoast's pods for the season. Mind you, her first quarters hadn't quite been like Emily's.

Tie had been the one to welcome Mac to Norcoast, although it hadn't seemed much of a welcome at the time. Mac hadn't known what to make of him. The tool belt over torn shorts said one thing; the casual first-name basis with which he greeted everyone another. As he'd led her down sidewalks that bobbed alarmingly, he'd lectured her dolefully on the proper care of equipment she'd never used in her life, seeming convinced scientists and students were equally inept with any technology and it being his thankless duty to make sure it all worked regardless.

At the residence pod, Tie had broken the unpleasant news that Mac would share her living quarters with four other students, the new pod being delayed in construction, that delay caused by other individuals also hopelessly inept with any technology whatsoever. Mac hadn't dared venture an opinion.

"You'll miss all this, soon enough," Tie had pronounced as he'd watched her thread her way among the shoes, bags, and general paraphernalia of the others to reach the bed with the least number of books stacked on it. Hers, supposedly.

Mac had desperately wanted to appear dignified and knowledgeable; she was closer to homesick and anxious. "Miss what?" she'd asked. "Why?"

"A bed. A roof." Tie had laughed at her expression. "They didn't tell you? A tent and sleeping on the ground. That's the routine here, while the rivers are free of ice. You live with the salmon."

Mac brought herself to the present with a shake of her head. *Tie had been right, as usual. What was she doing, worrying about something as trivial as where she slept? Must be getting old.*

"Brymn isn't news?" Emily scoffed, as if unaware Mac's thoughts had wandered. "I'd say he's more newsworthy than that delicious graphic opera star you entertained here last year. Weren't you the one telling me you had to call in the coast patrol to get rid of the reporters who followed him?"

"Two years ago," Mac corrected, waiting for Emily to unlock her door. "And there was no entertaining involved. He claimed to be making whale documentaries and had heard about our work. I offered him a tour."

"Tour." The word oozed innuendo. "Really."

"Dibs on the shower," Mac said quickly, taking advantage of her smaller size to squeeze by Emily and dash for the washroom.

There were times to linger over the sheer hedonism of hot water after living under field conditions. This wasn't one of them. Mac hit the air dry the instant her hand skimmed the last clumps of lather from her head, bending over so the jets meant to dry her skin did double duty on her hair. The locks were still damp enough to stick to her fingers when she shut off the shower and stepped out, her other hand snagging the navy blue Norcoast coveralls Emily had found for her.

They fit, in the way shapeless, untailored, thoroughly practical clothes did. Mac rolled up the cuffs at ankle and wrist, securing each by pinching the mem-fabric in their hems. She'd had everything else she needed, including dry sandals, in her backpack.

"Your turn, Em." Mac kicked her 'pack into Emily's living room, her hands busy sorting her hair into its customary braid, twisting the result into a knot to lie at the base of her neck. "Don't dawdle."

Emily was stretched out on the couch, one arm trailing on the floor as if she'd melted into the furniture, the other, with its cast, resting on the couch back. She lifted her head from a cushion, her expression one of complete disbelief. "What did you do? Skip the soap? I just got comfy—"

"I know. Sorry." Mac pulled the envelope from a pocket, its dark blue veined with green like some exotic shell. Her name, in lighter mauve, looked ridiculous. "This shouldn't wait much longer.

And—" Mac paused, then gave words to the unease she'd felt since first touching it, an unease she'd postponed acknowledging as long as she could. "I don't want to read this alone."

"Of course not," Emily agreed, rising to her feet in one smooth motion. She took a step toward the washroom, then stopped, looking at Mac. Her eyes dropped suggestively to the envelope.

"Fine," Mac said, just as relieved. "I'll open it now." She chose to sit cross-legged on the carpet. Emily joined her.

"Do you know how?"

Mac turned the envelope over, running a fingertip along each edge. There were no seams. It might have been a wafer of mother-of-pearl, solid to the core. "Any ideas?"

"Not I." Emily leaned forward, studying their problem. "I won't touch it either. Not with your name on it. Maybe you should call our friend Nikolai."

Mac remembered the searching look the bureaucrat had given her—the way he'd obviously decided not to talk to her. "He expected me to have opened it already," she concluded out loud. "So there's nothing high tech about it." Before she could hesitate, Mac grabbed the envelope in both hands and ripped it in half.

A tiny multifolded sheet slipped from the portion of the envelope in her right hand, landing on her leg. Mac put the halves aside and picked up the sheet, opening it slowly. Mem-paper, if a far finer, thinner version than those in Lee's books. The sheet was smooth between her fingers as she angled it to read:

TO: **Dr. Mackenzie Connor, Norcoast Salmon Research Facility, British Columbia, Earth.**
FROM: **Muda Sa'ib XIII, Secretary General, Ministry of Extra-Sol Human Affairs, Narasa Prime.**

Dear Dr. Connor:
   Our Ministry has been advised of a potential Category Zeta threat. This is a hazard to life on an intersystem, planetary scale. The appropriate agencies representing all signatories of the Interspecies Union have been notified and have agreed to share any findings in this matter.

This threat, if confirmed, could affect a portion of space which includes over three hundred Human worlds and even more extraplanetary habitats. It could impact Earth herself. This threat must therefore be considered as a threat to our species' survival, authorizing the most extreme measures, should they be necessary.

Among the investigations being conducted is one by a Dhryn scientist who has requested access to your facility and your research, claiming it has relevance to our mutual concern. While he has not yet explained that relevance, citing its preliminary and speculative nature, his request has, of course, been granted. We expect you will offer him all possible assistance.

We ask that you keep this information, and any findings you and the Dhryn obtain, confidential until such time as our Ministry reaches a conclusion concerning the existence of this threat and what action, if any, should be taken. While we hold little expectation for this particular line of investigation, we have nonetheless assigned a diplomatic liaison to you, who has identified himself by giving you this message. Through him, you may communicate with my office at any time.

It is our sincere hope and belief that this threat will turn out to be spurious, another rumor to be dispelled as quickly and quietly as possible. If not, we will rely on you to provide your assistance, however and as long as required.

Thank you, Dr. Connor.

See Attachment

"You look as though you've eaten some of Ward's scrambled eggs. It can't be that bad."

Mac shook her head, more to postpone Emily's questions than in answer. "It doesn't say much of anything," she puzzled. "There's more attached." A light tap on the page and the memo was replaced by a list of reports. *This mem-sheet was definitely more sophisticated than those in Lee's novels.* "Grab your shower, Em," she suggested, looking up to meet her friend's eyes. "This is going to take a while to read."

The other woman didn't budge. "Not until you tell me if we're all going to die before the weekend. If so, I've got plans to make first."

"I think your weekend is safe."

"Not good enough."

Mac's lips quirked. "Fine. It's from the Ministry of Extra-Sol Human Affairs—"

"Whoa." Emily's eyebrows rose. "That's weird. Earthgov, I expected. The Consulate, I could see. Any alien entering our air has to go through them. But the Ministry? To state the obvious, they don't deal with Earth at all."

She was right, of course. Mac knew that much history. Humanity's spread throughout its own solar system had produced another layer of governance, to speak for the differing needs of those living without gravity or biosphere. The Ministry, as most now called it, had served as the conduit for both complaint and accommodation. As the populations living off the planet had increased, so had the Ministry.

In a way, that exponential growth had prepared humanity for its next great leap outward. A mere 150 years after the first Human birth on Mars, Humans gained the technology to expand to the stars. Oh, it wasn't theirs. *Very little*, Mac thought ruefully, *from imp to broadcast power, was.* When the first non-Human probe arrived, with its standard invitation from the Interspecies Union to build and maintain transects to bypass normal space, and thus participate in its economic community of other intelligences, humanity hadn't hesitated an instant. The Ministry, for its part, moved outward with every Human starship and colonist, a familiar safety net—and occasionally useful bureaucratic aggravation—for those brave souls venturing into the true unknown. Mind you, it turned out that much of the galaxy in Earth's vicinity was very well known and populated, so over the last century, the Ministry had quietly evolved into a convenient way of keeping Earth's far-flung offspring in touch with home.

Meanwhile, the Interspecies Union, or IU, hadn't left that home alone. It had requested, and been granted, property on Earth to build a Consulate. In New Zealand, in fact, due to the variety of climates readily available. There, visitors of any biological background could be welcomed, briefed on local customs, checked for transmissibles, and sent off to conduct whatever business they deemed worth doing on the Human home world. Little about Earth wasn't of interest to someone or something, although Saturn's moons boasted more alien traffic on an annual basis.

In return, Humans continued to feast on the combined technology of thousands of other races, many more advanced in one field or another, the whole benefiting from the cross-pollination of ideas. The IU wasn't composed of fools. Not entirely, anyway. There were always stories—

Not that Mac paid attention to stories about aliens or their business, content to use the latest tools and stay within her field and species. *Until now.*

"You'll see why it comes from the Ministry, Em," Mac said soberly, then read the rest of the message out loud. When done, she added thoughtfully: "I'm not downplaying the threat, but this part about Brymn coming to me? Does it sound like a plea for some diplomatic nuisance-sitting to you?"

"Oh, as if diplomacy is your strong suit," Emily quipped, but looked only faintly reassured. "You read the rest while I clean up. Then I want to know everything else that's in there. Deal?"

Mac hesitated. A little late, her conscience was bothering her. "The message said confidential."

Emily flashed a grin. "So don't tell Tie. You know he spreads gossip faster than the com system—"

"Be serious, Em."

A sudden, very sober look from those dark brown eyes. "I'm nothing but serious, Mac. A possible 'Category Zeta' threat? We can't let word of this spread in any way. You probably shouldn't have told even me—but now that I'm in it, I'm damned if I'll sit by and wonder what's going on overhead."

Mac acknowledged the truth of that with a single nod. "We need to talk to Brymn. Go shower. I'll start going through this."

"On my way, boss." Emily shed clothing as she went, apparently determined to challenge Mac's speed.

Once the door closed, Mac stretched out on her stomach, laying the mem-sheet on the floor in front of her. Unconfirmed rumor or crackpot notion, Em was right—this scale of threat had to be taken seriously until prove otherwise. Obviously, she and Em weren't the only ones to think so.

She was, however, the only one to poke the scientist she was supposed to help in the midriff, shoo him from her field station, then attempt to drown the man sent by the Secretary General to assist them both.

Not the most auspicious start to their relationship.

Resisting a quite remarkable level of guilt, Mac began to read.

Mac tapped the com. "Dr. Connor to Pod Three, please." While she waited, she frowned at Emily, who'd settled on her outfit of choice with unusual alacrity and was now resplendent in a black evening jumpsuit that oozed sophistication and personal style. She'd given up on the sling and wrapped the cast in matching fabric. At the moment, the other biologist was holding out a similar garment in red, a gleam in her eye. *Over my dead body,* Mac mouthed at her.

"Pod Three."

No mistaking that voice. "Tie? What are you doing on coms?"

"Oh, it's you. Hi, Mac. Yeah. Everyone else has headed for the gallery to get a good seat—I pulled short straw, having met our guest. Should be quite the affair. Why aren't you down there yourself?"

Emily shook the red jumpsuit suggestively; Mac stuck out her tongue. So much for her hope to arrange a private meeting with—and apology to—both Brymn and Mr. Trojanowski before supper. "We'll be there shortly," she said. "I wanted to check that everything was on schedule." Emily rolled her eyes.

"On schedule?" Tie's laugh was a bark worthy of a sea lion. "No problem. It's been the Pied Piper and his rats around here. Last I saw, that Dhryn was walking through Admin, collecting people as he went. Cooks will have to hustle to be ready, that's my guess."

Disrupting everyone else's research, Mac thought, changing her mind about the apology as she closed the connection. "Let's go."

"Dressed like—that. You can't be serious. Now that we know it's for supper—"

"Supper?" Mac raised both eyebrows. "Em, it's Pizza Tuesday."

Emily appeared to struggle with the concept, then spat out something frustrated in Quechuo. "You're meeting with a scientist of another species and a representative of the Ministry of Extra-Sol Human Affairs! What kind of impression will you make in those?"

Mac brushed nonexistent dust from her borrowed coveralls. "No worse than I've made already. You impress them. I want to get this over with so we can get back to work."

The rejected jumpsuit sailed across the room to drape itself over the couch. "So you've made up your mind about this so-called threat to humanity." Emily's voice was studiously neutral. She'd read the reports after Mac and had had nothing—yet—to say.

Not knowing what to do with the pieces of the secret envelope, Mac had slipped them over the refolded mem-sheet, intending to save all three. To her astonishment, the two halves had immediately mended themselves into an unblemished whole, once more winking with her name. The envelope now seemed to burn a hole in Mac's hip pocket. "What threat?" she asked. Mac walked over to the window wall and stood peering out through the droplets, then refocused on them. With a finger, she traced imaginary patterns between drops picked at random, touching each as she recited the list from memory. "A group of climbers disappears from a mountain on Thitus Prime. A cruise barge on Regellus drifts ashore, empty. Balloonists never land on N'not'k. An eco-patrol vanishes from a forest in Ascendis. A harvesting crew isn't seen again on Ven Twenty-Nine—"

"Don't forget the Dhryn."

"Ah." Mac left her finger on one particularly large drop. "The Dhryn misplace an entire field trip's worth of students on their Cryssin colony." She let her hand fall to her side and faced Emily.

"Don't get me wrong, Em. I sympathize with everyone involved. These are all tragedies. But nothing from the Secretary General explains why a handful of missing person reports put Brymn in my quarters and our population survey on hold."

"There's more missing than these people. Information on our Nikolai, for one."

Mac blinked. "What information?"

"Exactly. There isn't anything in the message about either Brymn or Trojanowski. Why?" Emily lowered her voice. "Or was it there—and someone tampered with it?"

For an instant, Mac seriously considered the notion. Then she laughed. "You, my dear Dr. Mamani, have read far too many books of the wrong sort. It isn't there, because it isn't necessary. Brymn will enlighten us tonight on his credentials and, hopefully, why he's here at all. As for our 'field operative'?" Mac paused, then shook her head. "To land this choice assignment, he's either offended the wrong people or is lousy at his job. Or both. In any event, there's no reason to believe we'll be stuck with them long enough for their backgrounds to matter."

Emily's long fingers played with the oversized emerald of her necklace, a family heirloom she never bothered to lock away, confident no one would believe she'd wear something so rare and expensive at Base. Mac had to concede her logic, even though she couldn't help occasionally translating the bauble's worth into an upgrade to the docking pads.

She knew the signs. "I take it you disagree, Em."

"You did take note of the locations and dates," Emily said in an odd voice. "The disappearances do not appear random."

"It's not like you to jump to conclusions from so small a sample—"

"It's not like you to put your own convenience ahead of the data."

"My—" Mac closed her mouth over the protest and stared at Emily. Rain drummed on the ceiling and walls like so many impatient fingers. "Is that what I'm doing?" she asked finally.

Emily raised one eyebrow and waited.

"Damn."

"We each have our failings at times. We won't mention your fashion sense, *sí*?"

Mac pulled out the envelope and waved it in the air. "Just show me what I missed."

"I can tell you. All of the locations are along the Naralax Transect." Perhaps sensing Mac's confusion, Emily shook her head, then drew a line in the air between them. "You never travel, do you? There are thousands of transects maintained by the Interspecies Union—"

"No-space corridors," Mac said dryly. "A.k.a. instant travel between connected solar systems. I may not gallivant like some, but I do know a bit about what's outside the atmosphere. So where does this Naralax Transect go?"

"Your ignorance is astounding."

Mac raised one brow. "I prefer to think of it as selective. So—are you going to tell me if there's anything special about the Naralax or continue to berate my choice of sciences?"

Emily shook her head in resignation. "Special? Depends on your definition. Home, for some. A dozen Human colonies. A few hundred non-Human systems, including our friend Brymn's. A record, of sorts. Our most distant trading partner, Thitus Prime, is reached via the Naralax. Beyond Thitus, the Naralax extends—oh—a few systems more." Emily's light tone gave no warning. "One famous. The Hift System. The rest, infamous."

"The Chasm." As she uttered the words, Mac felt the hairs lifting on the back of her neck.

"Ah, she does know something. Yes, the Naralax is the only transect that extends into the Chasm. There's a special destination for you, if you're a prospector, archaeologist, or tourist with a taste for the macabre."

Oh, she knew about the Chasm. Every biologist, every religious order—probably every being who learned of it—worried over its very existence at some point in their lives. "There's nothing in the Chasm," Mac said. Except for system after system containing life-capable planets, all completely without life.

Oh, it had been there once. It had—disappeared—three thousand years ago. That much, and only that, they knew.

She shook off a chill. *Stuff of fables.* "Don't tell me," Mac continued, raising her voice into a falsetto. "Chasm Ghouls have kidnapped all these beings and are on their way to Earth next. We're the only ones who can save the day." Before Emily could do more than begin to look offended, Mac relented. "That was uncalled for—"

"That's for sure—"

"I am grateful for any insights you have, Em. Frankly, if it were up to me alone, I'd stuff this message down your Nikolai's throat and let him look after our guest."

"Thus causing an interspecies' incident before supper?" Emily said, the corners of her lips curving up. "One would think you enjoyed notoriety. The vidbots would be here before dessert." Her smile faded. "Mac. The locations and dates matter because they occur as if whomever or whatever was behind the disappearances is traveling the Naralax from Thitus Prime toward Human-dominated space. The affected Dhryn colony is only systems away from our outermost settlement. If this pattern continues, the next beings to disappear may well be Human. I'd say that's valid reason for the Ministry and us to take this seriously."

"Serial murders. Mysterious disappearances. They happen all the time," Mac protested, stuffing the message back in her pocket. "We're talking thousands of worlds. Trillions of beings. Standards of morality that vary from incomprehensible to those that would make an alpha shark swim deep and fast. Let alone species like the Ehztif and Setihak . . . Sethilak . . . or however you say the damn name—you know, the ones who eat one another given half a chance and a dark alley. With all that, what makes these few incidents so significant?"

"Your first question for our dinner guests, I presume," Emily said, gesturing to the door. Then her slim hand turned palm up, stopping Mac before she could take a step. "The hair. At least the hair. Please, Mac."

"You've got to be kid—"

"Think of it as camouflage."

"You're going to be a pest about this, aren't you?"

"I'm right and you know it." Before Mac could move out of reach, Emily had grabbed her braid's end and tugged smartly. Hair, still damp enough to smell faintly of soap, cascaded over Mac's shoulder and threatened to cover one eye. "There," Emily pronounced with satisfaction.

Mac shook her head to settle the mass down the center of her back, shoving the strand over her left eye behind her ear. "Happy now?"

Emily's wolfish smile wouldn't have looked out of place on one of the Haida totems that still startled visitors to the shore. "I will be."

- Portent -

THE FIRST drop plunged into the fine sand, coalescing grains into a tiny, glistening ball, green against the dusky red of the dune. The ball slipped downslope very slightly, drawing a shallow line behind.

More drops fell, more balls formed, more lines clawed at the massive upcurve of the dune.

More. Drops struck already dampened balls, shattering them into smaller, darker portions that spread the green tint, the lie of life, across the sand.

Each impact sent its vibration coursing through the dune, the sum of all the drops a siren call to those who spread sensory hairs and waited for opportunity.

Serrated claws pushed through the sand, their owners as eager to sip from the rare cloudburst as they were to hunt others with the same intention. Slender whiskers trembled in search of imminent danger as other, barely larger creatures were drawn into the evening air. Writhing nodes of worms collected beneath what should have been the moisture they needed to reproduce.

It was not.

More drops fell, dissolving claw tip and whisker, searing away fur and flesh, melting everything they touched or that touched them into more balls of sand.

As the balls slipped downslope, the mouths were waiting.

- 4 -

ENCOUNTER AND ENLISTMENT

T HE GALLERY was on the main level of Pod Three, located there by practicality, since Three was the only residence pod in operation year-round. There were smaller cafeterias within the other residential pods, where students and staff could make their own meals. Most came here, saying they preferred the convenience and camaraderie of eating together. As a former student herself, Mac knew it had more to do with having someone else wash dishes.

The gallery was large enough to accommodate everyone on Base, but Mac had never seen this many filled tables on a late summer afternoon. *Was no one but Tie working?* Hopefully no ongoing experiments—besides hers and Emily's—were being ruined by neglect.

Not that she blamed the excited crowd. Most students had been here since spring thaw and novelty was a treasure. Their "guest" was the former, if not necessarily the latter.

He was sitting at the head table already—or rather beside it. Someone had done some quick work to modify a second table for the Dhryn so it sloped at an angle parallel to the alien's normal posture. Holes had been cut in the tabletop to support a variety of bowls and other utensils. The table leaned in the other direction as well, there being only enough room on the raised dais that held the head table for one end of it. Mac hoped the Dhryn could manage. The head table was supposedly for the research leaders, but was usually commandeered by whichever students got there first. The dais' elevation gave those sitting there the best view of the wallscreen during hockey games and other events.

No students up there now, Mac noted, wending her way through a maze of chairs, bags, and long, and some quite hairy, legs. She nodded and smiled in greeting, but didn't stop to chat with anyone, reasonably sure Emily would prod her in the back to get to where she was expected. Mac would have happily sat with the students, but there were two empty places beside the Dhryn.

The rest of the seats were already taken by Mac's fellow lead scientists: Lee Fyock, Martin Svehla, Kammie Noyo, Jirair Grebbian. The order in which they sat had nothing to do with relative seniority. Mac's and Kammie's work was year-round, which was why they split the administrative duties for Norcoast. The rest arrived each spring with their own teams of scientists, techs, and students, cluttering up available space and demanding more than their share of equipment. Once the resulting waves stopped crashing about, everyone slipped into research mode. The only command structure, as such, lay between the students and their supervisors and, by early summer, that typically degenerated, leaving only a group of individuals focused on their work.

There was, however, an unspoken acknowledgment that lovestruck Lee could sit beside Emily—who tolerated his attention because he lent her books—and Jirair, who tended to wander absently from any meal halfway through, always had an end seat. The other researchers would be either sitting with their students, in the field, or in a few cases, taking their meals in their lab. There were always some who remained blissfully oblivious to anything outside their work.

Mac glanced around the room. Trojanowski was conspicuously absent. She nodded to her bright-eyed colleagues as she took the seat closest to the Dhryn's table. No doubt they were brimming with curiosity. Mac paused to admire the cutlery, not having seen this many pointy objects on display in the gallery since Jirair's students had built a ceiling-high castle from sea urchin husks and left the remains to fumigate the entire pod. Emily sat beside her.

The room, which had been buzzing with voices and the tinkle of utensils as students experimented with theirs, fell silent.

"Welcome, Mackenzie Winifred Elizabeth Wright Connor!" The Dhryn's deep boom shook the windows. "Welcome, Emily Mamani Sarmiento!"

Definitely infrasounds under there, Mac told herself, now obliged to look directly at her guest for the first time since poking him in the whatever.

The Dhryn had reapplied his makeup, adding sequins along his ear ridges. The bands of silk wrapping his torso were now bright crimson, a color that went rather well with the Dhryn's mottled blue skin. There were gilded bobbles hanging from those bands showing above the sloped tabletop. *Dressed for the occasion.* As were, Mac registered belatedly, everyone else who possibly could be. Even the students were in their civvies, looking en masse like a riotous garden of floral shirts punctuated by the inevitable black T-shirts. No coveralls in sight.

Mac could feel Emily's *I told you so.* She sat a little straighter, taking what comfort she could in being clean. At least her hair wasn't trying escape its usual asymmetrical lump at the back of her head. Despite her cast, Emily had managed to pull the mass upward into a tight French braid, leaving only the length down Mac's back free to cause trouble. While it felt as though something with little claws and attitude was sitting on the top of her head, even Mac had to admit she looked more dignified than usual. Maybe she should wear it like this for her next meeting with Mudge, which now seemed by far the simpler half of her life.

"It is we who welcome you, Honorable Delegate," Mac responded, unsure if she was supposed to use his name in public, since even the Secretary General hadn't used it in the message. As she sought frantically for anything else to say, well aware the entire room was listening, she found herself transfixed by the alien's goldirised eyes. They seemed to hold a great sadness, despite the polite smile the Dhryn wore.

Could the disappearances of the Dhryn on Cryssin have involved individuals close to Brymn? His family, perhaps? Mac hadn't the slightest idea what a Dhryn family unit might be, but she trusted her instincts. *Whatever reason brought Brymn to her*, she decided, *it was something personal.* "We will help you," she promised quietly, "if we can."

Brymn's lips formed a small, closed circle. A bead of glistening yellow moisture trembled at the opening of one large nostril. Even as Mac hoped this was an indication of a positive emotional response and not a virus, the Dhryn flung his uppermost arm around her shoulders. "I knew I was right to come here. *Slimienth om glathu ra!* Thank you, Mackenzie Winifred Elizabeth Wright Connor! Thank you, all!" Brymn's voice vibrated the glasses on the table.

With each "thank you," the arm squeezed tighter. Forget bruising. Mac began to seriously worry if her bones could take the pressure. She managed a little squeak of protest which the Dhryn fortunately understood. Or he was about to let her go anyway. She was, Mac decided, saved from damage either way.

The buzzing of voices started up again as the students spotted the food trolleys being wheeled from the back. The buzz rose to near-deafening levels. *An extreme reaction to pizza, even from this group.* Mac squinted, trying to make out what was coming.

" 'My treat.' Is that the expression?" One of the advantages of multiple limbs was apparent as Brymn gestured grandly in all directions at once. "There was to be a grand supper at the Consulate for me tonight. I insisted the food be sent here instead. This is acceptable?"

From the exclamations of rapture spreading across the gallery, Mac had no doubts at all. "Thank you. Although I hope this won't cause you any difficulties." She wondered what a formal meal would be like at the IU Consulate and was ashamed when the first image in her mind was feeding time at an old-fashioned zoo.

"Difficulties, no." The Dhryn tilted forward conspiratorially. "But I suspect the consular staff would like to serve me for supper," he told her in what was presumably his notion of a whisper.

She almost smiled. "Here's hoping that doesn't happen."

"Indeed," Brymn agreed, leaning upright again. "I imagine there could be considerable discomfort involved!"

Mac chewed her lower lip for a second, then decided. She turned in her chair to more directly face the alien. "I want to apologize for—for—"

"What? Not letting me bully you?" His small lips could fashion quite an infectious grin. "Dear Mackenzie Winifred Elizabeth

Wright Connor, I'm lucky you don't work for the Consulate, or there'd be no treat on these tables tonight!"

"Why, you—" Mac shook her head, then found herself smiling. "You had me worried, I'll admit."

Brymn picked up two water-filled glasses, passing one to her. "To mutual understanding," he offered, lifting his glass to hers.

"Psst." Emily's breath tickled her ear. "Check out Seung and the rest of the Preds."

As she sipped her water, Mac let her eyes drift across the tables. They'd doubtless been arranged in tidy rows before the students arrived and 'modified' their environment. Now, they were clearly in clusters by research preference.

The Harvs were near the back wall. *She was slipping,* Mac told herself, not to have noticed those who should have been in the kitchen to help prepare food were sitting with the rest. Missies, catch-all slang for other, miscellaneous topics, filled the bulk of the room, subclustered by interests in benthic organisms, competition, long-term climatic trends, water or soil chemistry, and so on.

The Preds had claimed a group of five tables to the far right of Dhryn's table, aligned so they could run for the nearest exit if whales sang into their hydrophones. They were busy tossing buns to—or at—the occupants of one of their tables.

Clad in a black T-shirt, likely a loan from a student, and hefting a bun himself, Nikolai Trojanowski had blended remarkably well. Mac appreciated the effectiveness of Emily's radar for the new and male. She took another sip as she studied him. At least he had his glasses.

Coincidence, perhaps, that Trojanowski chose that moment to glance at the head table and catch her eyes. From this distance, Mac couldn't make out his expression. Not that she wanted to. Her face and neck flooded with heat as she remembered everything from the prickly softness of his suit under her hands to the splash when the poor man hit the water.

Make an impression indeed.

"What a wonderful color change," Brymn commented. *It begged the question of whether his vision included the infrared or the color red,* Mac thought glumly.

"She's very good at it," Emily said, leaning over the table to speak past Mac as if that worthy wasn't there and glaring.

"Is there significance? A hormonal state, perhaps?"

Mac aimed a kick under the table at her oh-so-amused friend, then decided against further physical reactions for the time being. "I'm a little warm," she assured Brymn, then went on quickly. "What's your preferred ambient temperature?"

"This is comfortable. A warmer and drier climate would be agreeable. Not that I'm complaining, but does it always rain here?"

The boisterous agreement from all within earshot seemed to startle the Dhryn, but he recovered quickly and waved his upper arms again in what Mac took for pleased acknowledgment. She edged her chair closer to Emily's, in case the Dhryn needed more room for such self-expression.

"Do you not have technology to modify your climate?" Brymn asked. "If this isn't what you prefer yourselves, wouldn't that be the obvious course? It is the first installation on any Dhryn colony."

"We do. There are control mechanisms in place to reduce the intensity of storms that threaten lives, or to end excessive drought in agricultural zones. Otherwise? No, we leave Earth pretty much as she is and complain about the weather." The trolley for the head table was now behind Mac. She sniffed appreciatively, leaning to one side to let the waiter-of-the-day, a skim-tech named Turner-Jay, deposit a steaming plate in front of her. Mac's eyes widened. *If this was the appetizer, they were in for a five-star feast.* Her stomach rumbled.

"Now you and I can leave." Brymn's low voice was almost lost beneath the clatter of knife and fork. She hadn't known he could speak so quietly.

Mac swallowed the saliva filling her mouth and looked at the Dhryn in disbelief. "Leave?" she echoed.

"A good time to speak privately is when others feast, is it not?"

She had to concede no one appeared interested in them at the moment. Even Trojanowski had his head bowed over Brymn's "treat." *Which now seemed something other than generosity.*

"As you wish." Mac folded her napkin beside her plate and inhaled the rich aroma one last time before standing.

The rain had stopped. Not only that, but the clouds were lifting, revealing foothills and shoreline, a hint of gray-mauve cliff, and, to the southwest, a glow where the sun would kiss the sea in another two hours. A westerly breeze chuckled through the pods and walkways, teased Emily's braidwork, then left to stir up waves in the distant heart of the inlet. Mac drew the smell of sea and forest into her nostrils, savored it, then promised her stomach something more substantial later.

There could be leftovers.

She led the way down the ramp from Pod Three to the walkway, glancing back to be sure her otherworldly companion could negotiate passages designed for Humans and their gear. Brymn moved like someone cautious of his balance, wise given the tendency of the walkway to rock from side to side under his greater mass. He could also have been unhappy about the ocean underfoot.

A valid conclusion, given his next request. "Could we go onshore, Mackenzie Winifred Elizabeth Wright Connor?"

"Call me Mac."

"Amisch a nai!"

Whatever the words meant, it wasn't something happy. Mac stopped and turned, her fingers wrapping around the rope rail. She narrowed her eyes as she stared up at him. "You aren't planning to make that abominable noise again, I hope."

The Dhryn was holding onto the ropes on both sides, using all six available hands. His seventh limb remained tucked under a red band. *Just as well*, Mac thought, remembering its sharp digits. Not helpful for rope grabbing, that was certain. "Are you all right?" she asked. "Should we go back inside?" Her stomach growled eagerly.

"I am well, Mackenzie Winifred Elizabeth Wright Connor. I will be even better if we can hold our discussion somewhere more private. And onshore."

Mac weighed the pleading note in the Dhryn's voice and the message in her pocket against the rules she'd have to bend, then shrugged. *It shouldn't be a problem.* She pointed down the walkway to Pod One. "Land's that way."

Norcoast's floating pods, like most of the homesteads, harvester processing plants, and other buildings along the coast, were kept upright and in place with anchors; ballast kept them submerged at the desired depth. In winter, Pods Three and Six remained as they were, protected from ice floes and storm winds by inflated barriers. Similar barriers, placed beneath, were used to lift the other pods free of the water until spring. The experience tended to startle those students who'd lingered through late fall to write up their theses and hadn't paid attention to the move-out date in their calendars. Someone always had to be plucked from a rooftop.

The complex of pods was linked to shore by one walkway, also removed from service during the winter months. Mudge, in his persona as Oversight Committee, had tried and failed to prevent a physical connection to the lands of the Wilderness Trust.

But it was access that could, and would, be rescinded at the first sign of complacency. All of the protective restrictions could be summed up by one phrase: no avoidable contact. Any unavoidable contact, such as the walkway holdfasts on shore, had been carefully planned for minimum impact and thoroughly documented so future researchers would be aware of all perturbations made to the area.

Which had led to some unique features in design and construction.

"It's perfectly safe," Mac assured the Dhryn when they reached the transition between the interpod walkway and the segment leading toward land. The former was built from slats of mem-wood, grown so that each piece would fit into the next like a giant puzzle and could be dismantled as easily. The shoreward walkway was something else again.

Seeing it, Brymn came to an abrupt halt, gripping the rope rails again. "Mackenzie Winifred Elizabeth Wright Connor," he rumbled somewhat breathlessly. "I do not wish to doubt, but are you sure?"

"I'm sure. We roll heavy equipment along it all the time." Mac stepped forward, trusting the anxious Dhryn would follow.

Trust was essential. To the eye, there was nothing between her feet and the white hiss of incoming surf four meters below. At least it wasn't high tide and the water almost underfoot. She did a little shuffle step, the effect as though she danced in air. "There's a bit of spring, but it's solid," she assured the Dhryn. The walkway material was a membrane, completely permeable to visible light, radiation, even water droplets—another way of reducing the impact of human structures on the shore's inhabitants. Mac could taste the spray on her lips and wondered what Dhryn thought of salt.

There was a railing of the same substance, continuing from the rope but invisible. Brymn found it by virtue of moving his hands forward two at a time, so he never had to completely let go. First one leg and footpod gingerly tested the walkway, then the other. "This is quite—remarkable," he said, his small mouth pursed as if in concentration.

Then he released his grips and sprang up into the air, dropping down with a bass "*Whoop!*" to meet the flex of the walkway, for all the world like her nephew on his backyard trampoline. Arms flailing for balance as the walkway pitched, Mac managed to find and grab the rail herself. "What—?"

The Dhryn's massive legs bent backward at a hitherto unseen joint, absorbing the energy from the walkway so it settled. "My apologies, Mackenzie Winifred Elizabeth Wright Connor." His eyes blinked slightly out of sync. "We have a *symlis*—a fable—of individuals who jump on air. I couldn't resist."

Play? Another congruence between their species? Mac filed the possibility away for later examination. *Much later.* "I take it you don't have a problem with heights."

Three arms waved in an extravagant gesture that, in a Human, dared her to do her worst.

The walkway carried them up and over the shore as it rose from the sea, the dark wet stone beneath giving way to a confusion of pale tree bones laced with drying strings of kelp. Crabs scuttled along, seeking shadows. A real gull, prospecting among the rocks, tilted its head to center one bright black eye on the spectacle of Human and Dhryn passing overhead, walking on air. That much interference couldn't be helped, although a low-level repeller kept flying things from collision or perch on the walkway itself. *Or web-building*, Mac mused, rather fond of the strands that glistened throughout the rest of the complex, beaded with crystal after every fog.

An artificial web faced them now, strung between the holdfasts as a token barrier. The tiggers pretending to roost in the staggered rows of forest ahead were the true guardians of the place, active night and day, programmed to accost anyone whose profile didn't appear in their data files. Given their lack of attention to Brymn, Mac concluded Tie had taken care of that detail. *Or Trojanowski.*

She pressed her palm over the lock on the right-hand pillar, then keyed in this season's code, waiting for Norcoast to send confirmation. The web folded itself away, a course of lights from beneath their feet briefly illuminating the choices currently in place: a path leading along the inner arm of the inlet, one rising to the treetops ahead, and a third swinging high over the rock to the left. The first two flashed red, indicating they had been reserved for specific projects. The last shone green.

In spite of everything, Mac grinned as she clawed wisps of hair from her eyes. She wasn't sure how much privacy Brymn wanted for their conversation, but she'd take any excuse to climb the inlet's outreaching arm. It had been two seasons since this particular area had been accessible. "Follow me."

The walkway was more rigid here, taut and formed into a series of steps. Each rise courteously drew itself in the air with a flash of green along its edge as they approached. Mac, curious, stood aside at the second step to let the alien take the lead. He didn't hesitate, lifting his ponderous foot the required amount to clear the illuminated line. *So.* The Dhryn's large eyes perceived at least that color.

Mac held tight to the railing as the walkway took them beyond the protection of the inlet's stone arm and they met the westerly wind straight off the Pacific. In the fall, those winds would shift east and intensify into storms. They were strong enough now. Her coveralls flapped against her skin and Emily's braid gave up the fight for dignity. Mac grabbed her suddenly free hair with one hand, turning to check on the Dhryn.

His eyes were no longer golden yellow and black. A membrane, perhaps an inner eyelid, now covered each. The result was as if his eyes had been plucked from their sockets and replaced with gleaming blue marbles. His silks, plastered tightly to his body by the wind, showed no signs of coming loose. Mac was mildly disappointed, having wondered what might be revealed of the alien's anatomy. Brymn waved her on.

Mac nodded, not bothering to talk over the rustling of her clothes, and led the way.

The outer side of the inlet's protective arm boasted a different shoreline, one that plunged like a knife into the ocean. Immense fingers of kelp, knuckled by shiny round bladders, stroked the waves into a dark, smooth rhythm. Salmon would be slipping through that underwater forest, drawn by the tastes of home flooding mouth and nostrils.

Mac could smell them, over the tang of cedar and fir.

The tide was on the move, too, its powerful eddies fighting the wind and each other with a roar and crash. Mac squinted, hoping to spot the sharp upright fins of orcas in the distance and seeing only the deceptive edges of waves to the horizon. She should have brought her 'scope.

They weren't here to sightsee. "Let me go first here," she advised Brymn, making sure the alien paid attention. He seemed as caught by the view as she'd been.

Four steps down, one after the other limned in black as the walkway compensated for the light now striking low and from the west. At the bottom, a mem-wood platform waited on pylons, complete with built-in bench and rails. From the way the wind stopped when they reached it, it must be surrounded by a curtain of the membrane that formed the walkway.

Probably Svehla's work. The joke around Base was that the talented carpenter would build everyone's retirement cottage instead of ever retiring himself. Mac explored the small area, then ran her hand along the rail on the ocean side. Regular holes marked where Preds had fastened their recorders and 'scopes.

Brymn came up beside her. She forced herself to stay still, even though his bulk intimidated this close. "Private enough?" she asked.

"Private and most spectacular. Thank you, Mackenzie Winifred Elizabeth Wright Connor."

She gritted her teeth. His continued use of her full name was becoming supremely annoying. *At least he didn't have a discernible body odor*, she reminded herself, trying to look on the bright side. She turned away from the Pacific to stare up at her visitor, noticing that his eyes had returned to normal. "Now. Why me?"

The Dhryn pursed his small mouth. "Sit. Please."

Mac walked over to the bench and obeyed, but hugged her knees to her chest so she could rest her arms on top. "I'm sitting."

He faced her, then slowly settled his backside to the platform by bending his legs at their uppermost joint. His two lower hands pressed against the wood, arms stiffening to form a secure tripod. "Ah. I've wanted to do this all day."

"You didn't have to use a chair," Mac noted dryly.

A cavalier wave. " 'When visiting a species . . .' You know the rest of the expression, I'm sure. Still, it does the body good." Before Mac could attempt to swing the conversation back to the note in her pocket, Brymn grew serious, his voice lowering in depth until she felt it through the bench. "Evolutionary units."

Mac blinked. "Pardon?"

Brymn looked worried. "You are the Mackenzie Winifred Elizabeth Wright Connor who has published extensively on that topic, are you not? There can't be two Humans with that same name, surely."

"Yes. To being the one, that is." Mac frowned. "I thought you were investigating the disappearances."

"I am. You've read the report, I see."

An eagle skimmed past them, the head and spine of a salmon locked in its talons. Mac suddenly empathized with the fish. "Forgive me, Brymn, if I seem confused, but I don't see any connection between my research and these missing people. Tragic as those losses are," she added hastily.

"People?" he echoed, eye ridges rumpling. "Far more than people are missing, Mackenzie Winifred Eliz—"

Enough was enough! "Please. Stop doing that. Humans rarely use their complete names. Never in conversation. Call me Mac." As Brymn opened his mouth again, Mac pointed at him and shook her finger warningly. "Mac."

"It would be highly disrespectful for me to omit any of your earned names. *Amisch a nai.*"

His distress was palpable. Mac rubbed her chin on her forearm. "A compromise to keep me sane," she offered. "Call me Mac when it's just you and me. Like this. No one else need know."

"If you insist." Brymn's lips pressed tightly together for an instant, as if over a bad taste. "Mac."

"Perfect. See how nice and quick that is?" Mac lifted her head. "So. What else was missing?"

"Everything."

"Equipment, transports—" she hazarded.

He shook his head. "Those remained, though damaged. Everything alive. Everything that had been alive. Gone."

Mac sat up, her feet thumping down on the platform. "Over how large an area?"

"The largest discovered so far involved almost twenty square kilometers. A valley. Scoured clean to the overburden. Even the soil was empty of life or its remains."

"Like the worlds in the Chasm," Mac said, her lips numb.

"Like the worlds in the Chasm," the Dhryn repeated. He rocked back and forth, his ridged nostrils flared. "So I come to you, Macken—Mac—because those aware of these disasters have good reason to believe we are all in the gravest of dangers. And I believe your work may hold a key to our survival."

Mac shook her head, sending hair tumbling over one shoulder. Automatically, her hands began braiding the tangled mass into order. She wished she could do the same with her thoughts. *Why hadn't the so-secret report contained this information? How could such a thing still be secret at all?* She focused on what she did know. "I work with salmon. An Earth species."

A low hooting sound. Frustrating, not knowing if it was laughter, a sob, or alien flatulence. *She had to read more.* "Your interest is in a bigger question, is it not? One that applies to all living things. What is the minimum genetic diversity required in a population to respond to evolutionary stress? What is that evolutionary unit for a species, a community? For a world?"

"You can't simply extrapolate . . ."

Brymn rose to his feet. "Do you deny the importance, Mac, of knowing how many of us must continue to live, if our species are to survive the doom threatening us all?"

The Dhryn had a distinct flare for melodrama, Mac decided. Her eyes narrowed in suspicion. "Exactly what do you do, Brymn?"

"I study the remains of the past, to better understand what may be to come."

"A—paleontologist?"

Another low hoot. *Surprise or humor*, Mac concluded. "No, no. An archaeologist. I thought you might have heard of me. Read my work? I'm quite famous in some circles."

"I study salmon," Mac found herself emphasizing, as if the words anchored her to something saner than this conversation. "I don't get outside my field much."

"You study life! That's why I need your expertise."

"Why come all the way here—to me?" she asked reasonably. "Why not work with a Dhryn biologist? Surely some of your scientists are working on the same questions."

The Dhryn became utterly still, his large eyes regarding her with what Mac could only interpret as a wistful expression. Then he said in a voice only slightly louder than the slap of water on rock: "This is something you need to know, Mac, but I can only tell you if you agree to keep it in the strictest confidence. Not even my assigned companion, Nikolai Piotr Trojanowski, may learn this. May I tell you?"

As if she'd refuse? Mac gave one quick nod.

"I am ashamed to admit there are no Dhryn biologists. The study of living things has been forbidden throughout our history. It remains so. I would be refused *grathnu*, Mackenzie Winifred Elizabeth Wright Connor, should any of my lineage learn I was speaking to you about such things, or that I had read and understood any of your work."

Mac tried to wrap her brain around an entire civilization without biology and failed. "What about medicine? Doctors?"

Brymn sat down again. "*Nie rugorath sa nie a nai.* It translates roughly as: 'A Dhryn is robust or a Dhryn is not.' There are other such sayings. Suffice it to say there are no sick Dhryn."

"Agriculture?"

"We consume varieties of what you would call fungi, Mac. Long ago, our leaders conveniently ruled that what is grown for this purpose is not alive. Today, these organisms are considered components of a chemical manufacturing process. Their study is part of engineering, not life science as you know it." He paused, seemingly thoughtful. "Truly, we don't have many scientists at all. The most proper study for a Dhryn is what it means to be Dhryn. Our brightest minds are urged to become artists, historians, or perhaps analysts. Our advances in applied science and technology, like many of yours, are purchased from those who possess that cultural priority."

Fascinated, Mac started to reply, then abruptly signaled the Dhryn to silence.

Anywhere else along the coast, the sound of gulls would signal the arrival of a harvester, or a run of pilchard or candlefish. They'd gather and bark in their hundreds over the bubbles of a humpback's fishing trap.

They wouldn't sound like these gulls. This vocal outrage was too regular in pitch and pacing, a deliberate mismatch to nature so these calls wouldn't distract or lure the real thing. *Tiggers*.

"Is something wrong, Mac?" Brymn asked.

"Wait here."

Mac ran up the steps, her hands shoving her braid under her collar. As she left the protection of the membrane, the wind gave her a too-helpful push. She grabbed at where the rail should be but missed it, the result being a drunken stagger to the next step. Of course, the Dhryn would be watching all of this grace in motion.

She found her footing and continued to the top of the rise.

The reason for the outrage was clear enough. A solitary figure was climbing the walkway toward her. Brown hair and a black T-shirt. The glint of glasses as the head angled up. *Trojanowski*. He dared wave at her, as if they'd arranged to meet.

The bureaucrat wasn't the target of the milling tiggers, however. They were massed over a flotilla of kayaks attempting to dock near Pod Two. Attempting, because the tiggers were programmed to prevent that as well, so they were flying directly at the faces of those paddling before dropping their tags. Mac could almost feel sorry for them.

Almost. She scowled. "Tourists."

Or worse. The gleefully clashing colors of life jackets and kayaks might shout summer rental, but Mac didn't forget Emily's prediction that the media would be interested in her guest. *Guests,* she sighed to herself, glaring at the man below.

"Guests?" Brymn boomed in her ear.

Mac gave a yip of surprise at having her thoughts echoed in a deep bass. Either the Dhryn could tiptoe, or the wind flapping her coveralls had overwhelmed whatever noise the creature had made.

She recovered, indicating Trojanowski, who'd turned to watch the show in the inlet. "I don't understand how he got in—takes the gate code and confirmation. No one at Base would give it to him without asking me first."

Brymn "sat" beside her, putting his head on a level with hers. "Nikolai Piotr Trojanowski was assigned to me at the Consulate, upon my arrival. We have not been traveling together long enough for me to assess his technical capabilities. I think we must assume they are considerable, given the importance of my investigation." There was a note of what would be pride in a Human voice.

Mac came close to telling the Dhryn the assessment of his investigation expressed in the Secretary General's note, then changed her mind. She'd defended her share of research that seemed esoteric and irrelevant to the layperson. The uncommon, unpopular questions were, in her experience, worth asking. More than once she'd seen them generate new schools of thought and previously unimagined applications.

More than once, she'd poured time and energy into an idea that turned out to be riddled with holes, but she preferred that risk over the chance of missing something significant. She would make her own judgment about Brymn's investigation.

And about something else. "Let's not assume anything about Mr. Trojanowski, Brymn, until we know him better," she suggested. "Keep things between the two of us for now. We can continue our discussion later—come to my office when you get a chance."

"Then, Mac, we are truly *lamisah*—allied?"

Yesterday, Mac would have laughed at anyone who said she'd be standing here, talking to an alien—an archaeologist, yet—about an alliance that included keeping secrets from a representative of her own government. *Hell*, she told herself ruefully, *she'd have laughed off any suggestion she wouldn't be deep in observations at Field Station Six right now.*

She gazed at the inlet, seeing how the clouds had lifted so they draped languidly over the white shoulders of the coastal peaks, the sun intensifying the necklace of forest green below, begemmed by the gold and oranges of early turning trees. The glittering blues, blacks, and greens of the ocean, stirred by the breeze, refused to reflect that glory, as if more interested in the life surging beneath its waves. The pods, full of humanity probably now enthralled by dessert trays; the kayaks, filled with the curious . . .

Yesterday, she would have scoffed at any threat to this place.

"*Lamisah*, Brymn," Mac agreed, wrapping her arms around herself, as if the wind had grown cold.

DINNER AND DISCORD

"**S**O THEY are the damned media!" Mac lowered her voice with an effort. She hadn't thought her life could become any more complicated, but Trojanowski's confident nod left no doubt.

"I recognized a couple of faces from press gatherings at the Consulate," he told her. "Someone must have leaked the Honorable Delegate's itinerary. First Dhryn on Earth, you know."

"Must be a slow news week," Mac muttered under her breath. Louder, "I'll call the coast police to—"

"I don't advise it, Dr. Connor. That would only fuel their interest. They'd be back tomorrow, in larger numbers."

Trojanowski had escorted her and Brymn back to Pod Three, which had meant passing the crowd of angry, miserable-looking kayakers, their bodies and heads splattered with tigger droppings, their boats trapped between Norcoast skims. The Dhryn had seemed fascinated by all the shouting, although they didn't stay in range long.

Mac had caught Trojanowski waving at Tie, who'd been standing in one of the skims. Tie had offered back an unusually cheerful "thumbs-up."

So. The bureaucrat must have delayed in following her and Brymn, presumably to give Tie instructions on how to deal with the intruders. Mac wasn't sure if she approved of Mr. Trojanowski ordering her staff around.

She did realize she didn't have much say in the matter.

Now, standing outside the closed door to her own quarters, which presently housed a large, blue alien, Mac did her best to regain some control of the situation. "If I'm not to call the police, Mr. Trojanowski, what are you suggesting? That I leave them in their kayaks to keep swearing at my staff?"

"And what kind of reports would they make about the Honorable Delegate's trip, Dr. Connor, or your facility?" He lifted his hands and shoulders, as if asking her to admit defeat. "I've made arrangements for them to stay here overnight. I'll be setting up interviews with the Honorable Delegate in a couple of hours. Hopefully, that will satisfy them."

"A couple of hours?" *So much for Brymn coming to her office later.*

Trojanowski's eyes twinkled behind their lenses. "They'll need time to shower first, don't you think?"

Tigger glue. It had a deliberately pungent odor. Mac's lips twitched involuntarily at the image. "A soak in solvent's more useful." She conceded the inevitable with a shrug of her own. "Seems you have this well in hand, Mr. Trojanowski. But I'd better not meet one of them—or hear they've interfered with anyone's work."

Trojanowski gave a crisp bow. "Leave it with your diplomatic liaison, Dr. Connor. That's why I'm here."

"Among other reasons," she dared add. The corridor outside her quarters was deserted. "I've read the message."

"And you have questions," he guessed. "Let me walk you to your office, Dr. Connor. If that's where you were heading?"

Mac sighed. She'd hoped to go back to the gallery and hunt leftovers, but the large central hall was undoubtedly filling up with filthy media eager for a target. They'd probably spilled into the lower corridors already. "I'd better check in with the Admin staff first—smooth whatever feathers were ruffled by our visitors and see what, if anything, the Oversight Committee has to say on the subject." *Not in a hurry to find that out,* Mac decided. "We can go on the terrace and take the stairs," she suggested.

"Excellent idea." He held up the pouch he'd been carrying, the one that held his portable office. Mac was beginning to believe he slept with the thing. "I've enough for two."

"I beg your pardon?"

Trojanowski refused to explain, leading the way to the terrace door and holding it for her.

Mac licked a crumb from her lower lip and smiled blissfully. "That was—that was great. Thank you." *Who'd have guessed?* Yet here she was, halfway down the stairs curving around Pod Three, legs outstretched, back comfortably against the wall, sitting shoulder to shoulder with Nikolai Trojanowski to share his stolen supper. Strips of savory duck, asparagus tips, salmon puffs, the list went on and on, each having appeared like magic from his pouch, each disappearing in what Mac had to admit was one of the most relaxed and companionable meals she'd had in a long time.

The view didn't hurt. Mac gazed contentedly out at Pods Five and Six, their curves catching the setting sun, the opposite halves deep in shadow so they looked more like natural islands than usual. The waves beyond were gilded as well. "Pod Six is the newest," she informed him, pointing to it. Their conversation had proved as easy as the meal, on her part, anyway. Answering questions about her home was always a pleasure. Mac only hoped she wasn't overdoing it. "Not that it's that new—I spent a summer there doing a special project."

"Salmon acoustics with Professor Sithole."

Mac looked at Trojanowski in surprise. "We didn't publish anything. How did you know?"

He grinned. "The wonders of record keeping, Dr. Connor. You received a grant to work with him. Money leaves tracks, as the expression goes."

A satisfied stomach helped calm Mac's initial reaction to being "tracked," but there was still an edge to her: "Professional snoop, are you?"

"I like to know who I'm dealing with," he admitted, unrepentant. "So tell me. Did you enjoy listening to your salmon?"

Mac looked back at Pod Six. Her voice grew wistful. "Of course. But I did it to work with Jabulani—Dr. Sithole—while Norcoast still had him. He could do incredible things with sound. Which is why he moved to bigger and better labs years ago."

Trojanowski was rooting around in his pouch. "Looks like we're done," he announced. "I'll have to run this through the sonic shower."

"I still can't believe you took the butter," she commented, watching him smear the last of it on his half of a bun.

"I wasn't the only one," Trojanowski said cheerfully. "Those students of yours probably stripped the table. Besides, I had time as well as opportunity. Your Dr. Mamani wasn't in a hurry to let me get up and follow you."

"Em?" Mac laughed. "You're lucky you escaped. Few men—" She stopped, remembering who she was with. Outside in familiar surroundings, the casualness of sitting on mem-wood, even his borrowed black T-shirt and pants fooled her, as if Trojanowski was just another student. Nicely snug shirt and pants, as Emily would doubtless notice. Mac blushed and pulled her knees to her chest. *He wasn't a student; she didn't notice such things.* "I meant to apologize for pushing you off the walkway," she said, to cover the moment and because she meant it.

His shrug brushed her shoulder. "No need. I'd have lost my temper, too. I regret we came at such a crucial time in your work, Dr. Connor." A pause while they both watched an eagle circle high above the pod. When it was little more than a black speck, he went on: "I hear you left your equipment at the river. Does that mean you'll be able to continue?"

Mac stared out across the inlet, at the mountains beyond. The mouth of the Tannu was hidden from sight behind tree-coated islands. Her salmon would find it, no trouble at all. They could be there now, in their hundreds of thousands, in their millions.

But what she'd learned from Brymn—what might be happening— that mattered, too. "How soon I go back depends on what you want from me, doesn't it?"

Trojanowski closed the pouch and stood, reaching down one hand to pull Mac to her feet. She had the impression her question troubled him. "It isn't what I want—or the Ministry," he began. "Brymn's the one who asked for you, Dr. Connor. He hasn't told us why. Did he tell you? That is why he insisted on your missing supper, wasn't it? To talk to you without me."

Mac didn't answer immediately, distracted by the way he'd kept her hand in his. *Social quandaries weren't her strength.* Should she tug her hand free, in case he'd simply forgotten to let go, or leave it there, in case he wanted to hold it even longer—which led to another complicated series of possibilities she really didn't need to consider under the circumstances. *What if he thought* she *was holding on to* him *and was going through the same choices?* No, definitely he was the one holding. Her hand was just lying there, innocent of any intention.

"Dr. Connor?" Trojanowski gave her an odd look.

What would Emily do?

Mac eased her hand back the tiniest amount, not hard enough to say she was offended, but enough to remind him it was there. He let go, his hand staying palm up between them for an instant longer, as if surprised to be empty.

Mac wrapped her fingers around the railing and coughed her voice back into existence. "Brymn's obviously familiar with my work. Some of it, at least. But nothing he said explained how it might help investigate these terrible disappearances. I don't see any relevance."

"Frankly, neither do I. I've sent a complete set of his publications to your office. Maybe you can find a link we can't."

Mac gave him a dismayed look. "Brymn is an archaeologist. I study salmon." *Why did she have to keep explaining that?*

"You'll be back to your fish sooner, Dr. Connor, if you can establish that Brymn's line of investigation is—invalid. If he even has one."

The sun was dipping into the ocean. Where the pod wall shadowed the terrace, lights began to glow along the underside of the railing, more outlining the steps of the stairs. It reflected in his glasses, hiding his eyes.

"And you won't have to baby-sit," Mac said, sure she was right.

"We both have other duties being neglected, Dr. Connor. I have to consider the possibility that the Honorable Delegate is, intentionally or not, playing tourist at our expense."

"What if Brymn is on to something significant?"

Trojanowski gave an expansive gesture, including the inlet and pods. "We are here," he reminded her, "in hopes he is. What else did he tell you?"

The impromptu feast had brought them closer. *Such moments never lasted*, Mac told herself. "I can't say," she said firmly.

She might have thrown a switch. Trojanowski frowned, his voice sharp and officious. "Can't—as in won't?"

Mac nodded.

"You must know that's not an option, Dr. Connor. The Ministry expects your full cooperation." Trojanowski took the next step and turned to face her, his hand on the railing below hers. The move effectively blocked her path down the stairs.

It also started her temper rising. *She hated being trapped.*

"I told you, Mr. Trojanowski: I can't say," Mac pressed her lips together, then settled for: "It was nothing that would matter to you."

"Let me be the judge of that, please. It's my job, Dr. Connor." No antagonism, no threat. Just an implacable purpose sheathed in courtesy.

He wasn't a Charles Mudge she could outshout or bluff.

Honesty, then, Mac decided. "I'm sorry, Mr. Trojanowski. But Brymn asked me to promise I wouldn't share our discussion. I did and I won't."

"I see." He took his hand from the rail, and backed down another step, giving her room, not a sense that he was giving up. She hadn't expected he would. "It's not possible to fulfill every promise we make, Dr. Connor," he said reasonably. "In this case, I think you must realize—"

"I keep my word, Mr. Trojanowski," Mac interrupted stiffly. "Don't you?"

He turned his head to look out over the inlet. The sun was almost down. Mac doubted he could see much more than the silhouettes of ocean and land against the dusk-washed clouds. *Or*, she wondered abruptly, *was he looking at something else entirely?*

"I don't give it, Dr. Connor," he said at last. "Not anymore." Then he met her eyes. His own were warm behind their lenses, their hazel darker in the changing light. "That doesn't mean you should stop. For now, I'll rely on your judgment to know what to pass along from Brymn."

"I didn't do this to cause a problem," Mac said uncomfortably. "Brymn was anxious, embarrassed. It was the only way to reassure him he could talk to me." She frowned. "But that's exactly what you wanted. Brymn and I, away from anyone else. Otherwise, you would have stopped us before we left the gallery."

His lips quirked. "You've got me there, Dr. Connor."

"Hmmph." Mac shook her head. "You could have just said so."

"We weren't on the best of terms earlier today." Definitely a grin—an infectious one. "I confess to fearing you'd toss me in the drink again, Dr. Connor."

Mac snorted. Skims were unloading by Pod Five and she stepped down to stand beside him at the rail to watch. "You mentioned other duties," she ventured, a peace offering of sorts. "What do you do when you aren't looking after traveling aliens and delivering scary envelopes to unsuspecting biologists?"

"Oh, that's pretty much my full-time job." His voice was deeper when amused, feathered a bit along the edges. Mac rather liked the sound.

"There you are!"

Of all the voices Mac hadn't wanted to hear at this moment, Emily's cheerful call was at the top of the list. *What were the odds?* Trojanowski turned to give the approaching woman a pleasant smile. As turning put him closer to Mac, something Emily acknowledged with a sly look the moment she reached them, all Mac could do was hope the darkening sky would hide any blush. "Hi, Em."

Gone was the sophisticated jumpsuit Emily had worn to supper with Brymn. Now her sandals kicked aside panels of a wild floral print skirt as she came up the stairs to join them, the fabric gathered in a knot low on one bare hip. Her top was a relatively conservative yellow shirt, with huge buttons shaped like letters spelling 'YUM' down the front. The same word was scrawled on her cast.

Camouflage, Mac judged it. Emily dressed as she wanted to be seen. This version was the "brain-on-hold" party animal. The question remained, was it for the media, Brymn, or the man standing beside her? *Could be all three.*

"And you must be what's been keeping our Mac busy. I don't believe we've been properly introduced." Em proffered her right hand to Trojanowski, eyes sliding up and down his lean frame with obvious approval. "I see you're nice and dry."

"Nikolai Trojanowski, at your service, Dr. Mamani." He touched his fingertips to hers, but didn't take her hand. Instead, he bowed his head briefly.

Emily narrowed her eyes. *Assessment*, Mac decided. "So formal. Emily, please."

"My duty as liaison requires formality, Dr. Mamani."

Mac knew that glint in those dark eyes. *Trouble.* To forestall it, she nodded at the stairs. "I'd better get going. I've some—reading—waiting for me."

"Kitchen first," Emily ordered brusquely. "You will help me make sure Mac gets something in her stomach, won't you . . . Mr. . . . Trojanowski?"

"Already taken care of," he said.

"Really?"

"I really need to get going." Mac suited action to words, hurrying down the remaining flight of stairs. She reached the walkway at the pod base before the other two could catch up, and headed around its curve to the entrance, only to halt in dismay. The main door was open to the night air and presently filled with strangers.

Nothing for it but to reach the admin office the back way, which meant going back upstairs. Mac spun around, only to collide forcibly with those coming behind her.

No one was hurt. In fact, Emily laughed, loudly enough to attract attention from Pod One, let alone the curious horde waiting by the door, doubtless equipped with vids and recorders. Mac hurriedly shook off the hands that had saved her from bouncing on her rump and pushed by both of them.

"Hey, Mac. Mac! Slow down. I'm sorry!"

Already on the third step, Mac glanced back. Emily was hurrying after her, but she'd expected that. Her friend was typically—and charmingly—contrite after embarrassing her. Trojanowski was there too. He pointed to the entrance. "They'll be gone any minute, Dr. Connor. Mr. McCauley's there—I assume to take them to their quarters. We can just wait, if you like."

She would like *to run up the stairs and avoid any chance of being interviewed.* Instead, Mac sighed and sat down where she was. *Mature behavior was expected from the coadministrator of a world-class research facility.* It was a lovely night, now that the breeze had died away. "Good idea."

Trojanowski sat one step below hers, leaning back against the pod wall. Emily picked the same step, but closer to the railing. *The ensuing silence could only,* Mac decided, *be called painful.*

There were reasons, she thought grimly, *to avoid social interactions.*

Trojanowski spoke first. "I understand you're quite the traveler, Dr. Mamani."

"I like to go places," Emily said, imbuing the phrase with more than one meaning. *No chance she'd tone down the innuendo,* Mac knew. Not in this mood. She leaned back on the rail support to listen, only to sit up straight again as Emily went on: "Not like our Mac, here."

"What?"

"C'mon, Mac. You know it's true. Your idea of an exotic landscape is anything with traffic control. You haven't been *anywhere.*"

"I just got back from Vancouver, thank you very much," Mac retorted.

"I make my case," Emily crowed. "Mr. Trojanowski, you work with the Interspecies Union. I'm sure you're a very well-traveled man yourself." *Amazing—or was it appalling?* Mac debated numbly—*what that sultry voice could do with a phrase.* "Did you know you were in the presence of a woman who's never left her continent, let alone her planet? Nor plans to?"

That again? "I'm perfectly happy here," Mac replied somewhat testily. Emily was forever trying to convince her to travel offworld. She should have known it wouldn't stop because they had company. Of sorts.

Polite company, at least. "Not everyone enjoys space flight," Trojanowski pointed out. "I take it you do, Dr. Mamani?"

A broad smile. "I'm the adventurous sort. But then again, I like knowing what's around me. But not our Mac. Oh, no."

"Drop it, Em," Mac said under her breath, doing her best to glare without being obvious.

Emily ignored her, words coming more quickly as she warmed to her topic. "What if I told you, Mr. Trojanowski, that you are in the presence of a woman—a biologist!—whose willing experience with non-Human intelligence can be summed up by a handful of entertainment vids and news clips, until the arrival of our being in blue? Who can't name the three systems closest to ours . . . who has absolutely no interest in any intelligent species but her own!" Emily stopped, the "Y" button on her shirt threatened by her deepened breathing. The light from the railing shone in her hair, but didn't reach her face.

Mac knew what was happening, if not why. For whatever reason, Emily didn't like Trojanowski—or was it his questions—and was tossing Mac between them as a diversion. *Which would have been fine, except*— Mac stopped the thought. "Are you quite finished?" she asked instead.

Emily tossed her head. "Not yet. Mr. Trojanowski is an expert— the kind we never see on Norcoast. I want to hear his opinion of such a person."

He didn't seem to notice Mac's discomfort. "My opinion? There isn't anyone alive who doesn't have something left to learn." He brought up one knee and rested his arm on it. "And I submit that the opposite is true. There's no one alive without something they'd like to unlearn—to forget. Wouldn't you agree, Dr. Mamani? Care to us give an example—something recent, perhaps?"

Check and challenge.

"We're talking about Dr. Connor, not me. Come on. You must see the waste. The least you can do is help me yank Mac's head out of her river—make her see there's a universe nearby."

"I am sitting right here," Mac protested. "On the off chance you decide to talk to me, instead of about me."

Whatever had Emily in such fine and difficult form, it was more than Trojanowski. Em turned and stared up at her, her eyes shockingly brilliant, as if moist with tears. "I've tried talking to you,

Mac," she said, her voice low and intense. "I've tried for three years and you haven't heard a word I've said. Not a word. I might as well be shouting in a vacuum. And it's going to be too late, Mac, by the time you wake up. Too damned late for anything."

With that, she stood and walked away, skirt whirling around her long legs.

Mac froze, torn between following Emily and demanding an explanation, and the patent need to explain to the now silent man beside her on the stairs that this wasn't what Emily was like.

Until this minute, anyway. *What was going on?*

Mac decided she didn't want to know. "Mr. Trojanowski. Let me apologize for Emily. Dr. Mamani. She's usually more—" *tactful wasn't really the word,* "—considerate."

The railing light caught the lenses of his glasses, the curls in his hair. Nothing more. "Was she right about you?"

Did it matter what he thought? Mac hesitated, then again decided on honesty. She wasn't ashamed of her way of life. "I frustrate her because I made a choice long ago. You talked about having more to learn. Well, there's more to learn, right here, about this world, than I could fit into a dozen lifetimes. So I chose to focus. That's all. But Emily believes I'm deliberately ignoring what she considers important."

Another quiet question. "Are you?"

"Maybe. To some extent, yes." Mac patted the mem-wood stair by her foot. "What happens here is my business. If I believed it mattered to what I do here, I'd pay attention to other sentients. I tend to treat politics and—social situations—the same way." Mac sighed. "Come to think of it, that gets Emily angry, too."

"Yet you're good friends."

"The best!" Mac shook her head. "But stubborn. Em tries to improve me. I'm the way I am." Nervously, she unknotted her braid and began to undo it. *She had to know.* "Are you sorry you brought your Honored Delegate to someone with her head stuck in a river?"

"Not when I consider that in less than a day, Dr. Connor, you've learned his name and gained his confidence, all while sacrificing your own work to help investigate a possible threat to our species. Dr. Mamani would be impressed by that, don't you think?"

For an instant, Mac thought he somehow knew she'd shown Emily the message, then she realized Trojanowski was simply being kind. "Emily will be fine," she said confidently. "Ten minutes from now you'll never know she'd been angry."

"What about you?"

"Me?" Mac watched a spider starting to spin her web under the railing, taking advantage of the light. Were personal questions part of his job? *Probably.* "I can hold a grudge a while," Mac said lightly. Permanently was more like it.

"I'd never have guessed."

She laughed. "You?"

Trojanowski put one hand over his heart. "They set civil servants to run on neutral—didn't you know?"

Like a signal, the bar of light marking the door dimmed and brightened as people walked through it. Mac could see small groups heading to Pods Four and Five. "Tie's putting them in with the students," she observed. "I wish them luck getting any sleep."

"I'd better grab a few for interviews now. Brymn's eager, at any rate."

They walked around the curve to the entrance, finally deserted. Before she opened the door, Mac stopped to look up at him. "I'll read his publications over tonight," she said. "Maybe I'll find something there."

"Here's hoping. Good night, Dr. Connor."

"Good night. And thank you. For the meal and your company." Mac reached out her hand. "I enjoyed both."

Maybe it was the growing darkness that dislocated time. Maybe it was lapping of waves and distance-muted voices that created a bubble of stillness around them. Maybe that's what made it seem they'd known each other much longer than a day. Whatever the reason, Mac somehow wasn't at all surprised when Trojanowski not only took her hand in his, but lifted it to his lips.

"As did I, Dr. Connor," he said quietly, his breath warm on her fingers.

- 6 -

STUDY AND SUSPENSE

"And . . . ?"

"That's all of it."

Emily's eyebrows disappeared under her bangs. "You've got to be kidding. A doom like the Chasm spreading through known space, and all Brymn told you was how ashamed he was at his kind's lack of scientists? Nothing more?"

"I told you, Em," Mac said, digging the knuckles of two fingers into a tight spot on her neck. "We were interrupted. Brymn shut up tighter than a drum when Trojanowski reached us. After that—well, we took him to my quarters to temporarily protect the Honorable Delegate from the less than honorable intentions of the world media. Reasonable, I suppose."

"Considering what it's been like dealing with seventeen of them covered in tigger spots, three claiming we tried to drown them, and one locking himself to the nearest vidphone?" Emily grinned suddenly. "I'd want to be protected, too."

"As if you'd need it. Brymn will come here when he can. Which may not be until tomorrow. Till then . . ." Mac dropped her imp into its slot, then put her bare feet up on her desk and leaned back her chair. She toggled off her deskside privacy mode and the workscreen formed in the air before her eyes. The 'screen adjusted its distance and brightness according to the level of eye fatigue it detected. It compensated for ambient light as well, tilting to avoid competing with any beams of sunlight coming into Mac's office—

not a problem at this hour. All well and good, Mac decided, except that the optimum distance grew slightly every year, as the 'screen tactfully compensated for the aging of human eyes. At the rate it was traveling down her legs, it would be hovering over her toes before she retired.

The Admin office had been surprisingly peaceful, under the circumstances; Mudge as well, apparently uninformed about the kayak invasion. Mac saw no reason to enlighten him, since none had approached shore. On returning to her office, Mac hadn't been surprised to find Emily already waiting, eager to talk about Brymn. Back to her normal, cheerful self as if nothing had happened.

If there was an explanation to come, Mac wasn't going to hold her breath waiting for it.

She began calling up data, then asked absently: "Is he unlocked yet? The reporter?"

"No one was rushing, let's put it that way. Let me see." As Emily was peering over her shoulder, Mac sent a duplicate 'screen to hover over the other chair in her office.

Her friend took the hint and the seat, body passing through the 'screen while her head swiveled to keep reading its display. "Dhryn physiology. Why? Planning to poison him? A little drastic over missing the salmon run."

Mac ignored her, busy scanning down what turned out to be a disappointingly brief list of references. She called each up in turn.

Emily read along. "Great. Now we know they pay their dues to the IU on time, have colonies on forty-eight intensely dreary planets, and prefer their privacy. No other species says bad things about them. No one says good things about them. How boring can a race be?"

"Surely not this boring." Mac was keying in other parameters without success, her curiosity engaged. "Odd. We seem to have found out more for ourselves than has been recorded about the Dhryn. You know what little that is. You'd think there'd at least be dietary info . . ."

"Well, Brymn's supper was wonderful. Shame you missed it."

"Didn't," Mac said absently. " 'Cept the dessert."

"Maybe there's something in the stas-unit?"

"I cleaned it out before we left for the field. You do remember what happened last year . . ."

Em wrinkled her nose in disgust. "I still say you should have made that a project for one of the pathology postdocs. Maybe I should send to the kitchen? Can't have you starve, Mac."

"Emily. I'm not hungry." At the knowing smile greeting this, Mac rolled her eyes and sat back, knowing Em would persist until satisfied. "Fine. For your information, Dr. Mamani, Mr. Trojanowski grabbed what he could of supper before following us onshore. We sat on the terrace and he kindly shared it with me before you showed up. That's all."

"Oh-ho. That's not all by a long shot, Mac." Emily perched on Mac's desk. "I want details."

"Asparagus, duck, little puffy things—"

"Not those details."

Mac felt herself flush. "We just sat and ate cold leftovers. There are no 'details.' "

"*Ai!* You're blushing!" Emily planted her hands on the desktop and leaned forward, her face pushing through Mac's 'screen. The image retreated in self-defense. "C'mon, Mac. Spill it."

Avoiding Emily in this mood was like jumping out of the way of a crashing t-lev. *You might survive, but there'd be a wreck to clean up.* Mac sighed her surrender. "It was nice. He was nice. I enjoyed his company—when we weren't talking shop."

"Not to mention those pants."

"I didn't notice," Mac insisted.

Emily laughed and sat up. "You are hopeless, girl."

"I am not. In fact—" She closed her mouth in time. Emily arched one eyebrow interrogatively, but Mac shook her head. "Okay, I'm hopeless," she agreed. *She didn't want Emily's opinion of how the evening had ended.*

Then, something about that evening, or that afternoon, niggled at Mac. She narrowed her eyes in thought. "Emily, Brymn didn't eat supper."

"*Ai.* Changing the subject?" With a wave of her hand, Emily gave up the chase and returned to her seat. "You think Brymn avoided eating deliberately? Interesting. I'd love a skin sample."

"And you accuse me of trying to start an interspecies' incident?"

Emily chuckled. "I said I'd love a sample—not that I'd attack the Honorable Delegate with a scalpel. Sentients tend to be sensitive about their inner workings. I worked with a Sythian once who cremated her mandible trimmings in a ceramic pot every night, just in case—"

"Spare me." The moment the words were out, Mac regretted them. The last thing she wanted was to set Emily off again tonight.

Sure enough, a disapproving finger wagged in her direction. "Tsk, tsk. You see? You stick yourself to one planet and one biosystem, and this is the price. Do you know why you shouldn't put a Nerban and a Frow in the same taxi?" Em didn't bother to wait for Mac's reply, saying triumphantly: "Such ignorance of our fellow beings."

"I'm a salmon researcher, not a taxi driver," Mac muttered to herself.

"Seung could help, you know. He taught an intro xeno-sentient course on the mainland last winter."

Mac shook her head. "I don't need a course—"

"You need something, Mackenzie Connor." Emily's eyes were flashing again.

"Okay, Emily. I'll bite. Why is this suddenly more of an issue with you than usual? Why now?" Deliberately calm, Mac steepled her fingertips in front of her, studying her friend's angry face over that barrier. "What aren't you telling me?"

"You're the one with the Ministry envelope in her pocket. You're the one an alien traveled through three systems to meet. And you ask me why I think you should be paying attention!"

"I'm paying attention now," Mac said reasonably. "How did you know Brymn went through three systems?"

"Unlike you, Mac, I know what it takes to travel to and from this ball of dirt. I know the questions to ask and where to get answers. So while you were getting dewy-eyed with your bureaucrat, I was checking on them both."

Mac refused to take the bait, or offense. Emily on the warpath was a person who got results. "What did you find out?"

Emily's smile was wicked. "Your supper thief isn't in any Earthbound birth record. From his accent, slight as it is, I'd put him as no more local than a Jovian moon. I've a query out with the Ministry for details, but I wouldn't hold out hope for any answers. A man of mystery still, your Nikolai." She slowly licked her full lower lip. "Adds a certain spice, doesn't it?"

"Is that all you learned?"

"About Trojanowski." Emily's left hand made a fist. Her right opened, palm up. "Our Dhryn archaeologist, on the other hand, is anything but a mystery. Departed his colony to hunt relics from other species—a pastime I suspect was of no particular interest to his own kind, since Brymn hasn't been home since. It has. gained him some acclaim from other pot-hunters. He's sought after for lecture tours by a variety of system universities—one of which he canceled to come here. He's an accomplished linguist—shaming those of us who only learn Instella." Emily paused and her face turned serious. "Nothing I found says he's a crackpot."

"I never said he was." Mac refocused on her 'screen. "Here. Trojanowski sent me Brymn's publications."

The list of publications attributed to their guest filled each 'screen, then kept scrolling.

"Prolific fellow, isn't he?"

"How do you want to split it?" Mac asked.

"We have to read all that?" Emily saw Mac's expression and rolled her eyes. "We have to read all that. Fine. I'll start at the beginning. You start at the end. We should be done some time next year, given you have no social life and mine will be over."

"I'd put students on it, but . . ."

Emily had already settled deeper into the chair and called up her own 'screen, transferring the list from Mac's doppelganger with a finger-touch in midair. "I know," she said soberly. "End of the species. Need to know. All that, too."

Mac remembered her reaction to Brymn's news about the disappearances, the hollow feeling in her chest even now when she considered the Chasm and its sterilized worlds. "If it's true, we can't risk panic," she said, hearing the echo of it in her own voice.

"It won't come to that," Emily insisted. "We aren't alone, Mac. I keep telling you that. Others are working on this—have been working on it." She held up two fingers and pinched them together. "We Humans just have our small parts to play. After that? It will be over and you'll be back with your fish before you know it. Have some faith in your wise old friend, Em."

"We'll both be back," Mac corrected. "If you think I'm running that device of yours on my own, Dr. 'Wise Old Friend,' while you cavort with sex-crazed manatees . . ."

Emily didn't smile as Mac expected. "Have some faith, Mac," she repeated. "You know I'll do whatever I can to help you."

With the Tracer—or something else? Mac knew from experience that cryptic statements, from Emily, were never invitations to pry further. She shook her head and leaned forward again, peering at the 'screen. "I trust you to help me read as much of this as humanly possible before I see Brymn again, Em. If you don't mind?"

The room quieted as both became absorbed in their work.

Or tried to. *Concentrating would have been easier*, Mac thought, staring at the text, *if Emily had answered her question*.

Why the frustration, the outright anger, now?

It hadn't taken long before they found a problem in having Mac read the most recent articles first. Later articles referred to those before, some to the point of being completely incomprehensible— to a nonarchaeologist—on their own. Mac redivided the list so Emily was reading the dozens Brymn had published in the prestigious *Journal of Interspecies Archaeology*. She took everything else.

"Everything else" was an eclectic mix, at first appearing random. Letters to the Editor in *About Things Past*. Essays in collected works on topics ranging from statistical analysis to the emergence of interstitial recording technology, many dealing with findings from Chasm sites. Articles scattered in more than twenty different publications. Even a popular treatment, a vid script that had some-how found its way into a documentary series shown on transstellar liners, entitled: *Bringing the Past to Life*.

Then Mac noticed two commonalities. Although Emily had said Brymn was a linguist, these publications were in Instella, the multi-species' language that had to be learned by any member of the Interspecies Union who wished to leave their world. It was taught as a matter of course in Human schools; the same held true for the other species in the Union, to the best of Mac's admittedly meager knowledge. It made sense: a shared language was crucial to under-standing.

But Brymn had spoken to her in English. She hadn't paid atten-tion to that until now. Em was right to chide her for being blind to things outside her field. Mac bit her lip. *What else had she missed?*

There was nothing particularly unusual in Brymn publishing in Instella. It was the language of choice for any scientist addressing a multispecies' audience. What puzzled Mac was the lack of any ref-erence to publications in Dhryn. Did this mean there were none—or merely that Dhryn didn't permit cataloging of work in their language?

The second nonrandom characteristic was quality. Brymn hadn't exaggerated when he said his work had been noticed in "some cir-cles." With the exception of the vid script, all the listings Mac called up were in peer-reviewed, academic journals. Their Dhryn was taken very seriously by colleagues on many worlds. Just not by the Secretary General of the Ministry of Extra-Sol Human Affairs.

Or by his own species? Mac suddenly wondered if the Dhryn had the same prohibition on archaeology as they did on biology.

The workscreen winked out of existence, replaced by a soft green message at least two hands' widths high: "Can no longer compen-sate for fatigue."

Mac didn't argue. It wouldn't do any good. In a fit of self-protectiveness, she'd programmed the 'screen to ignore any requests to reinitialize for thirty minutes. It would doubtless take longer than that to find the password to change it.

She was startled to find the room dark except for the glow around the doorframes. The automatics had kicked in night illumination levels when she hadn't set the ambient to increase. There was just enough for Mac to see Emily was sound asleep in her chair, head twisted back at an angle impossible for anyone with a shorter neck, the sloppy old sweater she'd always borrowed around her shoulders. Every third breath was that soft little snore Em denied utterly when awake. Her 'screen was gone. It would have turned itself off after detecting her eyes had been closed for more than a few minutes.

So much for Brymn paying a visit. The media must have tied him up longer than she'd expected.

Keying on a low light, Mac stood and stretched, easing the kinks out of her spine. *Some,* she decided, *felt permanent.*

They probably were. Winter months, Mac lived in her office, analyzing data from past seasons, writing proposals for the next, daydreaming. It was her environment, her life, that surrounded her. She could forgive Brymn taking her quarters. They weren't as personal as this room.

She'd had the wall removed between the dry lab and her office space the first year, replacing the window side two-thirds of that barrier with what Tie affectionately referred to as the lousiest garden he'd ever seen. It had begun as a series of old barrels, cut in half, some on tables and some on the floor. Mac was in the habit of stuffing interesting local vegetation into her backpack, roots and all. Whatever survived her collecting method would be thrust into the nearest empty bit of soil in one of the barrels and more or less left to its own devices.

They were also abandoned to the local weather. The second winter, Mac had installed a microclimate around her growing collection. Far from creating a greenhouse, she linked the humidity, temperature, and daylight controls to those being experienced at any given moment along the shore of the spawning beds at Field Station One, some 700 kilometers northeast and 1100 meters higher than the pod. Even the wind conditions were replicated, making it not unusual for visitors to her office to be startled by a self-contained blizzard in the corner.

Tonight, the ceiling-high mass of young cottonwood, sedges, and orchids was peaceful save for the rustle of dying leaves. Field Station One's seasons, mirrored by those in Mac's garden, rushed ahead of those at Base. The urgency drew her closer to the living things she studied, who had to anticipate change or die.

Mac retracted the invisible barrier so she could feel the same soft breeze against her face. She closed her eyes and drew in the scent of soil and living things. A faint tinge of corruption on the back of her palate. Perhaps a lingering piece of salmon. She tossed a few corpses in each fall, challenging the air scrubbers. Or had one of the newer arrivals decided to rot instead of grow? *Fair enough.*

The patch of wilderness indoors wasn't the only unusual aspect of Mac's workspace. She'd had a load of stream-washed gravel delivered at the start of her fourth winter at Base. Instead of gaming or doing puzzles in the gallery, she'd coaxed the few other full-time staff into spending their evenings re-creating a spawning bed by gluing the stones to her floor. The result snaked through her office, its authentically irregular swath owing a fair amount to the number of beers consumed during its creation.

Needless to say, the cleaning staff wouldn't go near it.

Mac loved it. She'd meander along it barefoot, while the winter storms coated the pods with sleet, imagining the depressions she felt with her toes were redds, the holes scoured in the gravel by female salmon. The spawning bed ended at her garden, where overflow from rain spilled over the last few stones. When the garden froze, water eased drop by drop from under an icy rim, glazing each pebble.

Mac had a small warning buoy she'd salvaged to put on the icy patch, in case a visitor was careless when walking.

Almost everything else about her office was standard fare: chairs, desks, lamps, shelves, and tables. Posters, maps, and doors on two walls. The third wall and outer half of the ceiling were part of the pod exterior and could be made transparent or opaque at will. Wide doors led through the wall to the terrace that ringed the pod;

fair-weather shortcut to her neighbors, impassable hazard during winter storms.

There was, however, one other feature unique to this room. Mac watched its shadows dancing over Emily's sleeping face and looked up with a smile.

The transparent portion of the ceiling was festooned with wooden salmon, hanging so that they moved with every breath of air. When she'd first come to live on the west coast, Mac had found herself drawn to the stylized carvings of the Haida, their use of large, white-rimmed eyes and realistic form. She'd bought a few pieces, then commissioned more, with different species, different sexes.

All this, so she could stand on the gravel of a spawning bed, and gaze up at the starry sky past the silhouettes of dozens of salmon as they swam through the air, while hearing a breeze stir the vegetation onshore.

All this, so she could daydream about life and its needs.

A flash of brighter light played over her eyes. Squinting in protest, Mac wheeled in time to see the door to the corridor close behind the Dhryn.

Instead of speaking, he rose to stand almost upright, his eyes fixed on the ceiling. *Not the first time a visitor's had that reaction,* Mac smiled to herself.

She took advantage of his fascination to go to Emily and shake the other biologist awake. "Waasaa? I'm reading . . . oh." The incoherent muttering faded as Em saw who was there. She glanced quickly at Mac's desk. Mac understood. Em was checking both 'screens were off. *Not that Brymn should object to their reading his research—but still.*

Brymn probably wouldn't have noticed if they'd strewn his publications over the floor. He kept staring as he said: "This—This is what it was like, Mackenzie Winifred Elizabeth Wright Connor. When I swam in the river."

"You should have visited me here first, then," Mac observed, her mouth twisted in a wry smile. "I wouldn't have had to throw a rock at your head." She went to the wall control and raised the ambient lighting.

Brymn's torso returned to its more customary orientation. He gave a pair of low hoots. "That was you?"

"Mac isn't subtle," Emily explained, rubbing her left arm beneath the cast as she stood. She noticed Brymn's attention. "Arm's asleep."

"A figure of speech," Mac clarified, distracted by what the alien would make of creatures whose body parts rested at differing times.

"Ah." The sound was noncommittal. "I have brought this for you, Mackenzie Winifred Elizabeth Wright Connor." Brymn held out a small bag.

Mac took it, surprised by the weight.

"I regret you did not get to enjoy the supper provided by the Consulate," the alien explained. "So I obtained for you the food item which received the most praise."

"Thank you." Touched, Mac opened the bag and looked inside. At first, she couldn't guess what the gooey brown mass could be, then she sniffed. Chocolate. Rum. She stuck her finger in and brought out a trace to put on her tongue. "Soufflé?" she hazarded. *What remained of one, anyway.* Emily stifled a giggle.

"Yes! It is a masterpiece, I'm told."

Was. Mac closed the bag and gently put it on her desk. "You are very kind. I'll save it for later." Either Dhryn weren't concerned about microorganisms in their food or—given the lack of life science—this one didn't know what several hours at room temperature could produce.

Her stomach expressed its interest in chocolate, regardless. She ignored it. "How did the interviews go?"

"Interviews?" Brymn crisscrossed six of his arms. "Torture. Oh, not torture for me." Another series of hoots. "For them! I have discovered a skill of being utterly boring on any topic."

Emily laughed. "I like you, Brymn."

The Dhryn gave one of his tilting upward bows. "I am most gratified, Emily Mamani Sarmiento."

Mac frowned. "I thought Mr. Trojanowski was going to help you with the interviews."

"As did I. But he said he had to attend to other urgent business, leaving me surrounded in my own quarters." My *quarters*, Mac couldn't help but think. Brymn lifted his topmost elbows in what appeared an approximation of a Human shrug. "Perhaps the Consulate set these media persons to punish me. I believe they are still upset about the supper. Don't worry. I've attended many a lecture that put me to sleep. All I did was emulate the worst of those. Several individuals stopped recording after the first hour." He seemed pleased with himself.

Would he be as pleased to learn she'd shared his secrets with Emily? *Time to find out*, Mac decided. The two biologists had discussed how to handle the situation. They'd found no better approach than honesty, no matter its consequences. "Brymn. Emily is my closest colleague and friend. I trust her with my work." Emily's eyebrow lifted and Mac hurried on before her friend's irrepressible nature asserted itself. "Please accept her as your *lamisah*, as you did me."

The alien's arms unfolded and he sat rather abruptly. It didn't seem to bother him that he sat on the gravel of Mac's pseudo-spawning bed. "Why would I not?" he replied, sounding puzzled.

"Good," Emily said much too cheerfully. "Because Mac's already told me everything."

Before Brymn could respond to that, Mac stepped closer to the alien, hoping the earnestness of her words and expression translated into something comparable within his ridged blue forehead. "I can't work alone on this, Brymn," she told him. "I'll need Emily to cover for me if I have to take time away from my duties at Norcoast. More than that. I need her to talk to—to bounce ideas against. I can't know how you think. I don't know Trojanowski well enough. If you want my best, that includes her."

Brymn didn't stand, but he did reach one pale blue hand toward each of them. He'd found time to repaint his fingernails lime-green. "Then we three shall be *lamisah*." When the two women put their hands in his, he gave a heavy sigh. "I suppose this means Mac will insist I call you 'Em' in private. *Amisch a nai*." There was, however, an upturn to his lips, as if the Dhryn was attempting humor.

Brymn's hand was warmer than Mac had expected, softer in the palm than it had looked. There were three digits, equally opposed so the hand would spread like a flower. Each digit was flattened, with a faint ridging along its sides, knuckled in three locations like Mac's own. A nail, manicured, smooth, and presently green, covered the end portion.

His grip was gentle. She squeezed more firmly, assessing the bone and muscle beneath the skin. A powerful hand.

Under careful control. Brymn tightened his own grip only slightly before releasing her hand. His eyes blinked. This time Mac confirmed her impression that the right blinked a fraction of a second earlier than the left. "We don't have much time, my *lamisah*, to speak in private," Brymn said. "Is this place secure from eavesdropping?"

Emily perched on Mac's desk, swinging one long leg. "Who'd want to listen to Mac whistle to herself?" she asked. "You do," when Mac opened her mouth to object. "Off-key. Gets worse when you're happy."

Which she wasn't at the moment. *Eavesdropping?* "There are no vidbots or recorders running in my office, if that's what you mean."

Brymn looked around the room, his arms gesticulating nervously. "Then we must take the chance. There is little time."

"Little time? You've just arrived—" Mac paused. "Something's happened."

"Another incident. I received the news before the first interview."

"Along the Naralax?" Emily asked, eyes intent. "Closer to Human systems?"

The Dhryn nodded. "Yes. You have observed the pattern of the raiding parties, then."

"Raiding parties?" Mac put one hand on her desk, assuring herself it was nearby in case the room seemed to shift underfoot again. "No one's said anything about raiding parties."

Another one-two blink. "What else could the attacks be but the advance assaults of an invading species?"

Mac glanced at Emily and received that patented "let him run till he chokes" look. It usually applied to one of the grad students spouting a hypothesis, or a prospective date spouting a better-than-average line.

In this case, Mac understood the message. *They needed to know more before deciding if Brymn was to be believed.* "Who do you think is involved?" she asked.

"Who destroyed the worlds within the Chasm?" Brymn countered. The salmon hanging above their heads vibrated. The Dhryn's voice must have included another of the infrasound tones. Mac wondered what information it would have conveyed to those who could hear it. She had to bring an infrasound detector to their next conversation.

Emily looked skeptical. "There's no consistent evidence to prove the destruction wasn't a natural disaster—a plague or some unknown type of cosmic event."

"No?" Brymn looked around, the conspiratorial movement exaggerated by his ponderous body. Any other time Mac might have smiled. "I have that evidence. That is why They pursue me. That is why They pursue all Dhryn."

They? Smile gone, Mac felt the hairs rising on the back of her neck. "Who pursues—" A loud chime interrupted her question and startled Brymn to his feet.

"It's my dad," Mac said hastily, glancing at the clock on her desk. "I had no idea it was so late—excuse me."

Emily moved out of Mac's way as she went around her desk and activated the vid 'screen. "Hi, Dad," she said somewhat lamely.

"Hi, Princess." Her father, Norman Connor, had been smiling. He looked past her, and his smile faded. "Aren't you supposed to be camped along the river by now? What's wrong?"

Mac narrowed the field of view she was transmitting, in case the Dhryn became curious. "A little delay involving Emily's Tracer," she told him, ignoring Emily's sniff. "Nothing we can't resolve, but it means we're stuck at Base a while longer. How's everything with you?"

"Oh, the usual. Your uncle and I had to watch those knuckleheads blow an early lead again. You'd think they'd pick up some better pitchers. He says hello, by the way. The geraniums are filling up the balcony. My neighbor brought over some rainbow trout this morning. Next time you visit I'll have to cook you some."

"You're on." Mac's stomach voiced its opinion. "Pardon," she muttered.

"You could eat more than once in a while," her father noted, the twinkle back in his eyes. "That's what you tell me."

"We've had a busy day."

"Your visitor?" Mac's shock must have shown on her face, because her father laughed. "I do watch the news, Kitten. A Dhryn on Earth? It was the second lead, right after that freighter disaster over the Arctic this morning. What's he like?"

Numbly, Mac widened the transmitted field to include her entire office. "Dad, meet Brymn."

The alien opened his arms, keeping the seventh safely tucked away, and gave one of his bows. "I am honored to be introduced to the Progenitor of Mackenzie Winifred Elizabeth Wright Connor."

Norman Connor widened his own field, so they could see his slight form stand and bow. Geraniums in every color imaginable filled the background. *Calling from his balcony, then.* "The honor is mine, sir. I trust my daughter is treating you well. Lovely place she has there."

"Indeed. I have been most impressed. She must have already performed several fine and unforgettable acts to serve in *grathnu* so often for your betterment and pride."

Mac and Emily exchanged blank looks, but Norman Connor didn't hesitate. Parenting three very different if talented offspring easily took the place of diplomatic training. "Thank you. Yes, she's been a treasure."

"I, alas, have yet to so honor my Progenitors." The Dhryn's nostrils oozed yellow fluid. "I yearn for the opportunity, but it has eluded me."

Mac's father smiled reassuringly. "Don't worry, Brymn. I'm sure your time will come. You are the first of your kind to visit Earth— surely an accomplishment."

"Unfortunately, I come under a cloud, Progenitor of Mackenzie

Winifred Elizabeth Wright Connor. A dreadful cloud of foreboding and doom."

Mac wasn't sure what was more alarming: Brymn bonding with her father or what the alien was saying over a completely unsecured transmission. Before either could go further, she spoke up. "We have to get back to our meeting, Dad. I'll call you tomorrow, if that's okay?"

Her father nodded. "Any time after four, dear. The pool tournament's underway this week." He hesitated. Mac understood—he was alarmed by what Brymn had said, but didn't want to ask without privacy.

"Don't worry," she said. "Emily and I are looking after things."

Emily waved from the background. "She means I'm doing the work, as usual."

"Good for you, Em. Keep her out of trouble."

If there was more to the words than usual, if there was worry in his eyes, Mac could do nothing about it now. "I'll call," she promised. "Bye, Dad."

"Bye, Princess."

The 'screen disappeared. Mac couldn't take her eyes from where it had been.

"Thank you."

"What?" She dragged her attention back to Brymn.

His lips were trembling. "Thank you. I had no doubts of you before, Mackenzie—Mac. But to share the regard of your Progenitor with another is the highest courtesy among Dhryn. I am truly touched." Yellow fluid dripped to the floor and his eyes blinked repeatedly.

Congruence or coincidence? Mac had no guideline but her own reactions. The alien seemed sincerely moved. Gingerly, she patted one of Brymn's arms, feeling warm, rubbery skin. "Dad was pleased to meet you, too, Brymn." *Except for the "doom" part*, she added to herself, with a stern reminder to call her father.

Now, Mac thought. *Down to business.* She opened her mouth to ask Brymn more about his conjecture when Emily asked in an alarmed whisper: "What was that?"

"What was what?" Mac snarled, beginning to feel as though she was in a badly written spy thriller.

Emily was staring out the window into the dark. "That."

This time, Mac felt the tiny series of jolts through her feet. Relieved, she grinned at Emily. " 'That' was Hector. You should know the feel of him by now." The nightly routine of the elderly humpback whale who visited the inlet included a good belly rub along the pod floats.

"I do," Emily said softly, before Mac could explain to Brymn. "It's not him." She pressed her face against the window. "It's *him*." This with triumph and a slap on the control that opened the door to the outside terrace.

The night air rushing into the room sent salmon careening into one another, their wooden bodies meeting in a cacophony of musical notes. With a protest of her own, Mac followed Emily as she ran outside. "What do you think you're doing?"

Emily stopped, her hands gripping the rail, her head swinging from left to right and back again. "He was right here," she insisted.

"Who?" Mac fought to keep her voice down, uncomfortably aware of passersby on the walkway below.

"I saw a man, standing on the terrace, looking in. I swear it was him. Trojanowski."

"You saw his face?" There was no moon, and the only lighting was that which spilled from occupied rooms and traced the undersides of the railing. Mac could barely see Emily's silhouette against the glow from her office.

"Since when did I need a face to recognize someone?" Emily countered.

"Even if you saw someone—and it was him—this is public space. Anyone can walk here. It's a nice night for a stroll, Em."

It was, too. Warm and still, fragrant with forest and ocean. The sound of conversation and laughter drifted from somewhere nearby. Farther, but no less clear across the placid water, the unmistakable *chuff* of a whale blowing out air. Mac took a deep, calming breath. "We're all tired," she began.

"And you think I'm imagining things." There was real hurt in Emily's voice.

"I hope you are," Mac said honestly. "I've as much as I can handle going through my mind right now. I don't need visions of skulking bureaucrats before I try to catch some sleep."

Mac couldn't see Emily's face, but her quick hug around Mac's shoulders said enough. "Understood. As for sleeping? Sure you don't want to come back to my place? I've the couch."

"There's a mattress on the way," Mac assured her. "Tie promised to look after it. Anyway, we'd better get back inside and talk to our troubled friend."

Easier said than done. The Dhryn was gone.

"Think he was spooked by Trojanowski?" Emily asked once they were back inside. "Or whoever it was I saw?"

Mac held her tongue. Little good now to accuse Emily of scaring away their guest—*and they could be both be wrong.* "He might have needed a bathroom, for all we know."

This drew the rueful smile she'd hoped to see. "Well, he knows where to find one. Or us. Meanwhile, you get that sleep. You look ready to drop on your face."

"Thanks."

"Hey, I tell it like I see it," Emily said. Picking up the sweater from the chair, she started for the door, then paused, looking over her shoulder at Mac. There was a question in her dark eyes.

"Do I believe any of this?" Mac said for her, and shrugged. "I'm not ready to decide without more information. Tomorrow we'll talk to Brymn—and I'll talk to Mr. Trojanowski." She forestalled Emily's complaint with a raised hand. "I'll ask if he was peeking in the window, don't worry. I hope he wasn't," she went on uneasily. "I'd rather he didn't learn how much you know about all this, not yet anyway."

"If you're trying to protect me from fallout over that message—"

"I was thinking more along the lines of keeping you my secret weapon, Dr. Mamani."

The gleam of Emily's teeth was nothing short of predatory. "I had no idea you were so devious, Dr. Connor."

"Grant proposals," Mac explained wryly. They shared a smile, then Mac yawned.

"I can take a hint," Emily said. "Seriously, Mac. You should take me up on that couch."

"No, thanks. I'm going to read a bit more anyway. And since when did you want me hanging around your quarters at night?" Mac stared at her friend. "This isn't so you can berate me for another few hours, is it? Because I've had enough for one night, Em. I really have."

Emily reached out and gently tugged Mac's braid where it draped over her shoulder. "I know. I should have left it alone. Sorry." Then she seemed to search Mac's face, or for some odd reason was trying to memorize it. "You'll be okay," she said finally, in a strange voice. "When push comes to shove, you do the right thing, Mac. I should remember that more often."

"And the right thing is to send you to bed," Mac said kindly. "You're babbling. Go get some sleep." She gave Em a quick hug, then pushed her toward the door. "See you at breakfast." Mac went to her desk and activated her 'screen, fighting a yawn.

She was startled to look up and see Emily hadn't left. She'd stopped, one hand on the door frame, and was watching her. "Now what?"

"Promise me something, Mac."

Mac called up the next publication with a stroke through the 'screen. "If you'll go to bed—anything," she muttered.

"Promise you'll forgive me."

"I forgive you. Now go."

"No, not now. Not today. Promise you will forgive me."

The qualification was not reassuring. Mac leaned around the 'screen to get a better look at Em. "What are you planning to do?"

"Just—just give me a one-shot 'get out of trouble with Mac' card, okay? It'll help me sleep."

Mac was disturbed by the wildness in Emily's eyes, the same look she'd get before disappearing for days with some stranger she'd picked up at a bar, or before challenging one of the students to a drinking contest he couldn't possibly win.

Then, with a sinking feeling, Mac thought she understood. "You saw him kiss my hand, didn't you? Em—"

The other woman leaned her back on the doorframe, cradling her cast and sweater against her chest. "Actually, no. I missed that. Who knew pushing a man into the ocean would have a plus side?"

"Then what?" Mac let her exasperation show. "You aren't making any sense."

Emily rubbed her eyes with her right hand. "Forget it, Mac. You're right. I'm overtired. See you in the morning." She turned with almost boneless grace and left.

Mac hurried to the door, catching it before it closed. Her friend was already halfway down the night-dimmed corridor. "Emily."

Her name stopped her, but Emily didn't turn around.

"I don't know what's bothering you, Em, but you don't need me to make a promise," Mac told her. "There's nothing you could do I wouldn't forgive. You're my friend. That's what it means."

A whisper. "Thanks, Mac."

And Emily walked away.

The triumphant arrival of two students bearing a mattress pad and bedding startled Mac from a cramped curl in the armchair, where she'd moved to read more of Brymn's publication list and had fallen asleep instead. With apologies and an endearing lack of co-ordination, the pair insisted on making up her bed. Mac dimly remembered shooing them out the door, then tripping her way on to the promised comfort.

By that point, anything flat would have worked.

So she was vaguely surprised some unknown time later to find herself lying flat on her back, wide awake. It was dark, without even stars glowing overhead. Darker than it should be. The light rimming the doorframes was gone, as were the pinpricks of green and red from the indicators on various gauges she should be able to see in her lab.

Power failure?

She must be dreaming. Norcoast didn't have power failures. It broadcast its own power and there were backups and redundant systems galore—more than most major medical centers—

necessities in an environment subject to hurricane winds and the vagaries of summer students.

Her stomach mentioned breakfast.

Not dreaming, Mac decided, coming fully awake. Instinct kept her still.

Something *scurried* across the ceiling.

Mac's heart began to pound. She fought to keep her breathing quiet and even, as if she still slept.

She wasn't alone.

She had no idea what else was in the room with her.

Scurry, scurry.

Not a mouse or Robin's pet monkey, Superrat. The movement she heard had more in common with something insect or crablike. *No.* Too large for anything of that nature.

Skitter, scurry.

Silence. Sweat trickled maddeningly down Mac's neck and chest, but she didn't dare move to wipe it away. She'd always loved the dark; now, it had a weight, a suffocating thickness.

Her fingers walked across the floor, found a sandal, then threw it.

Water hitting a red-hot pan made that kind of hard *spit!* and *pop!* Right after those sounds, Mac heard the door to the terrace open and close.

The door?

Mac lunged to her feet, stumbling in the direction that should lead to the same door, her hands outstretched. Desk edge. *Feel along it.* Desk end. The door should be straight ahead. Two steps. *Nothing.*

She froze in place, then stretched out one foot. It touched the smooth irregularity of gravel and she sagged with relief, knowing where she was. A turn and three steps to the right. The door control was under her hand. Mac followed the cold night air outside.

Overcast. Not raining, but moisture immediately condensed on her lips and eyelids, beaded her hair. The morning fog was forming. *Dawn couldn't be far off.* Mac blinked, trying to see anything.

Again, her ears were her best sense. *Scurry . . . spit! Pop!* From the roof, this time, as if her unwanted visitor had climbed the curve of the pod wall. *Why not?* Mac thought numbly. It had been running along her ceiling. She hadn't imagined it.

Whatever it *was.*

She knew one thing. It wasn't getting away from her that easily.

Back inside, hands groping in the dark. Mac found her desk, pulled open the second drawer, and grabbed the candle lantern she kept in there. There were matches in the base. She closed her eyes to slits before striking one and lighting the candle. The wick caught, burning brightly. Mac waited until the flame was steady before lowering the glass shield. "Thanks, Dad," she whispered. The lantern had been a birthday gift.

Mac played the lantern's light over the interior of her office, shaking her head in disbelief. Trails of clear, glistening slime, a half meter in width, lay over the floor, walls, and ceiling. Some passed between the suspended salmon, a couple over her desk. Mac lowered the beam to the floor, following a trail that led over the bed where she'd slept. She checked her legs. Sure enough, the material below her knees shone with slime.

"I'm getting well and truly sick of alien biology," Mac muttered, using a clean section of blanket to wipe her pant legs.

She ignored the confused pile of her belongings stacked against the far wall, refugees from her purloined quarters, hurrying instead to the storage cupboard. Putting the lamp where it would shine on the cupboard's contents, Mac pulled out what she wanted. Slicker. Hiking boots. That really old wool sweater that had belonged to her brother William which she kept for winter nights when she was too busy to head upstairs to her quarters. Warm, too big, and itchy as could be.

Mac tried to activate her imp. Nothing, despite its supposed decade-worth of stored power. "Neat trick," she told her quarry, tossing the device aside.

It took Mac only seconds to bundle up—a side effect of innumerable excursions in the dead of winter to chip off ice and help unload surface or air transports. They'd never listened to her recommendation to bring in supplies underwater, where weather wasn't a factor.

Back out the door to the terrace. Mac opened the lantern and blew out her candle, tucking the unit into a pocket, then stood perfectly still, listening.

She knew her responsibility. To catch whatever had invaded her office and Norcoast—or at least get close enough to identify it. The too-convenient power failure had to be a ruse by the creature; waking up the rest of Base's inhabitants would only add a crowd of confused students, sure to get in her way.

Scurry.

Fainter. *The sound was different.* "Gotcha," Mac said to herself, making the connection. It was on the walkway below.

She ran along the terrace, guided by memory and one hand on the pod wall, heading for the stairs. Stealth wasn't as important as speed, but speed wouldn't matter if she broke her neck in the dark.

Her feet knew every centimeter, every rise and fall along the walkways.

A whiff of roses. *Dr. Reinhold's rooftop planter.* She was passing Pod Two. *Scurry . . . scurry.* It wasn't stopping. Mac wasn't surprised. Her boots made a solid drumming on the walkway. She wanted it that way. *Keep her quarry moving, panicked.* With luck, she'd corner it against one of the pod doors.

Ambush seemed unlikely—given its reaction to her sandal. Mac was sure her visitor was a thief or spy. Maybe even one of the media, sliming around for a story. She should have asked if all had been Human. *Not a question that would have occurred to her yesterday.*

Whether it knew her plan or not, the creature wasn't cooperating. Mac kept stopping to listen; the susurrations continued to move straight ahead. Not to a launch pad and waiting escape vehicle, as she'd feared, but retracing the path she and Brymn had taken that afternoon.

Toward land.

Mac kept her fingertips sliding along the top of the right-hand rail, moving as quickly as she dared through the darkness. There were sounds behind her now—perplexed voices as people began questioning one another about the power failure. A glow of new lights reflected on the water, candles and lanterns caught on each upward swell, enough to etch out the darker line of the walkway in front of Mac's feet, so she risked starting to run.

If the creature reached land first, it might be trapped by the web gate.

If it wasn't, it would have the entire coastal forest and a continent beyond in which to lose her.

- Portent -

THE FIRST drop hissed into the snow, its remains a crater, stained green, like a dead eye staring back at the sky.

Another embedded eye. Another.

The pristine snowfield became pocked with green, rotting under unseasonable rain. Rivulets began to form, eating deeper as they flowed.

More drops fell.

Beneath the snow, those asleep in their shells knew only the regular, once-weekly beating of their hearts, dreamed only of the coming warmth, when their world danced closer to its partner sun. Under the open fronds of the Nirltrees, they would teach their offspring. It had always been thus. It would always be thus. The Great Sleep was their salvation, the snow their protection.

They were wrong.

The green rivulets melted deeper and deeper. Soon, they flowed over what seemed a bed of immense pebbles, each regular in form and smooth, as if polished.

The pebbles were seamed, the edges held by ligaments laced together like so many fingers in prayer. Admirable defense against cold and predator, but the ligaments rotted away as the rivulets touched them. The halves of every pebble fell open, exposing the flesh within, flesh that dissolved in the flood before it could awake to scream.

The shells melted almost as quickly, washed away with the dormant stumps of the Nirltree grove, even the roots of the trees dissolving as the green drops penetrated the frozen soil. Drops and rivulets joined into a widening river, washing away the snow, dissolving all life that had sheltered beneath it, scouring the mountainside until all that remained was rock.

Where the river flowed into a cirque, becoming a limpid pool of green, mouths gathered.

And began to drink.

7

CHASE AND CONFRONTATION

MAC SMACKED her hand against the lock on the pillar. Of course it didn't respond. No confirmation signal for her code could come from Norcoast until Base's power was restored. The webbing of the gate remained in place, a default that would have pleased Mac immensely had her quarry seen fit to be delayed by it.

But no. She'd arrived at the gate between the holdfasts to find herself alone.

Maybe.

Remembering how easily the creature had hidden in her office, Mac put her back to the pillar and stared outward until her eyes burned. Warm yellow marked activity around the pods. Someone had already strung a series of lanterns along the walkway leading to Pod Three, probably anticipating breakfast. Which would rely on the ingenuity of those on duty if the power remained off. Mac wasn't worried. Enough students had stashed grills in their rooms to cook for the entire crew, if need be.

She willed herself silent, wanting to hear what was around her.

Waves licked the rocks. The fog was condensing in the forest, producing a combination of drip and sigh as leaves released their burdens. A cone dropped on the moss. A salmon leaped and splashed in the inlet. *All sounds she knew.* Mac listened for the un-familiar and was rewarded.

A low, regular *thrumming*. If she hadn't lived here for years, Mac would have dismissed it as the call of an insect, perhaps a large cricket rubbing its legs together.

Even as she became convinced she was hearing the creature breathing, she realized the sound was coming from over her head.

Mac swallowed, then took one step forward and turned around, keeping her movements slow and cautious. "I know you're up there," she said, hoping her Instella wasn't completely rusty. "Come down and talk to me."

Spit! Pop! The same noises as when she'd thrown her sandal. *Surprise?* Mac peered upward, wondering if she was imagining being able to see the outline of the holdfast pillar against the trees. Dawn must be fighting its way over the mountains. The fog would delay true light another hour yet. "I won't hurt you," she ventured, hoping for the same attitude.

"Dr. Connor!" The call came from Base, echoed by a series of anxious voices. Someone had probably gone to alert her about the power failure, Mac realized, and discovered the condition of her office.

She was reasonably sure shouting in answer would cost her any chance of seeing her visitor. There was definitely more light every minute now. *If she could only keep the creature here . . .*

It might have had the same thought. *Scurry . . . thump!* The odd clattering of its movement on the pillar ended in a rapid rustling through the underbrush. It had climbed over the gate and left the walkway for the forest floor.

"Damn it!" Mac smacked her hand against the lock again. *Nothing.*

"It broke the rules first, Oversight," she muttered, then felt her way to the edge of the walkway membrane and sat, boots dangling in midair. The walkway guide lights inside the Trust would stay off, since no access code had been confirmed to the gate. But, with the sort of luck Mac was coming to expect tonight, the repeller field was still active, being powered—like the tiggers—from an inland broadcast source owned by the Wilderness Trust. As she sat down, the field vibrated unpleasantly through her pelvis and up her spine, setting her teeth on edge, but its intensity was meant to discourage bats, wasps, and jays, not an adult and determined woman.

And probably a foolish one, too, Mac told herself, but that didn't stop her from jumping into the dark.

Scritch . . . whoosh.

Mac let out the breath she'd unconsciously held while striking the match. She lit her small lantern, then carefully wrapped the tip of the spent match in wet moss before tucking it into an upper pocket. *Minimal presence,* she reminded herself. The light was more welcome than she wanted to admit.

Its tiny flickering reminded her of another hunt through the dark.

Her dad hadn't been sure about bringing a very young Mackenzie on his owl survey. Her older brothers had talked him into it, probably so they needn't feel any guilt over choosing not to come. Mac hadn't cared about their reasons; she'd been hoping to go as long as she could remember. After all, what was the fun of staying in town with her aunts while the rest of her family went camping in the dark and perilous northern forests?

Not that they were either, but at seven, Mac had been nothing if not imaginative. To her, trees traded stories about you behind your back and, if they didn't like you, they would move to confuse your path. Moss-covered stones were worse. The little ones would try to trip you. The big ones would wait until you passed before turning into something else, something with long, thin fingers and sharp nails, something that snacked on children who didn't know the magic words. Mac was very proud of her ability to make up such words, each having proved most effective on past walks through the park near her aunts' house.

She'd been ready for anything the northern forest could offer. Until her father lost himself.

"Poppa?" Mac had been sure he was outside their tent, putting up the pack for the night, but he'd been nowhere in sight. She'd stopped shouting immediately, careful not to draw the attention of tree or stone. In this wilder forest, both were larger and stranger than any she'd seen before. *Where could he be?* She'd noticed her father was easily distracted. Why the very first day, he'd sat transfixed by the huge eyes of a large white owl, until she'd had to grab his hand to remind him he had a daughter to feed.

Glow in hand, she'd set off to find him, careful to say a magic word each time she passed a threatening stone, careful not to step on the exposed roots of trees and give them reason to spread dislike about her.

Mac had walked all night, longer than she'd ever walked in her life, a girl on a heroic quest. Her glow had dimmed until the moonlight was brighter, if only in clearings where there were more stones. Her voice had grown hoarse, then faded to a whisper, but she'd kept uttering the magic words, knowing she had to keep herself safe if she was to help her father.

And when she'd finally found him, surprisingly close to their campsite, his own voice had been strained to a whisper, his face pale and lined with fear. Tight in his arms, feeling him shake, Mac had decided not to scold him for getting lost. It could happen to anyone, alone in a dark forest.

Mac shook her head, smiling at the memory. *Gossiping trees and hungry stones?* At least she hadn't made up her visitor, invisible or not. She glanced up. The drop hadn't been far. If she stretched, she could brush the bottom of the walkway with her fingertips. It didn't show to her light.

It didn't matter. Mac needed to see the forest floor, not where she'd been. She hurried over moss-covered stones, grateful for her boots, holding the lantern low. *There.* A couple of meters past the holdfast pillar, lines of moss had been peeled up in a series of loops, as if the tines of a large fork had scooped them from the soil. Mac refused to speculate what body parts would leave such a mark, instead raising her lantern to look for more tracks. If the thing could climb from tree to tree, she'd never be able to follow it.

Another rip in the moss. Another beyond that. They led her to a row of similar marks scoring the top of an immense nurse log that loomed like a tanker out of the mist. Mac set her lantern on top and clambered over, her hands sinking into the decaying wood. She whispered an apology to Charles Mudge III under her breath as a clump broke free under her boot.

She wiggled on her belly over the log, no doubt damaging the tiny saplings growing there, and retrieved her lantern to hunt for more tracks. *There.* Leading upward. Away from Base.

Where they didn't belong, Mac thought, welcoming the anger that warmed her body. Bad enough she was ripping through the vegetation.

At least she was from this planet!

Hiking through a coastal rain forest was never a straight-line affair at best, even in full daylight. Myriad tiny streams, ice-cold and swift, flowed down every crease in the rock. The rocks themselves were the jagged shoulders of a new mountain range, untamed by time and unsympathetic to anyone who chose to climb them. Hunched over the spot of light from her lantern, moving from one track to the next, Mac felt as though she crawled across the forest floor like a slug.

The slope increased in jagged steps, but luckily never so steep that Mac couldn't follow the creature's spoor. Still, she often had to plant one foot firmly, then reach with her free hand for a branch that wouldn't come loose. Then pull. Her shoulders began to burn.

Abruptly, the tracks ended. Mac hunted with her lantern for a few moments, careful not to move too far from the last impression. *Nothing.* Finally, she sank to her knees to rest and consider what to do next. *How long until dawn?* she wondered, and closed the front of the lantern to assess the light.

Dawn might be touching the mountaintops by now, but not here. She hadn't expected it yet, not under the fog-laden mammoth trees and certainly not deep within this fold of land. "But what's this?" Mac breathed, staring at the ground. A faint, green fluorescence shone from under her knees, leading up the next rise. *The slime*, Mac exulted, surging to her feet.

Now she raced against the dawn. The fluorescence remained visible, barely, for mere seconds after her lantern activated it. She proceeded in sprints now, waving her light to memorize the terrain as well as energize the slime, then covering it so she could run along the glowing path.

Up the path was more accurate. The landscape had become punishingly vertical. Mac prided herself on her conditioning; even so, she struggled to make any speed. The footing was wet and slick, so her boots slid backward with every step. Progress was measured in altitude gained, not the number of strides it took. Achievement? How quickly she could stand after a fall that slammed her against tree trunks, not the number of times she slipped.

"I've got you now," she whispered to herself.

Every so often, Mac snatched leaves and licked the moisture from their surfaces. The lifting fog had condensed in the upper canopy, drops runneling down every branch and dripping from leaf tips. This time of year, it wouldn't be long before real rain followed, so dehydration wasn't a problem. The hollow feeling in her gut she could ignore. A good thing she'd shared leftovers with Trojanowski last night.

Her growing ability to see her surroundings was something else again. Mac blinked and stopped, leaning against a redwood wider than her last apartment. She blew out the candle and tucked the lantern away.

Not quite bright enough for color, but her dark-adapted eyes could easily discern the shapes of tree, log, and rock from the background mist. The slime's faint glow could no longer compete with the rising sun. *The morning rain would wash it away soon anyway*, Mac thought resignedly. She tightened the collar of her slicker, but left the hood down. She'd have to listen for her quarry now.

It helped that most birds were finished singing for the season. A few twittered sleepily around her. A squirrel complained about intruders in the distance. *That way*. Mac lifted her head from its rest against the tree like a hound taking point. She was willing to gamble the intruder was hers.

Crack.

From *behind*, down the hill. Mac pressed herself against the redwood again.

It might be nothing. Forests cracked and snapped all the time. She waited, hardly breathing. The squirrel continued to chatter furiously, not far at all. She could be gaining on the creature at last.

To take advantage of that meant moving. Mac shoved away from the shelter of the tree, feeling every muscle protest, and began to climb toward the outraged squirrel.

The clearing was new. Mac didn't need a vegetation survey map to tell her, she'd been able to smell the sap and bruised leaves, the spicy tang of freshly cut—or rather freshly smashed—cedar well before she'd reached it.

Poor Mudge would be horrified.

As she'd expected, the fog had slipped from under the forest canopy to make room for the rain that replaced it, the kind of steady, soaking deluge that promoted the lush growth of fern and moss and mocked even the best slicker's ability to keep a body dry. Mac shivered spasmodically as she crouched under the partial shelter of a leaning nurse log, distracting herself with daydreams of hot showers, hot towels, and hot sunshine.

She hadn't found her quarry. *Not yet.* But this had to be its destination. The clearing had been made either for or by a landing craft. Within the past day, she guessed. The broken vegetation was still green and unwilted. Dark exposed soil marked a too-regular series of depressions, now filling with rainwater.

Mac refused to believe she'd arrived too late. There'd been no sound or flash, no vibration. Even a t-lev on hush would have stirred the treetops on its way down.

Crack.

Only Mac's eyes shifted to search the wall of green and brown to her left. The contrast to the clearing, despite the low cloud and rain, was enough to darken the forest beyond into night.

Rabbit or deer, she told herself, licking water from her lips. *Grizzlies weren't so careless.*

A scrap of moss floated down past her eyes, like the tuft of a feather dislodged from a bird. Mac froze.

Scurry . . . scurry. The log above her vibrated. More moss fell. Mac launched herself from the shelter that now felt like a trap, looking around frantically for any sign of it. *Nothing.* She was alone. "The fun's worn off," she muttered, heart still pounding with shock. Louder. "Look—I just want to talk to you—"

"Get down—!"

The shout, in a man's voice, was lost in the roar of an engine where no engine existed. Mac stared into the empty clearing, hearing what she couldn't see. Wind from nowhere buffeted her, driving the rain sideways into her face. She staggered back, grabbing at branches to keep her footing.

But there was nothing there!

A blinding flash of light as heat struck her, both preludes to a wind that shoved her backward. Mac threw her arms in front of her face and turned with the force, throwing herself to the ground. The roar grew louder, then, as suddenly as it had started, ceased.

Mac spat out a mouthful of fern and dirt as she pushed herself up to sit. She opened and closed her eyes, fighting to see past the fiery specks blurring her vision.

"Are you all right?"

Her ears might be ringing, but she recognized the voice now. *Trojanowski?* She didn't waste time in "hows" or "whys." "Did you see what—who—it was?" Mac demanded.

"No." A wealth of self-disgust in the word.

Mac swore under her breath and fought her way to her feet, grateful to find her eyes sore but functioning. He was standing a couple of meters away, looking not at her but at the presumably now-empty clearing. There were new scars in the ground as if whatever had landed had put down feet. "An invisible ship?" she said in wonder. "Who has such technology?"

"Good question," he said, taking what looked to be an unusually small scanner from a pocket and walking into the opening.

So, Mac thought. *His device wasn't keyed to Norcoast's power broadcast, or Norcoast was up and running again.* She was inclined to believe the latter. A technology that could hide a ship from view? Once the need had passed, they'd probably restored power to the inlet with a nod—if they had heads and bendable necks. *No guarantees on either point.*

Mac followed, studying the man, not the place. Bureaucrat? Diplomatic flunky? *Not likely.* The glasses were gone, as was the apologetic slouch. This version of Nikolai Piotr Trojanowski was all business, stepping easily over the uneven surface, dressed in a jacket and pants that might have been made from the forest, their camouflage so perfect Mac found him hard to see even this close. He wore a pack on his shoulders and her stomach chose that moment to remind her about breakfast.

Mac fought for patience. Her eyes were improving by the minute; they weren't helping her make sense of any of this. "Anything?" she asked, watching him scowl at his device.

Trojanowski might not have heard. He made an adjustment, then crouched to pass his scanner close to the dark soil exposed in one of the scars.

With a shiver, Mac pulled her slicker tighter to her neck and followed. The rain had eased to the mist-in-your-face variety that could last all day. The sun was high enough now to add pastel colors to the trees and ground, if not send its warmth through the clouds. *Pleasant enough weather, if you weren't already soaking wet.* She tried again. "Do you know what it wanted?"

That drew a look. "You should go—" he began to say, then, perversely: "Don't move." He took three quick strides to stand in front of her. Mac fought the impulse to back away as he raised the scanner to the side of her face. His expression was cold, clinical.

This wasn't the man who'd laughed and shared his supper with her, who'd held her hand, who'd kissed her fingers like some centuries-past gallant. Yesterday might have been something she'd dreamed.

"What is it?" she asked, reaching up with one hand. "What's wrong?" The question was about more than her face.

"Don't touch your skin, Dr. Connor." He put away the device. "Minor flash burn. You didn't move fast enough."

Mac's fingers hovered near her cheeks. "I don't feel any pain," she said doubtfully.

He raised an eyebrow. "I suspect that's temporary. You'd better go and have it treated."

Go? Given the effort involved in retracing her steps downslope and in the rain, Mac was in no hurry. She looked Trojanowski over from head to boot-encased foot. No stains. No rips. Unlike her poor abused slicker. It meant he had transport of his own. *And something else.* "You didn't follow me," she deduced. "You were already here. Waiting. I want to know why."

His eyes narrowed, their hazel turning almost green. Mac supposed intimidating looks were part of his training. She was too full of adrenaline to be impressed. "Same side, remember?" she told him. "Protecting the species. Working with Brymn to solve this mysterious threat." She tilted her head back and gave him her own intimidating look. "Or are we?"

"You know the Secretary General assigned me to accompany the Honorable Delegate—"

" 'Accompany,' " Mac repeated, interrupting him. "Or was that a convenient excuse to come here? I don't think you or the Secretary General are paying any attention to Brymn's work at all. I think you are here because you expected this!" She waved somewhat wildly at the clearing, lacking any better idea of what *this* was.

"Is that why you're here, Dr. Connor?" *Oh, he was good.* The return accusation was sharp and slick.

Mac would have stomped her foot if it would have done more than splatter mud. "Look, this—thing—woke me. I followed it—"

"You what? Did you see it?" Trojanowski demanded. "Did you see anything?"

Mac shook her head. "Only its tracks . . . Hey!" She found herself talking to his back. His moving-away-from-her, you-are-irrelevant-and-dismissed back. She spat a rude phrase Emily had taught her and forced her tired legs in pursuit. "Wait! What did you expect to find here?"

That stopped him in the middle of the clearing. His eyebrows drew together as he glared down at her. "I didn't expect to find you."

Mac bristled. "What was I supposed to do, Mr. Trojanowski? The thing was in my office. It ran away when I woke up."

"Woke up? So, you were asleep in your office," he rephrased as if trying to make sense of what she was telling him, "and, when a 'thing' you couldn't see woke you, you chased it up here. Alone."

"I didn't see a choice. Someone had to follow it, find out what it wanted—"

"What if it had wanted you dead?"

Mac shook her head, soaking wet hair falling in her eyes. She tucked it behind an ear, careful of her numb skin. "Then I would have been dead," she said reasonably. "It wanted something else. What?"

"In your office," he echoed, in the same skeptical tone he'd used for "alone." His look became intense, as though he could somehow read the answer in her face, burned or otherwise. It was like being transfixed by a spotlight—an unfriendly one at that. "Why your office? And how could you possibly follow it here . . . unless you already knew where to go." Clear threat now. "Which brings us back to the key question. How did you know to come here, Dr. Connor?"

"And who the hell are you, Mr. Trojanowski, to stand here and ask me questions of any kind?" Mac retorted, despite feeling that arguing with a man who secretly skulked in the forest in camouflage gear wasn't necessarily wise. "You aren't who you pretend to be, that's for sure. Let me finish," she snapped, but quietly when he opened his mouth.

A wary nod.

"You're the one who handed me the message that dragged me away from my work, remember? You're the one who brought that Dhryn—and the media—into my life. You want to know why some weird, invisible alien was running across my ceiling in the middle of the night? Well, that makes two of us."

Trojanowski pursed his lips and considered her. She did the same, waiting. *He remained a contradiction*, Mac decided. The camouflage gear and pack, how naturally he wore them, his sudden shift in personality . . . clearly he'd been trained to handle situations other than ferrying diplomatic messages to biologists. For all she knew, he was some kind of spy, like those in Em's old movies, if less glamorous.

But Trojanowski's face didn't suit the man-of-action mode. When he was thinking, as now, little perplexed lines formed at the corners of his eyes and mouth. *He doesn't like mysteries*, she thought abruptly. *Neither did she.* So Mac wasn't surprised when his very next words addressed another. "How did you find your way through the dark, Dr. Connor? Please."

Mac put her hand in her pocket. He tensed and she blinked at him. "It's only a lantern," she said before pulling it out, in case he needed reassurance. "Combustible. A candle." She offered the lantern to him and he took it, giving her an inscrutable look. "Whatever—whoever—was in my office left a trail of slime that fluoresced under its light. The glow didn't last long; just enough that I could follow it. No mystery, Mr. Trojanowski."

He handed the lantern back. "Quick thinking."

His praise was unexpected. Mac had begun to believe "fool-hardy" and "stupid" were better descriptions of what she'd done. "Fair's fair," she suggested, replacing the lantern in her pocket. "How did you know to be here?"

Trojanowski frowned, *but not, this time, at her*, Mac thought. "There was a collision yesterday, northeast of here, involving a low-orbit freighter. All hands were lost. No evidence of what it collided with until this—" he nodded at the flattened clearing, "—appeared on the monitors. I was contacted to check it out as soon as I could get away from Brymn. I played a hunch and stayed."

"Do all diplomatic liaisons check out freighter crashes and holes in the forest canopy?"

"Not all." He had the grace to look embarrassed, a reminder of the man she'd met yesterday. "I'm not supposed to get caught like this, Dr. Connor. I'd planned a quiet investigation, no one the wiser."

"Why the pretense? I mean, it's not as if Base is full of—" She closed her mouth into a grim line.

"Spies?" Trojanowski's expression matched her own. "I'd say my precautions were well advised, given your visitor."

"Who was it? What was it? You know, don't you?"

"Even if I did, Dr. Connor," he said with what seemed sincere regret, "I couldn't tell you. Secrecy is more important than ever now." With that, he turned and walked away.

"Oh, no, you don't!"

Mac caught up with the bureaucrat-cum-spy at the opposite side of the clearing, where he'd started removing a camouflage net from what turned out to be a one-person lev. "We aren't done here, Tro-janowski," she told him fiercely. "Not by a long shot."

"Duty calls. I'm sure you know the way back." In one easy motion, Trojanowski straddled the seat and activated the lev. There was barely a whisper of engine noise. *Not your average off-the-lot weekend toy,* Mac thought, unsurprised. Probably maneuverable enough to fly under the canopy, out of sight. "Good day, Dr. Connor," he said, donning a black helmet and visor.

Mac stepped away as the lev lifted, contemplating several things, including what she'd transmit to Trojanowski's boss before the day ended. Her foot caught in a fragment of toppled cedar and she fell on her rump within its branches. *Perfect.* As she sat there, she glared up at the lev, which was now almost at tree height, and added a few others to the list to "speak to" about Mr. Trojanowski.

A breeze free to roam the new clearing slipped through her hair, scented with bruised leaves. Leaves bruised by the intruder in her office. Mac said "Damn," to herself, but squirmed to her feet. Once standing, she cupped her hands around her mouth and shouted: "I heard it."

The lev paused, then plunged groundward to rest over her head. Mac swallowed hard, but stood her ground. Trojanowski flipped up his visor and looked down, his expression noncommittal. "What did you hear?"

"Not words I could understand. Other sounds. When it was in my office, when I was following it, I heard—"

"That's enough. Stop," he ordered, emphasizing the command with a raised hand.

Mac obeyed, but pressed her lips together and scowled fiercely.

Trojanowski's expression became slightly more conciliatory. "Please don't take offense, Dr. Connor. You're right—this is important and I'll want your full report, but we need an audio expert to help reconstruct the sounds. Please don't talk to anyone else about what you think you heard until then—not even yourself. Premature verbalizing can distort recall. In Humans, at least."

He probably thought he was making sense, but Mac wasn't inclined to listen. Her toes were icicles, her legs ached, and her face was beginning to burn along the right side, from chin to forehead. "Then I suggest you call a transport to get me home."

"Call—? Does the concept of secrecy hold any meaning whatsoever to you?" Trojanowski actually sounded frustrated, likely the closest to an honest emotion he'd shown her since she'd arrived. "No one can know we've been up here."

Somehow, she doubted he was worried about the Wilderness Trust Oversight Committee. "Our 'visitors' already do," Mac pointed out.

"Which is more than enough. This isn't a debate, Dr. Connor. I'm very sorry, but you'll have to go back the way you came. I'll contact you as soon as I can."

Mac prided herself on keeping her temper. She found nothing productive or appealing in the furies the more volatile Emily would unleash without warning at targets ranging from slow drivers to political leaders. Now, however, she put her fists on her hips, stared up at Trojanowski, and let fly: "You're right. This isn't a debate, Mr. Trojanowski. You will arrange for me to be transported back to Base, or the moment I get back I'll be in touch with the Secretary General and everyone else I can find." She drew a shuddering breath, but kept going. "I'm sure some of the media are still around."

He lowered the lev until it brushed the ground, making it easier for her to read his expression. Not anger. *Regret*. Mac felt her blood chill as he spoke.

"You leave me no choice, Dr. Connor. One word about any of this—our encounter, what you chased, what happened here—and I'll have you arrested and removed from your facility as a threat to the species. And before you ask, yes, the Ministry of Extra-Sol Human Affairs has that authority, as an agency of the Interspecies Union. There would be no recourse or question. You would disappear."

What could she say to that? Mac stared at him, feeling as though her feet were sinking. *Which could well be*, part of her acknowledged.

He leaned forward. "I don't want to do that to you. But I will, if I have to—no matter how beautiful your eyes are at sunset. Your word, Dr. Connor, please, that you won't tell anyone."

Mac could only nod. Trojanowski's face was replaced by the black sheen of his visor. The lev shot toward the forest and vanished.

Her eyes were beautiful?

A squirrel complained furiously and Mac snorted, feeling—she wasn't sure what she felt. Angry, maybe. "Losing your temper never helps," she advised the squirrel. "Trust me."

She'd been about as effectual as the tiny creature. *Worse*, Mac realized with dismay, *she'd been wrong*. Trojanowski hadn't lied. There were secrets to protect, even if she hated being part of them. And it was her fault, no one else's, that she was part of them now.

She could already hear Emily's voice, providing a scathingly complete list of why she, Mac, should leave secrets and the pursuit of invisible aliens to professionals.

Like Trojanowski.

"Then she'll want to know how he looked without glasses," Mac told the squirrel. "Sorry, Em. I forgot to notice." *But he'd noticed her eyes.*

She made her way back through the clearing, dodging shattered stumps and piles of leafy debris. This couldn't possibly be overlooked by the Wilderness Trust and their satellite monitors.

"Who am I kidding?" Mac grumbled, about to step over another scar in the ground. "He probably has authority over Mudge, too. I'm so far out of my league it's . . ."

She paused. This scar was another that was too regular, forming an indentation longer than it was wide. Unlike the others, it was marked along one edge in a pattern of narrow scrapes similar to the one Mac had seen near the pillar, where the creature had dropped to the ground.

Mac sank on her heels to look out across the clearing. The other large depressions she'd judged the imprints of landing gear were at even distances from this one. She twisted on her heels to check behind her. The log where she'd crouched under the alien was in a direct line from this point. "I'll be . . ." she breathed. "This must have been the hatch."

They'd literally watched the creature enter its ship, and seen nothing.

Mac whistled between her teeth. "Now, that's camouflage." She unzipped the right-hand pocket of her slicker and shoved its contents—tissues, pencil remnants, and an unused t-lev ticket—

into the left with the lantern. Taking a piece of torn bark, she removed soil from the longest of the scrapes, putting as much into her empty pocket as she could fit. *A little present for Kammie.*

Mac smiled, wincing as it stretched the tender skin of her cheek. Now to see if Trojanowski's fancy scanner was as good as one of the top soil chemists on Earth.

Maybe she wasn't a professional whatever, with a fancy lev and helmet, Mac told herself. *But she was used to looking for answers—and finding them.*

The shadows cast by ruined branches and trampled ground abruptly lost their edges. The forest, already dim under the canopy, became as inviting as the door of an unlit basement and Mac heard the rain approaching through the trees. "Perfect," she said aloud, then pulled her hood over her head in time to keep her hair only damp, and stood.

Time to go home.

"Why sneak around my . . . *omphf* . . . office?" Mac muttered to herself as she slid down the next dip on her rump, grabbing whatever handholds she could find. It might not be dignified, but between the rain-slick slopes and her growing fatigue, she judged it safer than trying to climb down on her feet.

On reaching the next patch that was more or less level, she levered herself to her feet, casting an eye to what lay ahead. A choice between vertical rock or slightly less than vertical rock covered in wet roots. "This was all so much easier on the way up—and in the dark, so I couldn't see what an idiot I was." *Time to catch her breath.* Mac leaned on the nearest tree to mull the question troubling her. "Em," she decided, "your radar was off for once." She gave a lopsided grin, avoiding the damaged side of her face. The figure on the terrace last night hadn't been Trojanowski—he'd been here. But if the spy on the terrace had been the creature—or its more visible accomplice—then its search of her office later made an ironic kind of sense.

Mac shook her head. Had it thought the bag with the soufflé

contained some secret Brymn had brought her? "Well, that must have been a shock," she told the finger-long banana slug climbing the bark near her ear. An unhappy thought, an accomplice on Base, but it would have been easy enough. After all, they'd been invaded by fifteen kayak-loads of local media folk disguised as badly dressed tourists. *Even* she *could have infiltrated that group.*

Trojanowski's insistence on secrecy, however uncomfortable it made her trip home, suddenly seemed more reasonable.

The thought of more spies wandering around Base got Mac moving again, not to mention a distinct longing for the simple things in life. Although Mac couldn't make up her mind. "Shower, then breakfast," she decided, checking for the next foothold. "No. Strip and sleep, then shower. No. Breakfast, then more answers from that Dhryn."

She'd have plenty of time to work out the order. The return trip was less straightforward than the one up. For one thing, the trails she and the creature had left had been obliterated by the rain. For another, landmarks looked remarkably different viewed from above. *Oh, she wasn't lost.* Mac knew the overall shape of the landscape well enough to be sure she was heading toward the arm's inner curve, not the Pacific side. She intended to follow the ridge that led to the arm's tip, which should bring her out of the forest near one of the three walkways or perhaps the gate itself.

"With luck, Oversight will never know I was here," she reassured herself before starting her next, cautious descent. Mac wasn't proud of such a hope. She hung on tight, reaching with her boots for a foothold, and promised herself that despite Trojanowski's oath of secrecy she'd document every bruised leaf for Mudge, in case a researcher ever climbed this ridiculous excuse for a—

As if paying attention, the root clutched in her right hand chose that moment to pop free of the rock, ripping away with it an appalling number of connecting rootlets, ferns, and moss clumps. Mac wedged her boot in a crack in time to save herself from joining them at the bottom of the tiny cliff. "Oops," she said, staring down at what was undeniable proof of anthropogenic interference.

Then again, she could hope that Mr. Trojanowski had every bit of the authority he claimed when threatening her. He'd need it.

The amount of damage she'd done climbing up and back would be enough to rescind Norcoast's land access permanently. It wouldn't matter that the alien ship had smacked a hole the size of a transport lev in the forest.

She *was supposed to know better.*

"Aliens," Mac muttered darkly.

Hours later, Mac pressed her hand to the door release of Pod Three with a relief so close to pain she couldn't tell the difference. She'd half expected to find the walkways crowded despite the driving rain, but she'd staggered to the pod without seeing anyone but a family of orcas, breaching in the inlet. All she wanted from life at this moment was a roof and dry floor. And to get her boots off, if humanly possible. Everything and everyone else could wait.

Unfortunately, everyone else was waiting inside Pod Three.

Mac blinked stupidly at the sight that greeted her as the door opened. The corridor was lined three deep with people on each side, most shouting in confused, though joyful, unison when they saw her.

One shout penetrated the rest. "Mac! Where the hell have you been? We've got search parties out—the police—"

It took a second before Mac could put a name to the almost hysterical voice. *Kammie? The unflappable?* She winced with guilt as that worthy burst through the crowd toward her, arms flailing and eyes wild. "Ah. Sorry to alarm everyone," Mac said. "I'm fine. I'll explain later." *Once she found the energy to dream up a plausible story.* "Was Brymn okay through the excitement?"

"Brymn? Excitement?" Kammie seemed stuck on repeat.

Another voice interjected helpfully: "Still snoring."

Mac found herself grateful for the support of the doorframe. "Glad someone was."

The rising babble of concerned, relieved voices made it impossible to carry on a conversation. Several hands took over the work of the frame and her sagging muscles, guiding Mac forward into the blissfully dry and warm, if noisy, building. *But why were they all here?* She fought to stand still so she could search their faces, dismayed by what she saw.

And by who she didn't see.

"Em?"

She might have dropped a stone into a tidal pool, the way silence rippled outward from her question. The few faces turned her way seemed those of strangers.

"Where's Emily Mamani?" Mac demanded, shaking free of her caretakers.

Kammie, who looked to have aged a decade since yesterday, stared up at her. "We'd hoped she was with you, Mac."

8

DISPUTE AND DECISION

IT WAS A nightmare from which no one would let her wake. Mac turned herself into an automaton, answering questions in the order they arrived, steeling herself against any emotion, hers or those around her. As if authorizing a barnacle survey, she sent divers to search under the pods, and skims to follow the tide. As if making arrangements for the delivery of fresh fruit, she called Emily's younger sister and gave the story as it stood: *Emily is missing. There's been no contact from a kidnapper. Yes, you'll be kept informed.*

Mac didn't mention the slime coating every surface of Emily's quarters, the smashed furniture, or the blood. Kammie's report had been graphic. She'd been the only one inside Em's quarters and, given what she'd seen, it was no wonder she'd immediately called the local police. They'd ordered Em's quarters and Mac's office sealed. A forensics team had arrived and set up at dawn, their warn offs extending to corridor and terrace.

Mac had no doubt Trojanowski would be allowed to cross; she could not.

There was nothing more for her to do but wait.

She didn't do that well.

As if she'd lost her dearest friend, those around her lowered their voices and hovered when they obviously had other places to be. To be rid of them, Mac finally agreed to be escorted to the Base nurse.

Because she refused to believe she'd lost her dearest friend, Mac left the nurse the moment her face was treated for its burn.

Now, she stood before the door to her quarters, seeking answers in the only place left. *Emily had tried to warn her. Emily had known there was danger, that something was coming, that this wasn't about risks to aliens at distances Mac couldn't imagine, but to them, here, now.*

Emily had been afraid, last night. She'd asked not to be alone and Mac hadn't understood even that much.

What kind of friend was she?

It wasn't locked. Mac hesitated, afraid Brymn wouldn't be able to help, afraid of losing hope. Recognizing the weakness, she raised her fist and knocked.

No answer.

Mac pressed her palm on the entry. For no reason she could name, she let the door open fully before she took a step inside.

Her hands covered her mouth, a painful pressure on the mem-skin now coating her burn.

They'd said Brymn was snoring. She should have realized that none of them would know if a Dhryn snored in the first place.

From somewhere, Mac found the strength to snap the paralysis holding her in the doorway, taking three slow steps into the room. The form hanging in the middle of her living room was Brymn. She could tell that much by the patches of blue skin showing between the glistening threads wrapped around him, if little more. The threads led upward to form a thick knot stuck to the ceiling.

He was alive. That much was clear from the regular, low moaning. *It did sound a bit like snoring*, Mac decided numbly.

By rights, she should call the police immediately.

Instead, Mac locked the door behind her, then went to the com, leaning her back against the wall beside it. "Dr. Connor. Is Mr. Trojanowski back yet?"

"What are you doing out of bed?" Tie was back on com duty—a rock in a storm.

Mac rolled her head toward the familiar voice, her problem

solver when skims failed to run or pods developed a list, but said only: "Trojanowski."

Tie knew better than to argue. "Yes, he's back. He's been with the forensics guys. I'll hunt him up for you, Mac."

"Thanks. I'll be in my—in Brymn's quarters."

"There's been no more word about Dr. Mamani," he said, almost making it a question.

"Keep me posted, Tie."

Mac stayed propped against the wall beside the com, studying the Dhryn. The one eye she could see was closed. Unconscious—*or pretending to be.* The netting that held him had an artificial look, but she was no expert.

Emily had told her to take that xeno course from Seung.

Mac wasn't a fool. She understood she was experiencing shock, made worse by physical exhaustion. She understood her calm was a brittle coating over emotions she wasn't ready to face. It didn't matter, as long as it let her find Emily.

Then, she'd let herself feel.

Meanwhile, there was the problem posed by the netted Dhryn. Mac examined the threads. They looked sticky as well as moist. Stepping closer at last, she could see that each length had adhered to whatever it touched, puckering his skin into thick, tight creases.

"Explains the moaning," she said to herself. His silks were on the floor, but laid out neatly, as if the Dhryn had been undressed before the attack. It wasn't that his assailants had been tidy. Other than the fabric, the contents of Mac's quarters showed the same disarray as Emily's.

The same trails of slime coated ceiling and walls.

A knock on the door.

"Who is it?" she asked without moving.

"Trojanowski. You sent for me, Dr. Connor. I've been trying to find you—" A pause. "May I come in?"

"Are you alone?"

"Yes." Another pause. "What's that noise?"

"The Honorable Delegate."

His voice lowered a notch. "What's going on, Dr. Connor? Let me in."

Mac crossed her arms and stood beside the hanging Dhryn to wait.

Seconds later, her locked door opened. Trojanowski took a quick step in, then another to one side, slapping the door closed behind him. "Practiced that, have you?" Mac commented, noticing he was back to his student garb: T-shirt and jeans, complete with glasses. *The so-harmless look didn't play well anymore.*

"What the—?" His expression went from shocked to guarded. "Is he conscious?"

"I don't know." The "I don't care" was in her tone.

"Have you tried to find out?"

"I don't know anything about alien physiology, remember? I called you."

He took what looked like a pen from his pocket and used it to poke one of the threads holding Brymn.

"What's that?" Mac asked. "A weapon?"

"It's a pen."

"Oh." She wasn't sure why she was surprised. *Too many old movies with Em.*

His lips quirked to one side. "This," he pulled a black flattened disk from the same pocket, "is a weapon." It disappeared against the palm of his left hand. Then he raised that hand and pointed two fingers at the ceiling, where the threads combined into the holdfast.

A narrow beam of intense blue shot up. Where it touched the threads, they shriveled and broke apart, to become bits of soot drifting through the air. Trojanowski played the beam over the massive knot, flaking away more and more until Brymn's body shifted downward a few centimeters.

He stopped and put away the weapon. "He's going to fall. Help me put the mattress under him."

"That's my bed," Mac protested, although she moved to help. "Was my bed," she amended. It looked as though someone had attempted to shred the surface of the mattress, then glue it back together with slime.

They flipped it over before dragging it under the Dhryn. It was the work of seconds for Trojanowski to cut him down completely. *He fell like a salmon,* Mac decided, *limp but firm.*

Once Brymn was down, Trojanowski used his strange weapon to singe the ends of the threads wrapped around the being, careful not to ignite the mattress itself. Mac stood back and watched, her arms wrapped around her middle. She didn't remember breakfast. She thought she'd gulped something handed to her while she'd been at her desk. Her stomach wasn't happy about it.

Ungrateful organ.

Each singed thread continued to flake away along its entire length, as if losing some inner cohesion. Where they'd adhered to Brymn, the small dark pits of his skin oozed a clear liquid, presumably the source of an almost palpable odor, musklike and with a hint of sulfur, that began to fill the room. Mac took tiny breaths through her nose. *She'd smelled and seen worse.* Walking on bloated salmon corpses in July came to mind. No matter how carefully you put your feet, one would always pop.

"Good thing you checked on him," Trojanowski said, continuing to work. He'd been watching her, too. She'd seen his eyes slip her way every few seconds, their expression inscrutable. "I might not have for another hour or so—might have been too late."

"I wanted—how long until he wakes up? Until he can answer questions?"

The last thread fell away. "No idea. Is there any clean bedding? A blanket?"

Mac pointed to a cupboard. Trojanowski rummaged inside and returned with a sheet, which he laid over Brymn with care.

Then, he looked at her. "I'm sorry about your friend, Dr. Mamani." His eyes were presently more hazel than green, lending them an unexpected softness. Mac doubted she could look away of her own volition. She also doubted she could so much as flex her fingers without throwing up.

She managed to force words through her tight lips. "What are you doing to find her?"

Mac had the impression he was taken aback by the question. "The police will do all they can," he said after that almost imagined hesitation.

"You brought *him* here," she managed to say. "That—thing—followed. This is your fault. You have to find Emily." Tears welled up in her eyes. *She hated tears.* "You should have been protecting us—not—not—"

"Dr. Connor, you should be lying down. Wait." Trojanowski shut up and dropped to his knees beside the Dhryn. "Listen," he urged, waving her closer with one hand.

Mac copied his position, finding it all too easy to answer to gravity. *He was right.* The moaning had changed. She leaned forward, wary of her body's wobble.

The alien was muttering one word, over and over again.

"*Nai . . . Nai . . . Nai . . . Nai . . .*"

"Nothing . . . Nothing . . ." Trojanowski translated under his breath.

Oddly enough, that was the last thing Mac heard before Brymn's midsection rose from the mattress to smack her in the face.

"I don't bloody well care who you are, mate. You can't come in here like—"

From the thickening of his Aussie accent, the nurse, Dan Mandeville, was ready to do battle. Considering he stood slightly over two meters and was built, in Em's terms, like an antique forklift, that couldn't be a good thing. Mac's eyelids felt glued shut, but she found her voice somehow. "It's okay, Mandy. I'm awake."

"Then only for a moment. The woman needs rest!" A door closed with sufficient force to vibrate through the floor.

Her arm felt strangely heavy. Somehow, Mac brought her hand to her face, and scrubbed her eyelids until they cracked open. "What happened?" she asked, less than surprised to find herself flat on her back in what passed for a hospital room on Base.

Trojanowski pulled over a stool and sat beside her bed. "You passed out on me. They brought you here."

Wonderful. Mac tried to rise to her elbows, but the room tilted in the oddest way so she dropped back down. "Emily?" she demanded.

He shook his head.

"How long?"

"They've finished serving breakfast—not that anyone here seems to have much appetite."

She'd returned midday of what was now yesterday. *Nothing she could do about time already wasted.* Mac assessed herself, finding a musty taste at the back of her mouth. She remembered it from some minor surgery a couple of years ago. Mandy must have given her a sedative. *Hopefully, it was wearing off by now.*

Mac rolled on her side and swung her legs over the bed, using the momentum to pull herself upright. She hung on to the mattress with both hands, waiting patiently for the universe to finish sloshing back and forth. It helped to focus on her visitor.

There were dark smudges under Trojanowski's eyes and a grim set to his mouth. The plain black T-shirt and jeans he wore glistened in streaks. Slime from the rooms. *So he hadn't slept yet.* "Brymn?" she asked, resisting a certain amount of remorse. "Is he all right?"

"I don't know." Trojanowski gave a half shrug, clearly frustrated. "The experts at the Consulate were no help. Said to leave him alone until he recovered. They did offer to pick up his body, if he dies."

" 'A Dhryn is robust, or a Dhryn is not,' " Mac quoted. At his questioning look, she shrugged. "Something Brymn told me."

"This Dhryn better survive." He studied her. "What about you? You look awful."

"I'll do," Mac answered curtly.

"Good. Because I have some questions."

"About last night?"

"No. Dr. Mamani."

Even behind the glasses, there was something in his eyes that made her swallow, a distancing, as if he felt the need to somehow protect himself—or was it her?

Mac shifted on the bed, then realized part of her discomfort was an IV wrap around her upper arm. She ripped it free, in case the device was delivering more sedative.

Why was her arm bare?

Mac stared down at herself. Bad enough her legs and feet,

swinging freely above the floor, were bare, too, her toes and ankles decorated with lovely red blotches from her boots. *But this?*

Someone had dressed her in an orange, knee-length flannel nightgown, trimmed with purple lace and covered in vivid yellow spots. Spots with eyeballs and tiny, pointy teeth.

Where was dignity when you needed it?

"This is not mine," Mac assured Trojanowski, determined to straighten at least that much out. She knew better than to check her hair.

The corner of his mouth deepened, producing a dimple in one cheek. *Emily would probably notice something like that.* Mac's eyes started to fill and she blinked fiercely. "Ask your questions."

"Could Dr. Mamani have followed you that night?" he asked, his voice carefully neutral. "Become lost?"

Mac felt a thrill of hope. *Em lost in the woods would be an irritable, grumpy, miserable Em, but a living one.* Then she thought it through, and shook her head. "It was pitch-black around the pods. Even if she'd somehow seen me heading for shore, the gate wasn't working. Anyway, Em—Dr. Mamani—is a techhead. She'd have gone straight to the main power node to see what was wrong before looking for me."

He pressed his lips together, then nodded as if she'd confirmed his own conclusions. "A slim chance, at best. I had the police run scans for her genetic markers on the bridge and up the slope a considerable distance. Nothing."

Mac ignored the implications of the police doing what he asked, too dumbfounded by the concept of teams of non-Base personnel romping at will through the Wilderness Trust. "The Oversight Committee—" she began.

Trojanowski's face had a way of becoming still that sent a small shiver down her spine. "The Committee has no objections to any investigation we choose to conduct," he finished in a voice that left no doubt at all in Mac's mind about objections made and summarily squashed. She felt mildly envious. "In fact, this entire inlet——land, sea, air, and orbit—is now under the direct jurisdiction of the Ministry of Extra-Sol Human Affairs, although we'd prefer not to share that with the media. You can understand."

"I don't need to understand, as long as it means you are hunting for Emily."

"Oh, we're doing that."

His statement should have been reassuring. Mac wasn't sure why she abruptly didn't feel reassured at all. She narrowed her eyes. "What—who was in my office, Mr. Trojanowski? Who took Emily?" Despite her effort to remain calm, her voice failed her after: "Why—?"

A glint from his glasses. "Why did they take her and not you?"

It was the right question. The one she'd been asking herself over and over again since learning Emily was gone. Mac loosened her clenched hands and made her fingers toy with the purple lace crossing her thighs. "If you're asking me an opinion," she answered slowly, "I have none. I threw a slipper at it."

Trojanowski's eyebrows lifted. "Hardly a deterrent."

"It worked," she pointed out the obvious. "The thing ran out the door. It ran from me all the way to its ship."

"Dr. Connor—"

Shivering at the memory, Mac drew one leg up under the other and pulled the blanket around her shoulders. "I prefer Mac."

"Mac." Trojanowski didn't smile. He took off his glasses—which Mac doubted served any useful function beyond camouflage—and leaned forward, elbows on his knees. "I don't know what you've been told about the condition of her quarters, but Dr. Mamani—Emily—must have put up a significant struggle. We found her blood—" Mac had no idea what suddenly showed on her face, but Trojanowski shifted in mid-sentence. "Trust me. If they'd been after you, you'd be missing, too."

Mac stared at her feet. Red and sore, but no real blisters. There were the inevitable pine bits between her toes. Socks seemed irrelevant. With her luck, whoever had undressed her would forget to pull both socks and liners from her boots. *They'd take days to dry.*

"We can do this later." A reluctant compassion.

She raised her eyes to his. "No need. I'm worried about my friend and I'm angry. Neither affect my ability to participate in whatever will help find her—and those who took her. Please continue, Mr. Trojanowski."

"As you wish." He straightened, replaced his glasses on his nose, and took out a disappointingly ordinary imp which he made a point of consulting.

"I'm okay," Mac insisted.

He peered at her over his glasses, a curl of brown hair sliding down over one eyebrow. An artfully harmless look Mac didn't believe for an instant. "What do you know of Emily's life outside her work?"

Startled, Mac began to frown. "I don't see the relevance—"

"Please just answer the question." He passed her a bottle of water from the side table.

Emily's life outside of work? Mac opened the bottle and took a long drink, then another. "If you mean her life on Base," she answered warily, "the usual. During the research season, we're either at a field camp or here. Emily—" *Might as well be honest,* she told herself bitterly, *he probably has it all in some damned dossier . . . Emily's wealth of lovers, her own solitary years.* "Emily tends to be more social than I—" Her blush made the burn along her cheek throb and Mac ended with a lame: "You'd have to ask around."

He didn't seem to notice her embarrassment. *That didn't mean he hadn't,* Mac thought. "What about off-season, when she's not here with you?"

"She makes time for her—family." Mac knew if she said "sister," she'd hear Maria's voice again, those horrid flat tones reciting a number for the office, another for her friend, a litany of ways Mac could reach her at any time with news. *Would call her, as if the numbers were like magic, drawing answers from the air.* Mac coughed to clear her throat. "Em heads out to the Sargasso Sea for a month or two to work on her Tracer. It's a remote biosensor—do you want details?"

"I've been briefed. It's impressive technology, but not the concern at the moment."

"What is?"

His eyes were hooded. "Just keep going, please, Mac. What else does Emily do? Does she take vacations? Travel?"

Mac didn't bother arguing that hopping between the north Pacific to the south Atlantic twice a year was traveling, since he apparently didn't think so. "She mentioned shopping in Paris. A visit to Pietermaritzberg. That's near the southern tip of—"

"I know where it is. Did Emily tell you about going anywhere else? Even a hint? Think, Mac. This could be important."

"Nowhere else." Mac's left foot was asleep under her right thigh, and she was feeling a somewhat inconvenient desire to visit the washroom. Nonetheless, she narrowed her eyes at her questioner. "You were asking her about traveling. You know something," she accused. "What aren't you telling me?"

"Thank you for your time, Dr. Connor." Trojanowski stood, a fluid motion that belied the weariness on his face. *He doesn't move like that in public,* Mac thought, wondering what else the man was trained to hide. "I'm expecting the audio reconstructionist shortly after lunch. We'll resume our conversation then." As if they were finished, he headed for the door.

Not again, Mac vowed to herself. "This isn't the top of a mountain," she snapped. "I'll decide when we're done, Mr. Trojanowski— if that's even your real name." Mac jumped off the bed with every intention of following him out that door if he dared open it, obnoxious orange nightie or not.

Well, that's what she'd planned to do, but to Mac's chagrin, her legs crumpled beneath her. As if he had eyes in the back of his head, Trojanowski spun around with disturbing grace, reaching out to steady her before she could fall.

For a moment, they stood face-to-face, his fingers wrapped securely around her elbows, his forearms like warm, sturdy rails under hers, supporting a considerable amount of her weight. His breath stung the burn on her cheek as his eyes searched hers. *For what?* Mac wondered, suddenly more perplexed than angry.

Then, as if impelled by something he saw, the man she'd once thought nothing more than a messenger said in a low and urgent voice: "Mac, listen to me. Listen carefully. The best thing you can do right now is be yourself. Be the reclusive scientist. Be the private, careful person who doesn't let anyone close. Anyone." His fingers tightened with the word. "The only reason you're here and you're safe is because you weren't in your quarters last night. Do you understand me? They found poor Brymn—but I believe they came for you."

"For me? Why?" Involuntarily, Mac's hands closed on his arms, not for comfort, but to hold him there, to demand more answers. "What about the intruder in my office?"

"I wish I knew." Trojanowski hesitated, then went on: "My guess is that one of them was to search your office and he, she, it was to run if discovered. You were lucky."

"Emily wasn't." Mac stared at him, aghast. "Brymn wasn't. I must go and see him—"

"He's being monitored. Meanwhile, you," the spy said sternly, "will stay here." Before Mac could protest, he used his grip on her arms to heft her up on the bed and sit her there. "Get some rest. I don't want that rugby player you call a nurse chasing me down the hall."

As the room was elongating on two axes, Mac didn't even attempt to nod. "You'll call me when your audio expert arrives, Mr. Trojanowski," she told him firmly.

He looked back at her, his hand on the doorplate. "It is my real name," he said, without smiling. "But I prefer Nik."

Then he was gone.

Mac lay back, legs dangling over the side of the bed, her head spinning far too much for safe passage anywhere but horizontal. *He'd been briefed on more than Emily's Tracer.* She'd rarely heard a more precise summary of her life.

Her fingertips followed the lingering heat from his skin along the underside of her arms. *Nik, was it?* Did "Nik" think she'd missed his implications? Of course not. Mac doubted a single word came out of that man he didn't fully intend to say. So there was something she didn't know and he did about where Emily had been, something connected to invisible aliens and Brymn's being here, something that meant she, Mac, wasn't to become close to anyone. She was to keep up her guard.

Good advice, regardless of its source. "Against you, too, Mr. Nik," she muttered, sitting up more cautiously this time. The local representative of the Ministry of Extra-Sol Human Affairs might have access to a dossier of her work, life, and likely even a psych profile. *He didn't know her.*

Not if he thought he could put her aside.

Mac achieved vertical with no more than a momentary wobble. "Must thank our Mandy for whatever he pumped into me," she told the room. Not that there'd been anything wrong with her body a few calories and some sleep hadn't cured.

As for her mind and heart, well, her dossier should have warned Trojanowski that Dr. Mackenzie Connor was a person of action, not mood. Worrying about Emily meant finding Emily. Finding Emily meant getting to her feet and back into the game.

Now.

- Portent -

ISHT HAD hidden.

It was *isht's* only duty, to scramble into the smallest, darkest place *isht* could find. Quickly. Without hesitation. Without thought.

That place should have been the one of soft warmth, the one filled with the rhythmic rush of sound, moist with the sweet satisfying taste of *aisht* or perhaps the bitter tang that meant *isht* had mistakenly climbed into *oeisht*. Any *oeisht* would have forgiven *isht*, would have willingly provided shelter.

Isht shivered in *isht's* hiding place, hearing nothing, tasting dust.

Time passed, unmarked by light. *Isht* vibrated *isht's* distress, unfelt by *aisht* or *oeisht*.

Isht's thoughts couldn't form abstracts such as hope or despair. There was only the duty to hide, the need to breathe and seek nourishment, the urgency of survival. Slowly but inevitably, survival warred with duty.

Isht couldn't stay here and live.

The moment came when, trembling, *isht* climbed upward, one clawhold at a time. *Isht* reached the slit through which *isht* had first passed into the place and stopped to listen. Nothing.

The slit led sharply downward, a twist *isht's* narrow form negotiated with ease. Then, *isht* was outside the place, clinging with all its might, looking for help.

Isht was accustomed to climbing from *aisht* to find *ishtself* in a new and amazing world. This was different.

Isht vibrated with fear.

The world wasn't new; it was gone. *Isht* clung, its grip the only safety.

What had been *isht's* home was now a skeleton of metal and glass.

What had been a farm was now an ocean reaching in every direction *isht* could see. It filled *isht's* home, lapping at the column of *isht's* hiding place like a tongue seeking *isht's* taste.

A shadow sent *isht* scrambling into the smallest, darkest place *isht* could find. *Isht* heard the mouths begin to drink.

9

MEETINGS AND MISCHIEF

MAC GRASPED the terrace rail and leaned back, turning her face to the sun as if she were a flower. It prickled the mem-skin covering her burned cheek and seared bright dots beneath her closed eyelids. She hadn't expected a gift like this, one of those unabashedly perfect days, where the sky was saturated with blue and the breezes, full of cedar and salt, slipped over skin and hair like a warm caress.

It would do them all good. Mac pulled herself upright to look down at the walkways filled with students and their gear. Several teams were loading their skims; others were loafing on towels, waiting their turn. Business as usual in the latter half of the research season.

Or not. On her way to meet with Kammie, having delayed only to exchange the obnoxious nightie for clothing that was actually hers for a change, Mac had quietly asked Tie to head up to Field Station Six with a couple of volunteers to dismantle her and Emily's equipment. It would be brought back and stored for use next year.

She couldn't bear to think otherwise.

Now, Mac headed left along the terrace, the long way around, since the section outside her office was still off limits.

Dr. Kammie Noyo's office and lab was on the opposite side of the pod from hers, affording a stunning view past the tip of the inlet to the open ocean. Not that you could see it from inside. Rumor in the student pods was that the venerable chemist had opaqued her window wall because she was afraid of water.

Mac knocked perfunctorily on the door, propped open to the sunshine with an earthenware pot containing a surprised cactus, and walked inside.

Rumor, as usual, was untrustworthy. *Afraid of water?* Mac shook her head at the notion. Kammie Noyo was a deepwater sailor and had picked this very office for its view. Unfortunately, all that was left of the view was through her open door. She'd covered her walls with shelves to hold her growing collection of soil samples, adamantly refusing to move so much as a single precious vial out of her sight. "You never knew when you'd need one to compare," she'd say in her cheerful voice, hands shoved into her brilliant white lab coat. The window wall? Permanently opaqued simply to protect the samples from daylight.

Mac let her eyes adjust to the interior lighting, then followed voices through the empty office to the lab to find Kammie, hands in her lab coat, holding court with her latest crop of postdocs. They were a matched set: three gangly youngsters who had faith the pale fuzz on their chins would be worthy beards by the end of the research season and their theses would change the world. Months working with Kammie, whose head barely topped Mac's ear, had given them a distinctly stooped posture. Kammie professed herself pleased with their individuality and brilliance. Mac still couldn't tell them apart, but she trusted Kammie's judgment.

She needed it more than ever now.

Quite sure Kammie had seen her—the woman's peripheral vision was legendary—Mac waved to show she could wait, then went back into the office. She punched her codes into Kammie's desk interface to bring up her own main workscreen, directly linked to Norcoast's, then found a chair with fewer periodicals than usual, and sat carefully on top. Everyone at Base, starting with the cleaning staff, knew better than to mess with Dr. Noyo's furniture-based filing system.

Mac leveled her bottom with a careful wiggle, grumbling automatically over the chemist's continued fondness for paper, then tapped the air where her workscreen had decided to float. She brought out her imp and initialized its personal 'screen—smaller, self-contained, and able to reference only data carried within the imp itself. Layering one over the other, Mac got to work.

Kammie bustled in half an hour later. "Sorry to keep you waiting, Mac," she apologized cheerily in her soft, high-pitched voice. "The boys had an interesting problem." She stretched to tuck a small aluminum vial box back into its place on a shelf behind her desk, then, as if struck by a thought, she stayed there, tracing the labels of its neighbors with her fingers.

"You okay?" Mac asked, glancing up through her 'screens. Unlike yesterday, when she'd been so distraught in the hall of Pod Three, the other woman appeared back to normal, hair smoothly coiffed, round face wearing the patented half smile that Kammie joked she'd inherited from a wise grandfather.

"I'm supposed to be asking you that, aren't I?" Smile fading, Kammie turned and sank into her chair. Whatever she'd left on it raised her to just the right height for her desk. Her almond-shaped eyes were troubled as she called up her own 'screen in preparation for their briefing. "I'm worried about my students. Is it wrong to send them back to work so soon?"

"Look at us." Mac poked a finger through her 'screen. "I'd say it's the only productive thing we can do, Kammie. And Em—you know she'd be the first person to take our heads off for moping around."

The chemist looked wistful. "No argument there. So. What can I do for you, Mac?"

"This." With a slide of her hand through the air, Mac sent her Admin codes, schedules, everything she had pending on Base to Kammie's 'screen. "I want you to take over for me, Kammie. Indefinitely."

"You're kidding. I'm in the middle of—"

"I'm very serious, Kammie. I need you to look after all the admin, not just your half."

Kammie Noyo leaned back in her chair, studying Mac over her steepled fingers. "No offense, dear lady, but didn't you just say work was the only productive thing we can do? I don't see you, of any of us, taking a break right now." Kammie's delicate eyebrows met. "Which means you're up to something. What?"

Mac almost smiled. She'd never joined Kammie's seafaring adventures or visited her extensive family; she was well aware that

Kammie, for her part, considered Mac an eccentric workaholic who must be reminded at regular intervals that others had real lives. But when it came to what mattered, each knew the other very well indeed. "I was a witness."

Kammie's eyes widened. "Your office?" she breathed, moving forward again. "You were there? But—"

"I chased one of them out of it. Don't give me that look, Kammie Noyo. It seemed perfectly safe at the time. And turned out to be, except for some sore muscles. As a result, while I don't know how much help I can be to the—investigation," Mac had trouble with the word. "There's no doubt I'm going to be called away from my duties. In fact, I may be asked to leave Base without notice. We've been disrupted enough. I won't let my absence jeopardize anyone's work. I won't have the entire season lost."

Norcoast had never lost a season, although it had been a near thing the year of the "almost perfect" storm. Mac watched Kammie remember it. How could she not? To anyone who'd been there, it had seemed like the end of the world.

The storm had slid toward them from the southwest, a late October mass of subtropical moisture and wind the weather controllers had decided to leave alone. The tides would be unusually high, but the storm track was northward, so the predicted surge was minimal. Such storms had immense natural value, stirring the depths of the ocean to bring up nutrients, and flushing rivers as it drove up the coast. Coastal communities had been warned to prepare for several days of heavy rain and strong sustained winds. Many had viewed the chance to experience a major storm as a rare adventure. It was dubbed the "almost perfect" storm by those who didn't know better.

Some at Norcoast had been eager to document the storm's impact on marine life. Mac had viewed it as a major inconvenience. She'd been working on her postdoc, lingering at Base through the fall months to help ready the pods for the winter, store samples and data, and generally earn her keep while waiting for her next projects to be approved. But nothing was going to get done outdoors until the storm passed through.

It was more than inconvenient. The first day, 15 centimeters of rain fell, carried on winds that hit 100 kilometers per hour. Weather controllers admitted they'd let a hurricane slip through their net and began remedial efforts. Too little, too late. The second day, gusts reached 289 kilometers per hour, blowing down trees like sticks in sand, and another 30 centimeters of rain landed on the coast. The third day 20 centimeters fell . . . The fourth . . .

There was no need to pack up the pods for winter. The original four that had made up Norcoast's Base had been nestled against the mainland at the mouth of the Tannu, protected by surrounding islands from wave action, but directly in the path of both landslide and flood.

Students, staff, and scientists had huddled together on transport levs to watch the pods tip and sink within a thick soup of snapped trees, gravel, mud, rock, and water. Then they'd gone to work. It hadn't mattered what your credentials or research plans that winter. Everyone had pitched in to ensure the first replacement pod was constructed and anchored—in a new, safer location—in time for the spring salmon runs. They'd succeeded. In Mac's estimation, that winter's catchall phrase had come to define Norcoast: "we'll get it done."

The new pods in their new location had weathered far worse since without incident. *It remained to be seen*, Mac thought, *if its people continued to have that kind of determination.*

Mac waited anxiously as Kammie, never one to make a snap decision, scrolled through the data on her 'screen without changing her expression from that slight frown. With her in charge, the others should be able to continue. Mac didn't have students of her own this summer, other than a shared project with John Ward. Kammie could stand in her place as his adviser, if need be. "Well?" she asked finally.

The frown was replaced by a somewhat surprised look. "Of course, Mac. I was only checking who from Wet could assist with your stuff. John looks available."

Mac and Kammie split the administrative duties of Base along practical lines: dry versus wet. Dry included those researchers who worked on land, but also those who conducted aerial surveys, retrieved remote sensing data, or worked primarily in the labs at Base.

Kammie's highly technical criterion was that her people never had wet socks. Wet was thus everyone else, and Mac's responsibility.

"He can be," Mac admitted with an inner wince, although Kammie was right. The bulk of Ward's analysis work could be left for the coming winter. *His reaction, though?* she grimaced. Mac knew he'd arranged classes at Berkeley, in California, but this would mean he'd have to stay on Base another six months. *Surfing, skiing. Both sports where you rode on something flat, right?* Mac keyed the message to John Ward's workscreen before she could change her mind. "Anything else?"

"Why does that sound final? I will be able to contact you—I won't," Kammie corrected herself as Mac shook her head. "Well." She sat a little straighter. "In that case, I'll go under the premise you'll approve anything I decide."

"Within the operating budget," Mac cautioned, but with distinct relief. She hadn't felt the weight of keeping up with the concerns of Base and its researchers until this moment, when it was no longer hers to carry. "I'll do my best to keep you informed, Kammie. I—I never wanted to dump all this on you."

Kammie made a rude noise. "Tell me that next spring when you fly off to a field station and leave me to settle the new arrivals."

With a chuckle, Mac got to her feet. "There's one more thing." She put away her imp, 'screens winking from sight, and drew out a vial, identical to any of the thousands in the boxes lining the walls around her.

Kammie rose and came around her desk, hand reaching out as if the tiny thing were a magnet. "What's this?"

As much truth as she dared, Mac thought. "There may be something unique about this soil," she said. The idea that such secrecy could be for Kammie's protection didn't help. "I'd like to know what you think of it. Between us for the time being, please."

From the speed with which the tiny chemist withdrew her fingers, Mac might have offered her poison. "Oh, no, you don't. If this is something that could help find Emily, it should go to the forensics—"

"No. No. Nothing like that," Mac insisted. *Did lying become easier with practice?* She could ask "Nik" Trojanowski, doubtless an expert. "It's something I've been carrying around in my pocket for you." *All too easy to sound frustrated.* "I'd like to know at least something of my work is getting done."

Kammie's transparent features eased from skeptical to sympathetic. She took the vial. "Not a problem, Mac. Sorry I jumped on you. You leave this with me. I'll get on it right away." A smile. "Well, after I deal with the 'A for At Once' on the list you dumped on me. What kind of category name is that anyway?"

"I thought it was more tactful than 'A for Annoying.' "

A laugh that made Kammie wipe her eyes. "Oh, dear. I suppose there're more gems waiting in here. Thanks a lot, Mac."

Mac rested her hand on the other woman's shoulder and squeezed gently. "Thank you, Kammie."

Kammie's fingers, callused and warm, captured hers. "They'll find her, Mac," she promised, eyes brimming with tears that now had nothing to do with laughter. "And she'll be okay. Emily's smart and she's tougher than any of us. You know she is."

All Mac could do was nod.

During lunch, while a police officer from nearby Kitimat stood at the gallery entrance and politely resisted all attempts by incoming Pred students to inspect his weaponry, Mac sat alone. *Literally.* The gallery's tables were deserted, its few visitors opting for a bag lunch to take outside while the sun still shone.

The privacy was welcome. Mac alternated absentminded bites of her sandwich with glances at the small 'screen hovering over her plate. She'd finished copying what she and Emily had found into her imp, whether about Brymn or his species. Now, as she awaited her summons from Trojanowski, she reviewed the list of everything else she'd grabbed, in case she had to abandon her resources at Base for any length of time.

"Anyone reading this would consider me certifiable," Mac mumbled around a mouthful of fluffy barbequed salmon and bun. One of the distinct advantages to eating in the gallery were the samples brought in by the Harvs; any extras turned up on the grill.

Oh, her list did include reasonable, logical things: summaries of the most recent Chasm research, a simplified spatial geography of the Naralax Transect complete with traveler "must see" suggestions, and a copy of Seung's course materials on xenobiology. Mac could no longer afford the luxury of thinking in Earth-only terms.

Emily'd tried to tell her.

She'd tucked the more eyebrow-raising entries under the heading "Groceries:" reported sightings of Chasm Ghouls; the latest popular theories, scholarly or not, on the existence of the Chasm; a report on the feasibility of invisibility from one of last year's exchange students, inspired by another too-close encounter with grizzlies; occurrences of invisible aliens on Earth—more than Mac had ever dreamed—and, last but not least, Emily Mamani's personal logs.

Mac took a sip of tea, her hands wrapped around the mug to seek its warmth. It had only taken a quick call. Maria had sent Emily's logs without question, although she'd admitted to denying their existence to "those officials who have no right coming to my home, prying into private family business when they should be looking for my sister." Knowing Emily's passionate temper, as quick to fade as it was to flare, Mac guessed Maria had regretted her lack of cooperation the moment the "officials" left. It probably relieved her conscience to send the logs to Mac. Certainly they all believed in doing anything that could help the investigation. . . .

That damn word again. Mac knew why she hated it. You investigated a crime that had already happened, searching for the culprits, not the victim. But she couldn't deny that finding the culprits seemed the only way to find Emily.

The only way Mac accepted, ignoring the fact that search teams were still out, following the tide, scouring the shoreline, and bumping around underneath the pods.

As for the logs? She'd received them directly on her imp, keeping them away from Norcoast's systems. *Now?* Mac flicked a finger through the 'screen to turn it off. She sipped more tea, gazing out the window at the novel spectacle of white-capped mountains cutting into a blue sky, unable to deny what troubled her most. *Was there something in those logs Emily would prefer not be known, even by a friend?*

She'd asked Mac for forgiveness. And now Trojanowski's questions about Emily were like splinters Mac couldn't reach to pull out.

Thinking about him made her impatient as well as uneasy. Mac pushed to her feet, tucked away her imp, and grabbed her lunch tray to take back to the kitchen.

"There you are, Dr. Connor!"

Think of the devil, Mac said to herself. Outwardly, she gave a polite nod, waiting as Trojanowski, again resplendently civil in suit and cravat, came walking toward her. Then Mac saw he was accompanied by a very dark, very round man in an ancient yellow rain suit who began smiling the instant she did.

Mac dropped her tray on the table with a clatter. "Jabulani!" She launched herself into his arms, her hands barely reaching around his sides. Almost as quickly, she pulled back, needing to feast her eyes on one of the dearest, most brilliant, people she knew.

Jabulani Sithole had hardly aged. His tight curls had silvered before they'd met, she remembered fondly. His dark eyes still twinkled. *And the raincoat.* Jabulani had decided long ago the only way to beat the coast weather was to always dress for its worst. Sweat pearled his brow and beaded his generous nose, but Mac knew from experience nothing would pry the heavy coat and sweater from the man if he thought they'd be going outside again soon. "I can't believe you're here."

"You said he could do incredible things with sound," Trojanowski said, standing to one side.

"Did you really?" Jabulani planted a kiss on Mac's forehead. "You were always kind, Mackenzie dear. A treasure."

"Because I kept you in sandwiches," she corrected, with a fond smile, "so you'd let me listen to my salmon."

Jabulani turned to Trojanowski. "Even then, so young, she called them 'hers.' Is it any wonder she's in charge now?" His voice softened and he gazed down at her, wide mouth losing its smile. "Mackenzie, I am so sorry—"

Before the sympathy of her old friend could do more than mist her eyes, Mac patted Jabulani once more to make sure he was real, then said simply: "If anyone can replicate what I heard, Jabulani, it's you." *If she could bear to relive that night with anyone, it was him.* She shot Trojanowski a look of gratitude. "Thank you."

He nodded, once. "If you're ready, Dr. Connor? Dr. Sithole? We should start as soon as possible."

Mac caught Jabulani's longing look at her tray and snorted affectionately. *Some things never changed.* "We can pick up a bag in the kitchen," she assured him.

The audio lab was in Pod Six, relocated there during the sojourn of the lost whale so researchers could interpret the baby's linguistic heritage and find its family; left there because the lab's space had been "mistakenly" reapportioned between its former neighbors in Pod Four almost overnight. The unspoken rule at Base held that a clear bench was a bench ready for a new owner.

Audio hadn't protested. Pod Six was hollow, fixed to the ocean floor year-round, and everything above the waterline was now unofficially theirs. Every year since, new projects had grafted themselves to the interior of the dome wall, supported by whatever means the researchers could afford or create. Despite appearances, to date only one had come loose and fallen into the water, fortunately not harming the students who'd been using that platform for a moment's indiscretion, nor unduly disturbing the otters who'd again found their way inside.

Mac led the way into Pod Six. The access door from the walkway opened on a small platform offering a choice of stairs, one set dropping down to the inner ring that floated directly on the ocean, the other newer and curving up along the wall itself.

She sensed her companions' wonder and stopped obligingly, fond of the place herself. Six was, well, unique.

From the outside, its domelike walls had the same curved, reddish stone appearance as those of the other pods, albeit with no terraces or antennae to foil the illusion. From the inside, it was a bubble of calm floating in the midst of Castle Inlet, any wave that traveled past damped to the hint of a swell. The walls, except for some necessary supports and the audio platforms, were almost transparent. They opaqued under the rare full sun to keep the ambient light level no brighter than that at a depth of ten centimeters underwater outside the dome, save for spot lighting on stairs and platform. This didn't bother the audio researchers. The interior air temperature was matched to an outside standard as well, something they did complain about—particularly when they arrived in early spring to work space close to the freezing point—but to no avail.

The floating inner ring was currently a jumble of diving gear, sample cases, and other gear, a maze busily negotiated by upward of three dozen researchers at any given time. Some waved up at them; most were too busy to notice the new arrivals. This week, Pod Six was temporarily entertaining an entire school of smolts, a combination of young salmon born last year and the year before, their bodies busy adapting to life in salt water. Varied species as well. They couldn't stay in even this huge space for long, some being eager to head to the open ocean, others destined for the mouths of estuaries and the rich feeding there. The race was on to learn as much as possible before the eight great sea doors of the pod opened to release them again.

Abruptly, someone shouted and began running along the ring in pursuit of something sinuous and brown. "I see the otters are still up to their tricks," Jabulani noted with amusement as the student below stopped and threw up her hands in patent disgust.

"Brains enough for trouble," Mac agreed. The boisterous river otters weren't just after the conveniently trapped smolts. They enjoyed chewing on synthrubber fittings and made toys out of anything they could tip into the water. Mac didn't doubt the animals were well aware that inside the pod they were safe from anything but the insincere ire of a few researchers.

"Which way, Dr. Connor?"

Trojanowski shouldn't need to remind her they weren't here to watch otters. Mac flushed and took the stairs up two at a time. "You can use Denise's setup, Jabulani," she said over her shoulder.

"Perfect!" Despite the makeshift construction, Jabulani's weight didn't budge the stairs as he rumbled eagerly behind her. "I hadn't dared hope she was still here, too."

"You kidding? She takes fewer off-Base trips than I do."

"Hold on a minute—"

Mac stopped on the staircase, her head below the first and largest side platform. The ones farther up overhung the water itself, but here the inward curve of the wall was barely detectable. She peered around Jabulani's thick shoulder to meet Trojanowski's gathering scowl. "Dr. Pillsworthy has the equipment," she informed him, understanding immediately. "And she can help."

"Dr. Pillsworthy does not have clearance—"

"Fine." Mac shrugged and waved the two men back down the stairs. "We'll have to leave Base, then."

"Dr. Connor—" Trojanowski didn't budge. "We must make the recording as soon as possible."

"And I can guarantee you we won't be allowed anywhere near her equipment unless Denise stays, clearance or not. She won't let a soul, not me, not even Jabulani here, use it without her present."

"Is there anyone here who—? No, forget I asked." The patently exasperated Trojanowski actually ran one hand over his face before using it to gesture that she should continue climbing to the platform. "Lead on."

Mac hid her smile by turning obediently to face the platform.

A few steps later, they crowded together on what was no more or less than an extension tacked onto the existing staircase. The extension itself hung out over the water to form the floor for what looked like, and was, a converted t-lev cargo compartment now bolted to the wall. Someone had painted "aUDiOcellAR" on the dingy gray door.

"Nice touch," Jabulani noted, pointing to a painted window filled with a cluster of desperate faces trapped behind what appeared to be hockey sticks.

"We ran out of beer in the play-offs two years ago," Mac explained. She pressed her hand on the doorplate to request entry. No use calling ahead to Denise; the audiophile detested the existing com and refused to use it, relying on runners or insisting on in-person visits. Mac had, in her first year as coadministrator, asked

Denise to submit a budget proposal for the ideal system. Since that moment of weakness, Mac had agreed Pod Six wasn't too far to walk. Nor was a little company too much for someone as dedicated to her lab as Denise was to ask.

Not that Denise Pillsworthy was a gracious host, Mac grinned to herself as a strident: "Who is it?" came through the wall.

To let Jabulani go first, Mac squeezed against Trojanowski. "Trust me," she hissed, when he would have argued.

"One guess, Sweet Thing!" Jabulani shouted.

The door opened immediately. "It can't be—"

"Me!"

"Jabby!"

Jabulani disappeared inside the audio lab as if inhaled by a whale. Mac followed, Trojanowski right on her heels, to find the older man sitting on a stool, cradling a cooing Denise Pillsworthy in his ample lap, yellow raincoat and all.

Denise stopped cooing only long enough to toss out: "Hi, Mac! Who's that?" before continuing to pepper Jabulani's chubby cheeks with kisses.

"Dr. Connor." From behind, low and amused. "Is everyone who works here so—so—"

"Close?" Mac suggested. *He might be amused, but she wasn't.* "You form friendships for life working in a place like Norcoast—or enemies," she added, being honest.

Quieter still. "I'm not your enemy, Mac."

"I didn't say you were. That doesn't make us friends," she replied evenly. Before he could continue whispering, Mac raised her voice to carry over the giggles. "Save it for later, okay? We don't have time to spare."

Jabulani's head lifted. "Ah, Little Mackenzie is right, Sweet Thing. We have some reconstructions to record—to help find your missing friend."

Denise surged to her feet, poking at her hair. "You could have told me," she grumbled. "Honestly, Jabby, you never get to the point. We're on it, Mac. What do you need, Jabby?"

As the two audiophiles began to talk a language all their own, Mac leaned on the nearest bit of equipment that wasn't blinking

madly to itself. The lab was lined with cases and wires, the technology an eclectic mix of old and new—much like its operator.
Denise, gray-haired and bone-thin, wore a sleeveless, eye-piercing
pink sweater over a brown woven skirt of indeterminate hemline,
but three pairs of state-of-the-art headsets swung around her long
neck and her ears were studded with implants. Her pale blue eyes
were almost buried beneath lids colored to match her sweater, but
her hands were those of a concert pianist, long-fingered and
strong, callused by years of slipping over guitar strings and old-
fashioned wire.

Trojanowski had his own preparations to make. While Denise
and Jabulani assembled equipment, he closed and locked the lab
door, then came over to lean beside Mac. "Where were you when
you first heard your visitor?" Before she could say anything, he
brought out an imp and sent its 'screen to hover in front of her
face. "Show me."

Mac found herself staring into a view of her office, generated as
if taken from above, in daylight. It hadn't been searched—it had
been destroyed. Her garden was a pile of vegetation, dirt, and broken barrels. The stones had been pried from her floor. The salmon
models were heaped in a corner, most broken.

Nothing was untouched.

The forensics team. Trojanowski. *Or both.* She realized numbly
they must have been hunting for clues to her intruder. Everything
still glistened with slime, as if the material had hardened into a permanent coating. *Had they found anything else?*

She must have uttered a protest, for the image winked out of existence. "I'm sorry, Mac," she heard Trojanowski say. "I didn't
think of how it would look. I should have warned you—"

"It's only a room," she replied coolly. "Show me again." When
the image reappeared, Mac swallowed and ignored everything but
the task at hand. She put her finger on the mattress in front of her
desk. "Here. The first time." Trojanowski reached over to lock the
display. "I was out on the terrace the second time." He provided
that image. Mac showed where she'd stood, then: "The walkway to
the shore, the mem-wood section—and in front of the gate."

He locked in her locations for each, then nodded. "I have the time of the power shutdown, of course, but do you know when you first woke up and heard it?"

"Not much before dawn," Mac guessed. "The fog was starting to condense in the trees, but there wasn't any light on the horizon that I could see. The mountains, clouds," she shook her head apologetically. "It's hard to say. But only minutes passed before there were people moving about—lanterns going up near Pod Three behind me."

"Shortly after five, then," he said, giving a small, tight smile at her look. "The police did extensive interviews and we've cross-referenced every statement. The only time line I didn't have was yours." The 'screen reoriented itself in front of Trojanowski and he stroked through it several times. "Dr. Sithole will incorporate the appropriate environmental parameters into his reconstructions."

"You've worked with him before," Mac guessed.

His eyes sought the other man. Mac couldn't read their expression. "No, but I'm familiar with the process." Trojanowski looked down at her again and said quietly: "They won't need to know anything about the creature's—appearance—or its actions, just how it sounds, so please watch what you say."

"Or you'll have to lock us all up?"

"Hopefully not."

"I was joking," Mac protested.

His lips quirked, but all Trojanowski said was: "It might be a while yet. Keep your mind busy while you wait."

"No problem." Mac pulled out her imp and headed for the nearest stool. "I brought plenty to read."

Mac made it through five of Brymn's publications before Jabulani called them to the studio at the far end of the lab, learning little more than a respect for the Dhryn's grasp of nonlinear analysis. Trying to follow his reasoning for the dating of certain Chasm artifacts had taken her mind completely off what they were trying to do.

Standing in front of the cubicle where she was supposed to recreate the sounds of the alien, however, Mac began to wonder if she hadn't made a mistake not trying to remember the sounds beforehand. "I didn't hear speech," she told them doubtfully.

"You can't know that," Denise said firmly, pulling a headset over her ears. "There was a time people didn't believe orcas had local dialects."

"Any information might help," Trojanowski added, coming to stand beside her. "Do your best. That's all."

Jabulani smiled confidently and waved her inside. "Easy as can be, Little Mackenzie. You give me a starting point—whatever you can recall," he said as Mac stepped into the small soundproofed room in the back corner of the lab. "I'll echo it back. Each time I do, you tell me how to make what you hear now, more like what you heard then. Ask me anything and I can do it. I am a genius," he added with a sly wink.

She couldn't argue with him there. Mac took the only seat, a built-in bench. Two strides in any direction and she'd bump into a padded wall. When Jabulani closed the door, it blended into wall as well. Before she could react to the closeness of the space, his rich voice filled it. "We're ready to start. Your first sound, Mackenzie."

"Give me a minute," she asked.

How to start? Experimentally, she scratched her fingernails on the bench surface. *Definitely* not *that sound.* Mac tried sitting absolutely still, only to have her ears fill with the pounding of her heart, the air through her lungs. After a few seconds, she was convinced she could hear her stomach digesting the salmon sandwich.

She couldn't "hear" anything else. "It's too quiet," she complained, feeling foolish.

"Understood. Stand by."

Five slow breaths later, Mac abruptly realized she could hear the ocean under the pod supports. *Tide moving through,* she judged, finding that odd for the middle of the afternoon until she caught on to the trick. "Clever," she complimented Jabulani, who must have checked the charts for conditions that night.

"A genius, am I. Keep listening."

The ocean faded into background, in part because Mac was so accustomed to the sound in her life that she herself tuned it out.

Overlaying it came the babble of water over stone, with a touch of wind through drying leaves. *Her garden*. He even replicated the clink of her suspended salmon touching one another as they swayed in their hangers.

"Try lying down." Trojanowski's voice. "The way you were when the sound woke you in your office."

True, the floor space wasn't much larger than her mattress had been. Mac laid down, then, remembering, rolled on her back. "Turn out the lights, please."

Darkness pressed against her face. She drew it into her lungs, imagining the scents of her office. "The power was off when I woke up."

The water and wind from her garden died away. Only the lapping of the ocean and the occasional snick of salmon to salmon remained.

Mac concentrated. *Where to start?* "Rain on a skim cover," she suggested.

The room filled with an irregular drumming on metal and plastic.

"Softer." It quieted. "Only from the upper left of the room— and sharper, crisper."

Not bad, Mac thought, listening to the result.

"Now, short little bursts, not continuous." Jabulani obliged. "Vary the—the—" she hunted for a word and growled to herself.

"Pardon?"

"Sorry. I don't know how to describe it. It was as if the thing moved across different surfaces, so the noise changed in small segments, but very quickly."

This time, a sequence of sounds played through. Mac shook her head, although they couldn't have seen her in the dark even if there had been a window. "Stop!"

She listened to the silence and the echo came back through her memory. "Not rain. Ice pellets. Sleet."

The modified sound played again. *Skitter skitter*.

"That's it!" Mac shouted, sitting up in the dark. "Soften the edge on the last third." *Skitter . . . scurry!* "Yes. Yes. More of that ending sound. The other happened in between."

She listened to *scurry . . . skitter . . . scurry* and hugged herself tightly. Like this, in the dark, it was as if the alien had somehow crawled in with her.

Had it?

They wouldn't have seen it.

Mac controlled her imagination. "Okay," she said rather breathlessly, "you've got the first sound. It made that frequently. I believe it was from its movement. Body parts or maybe feet."

"Leave those determinations for later," Trojanowski ordered. "Can you give Dr. Sithole direction and volume?"

They played with the sound until Mac felt dizzy, but she was reasonably sure they'd mapped it as she'd heard it that night in her room. "Sound number one done," she said, standing up and fumbling her way to the bench.

"Ready for number two?" Trojanowski asked.

"Yes. A bit of light please," she asked.

"Whatever you say, Little Mackenzie."

The illumination came from the ceiling and floor—rose pink. Mac spared a moment to wonder what Denise had been thinking.

"This might be easier," she said hopefully. "A drop of water hitting a hot pan."

Splot . . . hiss.

"Or it might not." She leaned against the wall and closed her eyes. "A much hotter pan. Cut out the sound of the drop landing. It's what happens afterward."

Spit . . . Sizzle.

"Close. Keep the 'spit.' Lose the 'sizzle.' Add—add popcorn popping."

"Popcorn?" Trojanowski's voice.

"Try this, Mackenzie."

Spit . . . pop!

Now that she heard the combination again, Mac realized there had been another sound sandwiched between the louder two. Maddeningly, she could only tell something was missing, but had no idea what. "It's right as far as you have it," she told Jabulani finally. "There should be more to it, but I can't remember."

"No problem, Mackenzie. Locations and direction." They mapped the sound in her office.

"One more, Dr. Connor, unless you've remembered more than three."

Mac rubbed her neck. "Yes, I have. The first sound, the scurrying. It changed when the alien was traveling along the walkway. More of a 'shuh' to each scurry. Not as sharp."

Jabulani nailed it in one. Mac was relieved.

"The last sound." She looked up. The ceiling was low enough to touch if she were standing. "It's what I heard when—" she swallowed hard. "—when it was hanging onto the pillar at the gate, right over my head. I was worried I'd lost it, so I was standing with my back against the pillar to listen. I heard what I thought was its breathing."

"How did you feel at that moment?"

"Feel?" Trojanowski's tangential question surprised her. Mac took a moment to consider before answering. "Triumphant, I suppose. I thought I'd cornered it, could talk to it. But when I tried, it made sound number two—the spit/pop—then took off into the woods." She shrugged to herself. "At that point, I switched back to feeling annoyed."

"You never felt in any danger."

"No. Why would I? It was running away from me. What are you getting at?" Mac wasn't sure she liked being cross-examined by a disembodied voice.

"I don't know. But it could matter to the interpretation of what we re-create here. Thank you. Please continue with the last sound." His voice sharpened. "Doctors! When you're ready?"

Mac stifled a laugh, well able to imagine what was going on— not that the two couldn't restrain themselves, but they'd enjoy Trojanowski's discomfiture.

He shouldn't have worn the suit.

"Are you ready?"

"Impress us, Genius-Man." Mac, cross-legged on the audio lab floor, grinned up at Jabulani. He might have stripped off his raincoat and sweater, but the crowded space had been warmed by bodies and busy equipment to the point where even her shirt was sticking to her skin. The big man's well-worn khakis were drenched in sweat, but he was smiling from ear to ear. Denise played a tiny fan over the back of his neck, alternating with her own flushed face.

Trojanowski, Mac decided, sneaking another incredulous look, *couldn't possibly be Human.* His suit and ridiculous cravat were immaculate. There wasn't a drop of moisture on his skin. It made it impossible to argue with his insistence on keeping the door closed and locked. He repaid her look with a raised eyebrow, saying: "Oh, I'm ready, too."

"I've tweaked it so we should hear the creature as if it were here, with us."

Mac braced herself. "Go ahead, Jabulani."

They listened together, Mac watching Trojanowski for any reaction to the sounds filling the lab. His expression showed intense interest, nothing more. *As if he'd let his face reveal anything he didn't want it to,* Mac reminded herself.

The final sound. The *thrumming.* Mac's hands tightened around her knees in frustration. "I was so close," she said.

"Too close," Trojanowski commented grimly. "Move the sound files to my imp, please, Dr. Sithole. Thank you for your work."

Mac stirred herself. "Denise, erase any copies or records. This never happened, okay?"

"I'll do no such—"

Jabulani cupped Denise's angry face in his big hands and kissed her lightly on the nose, but there was nothing light in his voice. "Yes, you will, Sweet Thing. For all our sakes'. Trust me."

Denise pulled away and began smacking switches to power down the lab, muttering something that sounded like *"same old government covercrap."* Mac pretended not to hear as she got to her feet and stretched.

Trojanowski studiously ignored the agitated audio researcher as well, getting the files from Jabulani and pocketing his imp. "Time to go," he announced briskly. "Thank you again, Dr. Pillsworthy."

Before Denise could utter whatever was about to spill from her thinned lips, Mac interjected: "This could help us find Em."

Denise's fingers fussed at the nubs of her implants. "Not arguing with that, Mac," she said grudgingly, then scowled at Jabulani. "It's erasing records I don't countenance and you know it, Jabby."

"Of course I do, but sometimes it's necessary to protect those—"

Trojanowski went to the door and unlocked it, as if to avoid further argument. Mac, drawn by the rush of cool, ocean-scented air as the door opened, followed close behind. She was almost through the doorway to the platform when his hand shot back to hold her in place. "Shhh."

Mac knew better than to ask. Instead, she strained her every sense to catch what had alarmed him.

The platform was empty except for themselves. *Amazing*, Mac told herself, as the hairs on her neck rose, *how between one breath and the next, a place you knew as home could feel like a trap.* She could barely see over the rail to the stairway and down, but the activity below seemed normal enough, a reassuring cacophony of footsteps, equipment, and voices rising to where they stood. Mac lifted her gaze along the wall's curve. The next platforms were behind this one, out of her sight.

Meanwhile, Trojanowski was turning his head, so slowly and smoothly that Mac hadn't caught the movement until she glanced back at him, turning it so he could look toward her . . .

No, she thought, her heart pounding in her ears, *so he could look* above *her.*

A low, regular, *familiar* thrumming, from overhead and behind. Mac held her breath as Trojanowski completed his movement, his eyes tracking upward. She'd have taken more comfort from his calm expression, if his face hadn't been deathly pale.

His eyes lowered to hers; in the platform's lighting they seemed dark pits behind their lenses. *Back inside*, he mouthed.

She'd been wrong, he hadn't stopped moving for an instant. His shoulders were almost perpendicular to her now and she could see one of his hands pulling something out of his suit coat.

Mac eased her weight to the foot still inside the doorframe. It flashed through her mind to argue that they had a chance to capture it, to demand answers—as quickly, she remembered the two unknowing people behind her in the audio lab, and the dozens working below on the ring, and hoped Nikolai Trojanowski was as good with his weapon as he was at secrets.

Scurry . . . skitter . . .

Flash!

Even as Trojanowski drew and fired, Mac heard footsteps behind her and threw herself around to stop. Jabulani and Denise from coming out the door. Fortunately, they were so startled by the sight of Trojanowski and his weapon that they halted of their own accord, both shouting questions. "Stay there!" Mac ordered, whirling back to see what was happening.

"Did you—?" She shut her mouth on the words, seeing Trojanowski rush to lean over the rail.

"I don't know. It fell," he added unnecessarily as she came up beside him and could see for herself the commotion below. "Or jumped."

This side of the floating ring was being lifted and dropped with a smack by waves originating where the water was still churned white from an impact. Students and their supervisors were scrambling to keep equipment from bouncing into the ocean, yelling questions at one another. A couple jumped in, ruining whatever experiments were underway, but obviously concerned someone might be drowning.

Trojanowski's elbow bumped Mac's as he put his weapon away.

"Shouldn't we stop them?" Mac demanded, worrying about the would-be rescuers.

"They won't find it," her companion predicted.

He was right.

10

SEARCH AND SHOCKS

THERE WERE clouds forming on the horizon. Mac hugged herself tightly and watched them blur the line where wave met sky in a spectrum of heaving gray and black. Where she stood, outside Pod Six, the midafternoon sun scoured to a hard-edged gleam every section of mem-wood walkway, every rail, every ripple of ocean surrounding them all.

It did nothing to expose an invisible foe.

"They worried they'd have to stop looking at dusk," Trojanowski announced. "Then someone volunteered to rig lights." He'd removed his coat and cravat sometime in the last hour, pressing the mem-fabric of his shirt sleeves to hold them above his elbows. Mac hadn't seen him put his hands into the water, but they dripped on the walkway as he approached her.

As "they" referred to a cobbled-together team of enthused students and supervisors using skims and whatever diving gear was at hand to search the water within and around the pod, Mac was less than impressed. "You told me yourself there's no point," she protested, pressing her lips together. Finally: "I should stop this."

"And how will you explain why?" he asked mildly, shaking droplets from his fingertips and squinting at the line of skims. "Too many heard something fall in the water. A stubborn bunch you have here."

Enough was enough. Mac took a deep breath, then said: "I won't bother with explanations. They can be as stubborn as they want at home, where I don't have to worry about them. I'm going to order Base evacuated."

The look he shot her at this was anything but mild. "No. Under no circumstances are you to do that, Dr. Connor. That would be—"

"What? An act of treason against my species?" He might be taller by a head, but Mac had no trouble glaring at him. "I have no problem being bait for our intruder, Mr. Trojanowski, if that's what it takes. I draw the line at risking the people of this facility in any way."

He met her glare with a resigned sigh. "I know. But—"

Just then, a skim swooped to a stop above the water in front of them, disgorging a pair of soaking wet and begoggled students who waved happily as they jumped onto the walkway. Between them they carried a seaweed-coated length of pipe, with links of chain dangling from each end, that they dropped at Mac's feet. "Look what we found, Mac!" one exclaimed with glee. "Part of the old goal post!" Without waiting for an answer, they dove back in their skim and headed for the others.

Mac nudged the pipe with the toe of her shoe. "Well, you've been missing a while," she scolded, to keep her voice free of either laughter or sob. Then, to the silent man beside her: "These people have no idea what we're up against. Even if they did, they'd still try to help. We can't protect them here. You know that as well as I do."

"Dr. Connor. Mac. Walk with me, please," he said, a command more than invitation. "I've some things to tell you that shouldn't be overheard."

"Is one going to be a damned good reason why I shouldn't send my people to safety—right now?"

"You'll have to judge that for yourself."

Without another word, Trojanowski led Mac to the very end of the walkway, away from searchers and spectators, to where the mem-wood slats broadened into a platform that ramped down on either side to meet the now-empty slips of Norcoast's small skim and t-lev fleet. He stood with the sun and the end rail at his back. *To hide his expression or illuminate her own?*

"Well, this should be private enough," Mac commented, raising her voice to be heard above the slap of water and the raucous chatter of gulls roosting on the slips. She adjusted out of habit to the sway of the walkway as it rode the incoming swells, then tapped her foot smartly on the mem-wood. "Or is it? We've no way to know, do we?"

"No way to know," he agreed, but didn't seem unduly concerned by this or the shifting surface underfoot. He rubbed his hands together as if to finish drying them, then spread them wide apart. "But this isn't the first time. It's been like chasing a ghost, Mac. No images on record. A few traces of slime that contain no genetic information or cells. No clues, beyond the type of encounter we've just had. We call them 'Nulls,' for want of anything better."

"So there have been other—encounters," Mac said, finding his word choice unsettling. *What would they call murder? A meeting?* "Where? Was anyone else taken? Harmed? What—"

"Nothing as tangible as this, until now," he answered, cutting her list short. "Nothing as bold. The Nulls themselves were only a name until you heard one. We've been able to spot their ship landings, some anyway—damaged vegetation and disturbed earth. If we're lucky, there's slime."

Mac wondered how anyone could say that with a straight face, but didn't interrupt.

Trojanowski went on: "Neither the Ministry nor the IU is ready to make a direct connection between these beings and what's been happening along the Naralax Transect—the disappearances—"

"But you—you personally—think there is," Mac stated, shading her eyes to make out more of his face.

His shoulders lifted and fell. "Anyone who goes to this much trouble to hide themselves has a reason. And there have been landing sites in systems along the Naralax, on worlds where and when such events have taken place."

" 'Events.' " Mac shook her head in disgust. " 'Missing person reports.' 'Disappearances.' Why don't you say what really happened? The eradication of all life, of every living molecule, as if it had never existed—just like the worlds in the Chasm. A minor detail I had to learn from an alien! Why wasn't it in the report?"

"I'm sure the Ministry would have briefed you more completely had there seemed a need from the start." Almost by rote.

"You mean if they'd taken Brymn seriously."

"Yes, but it was more than that." He shook his head. "The decision to keep a lid on this was made in order to prevent panic. We didn't want to alarm you or anyone else, unnecessarily."

The wind, previously soft and steady from the west, chose that moment to send a spray-laden gust over the end of the walkway. Mac had already tucked the portion of her braid escaping its knot into her collar, but sufficient drops landed on her face and head to steal the sun's warmth. She licked salty lips. "I'll tell you what's alarming me, Mr. Trojanowski, the idea of my people being stalked by these creatures. I think that's more than enough reason to close this facility immediately and send everyone home."

A sliver of steel entered his voice. "And I say that would be premature. They've only shown interest in you, Dr. Mamani, and possibly Brymn. There's every indication they've attempted to prevent inadvertent contact with anyone else. The power failures, the late night intrusions. If we change the routine at this facility, we might spook them into disappearing for good—or into more direct action."

"Not good enough," Mac snapped. "A pile of conjecture that does nothing but serve your interest in finding these Nulls."

"They are after you," he repeated, as if she hadn't spoken. "The obvious conclusion is that, despite all our security, somehow they've found out you and Brymn are looking into the— eradications. But why Emily? You know something, don't you?" His voice softened. "I've seen it in your eyes, Mac. You're blaming yourself. Why?"

Mac walked around Trojanowski so he had to turn to the sun in order to keep her in view. As if sensing what she wanted, he took off his glasses, put them in a pocket, and waited, a patient, if determined, compassion on his face. *Each time they had stood like this, face-to-face,* Mac realized with a small shock, *something fundamental between them had changed.* Was it only the circumstances? Was it him?

Was it her?

This time, it felt natural to say to him what she could hardly bear to think. "Emily was trying to tell me something, the last—the last time I saw her. She wasn't angry at me. I know it sounded like it, when we were together on the stairs, but she wasn't. She said I needed to understand that we—she meant Humans—weren't the only people investigating the disappearances. She said we had our parts to play, but they were small and we'd be back to normal soon. She said all this as if to reassure me." Mac paused to firm up her voice. "But I think it was to reassure herself." Tears spilled over her eyelids; she let them fall. "She was afraid, Nik. I didn't see it until too late."

"What was she afraid of?"

"Something that hadn't happened yet. Something—maybe something she was going to do. Emily asked me to promise to forgive her, but wouldn't tell me why."

Nikolai Trojanowski put his hands on either side of her face, then brushed his thumbs over her cheeks, once, ever so lightly, to wipe away her tears. "Did you promise?" he asked gently.

"I didn't need to promise that," Mac sniffed. "I told her friends always forgive friends. What could she have meant? What was she talking about?"

"I don't know. To figure this out, I need you to tell me everything you can, Mac." Nik lowered his hands. "It's your choice."

A gull complained about ravens. A fish jumped in the distance, visiting an alien realm. Mac weighed promise against reality, and knew there was no choice left.

"I understand. Brymn. He called me his *lamisah*," she told him. "Do you know the word? He said it meant that we were allies."

"I haven't heard it before. But please. Go on."

"Emily was his *lamisah*, too." Mac turned and gripped the rail in both hands, staring out at the simplicity of the inlet's life, and then told Nikolai Trojanowski everything she knew, from sharing the Ministry's message with Emily, to Brymn's desire to speak to her privately and what he'd said, ending with the meeting between the three of them in her office. The only time she sensed a reaction from the silent form beside her was his stiffening when she mentioned the figure watching the three of them from the terrace.

"Emily thought it was you," Mac told him.

"Hardly. I was waiting for ghosts on the mountain."

Mac's hands tightened on the rail until she felt twinges of pain up both wrists. "You should have been here protecting us! Protecting Emily!" The fury of her own sudden outburst shocked her. She put one hand over her mouth, then drew it down slowly. "It wasn't your fault. You couldn't have known. I'm sorry. . . ."

"Don't be. You aren't wrong, Mac." His tone brought her eyes around to look at him. A muscle jumped along his jaw and his mouth was a thin, stark line. "I wish I'd been here," he said grimly. "I wish I hadn't completely underestimated Brymn and the situation I placed you in. I thought he was a joke. I thought having to come here with him was a waste of my time and my superiors were fools to let him convince them otherwise. Oh, I did all the right prep—made all the right motions. Backgrounds on you and your people. Checked, what I could, on the Dhryn." Twin spots of color appeared on his cheeks and his voice lowered. "Getting that call to watch for a Null ship felt like a reprieve—until I found out what had happened while I was gone. It's I who owe you an apology, Mackenzie Connor. As if words matter now."

Emily assessed people in an instant and was rarely wrong, an ability Mac now envied. Her own way was to avoid such judgments, to wait and watch while time spent working together revealed the quality of a person, or its lack. *A luxury she no longer had*. There was only the seeming sincerity of this man's voice and expression, his actions over the past two and a half days, and a supposedly counterfeit-proof message, carefully transferred to her pant pocket because nowhere in her home was safe.

Like rolling a kayak, Mac decided. You had to believe your first drive of the paddle would bring you up again. Without that confidence, the timing never worked and you stayed head down and flailing underwater. Embarrassing at best. Deadly at worst.

"Words matter, Nik," she disagreed. "I've one for you. *Lamisah*. Allies." Mac poked him in the chest with two fingers. He feigned a grab for the railing and she almost smiled. *Almost*. "Taking your advice, *Lamisah*, I won't shut down Base unless there is another incident. But if there's so much as a hint of a Null around, I'll empty this place and raise the pods so fast your head will spin."

He looked relieved. "More than fair, Mac. Meanwhile, I'll deploy more officers. For what it's worth."

"Appreciated. Now. Where do we go from here? How do we find Emily?"

An eyebrow lifted. "We?"

Mac shoved her hands in her pockets and stood braced against the now-gusting wind.

Nik considered her for an instant; *perhaps*, Mac thought, *forced into his own quick judgment*. Then he nodded. "We." His hazel eyes picked up some of the ocean's chill blue. "We start searching for your visible intruder," he told her. "But first, I think it's time we woke our sleeping beauty."

Nik hadn't exactly lied to her, Mac thought ruefully. He'd merely neglected to tell her they'd be making a brief stop on the way to see Brymn.

Would a warning have made this moment easier?

She stepped inside Emily's quarters, hearing the police barrier hum back into place behind her, and seriously doubted anything would have helped.

"What are—what do you think I'll see that you haven't?" she asked Nik, who was moving carefully through the remains of Emily's glass table toward her desk. Focusing on him, a person who didn't belong with her memories of this room, was better than remembering how it used to look. *How it* should *look*.

Emily defined her space, Mac thought, picking her way among pieces of brilliant fabric her eye refused to recognize as a wardrobe. *The delay Emily had coaxed from her on arriving?* In part so she could, as every year, disappear into her new assigned quarters to "scent mark the place" as she'd call it. One or more of her travel cases would contain oddments from home: a new ceramic sculpture, a rug, a watercolor, a colorful woven throw. Once it had been a set of stuffed llamas, in striking white and black, adorned with magenta sunglasses. The only commonalities from year to year were the confusion of cosmetics in the bathroom and satin sheets on the bed. The end result, regardless of scheme, was a space that had nothing in common with those of the other scientists in the pod, something that suited Emily Mamani very well.

Mac didn't look up again. She didn't dare. Looking at the floor was bad enough, littered with treasures become debris, glistening with hardened slime. Her first involuntary glance around the room had been trapped by the marks on one wall, a combination of deep gouges and a single, blood-red handprint. The marks had been linked within an irregular black outline, as if a child had thought to frame them.

There were other signs of the forensics team at work: labels and code numbers stuck seemingly at random around the room, vid-bots hovering in every corner to record any evidence tampering, accidental or deliberate.

Mac fought the urge to show her empty hands to the nearest lens.

Nik was looking through what was left of Emily's desk. "See anything that doesn't belong?" he prompted.

She considered several replies to this, settling for: "You're joking."

He glanced over at her, his face inscrutable. "I mean it. Look around. If something isn't right, you'll notice. Trust your instincts."

"How can you be—" Mac stopped what she was going to say and gave a nod. "I'll do my best," she said, wondering where or when he'd had occasion to prove that for himself. *She probably didn't want to know*, Mac told herself, raising her eyes at last.

It helped that the marks were behind her now. She pushed the emotions crowding her behind as well. Time later to worry about Emily, to be angry at the defilement of her things, to be afraid.

Fear was the hardest to dismiss. Slowly, insidiously, it sucked the moisture from her mouth and disrupted the rhythm of her heart. There could be another of the creatures clinging to the ceiling above her head, or in the shower stall. The walls could be crowded with Nulls, silent and waiting.

Let them wait, Mac told herself fiercely.

Nothing in the living room drew her attention. Mac made herself walk into Emily's bedroom. She felt Nik's presence at her back, as if he offered support but wouldn't interfere. *Scant comfort*, she thought. He couldn't shoot what he couldn't find.

Even prepared by the state of the outer room, Mac gasped. The bedroom, half the size of the living room, had been the site of battle. Streaks of slime crisscrossed others of rust-red. Numb, Mac bent and picked up a fragment of blue and yellow, all she could see that looked familiar. It was from a lamp Emily had "borrowed" from her office. A lamp that had been shattered against a wall—or a body.

"They left through the window."

Mac ignored the words as she ignored any attempt by her mind to reconstruct what had happened here. She edged around the mattress, sliced as had been the one in her quarters, hurrying her inspection over every surface. *Almost done . . .*

"What are you doing here?" she muttered in surprise, tugging at a piece of brown plastic that peeked from beneath a fragment of chair leg. The piece tore free and she brought it to her nose. The soufflé had smelled much better two days ago.

"What is it?"

Mac frowned in puzzlement as she held out the scrap to Nik. "Dessert."

"I beg your pardon?"

She dropped to her knees, digging after more pieces. "Leftovers," Mac clarified as she searched. "Brymn brought this bag of soufflé to my office that night. He didn't know I'd eaten . . . said he picked this to bring me because others praised it. I don't think he eats what we do."

Nik squatted beside her, helping to move aside the rest of the broken chair. "Dhryn diet aside, why does it matter that the soufflé ended up here?"

Impatiently, Mac pushed her hair behind one ear. She had a small pile of bag pieces now, several attached to dried clots of egg, chocolate, and cream. "It matters because the soufflé wasn't edible anymore. Em must have taken the bag to recycle it for me. I've had some—well, sometimes old food hangs around in my office." She coughed. "That's not important. Nik, what if whoever was spying on us through the window stayed nearby and saw her take the bag from my office. Maybe he—it—assumed it held something important, something secret. That could be why Emily . . ." She didn't finish the statement. The room around them did it for her.

"Not an unreasonable assumption," Nik replied approvingly, then made a clucking sound. "It doesn't explain why Dr. Mamani would bring a bag of dead soufflé all the way back to her quarters. I saw recycle chutes in every hallway."

"I don't know." Mac rocked back on her heels. "We were both tired. We'd said things, argued. I didn't even notice her taking it. She must have gathered it up with her sweater." Mac started to look around for the garment, but stopped herself with a shudder.

Nik produced a clear sheet from a pocket, unfolded it, then laid it over a fairly clean section of carpet. "Put all the pieces here," he ordered. "I'll have the forensics team reconstruct what they can."

Mac stared at him. He looked serious. "The soufflé?"

"And whatever else might have been in the bag."

She shook her head. "I looked inside—"

"Can you swear there was nothing else in it?" he interrupted. "Did you take it out?"

"Of course not, but—"

"That's why we'll have this analyzed."

Mac shook her head. "You aren't seriously suggesting that Brymn actually put something else in the bag? I was only speculating—"

Nik lifted the end of a drawer and exclaimed with satisfaction as he found another, larger mass of bag bits stuck to one another and to the floor. Rather than try to remove it, he drew out a knife and began cutting the carpet around the mass. "Speculating is part of good detective work, Mac," he informed her as he worked. "As a scientist, you should know that."

She knew she didn't like where this particular speculation was leading. Mac put her fingers on Nik's arm. "Wait." When he looked at her quizzically, she bit her lip, then went on: "What aren't you telling me about Emily, Nik? What's going on? Tell me what you know—what you think you know. Please."

The knife blade drove deep into the carpet to stand between

them. "I know she's your colleague and closest friend, Mac," he said evenly, meeting her eyes. His were troubled. "But that's not all she is. I can't explain here—" a deliberate glance at the hovering vidbot, "—but I believe she might have taken the bag from your office because she suspected Brymn of trying to pass you a secret message—"

"Whoa! Stop right there, Mr. Trojanowski." Mac snatched her fingers back as though his skin burned them. "Why would *Emily* want to intercept a message from Brymn? She didn't even know he existed until you brought him to the field station! I involved her in all this. She knows nothing about his species, or—" His stillness penetrated her fury. He was waiting for her, for something from her. *What?*

Mac took a steadying breath, then another before asking as calmly as if after the weather: "Why would you believe such a thing?"

He bent his head, lifting only his eyes to hers. The regret in them made her pulse hammer in her throat, an ominous drumbeat underlying his next words. "Because Emily Mamani has lied to you, Mac. By omission if not more. She visited at least two Dhryn colonies in the past year; three the year before. I'm quite sure she knows more about Brymn and his species than either of us."

A pause, and his regretful expression turned into something more akin to warning. "And, Mac? It's never just one lie. Not once you start digging."

"No change, Mac."

"Thanks, Tie." Mac curbed her impatience. After Nik had passed the wrapped bundle of dried soufflé and bag bits to the officer who'd been waiting outside Emily's door, they'd come straight here, to her quarters. *No time to process what Nik had told her. No time to do anything more than shove all thoughts of Emily Mamani out of her mind.* "We'll watch him for a while, Tie. I'll let you know when we need to be spelled."

While she talked with Tie, Nik was heads-together with the police officer who'd been guarding Brymn. *If that's what she was*, Mac wondered abruptly. She'd never asked for any identification. She was reasonably certain Kammie wouldn't have bothered either. You had an emergency, you called for help, real police came. Who doubted that?

Suddenly, she did. *If the police at Base weren't real, and the Wilderness Trust no longer ruled the landscape around the inlet, and Emily had lied . . .*

"Mac?"

"Sorry, Tie," Mac said quickly, quite sure her expression had been a study in itself. "Distracting day, as you can imagine. What were you saying?"

His rough, round face puckered in distress. Tie was at his best with engines, not people, but he'd done an admirable job keeping cool and focused through this crisis. An unconscious alien on the floor of her quarters was about the only thing he couldn't handle. Mac knew how he felt all too well. "I'm saying, Mac, we should've moved our 'guest' yesterday. This isn't right, you not having your own quarters."

"Don't worry about me, Tie." Mac put her arm around his shoulders and gave him an affectionate squeeze before letting go. "The last place I want to stay right now is in here. It's going to take weeks to clean this up—let alone put everything together again." She didn't bother adding that her office was worse. He knew. "Did you get all our gear packed up?"

"Done by noon." He found a smile for her. "Only problem I had was convincing McGregor and Beiz to stop sunbathing so we could get back to Base. If it wasn't for the situation—" Here his voice finally faltered.

"It's okay, Tie," Mac said softly. From the corner of her eye, she saw that Nik and the "officer" were finished with their private chat. "I'm heading to the mainland this evening anyway. They're putting me up in a fancy hotel, with room service. What do you think of that?"

He brightened. "I think it's a great idea, Mac. You make sure you take full advantage. Just don't be gone long."

Something she couldn't promise. "Kammie has the reins," Mac assured him instead. "You keep things working for her until I'm back. Deal?"

This didn't sit well at all. She could see it in the unhappy look in his eyes. But Tie wouldn't argue, not with Outside Authority in the form of the bureaucrat and police officer now moving their way. He ducked his head to her in mute agreement, then started to leave, only to turn back. "Mac. I'm sorry. I don't know where my head's been. Your dad called again."

Mac blinked, then remembered. She'd promised to call him back—what was it now, last night? Something so normal and sane as talking to her father seemed improbable. *She'd have to do it, though.* "Thanks, Tie. You didn't say anything about what's been going on, did you?"

He looked offended. " 'Course not, Mac. You know me better than that. I told him you were resting."

Mac hid a wince. Now she'd really have to call, and soon. *Resting?* Her Dad wouldn't believe that even without the bonus of an alien guest during her field season. *She'd be lucky if he didn't show up on the next t-lev out of Vancouver.* "Perfect," she told Tie, forcing a smile.

"Everything all right?" Nik asked, coming up as Tie made his exit.

"Perfect," Mac echoed, but gave the word a more appropriate intonation. When Nik looked interested, she gave a noncommittal shrug. "Nothing to do with this."

The officer, a stocky woman whose dark eyes, coppered skin, and straight black hair spoke of a heritage along this coast almost as old as the salmon themselves, gave Mac a look that likely memorized everything from braid to shoe size before saying to Nik: "If that's all, sir, I'd like to check on Simeon's progress."

"Yes. Thank you." Dismissed, the officer nodded and left without another word.

"So," Mac said as soon the door closed and they were alone. "What did your friend have to say?"

"Friend? Officer LaFontaine? There's been no change in Brymn's condition."

A shade too innocent, Mac thought, but didn't press the issue. "Tie said that, too." They both looked at the unconscious alien.

The Dhryn wasn't moaning anymore. Mac hoped that was an improvement. Otherwise, he lay exactly as she and Nik had left him, his arms curled over his torso, his thick legs bent back at their main joint and splayed. The sheet over him had soaked through with dark blue exudate in several spots. More liquid of that color puddled down Brymn's left side, the one closest to where they stood, flowing off the mattress onto the floor. It hadn't dried or congealed, suggesting it continued to flow. On the other hand, there wasn't enough of it to suggest the alien had lost a significant amount of a vital fluid.

Or maybe he had. Mac thought wistfully of the xeno course in her imp and promised herself time to read it before much more took place.

Unlike Emily's quarters, some effort had been made to push the remains of furniture and torn bedding aside. Mac assumed this had been to accommodate the various doctors and other Human experts trying to puzzle out the Dhryn's comatose state. There was only one vidbot, aimed at Brymn.

"However," Nik continued, "The officer did pass along one bit of news. The police think they've found your eavesdropper."

Mac looked at him, eyes wide. "And?"

"Human. Career thief. Several recent names. Born Otto Rkeia. He didn't come in with the media crush, but I imagine all the unfamiliar faces let him move around pretty much as he pleased. Probably swam in under cover of darkness."

"If he did," Mac said confidently, "we'll have a recording. We may not have much in the way of security from intruders, but we pay a great deal of attention to what moves in the water under the pods."

"Good. I'll have it checked. The more we can find out about Rkeia's movements, the better."

"You can't ask—" Mac stopped at his thumbs-down gesture. "Oh. Where did they find the body?" she asked, momentarily aghast at the calmness of her own voice. *Maybe she was learning to deal with repeated shocks. Maybe this is how the police—how Nikolai himself—dealt with such things as violence.*

"Your eager rescuers found it under Pod Six."

Yuck. Mac flinched. "I don't suppose it was an accident."

Nik snorted. "Not unless you can accidentally glue yourself to a support strut, thirty meters down. They're estimating time of death now." He shot a look upward, to where the remains of the adhesive netting still starred the ceiling. "Not too much of a stretch to believe our invisible friends were responsible."

"So they kill people."

"They *took* Emily, Mac," he responded, understanding her fear. "If they'd wanted her dead, there was no need for that."

As comfort, it was as cold and dark as thirty meters below the pod, but Mac made herself accept it. "Jirair—Dr. Grebbian—can help you determine when the body went in the water, if that helps." At Nik's interrogative look, she added: "He studies zooplankton, particularly those with a sessile component to their life cycle. Mr. Rkeia's body will have been colonized by several species. Jirair can tell how long each has been growing."

"That could be useful." Nik went to the com on the wall and passed a message to the forensics team to contact Grebbian. "Done," he said, coming back a moment later. "Thanks, Mac." He gave her a searching look. "How are you doing?"

She licked dry lips and gave a curt nod. "Better than he is. What can we do?"

He joined her in staring down at Brymn. "We have next to no data on Dhryn. Any thoughts?"

"I study—"

"—salmon," Nik finished for her. He smiled slightly. "Think of it as having no preconceptions in your way."

"I don't know," she replied slowly, but obediently walked around the alien on her floor. The first thing Mac noticed was a modest, regular expansion and contraction of his upper torso. *Great*, she mocked. *I can tell he's breathing*. There was a monitor on the floor connected to a sensor affixed to what corresponded to a chest. Its display was a confusion of peaks and valleys that bore no resemblance to any electrical rhythms Mac had ever seen in a vertebrate.

As she walked around a second time, she undid the knot of braid on her neck, then the braid itself. The third time, she started braiding her hair again, then stopped, fingers paused in mid-twist. "Play Jabulani's recording," she suggested.

Nik, who'd stood by watching her pace, obediently pulled out his imp, but didn't activate it. "Do you have a scientific basis for this experiment, Dr. Connor?"

Mac finished her braid and dropped it down her back. "Not really."

His mouth quirked. "Stand back, then. In case it works."

Scurry . . . scurry . . . skittle!

No reaction from Brymn that Mac could see, although her heart jumped. From the look on Nik's face, he wasn't too happy with the sound either.

Thrummmm . . .

Nothing.

"Here comes the last one," he warned her.

Spit! Pop!

A quiver raced along those of Brymn's arms Mac could see, starting from each shoulder and ending with a spasmodic opening of his fingers. Then nothing.

Spit! Pop!

An identical quiver. Nothing more.

Before Nik could play the sound again, Mac raised her hand. "That's it!" she exclaimed. "The missing part. I knew there was something between the 'spit' and the 'pop.' It wasn't something our ears could detect—but his should. It might make the difference." She hurried to the com. "Dr. Connor. Put me through to the Pred lab."

As she waited, she explained to Nik: "The Preds listen to infrasound all the time—from whales. They'll have something we can try."

"Predator Research, Seung here. What can we do for you, Mac?"

"I need you to play a single pulse, ten Hz, through the com for me. Fifty dB will do." She waved her companion over to the com. He understood, holding up his imp to catch the sound.

"Just a minute." A muttering of voices, some incredulous, then something bounced along the floor. Likely a basketball—the Pred lab wasn't the most formal. Mac shrugged at Nik's look. After "just a minute" stretched into three, Mac was about to signal again when Seung said: "Ready. Pulse in three, two, one . . ." The following silence made Nik look at her in question. She nodded confidently as the com came alive again. "There you go, Mac. Glad to help. Any word on Em?"

Mac met Nik's eyes. "Not yet," she said into the com. "Thanks, guys. Dr. Connor out."

"Now what?"

"I'm convinced Brymn's speech includes infrasound—sounds below the frequency detected by the Human ear. If he utters it, he should be able to hear it. When Jabulani was trying to recreate the 'spit/pop' sound I'd heard, that's what was missing."

"A sound you couldn't hear. How can you know?" he asked with a slight frown.

Mac stroked the hairs on her forearm. "If you're close enough to the source of infrasound, you feel it," she said, remembering. She pulled out her imp. "Send me your 'screen," she ordered, walking closer to Brymn. "I'll key the sounds through mine."

When nothing appeared in front of her eyes, Mac turned to frown at him. "I know what I'm doing," she argued.

"I'm sure you do," Nik countered, "but our devices aren't compatible. Tell me what you want and I'll do it." He approached, the 'screen from his imp disconcertingly afloat to the left of his face.

It looked like an ordinary enough imp to her, and he'd used it with Denise's equipment, but Mac didn't waste time arguing—although she did think dark thoughts about spies and their toys. "Play just the 'spit' of sound number three followed by Seung's pulse. We'll add the 'pop' later if necessary."

He nodded, drawing the fingers of his left hand through the display. "Now."

Spit! . . .

They might not hear a difference, but the Dhryn certainly did. As Nik played the sounds, the body on the floor convulsed upward, arching from neck to foot. Mac stepped back as the wire to the monitor ripped clear. Brymn's six arms stretched out as if grabbing for holds. His seventh arm shot straight up through the sheet, ripping it as if it were paper. An instant later, he went limp.

"I'd say that had an effect," Nik said dryly.

Mac walked over to the Dhryn and pulled the remains of her sheet from his body and arm, avoiding contact with any of the blue stains. "Insufficient. Didn't wake him," she said, shaking her head. "Add the final component of the sound."

"We don't know—"

She shot a look at Nik any of her students would have recognized in an instant. "That's the reason we're here, isn't it? Play the sequence."

"Move away first."

Mac obeyed.

Nik raised his hand to the 'screen in midair, then jabbed one finger into its heart.

Spit . . . pop!

For a terrifying moment, Mac thought they weren't alone.

She wasn't the only one.

Brymn let out a roar and surged to his feet. Nik leaped back, having come close to underestimating the reach of the Dhryn's wildly moving upper arms. For a moment, all Mac could tell was that the alien was alive and awake; she wasn't convinced he was sane or safe.

Then, like the branches of a great tree swaying in a storm, the six paired arms began to move in unison, from side to side, lower and lower, gradually coming to a rest at Brymn's sides. The seventh, always moving in opposition to the rest, tucked itself under an upper armpit. Then, finally, his eyes snapped open—along with his mouth.

Mac grinned at Nik as they both covered their ears. "I never thought I'd be happy to hear that again!" she shouted at him over the din.

As if her voice had been a switch, Brymn stopped keening. His eyes came to rest on her. "Mac—?" Then he folded at the knee joints, dropping into his tripod sit with a suddenness that probably hurt.

"*Lamisah,*" she said quickly, hurrying up to him but stopping short of touching any body part. "Are you all right? Can you talk to us?"

"Us?" He appeared to notice Nik for the first time.

That worthy turned off his 'screen and gave a quick bow. "Honorable Delegate. Is there anything you need?" Mac had no trouble interpreting the look he sent her: *let's be sure he's stable first.*

"A drink, maybe?" she added helpfully, looking in vain around her ruined quarters for an intact cup.

Brymn's eyes followed hers. Mac felt the floor vibrate. He must have made one of his low frequency sounds. "What has happened to your room . . . ?" his voice rumbled into silence as he looked up at the ceiling and saw the remnants of the adhesive webbing overhead. "Aieeee!" His shriek rattled everything loose in the room. "The Ro are here! We must run for our lives!" Even as he attempted to stand, he lapsed from English to what sounded to Mac like more of the Dhryn's own language, only so rapid that none of the words were remotely familiar.

They were going to get some answers at last. Satisfied, Mac leaned against the wall that had once held a set of shelves, the shelves in turn once holding a shell collection now shattered at her feet, and waited with some interest to see how Nikolai Trojanowski handled a bear-sized case of alien hysterics.

- Portent -

A STORM WITHOUT cloud brought the rain, sudden and hard. Its drops pock-marked the smooth rise of swells bringing the new tide, drops that tinted the ocean a deeper green.

Thrice daily, the tide brought life to life. Its return woke those who bided their time within airtight casings or hidden in moist crevices, so they might feast on the flood of organics. It drew to the shallows those from the depths who would, in turn, feed on the feasters. Yet they would leave their eggs behind in the protected pools, to begin a new cycle of life that would wash out with another tide.

Until this tide came in, storm-wracked and bringing only death.

First to succumb were those who opened their casings and extended fragile arms in anticipation, those arms dissolving with the ocean's tainted kiss.

Next were those who had risen in their multitudes to feed and breed in the shallows. Even as they tasted the layer of death above and would have fled, their flesh rotted from their bones, their bones washing into the tide.

The tide paused at its zenith, having filled the pools with quiet green.

Only those waiting onshore for the tide's departure were spared. They peered, bright-eyed and bold, from their holes in the rock face above. Some leaned farther out, into the daylight, tiny feet holding firm to the edge of the stone.

Shadows cut the sun.

In reflex, those leaning winked inside their shelters. Those who felt safe kept watch, chittering among themselves, then grew utterly quiet as the shadows surrounded what had been a tidal pool.

And began to drink.

11

INTERROGATION AND INVASION

IN THE END, it was the ruined mattress, not any particular heroics from Nik, that saved the day.

As Brymn prepared to run for his life, the man calmly reached down and pulled one end of the mattress. *Hard.* The mattress, already shredded, gave way entirely—taking one of the Dhryn's pillarlike feet with it. The alien toppled on his side like a crab tossed by a gull.

Before he could wriggle himself up again, Mac cupped her hands around her mouth and bellowed over his piteous—and loud—exclamations: "It was only a recording! You're safe. Brymn! Calm—" She found herself yelling into a quiet room and shut up.

Mac walked to where the Dhryn could see her. His small mouth was working, as if he couldn't help trying to speak. The vivid blue membrane flickered across his yellow-irised eyes with almost strobelike speed. She found it disconcerting and was glad when Nik joined her, going to one knee so he was face-to-face with the alien. "It's been two days since you were attacked," he informed Brymn, talking slowly and distinctly. "Do you require any care, Honorable Delegate?"

The flickering slowed. "Mackenzie . . . Winifred . . . Elizabeth . . . Wright . . . Connor . . . ?" the words came out punctuated by faint gasps. His eyes seemed to be searching for her without success; she wondered if the moving eyelids impaired his sight. "Mac?"

"I'm here," Mac assured him. *How remarkably tempting*, she thought, *to take his question for a Humanlike concern.*

Nik leaned forward, in range of those still-restless arms. Without the suit coat to disguise it, he was built like a swimmer, with that distinctively rounded cap of muscle on each shoulder and strong curves along both back and upper chest. Emily would approve, Mac knew. For a Human, his was not a small or insignificant form, yet he was dwarfed by the more massive Dhryn.

Mac restrained the urge to pull Nik back a safe distance. *Trained spy or whatever*, she told herself inanely, *while poor Brymn was, after all, an archaeologist.*

A very large, very anxious archaeologist. The eyelids slowed to a mere nervous-looking twitch. "Nikolai Piotr Trojanowski," Brymn said earnestly, his voice softer but prone to tremble. "We are not safe here. None of us. The Ro . . ." The violent shudder that accompanied the word seemed a reflex. "They are dangerous, evil creatures."

"Don't worry. These rooms were swept and sealed, with guards and a repeller field at every access."

He could have told her *that*, Mac grumbled to herself, feeling a knot of tension easing between her shoulders she hadn't noticed until now.

"Help me sit up, please."

It took both of them to steady the Dhryn as he rose, then settled back down more comfortably, two hands searching for and finding a bare patch of floor on which to balance his body. Touching his torso and arm was like taking his hand, Mac found. The skin was like sun-warmed rubber, dry and with an underlying musculature. This close, he had a delicate, floral scent. Mac recognized it. Her bottle of lily of the valley must have been a casualty of the attack.

"What happened?" she blurted. "After you left my office, I mean. And why did you leave?" she added, earning a slight frown from Nik, doubtless about to conduct his own, more professional interrogation.

Brymn folded his arms in an intricate pattern. Sitting, his face wasn't much higher than Mac's own. Right now, she couldn't read any expression on it that made sense to her. At least his eyelids had stopped flashing that blue blankness across his eyes. "I left because you did, Mackenzie Winifred Elizabeth Wright Connor."

"I did?" Mac considered this and felt herself blush. "Well, yes, I suppose we did. But we were only on the terrace for a moment—you thought we'd left you?"

"I did not think you had left. You did leave. Was I not to assume this meant our meeting had ended?"

Nik spoke before Mac could attempt an explanation. "Where did you go after you left, Brymn?"

"Here. I had a great deal of reading to do. The opportunity to access—" his voice faded, then strengthened, "—my apologies for my condition. I will require a few more hours to recuperate fully." A look of surprise. "You must have disturbed my *hathis*, healing sleep."

"Sorry," Nik said tersely. "As you were saying?"

"Ah. I was saying, I came here to read the Human journals I'd requested. When attempting to reconstruct the development of theories, I prefer to study the research in the original language of the author."

Implying he read more than English and Instella, Mac decided. Her species might appear—and act—united to those from other worlds, but there had never been a homogenization of cultures or tongues at dirt level. Part stubborn habit and part a celebration of distinctiveness. She'd read somewhere that humanity's extra-Sol settlements were pretty much the same: Instella with company and tradition at home.

The biologist in her approved. Just as a population's survival improved with a variety of inheritable traits, Mac suspected a civilization's ability to cope with change was enhanced by having a choice of approach. She'd lost the debate to Emily when she'd admitted to not comparing data on humanity with that of other sentient species. As usual, her friend had scoffed at what she called Mac's parochial attitude. There was more to the universe than opposable thumbs and nose hair, she'd insist.

What had Emily been trying to tell her?

Where did she break her arm . . . where had she been . . . ?

Why would she lie?

Mac snapped her attention back to the moment. Nik had continued his questioning. "What happened after you arrived in these rooms?"

"I do not wish to think of it." This with a tone of complete finality.

Nik sent her a warning look before Mac could say a word, then crossed his arms over his chest. *Meaningful mimicry of the Dhryn or thoughtless gesture?* Mac felt like tossing dice.

"We respect your wish, Honorable Delegate," the man told the Dhryn.

Brymn blinked and Mac thought he looked startled. *So was she.* She narrowed her eyes and studied Nik. He looked solemn, almost grave, but she thought there was a bit of smugness in his expression as well.

"Thank you," the Dhryn boomed, his voice closer to normal. "I—"

"It is, however," Nik interrupted without missing a beat, "my duty to inform you that your visitor's visa has been revoked—effective immediately. You will be escorted from Earth and Sol System within the hour."

"You can't do that. Mac?"

Mac nodded. "He can do that," she told the shocked alien.

Rather than distress, Brymn's face assumed a look of great dignity. He unfolded four arms and spread them widely. "You see, Mac? I told you your government considered my mission of great importance. They have assigned an *erumisah*—a decision maker of power—as my companion and guide." He proffered Nik one of his rising bows. "I am most gratified."

Mac wasn't surprised to see Nik take this in stride. *He must be used to dealing with cultures as varied as their biologies.* "Then you will understand, Honorable Delegate," he said, "why I cannot permit you to remain here, potentially drawing more dangerous attention from these 'Ro,' unless you are willing to provide whatever information you can to help us."

The arms wrapped back around the torso and Brymn looked at her, then at Nik, then at her again. "It is not permitted to speak of them," he began. Mac felt the vibration through the floor as he uttered something more in the infrasound and held up her hand to silence the Dhryn.

"We can't hear that," she advised him, then remembered what Brymn had told her about the lack of Dhryn biologists. "Our ears are not adapted to respond to the same range of sound frequencies as yours, Brymn."

He looked startled and glanced at Nikolai as if seeking confirmation. The man nodded. "We feel vibrations that tell us you are making certain sounds, but not what you are saying. If we need to hear them to understand you, Honorable Delegate, we'll have to bring in the appropriate audio equipment."

"This is fascinating. Let us find out—" The Dhryn uttered a series of hoots, each lower in pitch than the preceding. He hit some lovely bass notes Mac was reasonably sure no Human voice could reach unassisted, then went deeper still. Suddenly, though his mouth appeared to be making a sound, she couldn't hear it. Mac raised her hand at the same instant Nik lifted his. Brymn closed his mouth, his eyes wide with what appeared to be astonishment. "You're deaf!" he exclaimed.

Mac dredged up memories of choral practice, took a deep breath, and did her best to nail a high "C." From Nik's pained expression, she mangled it nicely, but Brymn's brow ridges wrinkled at the edges. "And I must also be deaf," he admitted. "This is most—awkward. You have never heard my full voice. Or the foul tongue of the Ro. Then how—?"

She understood. "For the recording you heard, we re-created the sounds I remembered hearing," Mac explained, "then added a very low frequency pulse."

Another shudder ran through his arms. "It was realistic enough. But do not worry about our conversations, my *lamisah*. From this moment, I speak to you as if you were an *oomling*. It isn't respectful, but you need not worry about being deaf."

Nik's mouth quirked, but he bowed slightly. "You are most kind. For our part, we'll avoid shrill." Mac might have blushed, but the man went on immediately. "Am I right to say one or more of these Ro were waiting here when you arrived?"

"I was ambushed," Brymn agreed, fingers spasming open and closed. "With no time to call for help, nowhere to flee. I regret the damage to your quarters, Mackenzie Winifred Eliz—"

None of this mattered. "Why did they take Emily?" Mac interrupted, well past impatient. "Where would they take her?" The redundant *Will they hurt her?* died on her lips. Nik had said the blood on the walls had been Emily's alone.

"Emily Ma—" Perhaps the Dhryn had learned to read Human expressions. "She's gone? This is dreadful!" Despite his promise to keep his voice within human hearing, Mac felt the hairs on her arms rising and the floor vibrate. *Emotional distress*, she guessed, feeling sufficient of her own.

Mac suspected Nik would have preferred to have other answers from the Dhryn first, but he gave no outward sign of it. "Dr. Mamani's quarters were left in a similar state," he told Brymn, indicating the ruin of Mac's living room. "We've evidence she was involved in a struggle with the same type of beings as left you bound here, possibly at the same time. We're very concerned about her well-being. Anything you could tell us to help direct our search . . ." He let his voice trail away hopefully.

"I am so sorry," Brymn said to Mac, his lips drawn down at the corners. Moisture glistened in his nostrils. More briskly: "You said this happened two days ago? Standard or Terran days? Wait, no matter. They differ by mere minutes. So." He lifted his supporting hands from the floor and rose to a stand. "I know little beyond rumor and legend, my *lamisah*, but we believe the atmosphere the Ro require can sustain our species. I presume this means yours as well."

There was a worry that hadn't crossed her mind. Until now. "Good to know," Mac said weakly.

"We also believe these dreadful creatures consume the flesh of other sentients."

A new nightmare. Mac looked desperately at Nik, who did his best to look reassuring. "It seems unlikely they'd take such risks if their goal was supper, Brymn," he pointed out.

"You said you needed information," the Dhryn said stiffly.

"And we appreciate everything you can tell us," Nik assured

him. "What about our search for Dr. Mamani? Can you give us the location of the Ro system?"

Mac held her breath.

But the Dhryn rocked his big head from side to side, a passable imitation of the Human gesture. "My people have searched for it, but to no avail. They are as much a mystery to us now as when they first began to harass our worlds."

" 'Harass?' " Nik repeated. "In what way?"

"They frighten our *oomlings*."

Mac had the rare privilege of seeing Nikolai Trojanowski completely flabbergasted. Before he could recover, she stepped in: "Where would you look for Emily, Brymn?"

Six hands pointed up. "They will have a dreadnought behind one of your moons. You have moons?"

"One," Mac said automatically.

Nik pulled out a portable com and spoke into it in a quiet but urgent voice. He waved to Mac to continue.

"What did you mean when you said these creatures frighten your *oomlings*?"

Brymn brought his arms down again. "We are both scientists, Mac. But I must tell you, there are things which defy logical analysis. Such is the terrible malady the Ro inflict on my species. They use their stealth technology to slip through our defenses, but not to steal valuables or attack our cities. No, they come to terrorize our *oomlings*, touching them as they sleep . . . waking them with their hideous voices . . . taking those they wish and leaving the others bound as I was." Mac couldn't help looking up to where the remnants of the painful webbing scarred her ceiling. "Only the most rigorous protections now keep the Ro at bay." A heavy sigh. "Beyond the vanishing of *oomlings* and those left to suffer, we know nothing more."

Nik had finished his call and was listening intently. When Brymn stopped, his passion spent, he asked: "Why haven't the Dhryn reported any of this to the Interspecies Union?"

A blink. "We do not wish to think of it."

Mac caught the phrasing. He'd said almost those exact words when first asked about the attack. In a Human, it would be a statement of emotional preference, a plea to avoid a difficult or upsetting memory. From an alien, might it mean something else—perhaps be literally true? Could Dhryn deliberately pick and choose what they would deal with in life, and refuse to think about the rest? A willing blindness?

They did it with biology, she thought, suddenly overwhelmed by the unhuman. *Why not with abducted children?*

And Emily.

Waiting didn't get any easier. While Brymn had packed and Nik made his "arrangements" for their move to the IU Consulate, Mac had sat here in the gallery. She'd managed to force down a tasteless supper, reading in fits and starts. She hadn't managed to ignore her fear of what was sending them away.

The Ro.

Over an hour. *She could have brought in a t-lev from Japan by now.*

Mac was struggling to focus on the next image when Nik returned. Without preamble, he said: "Nothing. No mysterious ship in orbit, behind the Moon or otherwise."

"That you could detect," she corrected, shutting down her 'screen. He didn't appear surprised. Neither was she. Brymn hadn't been able to tell them much more about the Ro or the Null or whatever she was to call them now. The Dhryn, as a species, apparently felt the taking of precautions to protect their *oomlings* was sufficient and the entire existence of the invaders should now be ignored unless annoying Humans insisted on discussing it. But one thing was clear. The technology that had hidden her intruder from her eyes worked very well indeed to evade any other form of looking tried so far.

"Where have you been?" Mac asked, glancing at her watch. "Was there a problem?"

Nik dropped into the seat opposite her, looking decidedly rumpled. It wasn't his clothing, back to its bureaucratic perfection, she thought, so much as the strain around his eyes. *Had he slept at all*

since arriving at Field Station Six? "Where have I been, my dear
Dr. Connor?" Nik echoed, just short of a growl. He leaned the
chair back, holding the table with both hands. "I've been doing my
utmost to convince several levels of idiots that there could be such
a thing as a starship able to fool our sensors. Then came the interesting part of convincing them that, even if they couldn't see it—
which they wouldn't—it was still most likely in orbit around our
Moon and did they not find it reasonable to tighten security at
every possible point? Which they wouldn't without seeing the invisible ship! Do you want me to go on?"

Mac grinned and shoved her bottle of iced guava in his direction. "Not really. I'm familiar with the rock and a hard place syn-
drome. Don't forget, I deal with the Wilderness Trust to find ways
to do research without breaking rules designed to prevent any such
thing."

Nik put the bottle to his lips and drank half in one long gulp.
Mac guessed he would have preferred something other than juice.
"Thanks. How do you manage?" he asked, handing it back.

"I find a way around. Or more than one. Conflict isn't my nature."

"You could have fooled me."

"Part of my charm," Mac replied, then froze, aghast.
She was flirting.

Emily was fighting for her life on an invisible alien ship, a mysterious threat was facing the Human, as well as other, species, at
any second she'd be leaving her home and responsibilities for who
knew what—and here she was, trading bottle and banter with
this—this . . .

Mac took another, deeper look. With this close-to-exhaustion,
rather decent public servant who was in all likelihood also trying to
find a moment without worrying about all of the above. *And likely
more.* Mac was very glad not to have the secrets that rode Nikolai
Trojanowski's back. So she eased her smile into something more
normal and added: "In case you haven't noticed, Nik. My charm,
that is."

But he undid all the good of her analysis and intentions by offering her no smile at all in return. Behind his lenses, his eyes, a

paler hazel in the gallery lights, were unreadable. "It doesn't matter what I notice, Dr. Connor. You can't afford to get close to *anyone* right now," he told her. "There's too much at stake. I warned you before, for your own good. I'll keep doing it." He stood. "I'd better see what's keeping Brymn."

Before she could do more than flush, he walked away.

What did you expect? Mac scolded herself. She was the first to admit she didn't do meaningless babble well, although she didn't think she'd said anything to send Nik bolting from her company. Mac's social conversations normally slowed to a cautious crawl the moment they meant something to her. Emily? She was a different story. Em had the gift of gab, as Mac's father called it, able to send any conversation into pleasant, freewheeling innuendo.

The gift of gab. Mac brought up her 'screen again, but couldn't concentrate on the list hovering before her. Don't get close to anyone? He hadn't meant himself, not entirely. He'd meant Emily.

Mac could understand her friend not bothering to tell her about offworld trips. Heaven knows, Mac had made her lack of interest in anything extraterrestrial abundantly clear on too many occasions. But not once Brymn arrived. It would have been natural—more than natural, unavoidable—for Em to offer whatever she knew abut the Dhryn to help Mac work this all out.

Unless, Mac blinked ferociously to clear her sight, *unless Emily Mamani had wanted to keep her in ignorance.*

If she'd asked where Emily had been these past weeks—why she'd been late—would Emily have told her, or would there have been more lies?

Mac shuddered. She'd been flirting with someone who thought such terrible things for a living. "Don't get close." Had Nik been warning her, or merely revealing his own survival strategy?

Whichever it was, Mac didn't like it. Any of it. She planned to give Emily Mamani a piece of her mind the next time she saw her. After they hugged to be sure each was whole.

A tear hit the back of her hand. Mac wiped it off hastily.

A pair of hands gripped her shoulders from behind, thumbs digging gently into exactly the right spots. "Hey, Mac. You okay?" a familiar voice asked anxiously.

She sniffed, detecting the distinct odor of old salmon and new soap, then found a smile, reaching up to pat Seung's hand on her shoulder. "I will be. Tired. Waiting for answers. Just like everyone else here."

Seung gave her a final squeeze, then slid into the chair beside Mac. He moved like the animals he loved so much, the great orcas and sharks, possessing a rare combination of grace and impulsive speed. His worshipful students regularly arranged athletic competitions with other research groups, counting on Seung to win the prize, whether pizza, beer, or mainland transport on a weekend. Unfortunately for their hopes, as often as not he'd be called away seconds before the finish, leaving the Preds to gaze wistfully after their defaulted winnings before following their professor back to work.

Years outdoors and both on and in the water had mottled Seung's naturally tan skin with mahogany. Against its rich color, his eyes were a startling blue. The eyes of a hawk, Mac had always thought, full of bold curiosity and challenge. Even now, when he was obviously concerned for her, she recognized both and smiled again. "You want to know why I asked for the pulse," she guessed.

His grin crinkled the skin around eyes, mouth, and nose. "It wasn't your everyday request, Mac. Sooo?"

"So. I was testing an idea. Could our non-Human guest hear infrasound?"

"Ah," a pleased sound. "I thought it might be something like that. And can he?"

It was hardly a secret. "Yes. Perhaps well below ten Hz."

"The AudioCell would love to get their mikes on him—he must emit in that range too, right? Wonder if he'd like to listen to some of our buddies out there." "Out there" for Seung being the white-capped Pacific showing through the gallery windows.

Mac warmed to the enthusiasm in his voice. *This was why they were here, to ask questions and puzzle out answers.* "He might. We've no time now—scheduled to head for the mainland tonight—but if you could send me a recording, I'd be happy to play it to him and let you know what he says about it."

"That'd be great. I'll get on it—" He got up. "By the way, Kammie sent this down. Probably already complaining about me." His face wrinkled in another grin as he passed Mac a curled slip of mem-paper. "You take care and we'll try not to burn the place down while you're gone."

"Thanks," Mac said, sticking out her tongue. She hoped he didn't notice her hand shaking as she took the slip.

She'd forgotten about the soil assay. Kammie must have started it immediately to have finished by now. Mac burned with curiosity, but tucked the slip away in a pocket that she buttoned closed. *Later.*

The weather had remained generous, bright, and warm—all of which promised heavier rains tomorrow. For now, long rays of afternoon sunlight streamed across the tables and floors, warming backs and gatherings. One ray crossed in front of Mac; she laid her hand within its cheerful glow. Through the window, she could see the light frosting the tops of waves as far as the horizon. The water might be rough for anyone skimming its surface, but the effect was breathtaking. Not a cloud in sight.

The ray of light across the back of her hand dimmed.

Another time, Mac wouldn't have noticed, but almost the first thing she'd read while waiting was the essay concerning invisibility technology. The refraction of light around an object was one technique. Not perfected, not by Humans at any rate. The student author hadn't been impressed.

But Mac now found her attention caught by anything about light that wasn't normal or easily explained. She kept her hand in the sunbeam, staring at it. The light brightened, then dimmed a second time. It dimmed slightly more. Her skin felt chilled.

Mac glanced up. The window, really a transparent wall, arched overhead to form part of the ceiling. The sky was that achingly blue color that looked ridiculous in paintings. No clouds. No haze.

Her shoulders hunched in reflex, her imagination painting a regrettably vivid image of the outer skin of Pod Three being coated by Ro. Ro about to find their way in . . .

"There you are, Mackenzie Winifred Elizabeth Wright Connor!" The bass bellow turned every head, including Mac's, to the doorway where Brymn stood resplendent in yellow and black silk. With his slanted body posture and multiple limbs, this choice cemented an uncanny resemblance to an overweight honeybee and Mac could hear several amused comments, albeit tactfully quiet ones, being shared around the room.

Hand bathed in a beam of varying light, Mac was in no mood to laugh. *Was she going crazy, or the only one to see it?* It took her less than a split second to decide that being wrong wouldn't matter—but being right? She lunged to her feet, making sure her imp was safe in another buttoned pocket, and ran for the alarm on the near wall. Ignoring the questions flying at her, she punched the control, then pressed her back against the wall, wondering what on Earth to do next.

The alarm had visual and audio components, both designed to rouse the most groggy student and penetrate every corner of Base. Yellow framed doorways and emergency exits. Strobes of red flashed across the floor. A modulated hum grated—against Human senses at least—pitched high and annoying, but changing rhythmically in volume so people could shout commands and be heard.

Not that commands were necessary. The gallery erupted in motion. Although there were false alarms every so often, usually after a bar run, the events of the last few days had left everyone on edge. No one hesitated now. The pounding of feet shook the pod floor as staff and students ran for the exits.

Not their feet, Mac realized in horror. She could feel a throbbing in the wall behind her back and jerked away. *The pod!*

The entire room was *moving*. Out the window, the horizon tilted to an impossible ten degrees and kept going . . . twenty . . . Mac wrapped her arms around a support pillar as tables, chairs, cutlery, dishes, and people began sliding toward the kitchen.

Impossible! Pod Three was permanently anchored to the ocean floor. Even a collision wouldn't lift it like this, and they would have heard one—felt it. Mac let go of the pillar and, ignoring the shouts of protest from those at the door, ran diagonally across the sloping floor toward the far end of the window wall. *She had to see what was happening to the rest of Base.*

Mac pressed her face against the transparency and cursed. Only Pod Two was visible from here, and it was . . . it was *rising*! The walkways, normally detached and stored before the pods were raised for the winter, were being pulled up as well, people clinging to railings for dear life. As she watched, unable to do more than pound her fists on the wall, the walkways twisted and split, spilling their Human contents into the Pacific. She could see heads bobbing in the water . . . water that was starting to lip at the wall in front of her.

"Mac!" It was the Dhryn beside her. "We must flee!"

She could hardly breathe, let alone move. Her hands felt glued to the window, as if she could somehow pass through it to help, if only she could press hard enough.

Then she was in the air . . .

Clutched by a giant bee . . .

A bee who *spat* at the window, then somehow charged right through it into the ocean.

Mac had barely time to take and hold a deep breath before she was plunged underwater.

She had even less time to worry if a Dhryn could float without a repeller suit.

12

DEPARTURE AND DECEIT

"PUT ME DOWN," Mac croaked for at least the hundredth time. Her rescuer paid no attention. It was as if she didn't exist.

It turned out a Dhryn couldn't float unassisted, but it hadn't mattered. He'd lain on his back, holding her wrapped in that almost boneless seventh arm, while the rest of his limbs churned the water in furious strokes, their sheer power driving them through the waves when anything Mac knew of anatomy said they should capsize and drown. Once she'd realized what was happening, she'd tried to convince him to turn back to Base. But to no avail. He was taking them to shore.

She'd protested and struggled until common sense took over. Whether the Dhryn was hysterical or sane didn't matter, as long as he could keep swimming. The water was choppy and rough; the Dhryn wisely riding the swell of the waves in, but they'd been chased by the rest of the Pacific. Mac had held her breath each time she saw a crest about to catch up and douse them, gasping for air as her head broke the water again. Each splash stole body heat and she'd soon been shivering uncontrollably. Thankfully, the Dhryn's body had insulated her back.

What was happening to Base? Mac had tried to see past the waves, but it had been impossible—the Dhryn almost submerged at best and the water too wild around them. She'd grown sick with fear. For her friends, for her colleagues, for what they'd built.

For herself.

It wasn't much better now, on land. The Dhryn had brought them to shore by virtue of crashing into the rocks with a higher wave than most. Before the water washed them out again, he'd taken hold of a skeletal log jutting overhead. Mac had seen the wood compress and splinter under his three fingers. With that one arm, he'd pulled them both clear of the waterline.

The part of her mind still capable of analysis had put a check mark beside the idea of the original Dhryn home being a heavier gravity planet.

Without a word, he'd shifted her to two of his common arms, tucked away the seventh, and started to run.

He was still running, quite a bit later. *After almost three hundred and fifty years of complete exclusion, the Wilderness Trust might as well open the inlet's forest to the general public,* Mac decided, wincing at the trail of ruined vegetation in the Dhryn's wake. His method of locomotion had a great deal in common with a crashing skim, straight through what could be broken and rebounding from anything more solid.

Despite what had to be hysteria, he seemed aware that he was carrying someone more fragile. *More or less.* Mac yelped as a branch snagged some of her hair and won the tug-of-war. She blinked away tears of pain, thinking of Emily. *Had she felt like this? Been imprisoned by alien hands and arms? Dragged to a destination she couldn't know? Unable to communicate with her captor?*

Mac pulled her mind back to the present—her present—assessing herself as best she could. They'd probably been running no more than a half an hour, though it felt longer. Any exposed skin was scratched. Her clothes had suffered, torn along the right leg and arm by exposed, reaching roots. She'd learned to keep her arms tight to her body after that. She'd lost a shoe. There would be bruises, perhaps a cracked rib, where his arms folded around her. But nothing worse—so far. It was almost miraculous, given the pace the Dhryn was maintaining as he raced through the rain forest.

He did slow to climb, although not as much as she would have. Two pairs of powerful arms and semiadhesive feet were distinct advantages, even if another pair of arms had to balance and protect her.

The next time he slowed, she tried again. "Put me down," Mac pleaded, doing her best to kick. "Stop. Please. We have to go back . . . I . . ." The words buried themselves in heavy, painful sobs as her frustration and rage took over.

He stopped.

Mac's hiccup echoed in the sudden silence. She tried to find her voice again. "Brymn?"

With a thrill of fear, she realized he hadn't stopped for her.

The forest around them swallowed the sun, disgorging dark shadows of every size and shape. *You wouldn't need invisibility to hide here*, Mac thought. Sound was smothered as well: birds waiting for twilight, insects too cool to buzz, no rain pattering cheerfully through the leaves.

The Dhryn's body was canted at its usual angle, and she was underneath, her head near his neck. From that position, it was impossible for Mac to look up when she thought she heard a familiar sound. Not the Ro; a lev, with a powerful, unusually quiet engine.

Trojanowski!

"Nik!" she shouted. "Down here—"

The rest was muffled by one of Brymn's free hands. The Dhryn finally spoke, a whispered, anxious: "You don't know who it is!"

He lifted his hand away and Mac spat out the taste of bark and salt. "Put me down!"

The relief when she landed on the mossy ground was so great, Mac fought back another sob. She rolled quickly, partly to get away from Brymn before he could change his mind and partly so she could look up.

There! A shadow in the canopy, moving in a reassuringly unnatural straight line.

"It is Nik! Brymn, call him. Your voice will carry. Hurry!"

The Dhryn stared at her, hands hanging limply as if, having stopped running, he'd finally succumbed to exhaustion. His blue skin was marked with scrapes and gouges, each a darker blue as if they cut into another layer; his fine silks were in tatters. "*Lamisah* . . . are you sure?" he whispered.

"Now!" She didn't wait for the Dhryn, cupping her hands and shouting: "Down here! Here we are!"

Her voice disappeared under a startling bellow: "NIKOLAI PIOTR TROJANOWSKI!"

Mac dropped back on the moss to catch her breath. If Nik hadn't heard *that*, nothing short of an explosive charge would catch his attention.

He'd heard. She watched as the machine resolved itself from shadow and branch, sinking down more cautiously than she remembered. Mac climbed to her feet, wincing at bruises she hadn't felt until now. Brymn backed away, but not to run as she first feared. He was leaving the most level patch of ground for the lev to land. Together, they waited until it touched down.

Somehow, Mac couldn't believe until the black helmet rose and she could see his face, pale and grim. "How—is everyone all right?" she asked him, hands out as if the answer was something she could hold.

"Help's arrived," Nik said cryptically, climbing down. A quick assessing look at Brymn, then back to her. His voice gentled and he went on without her needing to ask. "The alarm gave everyone a fighting chance. Best thing you could have done, Mac. So was vanishing into the sea—although that did upset your friends in the gallery. I assured them you'd be all right. And you are." *Did she hear relief?* "My only doubt was if I'd find you two before nightfall. The bioscanner works fine, but there's the issue of navigating in these trees."

Mac shook her head to dismiss what was irrelevant. "Was anyone . . . hurt?"

"We cannot stay here!" This from Brymn. The Dhryn lifted his head and shoulders, then lowered them, rocking his body up and down the way a Human would rock from one foot to another.

She ignored him, walking toward Nik until she could put both hands against his chest and stare up into his face. "Please. Tell me."

He hesitated, then took her shoulders in his hands. There was a darkness in his eyes that had nothing to do with twilight. "There were casualties, Mac. Not many," he added, tightening his grip as she flinched involuntarily, "but I won't lie to you. There may be more. I don't know how many injuries were life threatening and—" he took a long breath and Mac held hers, afraid. "—and they've sent divers into Pod Six. It was totally submerged."

"It heard us play the recording," Mac said, lips numb. "It knew I was responsible."

His nod was almost imperceptible, as if he wanted to spare her, but knew she expected the truth. "They were after you, Mac. Once you were gone, there was no sign of them. As I said, leaving was the best thing you could have done."

Brymn burst out: "We must go!"

Without taking his eyes from hers, Nik replied with unexpected heat. "Where? Where will she be safe from them? Not here!" Only now did he turn his head and glare at the alien. "This is where they landed the first time! What were you thinking, Brymn? Were you saving Mac—or bringing her straight to them?"

"They were here?" Brymn shuddered. "I didn't know. I was trying to reach the nearest spaceport." He flailed two arms over his head at the forest. "Is there no civilization on this planet?"

"A spaceport? You wanted—you were going to take me to a Dhryn world," Mac said faintly, understanding at last. She leaned forward until her cheek rested on the cold hardness covering Nik's chest. She wasn't surprised. *Armor for a black knight.* His arms went around her, a welcome Human comfort, despite the flash of pain it sent through her damaged rib. She fought to focus on what mattered, fought to overcome a terror greater than anything she'd faced before.

Leave Earth?

"The Dhryn protect their—their *oomlings*," she reminded Nik—and herself—in a hoarse whisper. "They can protect me."

"Yes. Yes. Yes. Now," Brymn insisted anxiously. "Without the gift of more time to our enemies. They hunt Mac because of the importance of her work to mine. They will never stop! We must keep Mac safe!"

"I study salmon," Mac muttered out of habit.

A hand, five-fingered and Human, stroked the back of her head. Words, hushed on warm breath, stirred her hair: "Mac. You don't have to do this. We'll find another way."

"Before the Ro attack again?" she asked. "Before something worse happens to anyone in the way?" Mac pushed gently and Nik let her go. She offered him a smile. From his worried expression, it wasn't a very good one. "Emily is always telling me to travel more. Here's my chance."

He understood what she wanted him to—Mac could see it in the way his gaze sharpened on her face. Emily had visited Dhryn worlds. Here was an opportunity to find out why, perhaps find a clue to why the Ro had taken her and where.

And if leaving home protected her friends, her family? Mac straightened to her full height: "Get us tickets. Or a ship. Or whatever one does to go—thaddaway." She blithely pointed up to the canopy.

And beyond.

13

GOODBYES AND GENEROSITY

THE ADVICE of a blue-skinned archaeologist had brought Mac to the one place on Earth she'd never planned to be. The orders of a hazel-eyed spy had locked her in a box and so prevented her from seeing any of it. The fabled Arctic Spaceport, one of fifteen on Earth, was reputed to be an impressive spectacle, blending the awe-inspiring tundra landscape with the world's longest slingshot track, capable of heaving freight directly into orbit.

Of course orbit was the other place Mac had never planned to be, and one she also doubted she'd get to admire through a window.

"Are we there yet?" Mac asked after a novel series of bumps announced something different from the steady vibration of the t-lev.

The woman, older but fit-looking, dressed in a suit twin to Nikolai Trojanowski's usual disguise, had been reasonable company, if you liked your company silent and preoccupied with reading what appeared to be streams of mathematical data. At the question, she looked through her 'screen, blinking her dark brown eyes as if surprised Mac had a voice. "They'll let us know, Ma'am."

Ma'am. Mac didn't have a name. Nik had been clear on that. She wasn't to give information about herself to anyone. She wasn't to bring out her imp where it could be scanned. She was, as he'd so tactfully put it, luggage on a conveyor belt.

Filthy, damp luggage, with scratches and scrapes that itched furiously. *Probably getting infected.* "Will there be a place where I can clean up?" Mac asked, drawing the woman's attention again.

"I'm sure I don't know, Ma'am. Would you like a drink?"

Not without a bathroom in the offing, Mac grumbled to herself. Mind you, this place might be one of the armored cubicles in a city transit station, for all there was to look at or do. The box held only two chairs with straps, bolted to the floor, a small table, also bolted, and a bag tied to the table, from which her nameless companion would produce bottles of water. And, of course, the two of them, locked in for however long the journey from Hecate Strait to Baffin Island to orbit would take.

If he hadn't lied about where she was going.

Mac squirmed, the thought as uncomfortable as the chair. Like all uncomfortable thoughts—and the damned chair—it refused to be ignored, cycling back and back through her consciousness until she paid attention to it.

The last hours had been a blur in which the world moved past her. Mac had followed Nik's instructions, without question or argument, grateful not to think, clinging to the anchor of his calm voice. She'd waited for the two-person levs to appear in the forest, then sat behind a stranger. She'd flown between trees whose girths made her feel like an insect, then been swept out over the ocean as if in pursuit of the setting sun. They'd met a t-lev larger than any that came close to shore, towing a dozen barges laden with crates and boxes.

There, still lacking a shoe for her right foot, she'd climbed into one of those boxes with this tall, dark stranger. The box, Nik had told her, would join a procession of identical boxes, only the others would contain refined biologicals for shipment offworld. The boxes would be lifted to orbit—here he'd cautioned her about the sometimes rough treatment the slingshot provided cargo—then scooped up and brought to a way station. There, she'd enter the transport taking them along the Naralax Transect, bound for the supposed safety of a Dhryn world. Once safely "loaded," Mac would be free to move around like any other passenger. Brymn would meet her there.

What if he'd lied, Mac's thoughts whimpered. *What if this box was taking her straight to the Ro? What if it opened to vacuum? What if . . . ?* She looked at her companion and gave herself a mental kick in the pants. They'd hardly bother with someone to keep her company if this was anything but what it was: the way to move her that risked the fewest lives.

"Thank you."

The woman looked up, frowning slightly. "For what, Ma'am?"

Mac gestured to their surroundings. "Good to have some company in here."

Her companion's sudden smile was magical, transforming her face from grim to gamin. "I know you wouldn't catch me in one of these alone," she confided with a wink. "Bad enough as it is."

"Could use a little decorating," Mac smiled back. "A cushion or two wouldn't hurt. Not to mention a mirror or—" she felt the tangled lump where her hair should be "—or maybe not."

The other woman gave another wink, then reached into her suit pocket and produced a thick-toothed comb. "If it works on my mop," she said, giving her tight black curls a tug, "it will work on yours."

"If you say so . . ." Mac yanked the rest of her hair from its hiding place down the back of her shirt, holding her hand out for the comb. The other woman tsked and, leaving her chair, came to stand behind Mac.

"Lean back and close your eyes, Ma'am," she ordered softly, her voice low and rich, spiced by some accent Mac couldn't place. "Relax a while. Excuse a personal comment, but you look like you could use the rest."

Mac wriggled as deeply into the chair as she could, careful of the rib she'd decided was more likely bruised than cracked, and closed her eyes with a sigh. "There's likely bark," she warned, *though hopefully none of the blue that had oozed from the Dhryn's scratches.* "Sap's a distinct possibility. Insects." This last a mumble.

The comb slipped into the hair at the top of her forehead and worked back, firm yet gentle, making slow progress. "If I find something interesting, I'll start a collection."

Mac felt some of the tension leaving her shoulders and neck. Whoever this woman was, fellow passenger, spy, or guard, she'd combed out tangles before, for someone she cared about. *Or for a horse in from the range*, Mac told herself, laughing inwardly.

As each crackling lock came free, her "groom" carefully twisted it into a miniature braid, then laid it over Mac's right shoulder. Lock after lock, braid after braid, until the mass rippled down Mac's chest and lap, and wisps tickled her ear.

Although there wasn't much but hair in the tangles, the process took time. Mac found herself drifting in and out of sleep, too uncomfortable in the chair to truly rest, but too exhausted to be anything more than a boneless lump. When she was finished combing, the woman gathered the tiny braids by the handful and began twisting those together, humming to herself all the while.

"You've lovely hair, Ma'am."

Mac didn't open her eyes but snorted. "Has a mind of its own. As you can tell."

She felt the larger braids being pulled up into one long rope. *Interesting.* The woman gave it a gentle tug. "Yet you haven't cut it."

Because I promised. Mac remembered when. It was like yesterday.

Behind her closed eyelids, she could see the party lights strung along the Jacksons' dock as if she stood there again, admiring how they reflected in the tiny ripples across the lake. She could hear the band playing back at the cottage, something loud to get everyone dancing.

To help everyone forget what was happening tomorrow.

As if the memory had to replay itself to the smallest detail, Mac remembered how she'd smacked her neck to dislodge a mosquito from her bare shoulder, her new, daringly low-cut dress an invitation insects accepted, if not him. She'd gone down to the dock to escape both the effort and the reason for it.

Sam hadn't noticed she was a girl before, in all those years they'd been best friends and classmates—why would he now, the night before he left Earth?

She'd glared at the stars until they blurred. Why was he going? What was out there in the cold and dark that could match the splendor right here? They'd been accepted to the same universities. Were those schools not good enough? Not challenging enough?

Was the Earth not big enough?

"There you are, Mac. Seneal said you'd gone home."

Mac had stiffened at Sam's voice, as mortified as if he'd somehow guessed her thoughts. "Wanted some air," she'd managed to say.

"Know what you mean." He'd come to stand beside her, gazing out over the lake. The night air had carried the scent of him, brought his warmth to her skin. "I'm going to miss this place."

Then why go? had trembled on her lips. But before she'd dared speak, Sam had playfully tugged her hair loose from the mem-shape she'd paid a week's salary from her summer job to have installed for the party, hoping its uplifted complexity would make her seem different, older, so he'd notice at last.

Then: "There. It looks happier."

"My hair?" She'd felt stupid.

Then, wonder of wonders, Sam had run his hand through her hair, from forehead to shoulder, leaving his fingers there to burn her skin with their touch. "Always loved it. Don't cut it while I'm gone, okay?" Before she could speak, he'd kissed her, so quickly she might have imagined it but for the tang of salsa on her lips. "C'mon back to the party, Mac. We're supposed to be celebrating, remember? I can't do that without you."

She'd kept her part of the promise.

Wearily, Mac shook free of the past. "Never seem to get time for a cut," she told her companion in the box stealing her from Earth. "As long as it's out of my face I'm happy."

She'd be even happier once she was home again, for good.

When a light jostling marked their box being lifted into position, Mac hurriedly strapped herself into her chair, mimicking the actions of her companion. For an interminable length of time, she waited, hands locked on the chair arms and doing her best to emulate the outward calm of her companion as well. *She wasn't*, Mac thought ruefully, *fooling either of them.*

The slingshot itself was an anticlimax after Nik's caution of a rough ride. No warning sound, no sensation of movement, just a feeling of increasing pressure against her entire body, the pressure smooth and building to a point that was certainly no worse than she'd experienced in a dive. Perhaps the interior of the box was protected somehow from the worst effects of fleeing Earth's grip.

Mac thought of her salmon, leaping from pool to pool, defying gravity with only their strength and determination. They couldn't see what awaited them until making that final commitment.

She wished she had their courage.

The pressure lessened abruptly, signaling launch—the moment their box joined the line of containers curving upward through the Arctic sky, another ball tossed at space.

Courage or not, she'd made her leap, Mac told herself, determined to hope for the best. She began to unbuckle her straps.

"Don't do that yet, Ma'am. The snatch can be bumpy. Should happen the moment we break atmosphere."

Snatch? Mac didn't like the sound of that. Of course, she wasn't very happy about the idea of breaking atmosphere either, so it was probably just as well someone was waiting to "snatch" them. Mac's ever-helpful imagination stuck on the image of a ball reaching the top of its arc then plummeting back to the ground. Fortunately, she was soon startled from that less-than-helpful thought by sounds from "outside" the box, a sullen series of thuds, as though a frustrated bear was trying to break open a waste container.

"They've got us, Ma'am."

On the surface, the explanation was reassuring, but Mac had to ask: "How do we know who has us?"

"That's my job, Ma'am." Her companion turned over her hands, which had been resting lightly on the arms of her chair. A weapon like Nik's nestled in each, colored to match the paler skin of her palms. "Welcoming committee," she announced with an easy smile, flipping her hands to lie innocently again.

Odd how one's view of the ordinary could spin on an instant. The woman in front of Mac was no longer companion, but warrior. The arrangement of chairs was no longer haphazard, but deliberate, to give her protector line of sight to the only entrance.

And Nikolai Trojanowski obviously didn't trust to subterfuge alone.

"Is there anything I should do?" Mac asked, her voice sounding normal to her own ears.

Perhaps not to others. The other woman's smile broadened. "Nothing would be safest, Ma'am. Don't even worry. I'm sure— There." This reassuringly as the thuds were replaced by a staccato series of high-pitched tones and Mac jumped as far as the straps allowed, jarring her rib. "See? On schedule and with the right code. In a few minutes, you'll be on your way."

Mac made herself relax, made herself focus on the next steps. *One at a time,* she told herself, the way she would when climbing a rock face to check its ledges as potential field stations. Normally she wasn't much for heights, but necessity was admirable motivation. That attitude helped now. "The shuttle takes us to the ship?" *She didn't know what to call the damned thing,* Mac realized. Starship? Transport? Prison?

"Not directly, Ma'am. Too many variations in freight handling in the Union, despite standards. We're being taken to a way station. You'll transfer to the—to where you're going." A smooth slip past what she was probably not supposed to say.

Mac didn't press the point. She'd be wherever it was all too soon anyway. "What about you?"

The other woman hesitated an instant too long, her cheerfulness too forced as she answered: "Paid leave, Ma'am. Nice gig if you can get it."

"Is everyone who helps me getting a similar—vacation?" Mac asked. *Was Nik?*

A sharp look. "I wouldn't know, Ma'am."

A warning she'd trespassed? Mac disliked games and secrets. Now it seemed she was to be surrounded by them. It left a foul taste in her mouth as she waited through the next half hour; she kept swallowing to rid herself of it.

But when another round of bear-thuds marked arrival at the way station—whatever that was—and the other woman unbuckled herself, then came over to help her, Mac patted her crown of tidy, if slightly sticky, braids. "Thank you," she said, for the protection as well as the hair.

Another of those brilliant smiles. "All part of the first-class service on Box Airlines, Ma'am."

Mac's laugh twanged her rib, so she rather breathlessly reached for help standing up. "I'll be sure to recommend you," she said, as the other woman hauled her to her feet. "Although I can't say I plan to do this again soon."

A shrug. "If you need us, we're here." It wasn't as casual as it sounded. Mac looked up into a pair of somber, worried dark eyes and could only nod.

Then, the side of the box fell away.

Revealing total darkness beyond. *Vacuum!* But when her guardian reacted by standing at ease, as if this had been expected, Mac could hardly do otherwise. But she moved ever so slightly closer to the other woman and tried not to hold her breath.

"Clear!" The darkness had a voice, male, loud, and authoritative. "Lifting shroud on three. One, two, three."

The darkness was gone, replaced by a whole new world.

"Go ahead, Ma'am. It's safe."

Mac's first impression was of being outdoors again. She stepped forward, blinking in what seemed full spectrum sunlight. When she was out of the box, however, and could squint upward, she could see, far above, that the "sunlight" was coming from myriad sources. *A lie*, she thought, aware of the irony.

Scale was hard to grasp. The box she'd traveled in might be a child's toy, left lying on the floor near towering piles of others. Skims of a style she'd never seen passed overhead in multiple lanes, sending their shadows to the floor. The floor itself, drawn with broad lines of yellow, black, and green, wasn't of metal or any substance Mac could identify. A heap of what appeared to be fabric lay nearby, black yet with a sheen to it. *The "shroud?"*

Dismayed, she searched for anything familiar. Surely this was a Human station. Emily had traveled like this. Millions did every week. But the figures waiting for her were Dhryn.

Not all, Mac realized with relief, as two men—Human men— came toward her. *Odd, she'd never needed to make that distinction before now.* They were both wearing an alarming amount of protective gear and each cradled an item of weaponry Mac concluded had been designed to intimidate an enemy into surrendering without a fight, given the number of wicked protrusions and glaring red lights on each bulky device.

"Welcome to Way Station 80N-C, Ma'am." His had been the voice in the darkness. Shorter of the pair by a hand's breadth, older by several years, with a face sporting implants on almost every possible surface of his caramel-toned skin. *Career military was a safe guess*, Mac concluded, swallowing hard. "Sorry for the delay opening your—" his eyes slid by her to the box as if seeking a helpful label, "—transport."

"We must leave this place at once!" An urgent boom that startled them all.

Mac didn't catch which of the five Dhryn spoke, but the volume and bass tones were familiar. She'd glanced at them once, quickly, expecting Brymn, but these were unfamiliar. Now she looked more closely.

Instead of colored silks, these Dhryn wore bands of woven fiber, either naturally the same cobalt blue as their thick skin, or dyed to match. No jewelry, but the upper portion of their middle arms bore what looked to Mac like black holsters, each holding a stubby cylinder. She had the impression they were smaller than Brymn, though that could have been their surroundings. Mac had never been inside anything so large.

Sam had loved to talk about way stations, she remembered, from how they were numbered for the Earth latitude above which they orbited, later given a letter to designate their sequence among the others in that orbit, to how they were the next logical outgrowth of Human cities. He'd set his family 'screen to receive live feed from the construction of 15S-C, the newest 'station of the time. Now Mac dredged her memories for those images, wishing too late she'd paid more than token attention.

The way stations were like the mining towns that had grown, or been planted, around points of access to treasures from Earth's crust, designed to process ore and house miners. Rather than ore, however, the modern incarnation processed materials being exported from or imported to the planet. They contained the refining and other industries no longer permitted within an atmosphere, as well as manufacturers who assembled products before shipment, or who specialized in repackaging for a varied species' marketplace. And they housed the teeming thousands required to run these operations, not to mention service the diverse shipping fleets that ferried both goods and people.

Mac had only the vaguest conception of the way station's ring shape, more a flattened doughnut than a circle, bristling with docking ports. She did know much of the structure was hollow, with buildings and industrial plants erected inside as required.

She hadn't known the reality would be sheer bedlam. She wanted to cover her ears. It was like standing beside a malfunctioning skim engine while Tie tuned it, only multiplied a hundredfold and with random explosions added. The larger skims roared around lumbering t-levs overhead, small skims passed both, all apparently lacking the mufflers required on Earth. Below them, teethlike racks stretched into the center from ports in the upcurved wall, ferrying boxes of various sizes from air locks to the receiving floor, the machinery complaining every step of the way. Shipping boxes were literally raining down atop the building-sized piles on every side of where Mac and the others stood, a cavalier treatment Mac was grateful their box had been spared.

There were automated shuttle trucks spinning among the piles like so many whirligig beetles on a pond, quiet enough on their multiple tires, but making their presence heard with a sharp *BANG* ... *Clang!* as each rammed the box of its choice in order to slide it up on its flat back.

It was a wonder any cargo survived intact, Mac thought, staring around in astonishment. There were no other people in sight. A pair of skims sat nearby, one larger than the other, explaining the arrival of her welcoming committee. Was everything in this section automated? *It would*, she decided with a wince at a shrill grind of metal to metal, *explain the racket.*

"We must leave!" The Dhryn were visibly agitated, limbs shuddering. *Not all*, Mac corrected, leaning to one side to get a better look at the Dhryn standing behind the rest.

He—she kept assuming male for simplicity—was maimed, his left lowermost limb a mere stub, jutting at an acute angle from his shoulder, his right lowermost missing below the elbow joint. *How did he sit?* There were nicks along both ear ridges, too irregular to be decorative. More proof, if she needed it, of the Dhryn disdain for medical care.

"Our friend's right, Ma'am," the Human said, though he looked none too pleased about agreeing. "Follow me—"

"We must leave NOW!" Two of the Dhryn jumped at Mac, arms out. Even as she opened her mouth to protest, she was grabbed and spun around so that her guardian could put herself between Mac and the oncoming aliens. The other Humans moved just as quickly to stand in front, aiming their weapons. The frontmost Dhryn stopped and, obviously nothing loath to escalate the encounter, used their uppermost hands to draw their weapons from their holsters and aim them at the Humans.

Cursing under her breath about trigger-happy fools of any biology, Mac shoved the other woman aside and stepped forward. She made eye contact with the maimed Dhryn and announced as firmly as she could, given the ominously nervous beings surrounding her: "Mackenzie Winifred Elizabeth Wright Connor is all my name. I thought we were cooperating."

The Dhryn, weapons still out, shifted aside so Mac and the maimed individual faced each other. She sent what she hoped was an "I know what I'm doing" look to her fellow Humans. At least they didn't budge. Unfortunately, neither did their weapons.

"I take the name Mackenzie Winifred Elizabeth Wright Connor into my keeping," that Dhryn said finally, giving one of those lifting bows. "Dyn Rymn Nasai Ne is all my name."

Four names. That would mean something to a Dhryn, but for all of Mac's research into the species, she'd yet to find anything to explain what that might be. *Best err on the side of being impressed*, she told herself. Mac remembered Brymn's reaction to her names and clapped her hands once. "I am honored to take the name Dyn Rymn Nasai Ne into my keeping." Courtesy having served its function and started them talking rather than shooting, she dropped it like a three-days' dead salmon. "What's going on? Why do you have weapons aimed at my companions?"

"We must leave," another Dhryn boomed.

"Fine. I don't want to stay here either. Put away those things!" This to all of them.

Mac wasn't sure who deserved the award for moving most slowly, but after everything stubby, pointy, or stealthy was off its target, she heaved a sigh of relief. "Thank you."

Dyn replied with a firm: "You must come with us, Mackenzie Winifred Elizabeth Wright Connor."

Tit for tat, Mac thought. She was spending far too much time lately arguing while filthy and tired. It made her inclined to be difficult, but in this case, being difficult might be safer. *Where was Nik? Where was Brymn?* were questions she couldn't ask strangers. "I cannot go with you. I require—" she stopped herself just in time. *No point saying "medical treatment" to a Dhryn.*

She was scrambling for something plausible the aliens couldn't provide when the other woman, who'd been silent until now, filled in with a perfectly straight face: "—the Rite of Manumission. It's required before she may venture farther from her home."

The Dhryn's tiny mouth flattened into a thin line of disapproval. "I have never heard of such a thing. Humans travel from this place constantly."

"Not one as important as Mackenzie Winifred Elizabeth Wright Connor."

Well done! Mac tried to keep a straight face. If the Dhryn didn't concede, it would diminish her importance after he'd just acknowledged it before witnesses.

And if there was one trait their species seemed to share, it was pride.

Someone had called ahead, Mac decided. *Ask no questions,* seemed the likeliest command given. Politeness was one thing; this bland acceptance of her torn clothing and barely scabbed scrapes by everyone they passed in the halls of this nondescript building was quite another. It was disturbing, as though in a way their inattention made her as invisible as the Ro.

"In here, Ma'am."

"Mac," she said, entering the door the woman held open. "It's hardly a secret now, is it? Please."

That infectious smile. "Mac. You can call me Persephone."

Mac gave her a suspicious look, but there was nothing but good humor on the other's ebony face. They'd all been relieved to squeeze together, Human to Human, in the small skim. Once the weapons were stowed beneath the seats, that is. The Dhryn had followed their rise into the traffic lanes, then kept pace around the rim of the way station to the inhabited area. For all Mac knew, the five aliens were still parked outside this building, whatever it was, waiting for her to finish the "Rite of Manumission."

"That was quick thinking, Persephone," Mac complimented as they walked into what appeared to be a deserted med-clinic.

"Part of the job description," came the offhand response, but she seemed pleased. "There should be a gown in the cubicle over there, Mac. I'll call the doc in to dress those cuts."

"Don't call anyone." Mac's smile and greeting died on her lips as Nikolai Trojanowski stormed into the clinic, his face dark with anger. "What the hell are you doing here?"

"Sir, the situation—" His look was nothing short of lethal. Persephone closed her mouth and, with a sympathetic glance at Mac, turned and left the room, shutting the door behind her.

Mac frowned. "I was *supposed* to let them take me away?"

"Shh!" From his suit pocket, Nik pulled a thin silver rod, giving it a shake to extend it to a length of over two meters. With his weapon ready in his right hand, rod in his left, he proceeded around the room, swinging the rod so that it brushed ceiling and walls, moving so quickly Mac found it hard to keep safely out of his way. She watched the anger fade from his face as he worked, replaced by concentration.

When Nik was satisfied, he shook the rod one more time to shrink it to pocket-size. His eyes found and fixed on her. Behind the glasses, they were smudged with exhaustion, but fiercely alert. *Probably stimmed to the gills,* she thought uncharitably. "Low-tech," he said, "but effective in an enclosed area."

"Whatever works." Mac couldn't believe she'd forgotten, even for an instant, that their foe could be hiding anywhere in plain sight. "You shouldn't blame your staff."

"You're right," he surprised her by saying. He leaned against the examination platform like a man conserving the last of his resources by any means possible. "I was trying to keep info splatter to an absolute minimum—which meant 'Sephe didn't know better than to back your decision."

"Info splatter?" Was no Human activity safe from jargon? "Have you heard anything more from Base?" she demanded, her voice feathering at the edges. "Any—names? Do they know I'm okay? What's . . . ?" Mac stopped herself. "I'm sorry. I'm anxious for news."

His expression softened. "I know. I've asked for the—for a list. I wish I could tell you more." When she kept looking at him, he continued, perhaps to comfort her. "Your people look to be good in emergencies: coolheaded, smart. I'm sure they did all the right things even before the rescue teams arrived."

"Real ones, or more of yours?" Mac asked. "I did figure out those police were nothing of the kind, you know."

A raised eyebrow. "Here we thought they were flawless. But yes, the rescuers were local."

Mac realized with a sinking feeling he'd avoided one of her questions. "You did tell them I'm okay, didn't you? And my dad . . . You'd promised to call him." Mac put a hand to her throat, something she'd thought only melodramatic movie heroines did until now, when it felt impossible to catch a full breath through the painful tightness of her throat. "Oh, God. You didn't tell him I was dead."

"Of course not!"

He could be lying and she'd have no way to know. Her father could be mourning her and she'd have no way to tell him the truth.

All her doubt and fear must have shown on her face, because Nik spread his hands out and said with unexpected honesty: "I would have, Mac, if faking your death would have thrown the Ro off your trail. Enough people saw you launched into the ocean with Brymn to make it credible that you drowned." When she began to sputter indignantly, he gave a faint smile. "Don't worry. Morality aside, it wouldn't have worked. Imagine the media uproar if the first and only Dhryn to visit Earth was killed. No, the Honorable Delegate had to make a very visible, very routine departure. When your friends catch the news and see Brymn escaped the attack at Base, and they know he took you with him, how could you be anything but well?"

Mac couldn't decide if she was more confused than relieved. "So what did you tell them? You had to explain my disappearance from the face of the Earth—" *literally!* "—somehow."

He looked insufferably smug. "*You*, Dr. Mackenzie Connor, have sent reassuring vid messages to Base and to your father."

Of course. As she'd spent years working with people capable of that type of forgery and more, if they hadn't been busier using their skills to investigate the natural world, Mac felt herself blush. "What did you—did I—say?"

"Oh, you explained how you'd been picked up by a police boat. Confirmed, naturally, by the 'police.' You related how Brymn was so unnerved by his brush with death—and you, so grateful for his help in escaping—that you accompanied him to the Consulate."

"And?" Mac prompted when Nik paused, as fascinated by this skewing of events as she would have been watching a skim about to crash. There was the same sense of inevitable disaster. *Her friends and family would never believe this.*

"And? As a parting gift," Nik told her, "Brymn arranged for you to access files he'd stored at the Consulate in hopes of finding something to assist the search for Emily and identify those who'd attacked Base. Because of understandably tight security there, you can only access those files within the compound and they will not let you leave, then return. So you are staying as long as it takes. There was more—your confidence in Kammie, condolences and wishes to be kept informed, reassurances to your father. I can arrange for you to view the recordings, if you like."

Mac gulped. "That's just—that's just—"

"Amazing?" he offered helpfully. "Brilliant?"

"Uncanny," Mac said, staring at Nik. "I *would* do that." They'd all believe it, too. Even her father, though he'd voice his opinion. She fought a wave of homesickness. "How could you know?"

His lips quirked. "You study salmon. I study people. Don't worry, Mac. We'll keep up 'your' messages and cover your absence as long as necessary. Right now, we'd better get you to the Dhryn.

They aren't the most patient beings and, with the Ro as adversaries, I can't argue."

"Where's Brymn now?"

"He's aboard the *Pasunah*, waiting for you." An unnecessary stress on the last word.

"He can wait." Mac went to cross her arms, then decided against it when her rib protested. "I'm not leaving to go anywhere—especially a Dhryn ship—until I've cleaned up and had a Human doctor seal these cuts."

He'd either anticipated her reaction or knew better than to argue. "Shower's that way," Nik pointed with his chin. "It's got a sterile field. Thirty seconds ought to do it." He swung the office pouch from under his shoulder to the platform. "Here. This is for you."

"Supper? Is there time?" Mac said, trying to smile at her own joke.

"Sorry." He patted the pouch. "Clothes, hopefully your size. The rest of your luggage is already on the *Pasunah*." At her highly doubtful look, he smiled. "We had staff do some discreet shopping in the way station's stores while you were enroute. Nothing fancy—don't worry. I did my homework."

For some reason, Mac immediately resented his assumption she preferred plain. *Not that Nik had any reason to assume otherwise*, she admitted.

The idea of being clean made every scratch and bite on Mac's body itch. She looked at the shower longingly. *But first* . . . "This is going to take time to undo," she waggled the end of the intricate braid at him.

"It's quite—thorough."

That surprised a laugh out of her. "That bad?"

"I confess I'm curious what you did to annoy 'Sephe."

Despite everything, Mac found herself grinning at him. "Let this be a warning to you. Never leave two bored women alone in a box."

"Warning taken," Nik said. "Here. Let me."

Mac turned to offer him her back, standing close enough that his knee brushed her leg. "Just get it started, thanks. I can work out the rest in the shower."

She felt him pick up the thick braid and run its length through his hands before his fingers began to puzzle at the knot at the end. "I had time to talk with Brymn on the way here," Nik told her. With each word, his breath tickled her neck in a way that made Mac suddenly aware of a problem.

She liked the way his breath tickled her neck.

She liked it in a way that sent waves of shivering warmth into places that should have been politely noncommittal, thank you very much, given where she was and who he was. *Not to mention the why of it all.*

Worse, she couldn't edge out of range of his breath without being obvious; by the movements of his hands, he'd found his way into the braid by now and was busy undoing it.

Mac gritted her teeth. *A cold shower.* "Did Brymn tell you anything more about the Ro?" she asked.

"Nothing to help us find or contact them. We'll probably learn more from the shroud the Dhryn used over your box."

The pile of dark fabric. "What was it?"

"Apparently the Ro can limpet themselves—more accurately, some kind of travel pod or suit—to other vehicles in either an atmosphere or in space. The Dhryn claim their shroud emits an energy pulse of some kind on contact that interferes with the attachment mechanism, shaking loose any such hitchhikers. It forms the basis of their defense for *oomlings*. They also told us they believe it stuns or kills any Ro inside, but that's never been confirmed. They haven't been able to retrieve any of these devices or their passengers."

Mac stiffened, fear rinsing away thoughts of warmth, in water or otherwise. "Then one or more could have come with us—could be on the 'station now."

"Given their capabilities?" She felt Nik spread apart the braids which had been twisted together, then begin to untwist the tiny braids of the one over her left shoulder. *No denying he was undoing the mass more quickly than she could.* "If not with you, then on any ship. All we can do is make sure we keep what secrets we can from them. It might be for the best that you refused to go with the Dhryn. That may have confused the issue, forced any Ro who were watching to decide which of you to follow."

Mac squeezed her eyes closed. Squeezed her hands into fists. Squeezed her thoughts into the tightest possible focus. Amazingly, her voice came out sounding almost calm. "I said my name. Outside the box. In the open. Anyone—anything—could have heard."

"Irrelevant." A tug. "They already know who you are."

"You could at least try to be reassuring," she protested, eyes flashing open.

"Could I?" a chuckle. Dozens of tiny braids tumbled free over her shoulder, a few spontaneously unwinding, and he went to work on the next twisted strand. "What's reassuring, Mackenzie Winifred Elizabeth Wright Connor, is that the Dhryn, particularly our busy Brymn, but also the captain of the *Pasunah* and apparently what passes for their government, also know who you are. And for reasons of their own, they are offering you what they never grant aliens—access to the heart of established Dhryn society, on a Dhryn-only world. Even your Emily didn't manage that, as far as we know." He sounded like a proud parent.

The lie had been larger than she could have imagined. Mac saw it with the stunning clarity of a lightning flash in a darkened room, her mind reeling with the afterimage of truth. Licking her lips, groping for calm, she said it out loud: "Which is exactly what you and the Ministry of Extra-Sol Human Affairs were hoping for all along."

His hands paused the barest instant, then kept unbraiding. "What do you mean?" Casual, but she didn't need to see Nik's face to know its expression. *Wary.*

"You—those who sent you—could have cared less about Brymn's reason for seeking me out. You never thought I'd be of any help either. It was the Nulls—the Ro—you've been after. You've known they were preying on the Dhryn. You let Brymn come to Earth and contact me to bring him where you could watch what happened! You were hoping he'd reveal something about the Nulls. You're probably glad they attacked us!" With that, Mac jerked away and whirled to face him, loose hair and unraveling braids flying in slow motion over her shoulders, breathing heavily with rage that finally had a target. She fumbled at the fastening of the pocket that had kept her envelope safe, drove her hand inside, then pulled it out and threw it at him.

It struck his chest and fell to the floor.

Nik held up the desiccated remains of a banana slug he must have found in her hair, then tossed it after the envelope. "You could be right," he said, each word slow and distinct. "I wouldn't know. I wouldn't have to know. And I wouldn't ask." His eyes became chips of stone in a face turned to ice. "A threat to the *species*, Dr. Connor. What part of that didn't you grasp? Where on the scale of that do you and I fall?"

"You put my people at risk—"

"They were at risk already. What's happening out here—" his violent gesture swept in an arc to encompass everything but the planet below, "—is destroying all life in its path. All life! If the Ro are responsible, yes, we'll do anything to stop them. I'll do anything. And from what I know of you, you would, too."

"I wouldn't put innocent people in danger—without at least telling them why! Without giving them a chance to protect themselves!"

Nik surged to his feet. "Haven't you noticed? We don't know how to protect anyone! I can't—I can't even protect you!"

The words rang in the room as they stood, eyes locked. Mac inhaled air warm and moist from his lungs and didn't know which of them moved first to remove any distance between them, didn't know whose lips were more desperate, whose arms held tighter.

She did know Nik was the first to break away.

He thrust her from him so quickly she staggered a step to regain her balance. His face—she might have imagined that flash of vulnerability—became cold and still once more. "It's time to go, Dr. Connor," he said harshly. "We can't risk the Dhryn leaving without you. I'll let them know you're coming; don't take long getting ready. There's a field med kit in your luggage. You'll have to treat yourself."

Treat herself? Mac pressed one hand over the thrill of pain from her rib, brought the other to her throbbing lips. When she pulled it away, there was blood on her fingers. She stared at it, her eyes wide.

His hand appeared in her sight, pressed the envelope into her bloodied one. Her name rippled across the surface in mindless mauve. "Keep that safe and with you at all times," she heard him say. "No matter what you think of how you got involved, this message authorizes you to claim help and equipment from any Human you encounter."

Mac lifted her eyes to his face, seeing a smear of blood on his mouth too. Heat flushed her cheeks, but she held her voice as steady as his. "I won't encounter any Humans, will I?"

Instead of answering, Nik went on with a rapid-fire briefing. Mac struggled to pay attention, to quiet the pounding in her ears and chest. "There's a beacon in the handle of the smaller piece of luggage," he told her. "When the *Pasunah* sets her transect exit, it will send us those coordinates. There's also an imp—use it instead of yours. It has an automated transmitter and whenever you enter a transect, it will squeal a burst containing your latest log entries, coded so only we can translate."

"How will you find me if I'm not entering a transect?" Mac asked, all too familiar with the unreliability of beacons and transmitters once out of the lab and in the field. *Not to mention some unique problems.* "The Ro can wipe out stored power," she reminded him. *At least in civilian equipment, like that at Norcoast.* "And what if the Dhryn take these things away from me? What will happen then?"

"There is a backup." Nik reached into an inner pocket of his jacket. He drew out what looked like a pen.

"I take it—this time—that's not a pen," Mac ventured, eyeing the thing suspiciously.

"No, it's not." He held out his empty hand. When she gave him hers, thinking that was what he wanted, he grasped her upper arm instead. "Don't move," Nik warned as he pressed the tip of the pen to her skin, taking advantage of the tear in her shirt.

Mac yelped as her arm went on fire from shoulder to wrist. *"What are you—?"* But the pain was gone before she could complete the protest.

Nik released her and Mac ran her fingers over intact skin. "Bioamplifier. The nans will replicate your DNA signature, then concentrate in your liver and bone marrow."

"So you can still find me if I'm in pieces."

He paid her the compliment of not disputing the point. "Yes. Potentially even a century from now, under the right conditions."

"Good to know." *But not the happiest thought*, Mac decided, rubbing her arm, although the technology had interesting potential for her work. She wondered if she could get the specs.

If she ever worked again.

"There are some important limitations," Nik continued. "The one of concern to you is that it only works reliably if you're on a planet surface. The artificial gravity of ship or station tends to blur sigs together."

She appreciated his candor, especially when it answered questions she'd been ready to ask. "So, my orders are to stay on the ground. You don't mind if that's in one piece, do you?" *God, she was getting punchy*, Mac thought. There'd better not be any important decisions in her immediate future.

He frowned. "We are doing everything to minimize any risk—"

"So you can retrieve whatever I learn from the Dhryn about the Ro. I know my value." The moment the words were out, a gauntlet between them, Mac flushed again. "Nik, I didn't mean . . . I know you . . . This is . . . I'm not . . ." He was looking at her in a way that made it impossible to finish any of it. Mac knew her face had to show everything she was feeling: the bewilderment, the longing, the fear, all served with a hearty dose of pine sap, scratches, healing flash burn, and dirt.

Awkward didn't begin to cover it.

"You can do this, Mac."

"If you say so, Mr. Trojanowski," she replied, fighting to stay calm.

It didn't help Mac's equilibrium when Nik traced her swollen lower lip with a fingertip, his eyes following his finger as if mesmerized. "Just don't get close," he whispered, as if to himself, then leaned forward and kissed her again, so lightly it might have been a dream.

But all he said next was: "Locating the Ro home system is the priority, Mac. If it helps to keep it personal, remember that's your best chance of finding Emily. We'll stay in touch through regular, open channels, but be aware none of those can be trusted. Don't initiate any contact."

This wasn't happening, Mac told herself. Knowing it was, she struggled to be practical. "I don't suppose you put a Dhryn dictionary in that luggage? Anything to let me know what to expect?"

"Hopefully, most can speak Instella. I wish we had a sub-teach ready for Dhryn to send with you, but outside of a few entries in an encyclopedia, no one's bothered to compile one. We're working on it now, believe me. Mac—" This with a glance at his watch.

This was it, then. The last chance she had to drop to the floor, kicking and screaming that they couldn't make her leave everything she knew, to go to where her only expertise was forbidden and her very species, the alien.

Emily had done it. *She couldn't imagine why.*

Mac, at least, had Emily for a reason. Keep it personal, Nik had said. *Good advice.*

"Let's not keep them waiting more than necessary," Mac said calmly. "Give me five minutes. Clothes, please?" She took the bundle he produced from his pouch then, without another word or look, without another touch, headed for the shower.

Nik's footsteps echoed hers, one for one. She didn't dare turn around to see if he was following her, but when Mac reached the door to the stall, she heard the door to the corridor open and close.

She pressed her forehead against the cool metal.

"Emily," she whispered, listening to the hammering of her heart. "What the hell just happened?"

- Portent -

THE CAVES WERE ancient, hallowed, and worn. Ancient, as measured in cycles of mineral and water; hallowed, as sites praised in prayer and storied memory; worn, as befitted the only practical shelter in these hills prone to violent wind. Throughout recorded time, the noblest and humblest cowered and wailed here together while nature unleashed her worst on the mountainside. It was said the caves refused no one.

Had such things mattered to him, Eah, night shepherd and litter runt, would have considered himself one of the humblest to ever set footpads within this, the nearest of the fabled caves to his pasture, the Cave of Serenity. But his was a simple soul, content to have a useful place within his kin-group, and, within that place, he felt all the pride of any Primelord.

No matter the fear raising the bones along his spine, no matter the nervous bleating of his flock, no matter the ominous strength of wind in the valley—that pride made Eah stop inside the entrance to light his torch and show proper respect. The ritual three spits into the dust at his footpads, a gift from his body. The ritual claw scrape along the tall stone godstooth, a gift of his might. The ritual howl—

Before Eah could properly prepare himself to howl, the great depth and resonance of his voice something which had always given him profound satisfaction, his flock, which had never appreciated his voice, bolted for the inside of the cave, running between his legs and past him on either side. They almost knocked him down in their haste. He would have chastened them, but they were mindless beasts, always finding ways to challenge his authority. Surely the gods understood such things and would not take offense. To be safe, Eah sprinkled three handfuls of sweetened grain from the bag at his side on the dust, clawed the stalagmite once more, then drew breath to howl.

A runnel of liquid green trickled toward him in the dust, like a finger reaching out of the darkness. Eah leaped sideways and away, clinging to the rock wall. His ability to jump was another that pleased him, if not his mothers, but this time he trembled. Did he now offend the gods by marking their soft glittering stone with his claws?

Before he could decide whether to drop down or remain, one of his flock staggered into the light of the torch, still burning where he'd dropped it in the dust. It was the Old One, whose ability to find water in the dry season was more valuable than her age-bleached hair or tough flesh.

Hair that had disappeared along with the skin beneath . . . flesh that was oozing away from the bones beneath. Her next and final step landed in the runnel of green, her sharp little toes melting so she fell forward.

And fell apart.

Eah trilled like a kit for its mothers, his claws digging deeper into the stone, hearts falling out of synchrony when he didn't leap away and run, as instinct screamed he should.

But the runnel, having washed away the Old One as Eah might wash dirt from his hands, stretched out its fingers across the entrance. There wasn't room for his footpads.

Eah was not one skilled with tool or words, but things he put his hands to usually moved. Now, he used that strength, holding himself with one hand as he stretched the other as far as he could reach along the wall in the direction of the cave opening. The coming windstorm would drive sand through clothing and skin, blind and deafen those without shelter, but it was a threat he knew, a threat sent by the gods themselves. He'd rather die there, where his kin-group would find his body and carry it home again so his mothers could wash him one last time.

He drove in his claws, released the other hand, then pulled himself closer to escape. Again. Again. One claw snapped, and he almost fell into the spreading pool of green.

Drive and pull. *Again!* This time, his arm was bathed in light. He was almost outside!

Even as Eah gasped with hope, he realized something was terribly wrong.

The storm winds had a new, strange sound.

As if they carried rain.

14

FAREWELLS AND FLIGHT

PERSEPHONE—'Sephe—was waiting for Mac when she stepped out of the shower stall, dressed though damp. "I don't think I've seen anyone quite that shade of pink before," she said with a grin.

As every portion of Mac's skin, scraped or whole, felt as though it had lost three layers then been soaked in salt, she considered several scathing replies, but restrained herself. "I take it my time's up?"

"Skim's waiting. Put this on," the other woman ordered, "this" being a huge and hideous mottled brown cloak with a hood. "It's Derelan," she added, then, at Mac's blank look, finished with: "—feels better than it looks."

"That's a relief." Mac whipped her damp, slug-free hair into its normal braid before 'Sephe could offer, tying a loose knot with the result. Feeling that much closer to normal, she walked over and accepted the cloak, surprised by its light suppleness. 'Sephe helped arrange the unusual garment over her new clothes.

They'd fit, not that Mac had expected anything less. And they weren't quite as plain as Nik's description had suggested either. A blouse, white with a gathered bodice and hem, long sleeves with actual buttons, not mem-fabric, to hold them snug to her wrists. A skirt, shimmering blue and sleek, falling to her ankles with thigh-high slits on either side giving her legs freedom to move. A slim waist pouch that could lock relieved her mind on the issue of pockets, holding, with a bit of squeezing, both her imp and the abused, but not yet studied, piece of mem-paper with the results from Kammie.

There was even new footwear, shoes with a soft, studded sole of a type Mac had never seen before that molded comfortably to her feet. *A relief after the boots.*

She hadn't expected to find frankly luxurious undergarments in the bundle, of the sort she'd never bothered buying for herself, though Emily would certainly know the labels. An intimate thoughtfulness Mac found somewhat distracting, given her last encounter with their source, but they'd provided a choice of secure locations in which to tuck her envelope.

The cloak rested on her shoulders and fell almost to the floor, the folds adding bas relief to the brown, so Mac felt disguised as a tree trunk. *Derelan.* The species was hopefully in her xeno text; it wasn't in her brain. *She'd look it up when the universe granted her time for things like breathing.* 'Sephe was already at the door, her stance just short of foot tapping.

Wrapping the Derelan cloak around herself, like hiding in a cocoon, Mac didn't try to fool herself that it was only the Ro's eyes she'd like to avoid.

"Put the hood up."

Mac complied, only to find the hood drooped over her forehead and face to her mouth. "Don't you think this is a little—obvious?" she asked, pushing up the hood so she could see Persephone.

The other woman looked serious. "Maybe to a Human. Hopefully not to our sneaky friends. We don't know if they use scanners, but the cloak's fabric is impregnated with a jigsaw puzzle of DNA fragments, which even our toys can't sort into anything more sensible than a platypus crossed with a clam."

Mac gathered the folds more tightly around herself. "I'm convinced. Now what."

"Your chariot awaits, Mac. We just have to retrace our way in: three corridors and a lift, all guarded. Nik—Mr. Trojanowski's in a mood, all right. We had to sweep them twice before he was satisfied."

Aware that the other was giving her a more than curious look, Mac pulled down the hood. "Then we'd better go."

It should have been easy—the walk through the corridors, the brief trip on the lift, all with 'Sephe's tall, strong presence at her side, in sight of two or more armed guards at any time. Mac did feel safe.

But every few steps, a tear would sting her cheeks, the skin scalded twice now. She was grateful for the hood's shadow.

These steps would be her last among Humans for the foreseeable future. Already the world she knew—of rocks, growing things, and water—seemed a dream, a vision of a paradise she'd lost. Here, nothing was irregular. Nothing struggled to survive. Nothing was alive but the people themselves—and they were encased in armor and caution.

Mac indulged in one final sniff, then stiffened her spine. She was, after all, a scientist. Here was a chance to add to a woefully neglected data set—the Dhryn. She had Brymn, if not a friend, then an ally, by his own words. And, as 'Sephe and another figure preceded her out the door of the building, she added to her list the backing, however many light-years removed, of the Ministry of Extra-Sol Human Affairs, in the person of Nikolai Trojanowski.

He was waiting for her, standing with feet spread and apparently relaxed between another Human guard and a Dhryn, with his suit, cravat, and glasses looking as bizarrely out of place in this gathering as she likely did in her ungainly cloak. Despite that, or perhaps because he hadn't bothered with armor, Mac didn't doubt he was the most dangerous one of them all.

As if rehearsed, the Dhryn stepped to the side of their skim and gave some signal that opened its side door. It was a bigger model than most, so a ramp slid out, clanging to a stop against the flooring.

Flooring. Mac peered up from under her hood, wanting another quick look at this amazing place. What she called a door in the building they'd just left could be an air lock, if the need arose. What she called a building was a portable stack of preconstructed forms, reassembled as needs changed. What she called a sky— Mac lifted her face to sunlight that wasn't, imagining the far-off lines of traffic were clouds.

A touch on her elbow. Mac nodded in acknowledgment and began walking toward the skim, her eyes on Nik. He gave her a look he probably thought was encouraging. It was a little too haunted for that.

The touch on her elbow pushed harder, as if to say, *no, that way.* Confused, Mac turned her head.

There was no one close enough to touch her.

Mac didn't stop to think. She threw off the useless cloak and broke into a run, arbitrarily picking the direction opposite to the one the touch wanted. "They're here!" she shouted to Nik, hoping he'd understand she hadn't lost her mind.

He began to shout orders, was already in motion.

Spit! Pop!

The sound electrified the Dhryn. The skim roared into the air, ramp still extended and hanging loose. The one left abandoned unsheathed his weapons and stood ready.

Mac caught all this in quick glimpses over her shoulder as she ran, arms pumping and grateful for a skirt that got out of the way of her legs. The twanging rib she ignored. She dodged around a pillar displaying notices to find herself face-to-face with a tall yellow barricade marked "under construction" in black.

Cursing the predictability of Human cities, Mac turned to run along the fence, hoping for a way around it.

Her skin crawled at the thought of another *touch*; her ears strained for any sound. *They must have cleared the area of passersby,* Mac fumed, slowing to a jog as she hunted in vain for a crowd or even an open door. *Nothing.* The place was locked up tight. Given a choice between a shadowed gap between two buildings and a wide, plazalike space, she ran into the open, hoping to be spotted.

"Mac!"

Well, that worked, she congratulated herself, panting as she stopped to hunt the source of that reassuring shout. Her rib throbbed in reminder and she pressed her elbow into her side to shut it up.

Scurry . . . skittle . . . scurry!

Mac launched back into a full-out run, dodging from side to side as though trying to make her way through a crowded soccer field.

Or like a salmon, trying to work upstream through rocks—only to find the flash and power of grizzly claws waiting.

She was halfway across the deserted plaza, still hunting the voice, when a figure appeared in the shadow of a building in front of her, frantically beckoning to her. Mac sobbed with relief and found an extra burst of speed.

"No, Mac! Stop!"

That voice she knew. *Nik, but from behind?* Mac stared ahead. *Then who was that?* The figure began walking toward her.

"Mac! Stop! Wait for us!" Now she could hear the thud of footsteps, his and others.

Who—was that?

Mac slowed to a walk, the better to see.

That shape, its easy grace? It couldn't be—

"Em . . . ?" The whisper tore its way up her throat as Mac started to believe her own eyes.

She was grabbed roughly from behind, held. "Mac, wait, dammit!" Nik shouted hoarsely.

She struck at him. "Let me go! That's Emily!"

Spit! Pop!

A sudden *whoompf* of sound, like a punch in the air. Mac felt Nik's body stiffen against hers, then go limp, slipping through her hands as she tried to support his weight. His eyes stared at hers, a terrible urgency in them. His lips moved. Nothing came out.

"He's hurt!" Mac cried, looking up desperately for help as she eased Nik to the floor.

She saw something else. Emily, dressed from neck to toe in skintight black, walking toward them while continuing to aim what had to be some sort of weapon at Nik.

This had to be a dream, Mac told herself. *A nightmare.*

"I am helping you," Emily insisted. "I told you I would. This isn't going to work, Mac. You have to come with me. Now. We won't hurt you."

We?

Scurry . . . skittle . . .

"Hang on, Mac!" More voices. Closer, with pounding feet as an underscore.

Beyond terror, past despair was a kind of numbness, erasing urgency and muting self-preservation. Mac sank to her knees, doing her best to keep Nik's head and shoulders off the floor. He'd lost consciousness. *Or worse*, that safe and detached part of her said. "What have you done?" she asked, as calmly as if she and Emily were still on that granite ledge, waiting for the first run.

"I'm trying to— *Ai!*" Emily dodged back as a huge shape descended on the plaza.

"Em!" A flash filled the air, bright enough to make Mac cry out in pain and close her eyes. She hunched over Nik's body, hoping 'Sephe and the others were responsible.

But the hands that tore her away were both irresistibly strong and very familiar.

Dhryn.

15

BOXED AND BOTHERED

SOMEONE had flung jewels at the night, the largest sapphire Earth, with her diamond Moon. There were others, smaller yet brighter, as if handfuls of cut gemstones had spilled over that black silk to catch sunlight and return it as fire to the eye.

Mac's fingers traced the cold metal outline of the vision. Her breath fogged the viewport and she wiped it clear. The Dhryn had given her this, a chance to watch as the *Pasunah* maneuvered from orbit into the appropriate orientation for the Naralax Transect.

She found a sharp burr on the metal and worried it with a fingernail.

They'd given her nothing more.

No comlink. No message.

No answers.

Mac drew her lower lip between her teeth, involuntarily remembering his taste, her tongue exploring the tiny cut along the inside of her mouth. Here she was, off on a mission whose primary goal—to her—was apparently safe, sound, and on the wrong side, not to mention back at the way station. And the Dhryn wouldn't or couldn't tell her if Nik was alive.

Well, Mac, she said to herself, bitterly amused, *here you are.* Same situation. Different box.

The transition from normal space into a transect might be worth watching, but they hadn't told her when it would occur. From what she'd seen through the viewport, Mac guessed the *Pasunah* was being guided into the required orientation by tugs. Once aligned with the desired transect, her engines would fire, sending the ship curving toward the Sun.

Not suicide, Mac assured herself. *Part of the journey.* Every schoolchild learned that the transects were anchored a few million kilometers outside the orbit of Venus and why. Inward and far enough from system shipping lanes—and the teeming populations of Earth, Mars, and the moons of the gas giants—to satisfy the most paranoid; close enough to make the trip to and from any transect itself economical. That this orientation also put outgoing freight from the Human system at the top of Sol's gravity well was a factor they didn't teach in school, but travelers foolish enough to buy round-trip tickets soon became acquainted with that reality. Mac had endured Tie's diatribe on that matter quite a few times following his first, and last, outsystem vacation.

Economics couldn't change where time was consumed in an intersystem trip. Travel through the transects was outside space-time itself. Mac couldn't quite imagine it, but she did know they'd leave this system and arrive in another with no perceptible passing of subjective time. The captain would enter the desired exit into the ship's autopilot just before they entered the transect—a crucial step since, in some manner fathomable only to cosmologists and charlatans, the act of specifying a particular exit created that exit.

Mac had read a popular article on the transects that compared their initial construction to training a worm to burrow outside space itself, leaving holes through which ships could slide. By that way of thinking, the Interspecies Union wasn't so much a political entity as it was a worm trainer, the result being the greatest collaboration of technology and effort ever conceived by any, or all, of its member species.

Conceived might be too strong a word. The transects owed their beginning to a discovery made hundreds of years ago, and millions of light-years away. The details tended to blur between various species' historical records—every species having members ready to claim they'd been about to make the crucial breakthrough themselves—but no one disputed that finding a key portion of the required technology, buried in the ancient rubble of a once-inhabited moon in the Hift System, had moved that breakthrough ahead by lifetimes.

Academics would probably always argue what might have happened if any species other than the Sinzi had made the initial discovery. But the coolheaded, cooperative, and highly practical Sinzi had been the ones to shape the Interspecies Union into its present form, perhaps due to their having multiple brains per adult body. The Sinzi had set the initial criteria for any species to receive a permanent transect exit, which was still in use today: desire for contact with other species, an independently developed space-faring technology, a demonstrated absence—or, at minimum, reliable control—of aggressive tendencies which might impact other species, and the willingness to adopt a mutual language and technical standards for interspecies' interactions outside their own systems.

All so most alive today in this region of space, including Mac, could take the ability to slip from system to system for granted.

Slip—through a nonexistent tunnel dug by unreal worms burrowing outside normal space?

On second thought, Mac decided, *maybe she should miss that highly unnatural portion of the trip entirely with a well-timed cough.*

Meanwhile, Mac had to endure the trip to the transect. No one had told her where the exit to the Naralax Transect was in relation to Earth but, being one of the less traveled and her luck staying its stellar self, it might be on the far side of the Sun right now. At minimum, they had about forty million kilometers to cover to reach Venus' orbit, and, to her knowledge, ships still obeyed the physics that involved staying below the speed of light. Maybe a week at sublight?

She had to read more, Mac decided. But it was like knowing the inner workings of a skim engine. You needed the knowledge most when the damn thing broke down, leaving you stuck where you couldn't possibly gain the knowledge you needed. And you had to walk home as a result.

Face it, Mac, she scolded herself. *You have no good idea how long you'll be in this box.*

Though calling her accommodations on the *Pasunah* a "box" was a trifle unfair, Mac admitted, finally relaxed enough to explore her new quarters. Her first observation proved she wasn't on a Human-built ship, had there been any doubt. There wasn't a truly square corner in sight, the Dhryn, or their ship designers, having built everything at what appeared closer to seventy degrees. Considering how the aliens themselves stood at an angle, this seemed a reasonable consequence. The lack of perpendicular didn't bother Mac. When she wasn't in a tent, she was in her office at Base, where the pod walls curved down one side.

Where there had been casualties. Plural. Pod Six had sunk. Who had been trapped inside?

Not Emily. She was alive.

Emily had shot Nik.

Was he a casualty, too?

As if it could quiet her thoughts, Mac pressed the heels of both hands against her closed eyes. The damn Dhryn could have told her. They could have let her contact those who did know. They could have told her where they were taking her.

But no. They'd brought her to their ship without a single word, either in answer to her frantic questions or to give her orders. They hadn't needed the latter. A Dhryn had picked her up as if she'd been a bag of whatever Dhryn carried home in bags, and only put her down here. While Mac had been sorely tempted, she'd kept her mouth closed over her objections and did her best to cling to the Dhryn, rather than struggle to be free. She'd preferred not to test her ability to splint her own limbs—or truly crack that bruised rib.

The skim ride had been fast and, from the frequent and violent changes of direction experienced by those within, probably broke every traffic regulation on the way station. *If they had such things.* Instead of stopping to argue with any authorities, the Dhryn must have flown right into their ship, because when the door of the skim had dropped open, Mac had found herself carried through a cavernous hold. The Dhryn had continued to carry her, reasonably gently yet with that ominously silent urgency, through tunnellike ship corridors to this room.

While such treatment alone might be construed as a rescue, there was the troubling aspect of the door the Dhryn had closed behind her—a door with no control on this side that Mac had been able to find.

That door, Mac corrected herself, slowing her breathing, consciously easing the muscles of her shoulders and neck. There were two others. She picked the door on the wall to her left, relieved to spot a palm-plate, similar to the Human version but set much lower. It was colored to match the rest of the room, a marbled beige. *Inconspicuous to a fault.*

The plate accepted her palm, the door opening inward in response. Mac looked into what was patently a space for biological necessities. She'd assumed that much physiological congruence, since Brymn had stayed in her quarters without requesting modifications. Still, she took it as a positive note that the Dhryn had made provision for her comfort.

The remaining door was on the opposite wall. Mac found herself taking a convoluted path to reach it, forced to detour around the main room's furnishings. She did a tally as she went: one table, six assorted chairs, ten lamps of varying size and color, and other, less likely items, such as a footbath and a stand made from some preserved footlike body part holding an already dying fern. Judging by the combination and haphazard arrangement, someone had shopped in a hurry. The Dhryn might as well have posted a sign outside the *Pasunah* saying: "Human passenger expected."

Not her problem.

It occurred to Mac that unsecured furniture meant the *Pasunah* maintained internal gravity throughout her run, not common practice on economy-class liners if she was to believe Tie's vacation story. That, or the Dhryn had a peculiar sense of humor. She tugged a chair closer to the table as she passed. While she was curious about Dhryn furniture, Mac was grateful for something suited to her anatomy. At least it looked more suited than the one in Mudge's waiting room.

The door opened into what the Dhryn must intend her to use as a bedroom, judging by the irregular pile of mattresses occupying its center. Spotting luggage on top, Mac wasted no time climbing up to see what had been provided for her.

Trying to climb up. She wedged her foot between two mattresses, but the ones above slid sideways each time she tried to pull herself up. Taking a step back, Mac frowned at the stack.

Five high, each mattress about thirty centimeters thick and soft enough to lose the proverbial princess and her pea, the sum between Mac and her luggage.

"Bring the mountain," she muttered, then grabbed the nearest corner of the topmost, and yanked. The result owed more to pent-up frustration than power. She dodged out of the way as both mattress and luggage joined her on the floor.

The two cases bounced to a rest, a mismatched pair of the type so common on Earth that frequent travelers on transcontinental t-levs knew to pack short-range ident beacons.

Mac kicked off her slippers, flipped up the ends of her long skirt, and sat cross-legged on the mattress, pulling the smaller case toward her. Her hands lingered on its so-ordinary handle. She had to take on faith that it contained the very long-range beacon Nik had promised, believe that beacon could identify the destination the *Pasunah* chose, and trust that identification would reach only those who—

Cared?

Such a dangerous, seductive word, fraught with risk even among Humans. Even between friends.

What had Nik said? "A threat to the *species*, Dr. Connor . . . Where on the scale of that do you and I fall?"

Mac drew an imaginary line along the handle, then circled her finger in the air above it. "We're not even on it, Mr. Trojanowski."

Oddly, the image steadied her. She may not have paid sufficient attention to astrophysics, but Mac understood the nuts and bolts of biological extinction, in all likelihood better than Nik—or most of humanity, for that matter. She was accustomed to attacking problems at the species' level, not dealing with betrayal and violent death among those close to her.

Nik had warned her not to let anyone close. *A little late.*

The luggage's lock was set to her thumbprint—easy enough to obtain from Base. Once she had it open, Mac gaped at the contents. Someone was obsessed with neatness. Each article was individually wrapped in a clear plastic zip, varying in size from the dimensions of her closed fist to the length of the luggage's interior. Picking a smaller one at random, Mac unzipped it, hearing a tiny *poof*. Almost instantly the contents expanded to several times its original size, startling her into dropping what turned out to be a yellow shirt.

Not neatness. Saving space to give her the most they could.

Maybe she shouldn't unzip too many items until safely off the ship, Mac decided, wondering how to get the shirt back into the case.

She took out each small packet, turning it over in her hands as she puzzled at what might be inside. Some, clothes, were easy enough. Lightweight, soft. Those Mac tossed behind her on the mattress.

A narrow hard packet claimed her attention. She unzipped it cautiously, giving it room to grow, but it stayed the same size.

"So there you are." The imp Nik had told her about. Mac wasn't the least surprised when it accepted her supposedly private code and a small workscreen indistinguishable in format from her own appeared in the air over her lap. "Snoop."

Well, it was his business.

She waved up a list of most recent files—nothing newer than her last link to her desk workstation—then shut it down.

So. Emily's private logs were still hers alone.

As if it mattered now, Mac thought. The Ministry staff had seen Emily shoot their leader, likely had her in custody within moments. They'd use whatever drugs it would take to obtain an explanation; somehow Mac doubted 'Sephe and her colleagues required warrants or permission.

Mac tucked a wisp of hair behind one ear. "Or did you elude them, Dr. Mamani?" she asked aloud.

Another question no one would answer. *Not that she was in a hurry to know*, Mac decided, given the lack of any good outcome.

She took her own imp from the waist pouch beneath her blouse and compared the two. Identical to anyone else's, at least on casual inspection. Her fingers unerringly found the dimpling along one edge of hers where she'd used a knife to pry off hardened drops of pine resin. *Fair enough.*

Mac put hers safely away again, then activated the other. Nik had

said any recordings she made would be transmitted whenever the
Pasunah entered a transect. If this was true—*when had she begun to
doubt everything she was told?*—she had a chance to communicate
that mustn't be wasted.

Mac sat a little straighter, a few plastic-packed clothes sliding off
her lap as a result, then poked the 'screen to accept dictation.

"This is Mackenzie Connor," she began self-consciously, stifling
the urge to cough. "The Dhryn have taken me on their ship, the
Pasunah, and we're heading for the Naralax Transect. Well, I don't
know it's the *Pasunah*—or the Naralax—but I'll assume so until I
have evidence to the contrary." Her voice slipped automatically
into lecture mode as she went on to describe her quarters and give
what details she could see.

Then, data recorded, Mac hesitated. *Who would hear this?* She
had no way of knowing.

She had no choice.

"Please tell my father I'm okay. Lie about where I am if you have
to, but don't let him worry. That's Norman Connor. Base—
Norcoast Salmon Research Facility—will have his contact information.

"Please tell Nik—Nikolai Trojanowski—that I have my luggage." Blindingly obvious, since she was using their imp to send
this, but it was easy to say. "And tell him . . ." Having reached the
hard part, Mac paused the recording. *Tell him what?*

That he should have protected her from the Ro? From the Dhryn?
Mac shook her head. *He'd never said he could.*

That he shouldn't have kissed her? She frowned at the display. As
kisses went, it had been spontaneous and as much her doing as his.
An impulse brought on by stress or something more? Probably best
forgotten.

Easier said than done.

Mac restarted the recording. ". . . tell him I wish him well."

"Now this is a problem."

Mac lined her water bottles—one half empty since she'd decided to drink first from a source she knew and two full—in front of her small pyramid of yellow-wrapped nutrient bars, then rested her chin on the table to check the result. She'd found the supplies in the larger luggage, along with boots, outerwear, and a daunting medical kit. Oh, there were self-help instructions on her new imp. They didn't make owning needles and sutures any less intimidating.

That wasn't the problem.

Mac rolled her head onto her left cheek, the better to see her predicament.

Beside her attempts at reconstructing an Egyptian tomb, the table held what Mac presumed was either supper, breakfast, or lunch. She'd lost physiological track of time hours past. It had been waiting here when Mac came out of her bedroom. She'd immediately looked for the provider, but the door to the corridor was closed and still apparently locked.

She studied the six upright, gleaming black cylinders. Brymn had said they ate cultivated fungus, but these looked like no fungus—or food, for that matter—she'd ever seen. They were arranged on a tray of polished green metal, each sitting within a small indentation—presumably so they wouldn't topple while being carried. Thin, hairlike strands erupted from the tops. At the right angle of light, the cylinders exhibited traces of iridescence, as if oil coated the outer surface. When she poked one with a cautious finger, it jiggled.

Mac squinted. It didn't make the cylinders any more appetizing.

She sat up, grabbing a nutrient bar from the top of her pyramid. Unwrapping it, she broke it into three pieces, popping one in her mouth with a grimace. *Oversweet, overfat, over everything.* Emily always carried a dozen in her pack. Mac couldn't stand the things. But they could keep you alive if you were lost in the bush.

Or worse, she thought, with an uneasy glance at the cylinders.

She started to wash down the crumbs of the bar with a drink but stopped with the bottle at her lips. *How much worse?*

Mac put the bottle down, capping it with deliberate care, and lined it up with the other two. A moment later, she stood in the Dhryn bathroom, her mouth already feeling dry. The "biological accommodation," as the Instella term generically put it, was of the suck and incinerate variety. The sink, lower and much wider than Mac was used to, presumably to fit all seven Dhryn hands at once, had no drain or faucet. She lowered her left hand into it cautiously, feeling a vibration that warmed her skin. Sonics. The shower stall, sized for a Dhryn with a friend, looked to be the same.

No water.

Maybe this was something done on ships, she assured herself. After all, water would take up precious cargo space, so minimizing its use might be a priority. Then Mac thought back to the dinner at Base. Brymn had toasted her with a glass of water. She hadn't seen him drink any.

Off the top of her head, she could name fifteen Earth species who obtained all the water their bodies required from their food. *What if the Dhryn were the same?*

"Great," Mac said aloud. Humans weren't. Worse, the nutrient bars were concentrated by removing water from their components. Digesting them would only add to her thirst. The three bottles from her luggage contained barely a day's worth of water.

There were mirrors on two walls, sloping toward the middle of the room. Mac licked her lips and watched her elongated reflections do the same. "Our friends will be in for an unpleasant surprise if they leave me here too long," she informed them.

Not to mention Mac, herself.

After a quick search of her quarters to see if she'd missed a water outlet or container, studiously avoiding the hairy, black sticks, Mac spent a few minutes reminding the Dhryn they had a guest. When shouting and knocking on the door to the corridor failed to elicit a response, she chose likely objects and began pelting the door with them.

Smash! Lamp with a ceramic base.

Crunch! Chair.

Shatter! Statue of three entwined bodies created by an artist with outstanding optimism concerning Human anatomy. Mac blushed as she threw it.

Clang! Footbath. Which wasn't going to do her much good without water to fill it.

Mac stopped, having run out of disposable objects and temper. She waited, listening to her blood pounding in her ears, her breathing, a low hum that might be the ship, and hearing nothing more.

The Dhryn weren't deaf—particularly to the lower frequencies caused by objects hitting a metal door. They were ignoring her.

Or the Ro had killed or bound all the Dhryn and they were ignoring her.

Or she was alone on the ship, heading toward the Sun.

There were times Mac really hated having a good imagination.

Without opening her eyes, Mac yawned and stretched. At the halfway point of her stretch, her rib reminded her yesterday hadn't been a nightmare and her eyes shot open.

And half closed. The lights were bright again. She'd discovered the hard way that the Dhryn ship observed a diurnal cycle, having been caught in the midst of compulsive furniture arranging when the lights went out. Not quite out. She'd remained still, letting her eyes adjust, and discovered a faint glow coming from the viewport. Moving with hands outstretched and a step at a time, Mac had managed to reach it and look out. Sunlight was reflecting from some protrusions along the hull. She'd decided to find the safety of her bed before the ship turned and the room was completely dark, given the shards of ceramic, glass, and splintered wood product now littering the floor.

Falling asleep had been as difficult as falling on the nearest mattress.

Now thoroughly awake, Mac rubbed her eyes and groped for her imp—the Ministry one, which she planned to use most. According to its display, she'd slept for eleven hours. According to the stiffness of her spine, most of that had been in one position. *Likely fetal*, she grinned to herself, even though her lips were dry enough to protest.

Amazing what a good sleep could do. Mac stretched again, with more care to the rib, then rolled to put her feet on the floor. *Deck.* She should start using ship words or Kammie would never forgive her.

Kammie. *The soil analysis!*

Mac muttered to herself as she hurriedly unfastened the waist pouch—doubtless another reason her back was sore—and pulled out the crumpled sheet. *Her brain must have been turned off yesterday.* Remembering Nik, she blushed furiously. *No excuse . . .* she started to read line by line.

Ordinary composition . . . expected nutrient levels . . . high moisture content, which Mac found ironic under the circumstances . . . pollen levels reflective of last year's poor conditions . . . and unfamiliar biological material from which had been extracted strands of DNA.

Nonterrestrial DNA.

Kammie had provided the nucleotide sequence without further comment, but Mac could well imagine what the soil chemist would say if she were here. For the first time, Mac was glad she was alone. She had to trust Kammie's discretion would keep her safe. "Sorry, Kammie," she whispered as she studied the results. If the Ro had started chasing her, destroying Base in the process, simply because she might have received information from Brymn, how would they react to Kammie having some or all of their genetic footprint?

Mac didn't want to know. She did want to get this information into the right hands—ones with five fingers—as quickly as possible.

"Regular channels aren't safe," she mused, turning the imp over in her hands. "Not that they're giving me one to use."

After some thought, and a carefully small swallow of water she held in her mouth as long as possible, Mac resorted to a trick so old it probably dated back to stone frescos on buildings. She activated the 'screen and went through her personal image files until she found the one she'd remembered: Emily, all smiles and arms wide, wrapped in some man's oversized T-shirt, the shirt itself peppered with risqué sayings Mac didn't bother to read. She avoided looking at Emily's face as well, enlarging the image so she could concentrate on replacing the letters of the sayings with the letters of the sequence Kammie had found.

It was long, long enough that Mac didn't try to make the substitution letter-by-letter. Instead, she had the imp transfer blocks. There were breaks in several areas. *Incomplete*, Mac realized as she worked, but perhaps sufficient to be the basis of a recognizable re-construction. She had never worked with alien DNA but was aware that some, like this, contained unique nucleotides. Those alone might suffice to identify a home world.

If they examined the T-shirt closely. Returned to its normal size, even she could hardly tell the words had been replaced by tiny, seemingly random strings of letters. "Let's see how smart you peo-ple are," Mac said grimly. Setting her imp to record, she spoke as clearly as her coffeeless throat allowed: "I found a picture of Emily that might help you find her. As you can see, she likes unusual clothing."

Feeling slightly foolish, Mac tapped off the imp and tossed the device on the mattress. For all she knew, Nik had obtained the same results during his scans of the landing site. It wasn't as if they would brief her on their findings. Still, as Mac told her students every field season, better found twice than ever overlooked.

Time to see what was new in the world of the Dhryn. Mac wrig-gled off the mattress, a process complicated by the fact that her skirt had done its utmost to tie itself in knots as she slept. Mac ex-tricated herself, salvaging the precious message in the process, and unzipped clothing packets until she found a pair of pants to ac-company the shirt she'd opened earlier. Both pale yellow, unless the Dhryn lighting was off spectrum from what Mac was used to, but she didn't care about the color. The style was loose enough for comfort and snug enough to move properly. *Good enough.*

Shower, then another mouthful of water. She'd gain the maxi-mum benefit from frequent, small drinks. Until the third, and last, bottle was empty. *Which would happen sometime today*, Mac re-minded herself unnecessarily.

As Mac padded through the main room, new clothes under one arm, she paused by the table. She'd had visitors again. A second tray of cylinders had joined the first, identical in every way. On the principle that if she was ever to eat them, it should be the freshest, she took the older offering—the tray closest to her pyramid—with her to the bathroom to dump it. *Emily would be impressed*, Mac as-sured herself.

Memory flooded her in darkness: the anguish of finding Emily gone, the horror of feeling Nik's body sliding through her hands, disbelief at hearing Emily urging her to leave him and come away.

There was never just one *lie—wasn't that what he'd said?*

Mac scowled at her reflections as she walked into the smaller room. "There has to be a sensible explanation," she told them.

Of course, any explanation that justified Emily shooting Nikolai Trojanowski in the back could very well condemn Nik himself, and, through him, all of those who'd put Mac on this ship. The same people she had to trust would get her home again.

"There's a choice for you," Mac growled with frustration. There was that other possibility, one she cared for least of all. *She shouldn't have trusted either of them.* "At this rate," she muttered, "I'll set a record as the worst judge of my own species."

A species who washed in water, whenever possible. Mac ran her tongue over chapped lips and glared at the shower.

Then, she stared at the shower.

Finally, she walked up to the opening and studied the shower.

The interior of the enclosure resembled the sink, coated in a rather attractive geometric pattern of finger-sized—Human fingers—tiles in beige and orange. But the shower had additional tiles, metallic and angled as if to focus something on whoever stood within. Mac had never seen such a thing in a sonic shower.

Crouching down, Mac shoved the tray with its jiggling, hairy cylinders along the floor into the shower and stood back to see what, if anything, would happen.

She wasn't disappointed.

The metallic tiles glowed fiercely, then what appeared to be shafts of blue-tinged light bathed the tray. The tiny hairs crisped and fell away; the cylinders themselves became limp and bent over. Before their tops hit the tray, they'd melted into puddles, producing tendrils of dark smoke.

Mac's first thought was one of calm analysis. The Dhryn had a thick, cuticlelike skin covered in glands. A brief burst of radiant energy could well be a pleasant way to sear off old skin cells and exudate, dirt and germs being efficiently removed at the same time.

Her second, less coherent thought involved imagining herself crisping and melting, all in the cause of cleanliness, and she couldn't help her outburst:

"Damn aliens! Can't you people even make a shower?"

Hours and ten sips later, Mac leaned her head against the door to the corridor, resting her eyes. Waiting was always the hardest part. She'd taken care of herself. Fresh clothing, although she herself was becoming somewhat ripe between anxiety and an ambient temperature above what her body preferred. A nibble of nutrient bar, those careful sips of water, no unnecessary physical activity beyond rearranging the furniture once more. Aesthetics hadn't been the issue; this time she was after clear passage between bathroom, window, and this door, along with a barrier of sorts in front of the table.

They were still on approach to the transect; she was still being ignored.

Mac's luggage was packed, locked, and beside her on the mattress she'd dragged from the bedroom, positioning it across the door's opening for her own comfort. She hoped it would also slow whomever might enter long enough for her to be heard—or for her to run out the door.

An ambush might not be subtle, but it was a plan. Mac was much happier having one.

The waiting? She opened her eyes, her attention reactivating the workscreen, and blinked patiently at the appendix to Seung's xenobiology text: "Common Misconceptions About Dining with Alien Sentients."

The material was fascinating, something Mac hadn't expected. In fact, under other circumstances, she would have tracked down the cited references to obtain the original sources for herself. It might be an introductory course, but Seung always challenged his students. She now knew enough about humanity's immediate neighbors and important trading partners to have questions whirling in her head. Sentience, it seemed, was a palette biology loaded with tantalizing variety. Let alone the consequences to culture and technology.

As for Emily's riddle?

"Why shouldn't you put a Nerban and a Frow in the same taxi?" Mac whispered. "Because the former sweats alcohol and the latter sparks when upset. Ka-boom!" It would be funnier over a pitcher of beer.

She caught herself giving serious consideration to a sabbatical at one of the prominent xenobiology institutions, like UBC, and brought herself back to the "research" at hand.

Predictably, the Dhryn had been mentioned in passing as "a rare visitor, largely unknown in this area of space," part of a lengthy list. The text claimed there would be over two thousand species added to the Interspecies Union before the end of the school term and recommended students sign up for Xenobiology 201 as soon as possible.

Reading the appendix on Dining proved amusing, especially the anecdotal accounts of what shouldn't have been offered certain alien visitors, but Mac was disappointed to find no clues to her present situation.

The fungus.

Putting away her imp, Mac snared the tray with her toes and dragged it closer, the cylinders jiggling gracefully as they came along for the ride. The kit at her side contained treatments for allergic reactions and food poisoning. The medical info in her imp hadn't said anything about their effectiveness on a Human who'd eaten Dhryn food.

Arguing with herself was pointless. Her natural desire to postpone the inevitable experiment couldn't override the simple fact that she'd be better able to survive an adverse reaction sooner rather than later. Another day and she'd be dangerously dehydrated. As it was, her persistent thirst showed she was close. And the last bottle was down to one quarter full.

No, Mac told herself, eyes fixed on the tray, *she might as well get it done.* She'd made a brief recording about the lack of water, to warn anyone else who might land in a similar situation. *And so they'd know what had happened if her recordings stopped in a couple of days*, Mac added with a twisted smile.

As for the food? If this was all the Dhryn would have for her to eat, she had to know if her body could tolerate it. If not, recording a call for help might be her only chance of survival—and that recording would only be sent when they entered the transect.

It wasn't every day you faced the point of no return.

Step one. After her experiment with the Dhryn shower, Mac wasn't going to risk herself without due care. She chose the outside of her left arm as most expendable and pressed it against one of the cylinders.

It felt cold, which didn't mean it was chilled. *Room temperature,* Mac concluded. She examined the skin that had touched the food. No reddening or swelling. She brought her forearm close to her nostrils and sniffed.

Blah! Mac wrinkled her nose. She wasn't sure if it smelled more like hot tar or sulfur. It certainly didn't smell edible.

Step two. She picked up one of the cylinders, doing her best not to react to its slimy feel or rubbery consistency, and brought it to her mouth. Slowly, fighting the urge to vomit—a potentially disastrous loss of fluid—she stuck out her tongue and touched it to the side of the cylinder.

Nothing.

Her tongue might be too dry. Mac brought her tongue back inside her mouth, letting its tip contact what saliva she had left, then, cautiously, she moved that saliva around so it contacted all the taste buds on her tongue.

BLAH! Mac barely succeeded in keeping her gorge in her throat. *God, it was bitter.* Putting down the cylinder, she crushed a bit of nutrient bar in her hand and licked up the crumbs. The sweetness helped, barely. She resisted the urge to take another sip. Thirty minutes until her next.

Step three. Mac breathed in through her nose, out through her mouth, centering herself, slowing her heart rate from frantic to tolerably terrified. Then she picked up a cylinder and took a bite.

BITTER! Before she could spit it out, moist sweetness flooded her senses as her teeth fully closed. Startled, she poked the jellylike mass around in her mouth. A tang of bitterness remained, but the overall impression was of having bitten off a piece of . . .

. . . overripe banana. Not that flavor, but the same consistency and texture. This taste was complex, more spicy than bland, and seemed to change as the material sat in her mouth. *A good sign*, Mac thought, chewing cautiously. The enzyme in her saliva was acting on what had to be carbohydrate. The moisture in the mouthful was more than welcome.

She swallowed. When nothing worse happened than the impact of a mouthful thudding into her empty stomach, Mac examined the cylinder. Where she'd bitten it, glistening material was slowly oozing onto her hand, as if through a hole.

Mac laughed. If the sound had a tinge of hysteria to it, she felt entitled. "I ate the damn wrapper," she said, wiping her eyes.

Choosing a fresh cylinder, Mac grasped the hairs coming from the top and pulled. Sure enough, they came up freely, the glistening interior remaining attached and rising too. What was left behind was a clear tube, with that oily sheen. She found she could pull the food completely from the tube, but it only held its shape for an instant before falling from the hairs.

"When visiting Dhryn, bring bowl and spoon," Mac told herself for the future. She experimented, finding the tidiest approach was to nibble the food from one side, while attempting not to eat right through the portion held by the hairs. The most effective was to dig in with her finger and lick it clean.

Step four would be the final test, but she'd have to wait a few hours to see how her digestive tract reacted to the alien . . . *what should she call it*? Mac concentrated on the taste and failed to find any one distinguishing flavor. The overall effect was pleasant, if strange.

A group of Harvs had tinkered with the supper menu at Base a few weeks ago. Mac hadn't believed it possible to make mashed potatoes one couldn't identify by taste or appearance, but the students had managed it. "You're officially 'spuds,' " she told the last three cylinders, using the silliness to control her relief at finding she could safely ingest the Dhryn food.

"Digest—that we'll find out." Mac wasn't looking forward to that part of the process.

Despite the moisture in the Dhryn food, water remained the

issue, and Mac stuck to her post, back against the door. They'd bring her more spuds eventually. She'd be waiting.

She brought up the next in her list of reading and raised one brow at the title: "Chasm Ghouls—They Exist and Speak to Me."

"Oh, this should be good."

She'd finished "Ghouls," unsure if it was intended as fiction or advertising for the country inn near Sebright where apparently such visitations took place, but only on summer weekends, and had started scanning through more of Brymn's articles when the door to the corridor abruptly opened. It did so by retracting upward, a fact Mac rediscovered when the support behind her back slid away. Before she could fully catch herself, she was falling, but only as far as the Dhryn standing there.

Mac, her shoulders grasped by the being's lowermost hands and her forehead brushing the woven bands covering his abdomen, looked up and gave her best smile. "Hello."

The being shifted his tray into two right hands and contorted his head so one eye looked down at her. "*Slityhni coth nai!*"

Mac's heart sank. *Not Instella.* What had been the name of the captain? "Take me to Dyn Rymn Nasai Ne!" she said, as forcefully as she could from such an undignified and uncomfortable position.

The Dhryn reacted by pushing Mac up and forward out of his way. She landed on her hands and knees, mostly on the mattress which bounced as the Dhryn stoically climbed on and over it to carry his tray of spuds to the table.

"Wait!" She grabbed her remaining bottle of water and scrambled to her feet. "I need more of this!" Mac shook it, the water within gurgling loudly.

Job done, he was ignoring her, walking back toward the door. Mac launched herself in his way. The much larger being stopped, staring down at her. She couldn't read much on his face, which possessed sharper brow and ear ridges than Brymn's. His mouth was in a thin line. *Disapproval? Dislike? Impatience?*

Bad spuds? Mac thought wildly. She held up the bottle, pantomimed putting it to her lips to drink. "Water."

No response, although he gave a look to the door that was, "I'm leaving as soon as I can" in any language.

She pretended the bottle was empty, then grasped her throat and made gagging noises, sinking down and rolling her eyes.

That seemed to get through. The Dhryn blinked, then said, very clearly, the only phrase in his language Mac actually knew: "*Nie rugorath sa nie a nai.*"

With that, he walked around her and left. Mac didn't bother to turn to watch him climb over the mattress and go out the door, locking it behind him.

" 'A Dhryn is robust or a Dhryn is not,' " she translated to herself, clutching the bottle and feeling fear seep into every bone. "Guess that means I've been adopted."

It was easier than admitting their ignorance of Humans might have just condemned her to death.

- 16 -

TRANSIT AND TRIBULATION

M AC KNEW she was stubborn. It wasn't her most pleasant characteristic, admittedly, 'though it had served her well in the past. She'd break nails before cutting a perfectly good rope to free a water-tightened knot. She'd wear out boots before wasting time to shop for new ones. And she'd exhausted the entire funding review committee at Norcoast with her seventeen-hours long personal plea to get Pod Six built and running the year she wanted it, not in a decade.

Since then, they'd been remarkably prompt with approvals.

Now, she might be dying. *But it would be on her terms,* Mac told herself again. It had become a mantra of sorts. *Her terms. Her way. If she died, it would because she decided to die.*

The lights had gone off again; she'd slept, fitfully this time and on the floor by the bathroom, having pulled the mattress there. The spuds had gone through her system, all right—and had continued to do so at distressingly regular intervals for much of the ship's night.

Moisture she couldn't spare. Making the Dhryn's food a source she couldn't afford.

To avoid the temptation to eat the moist things regardless of the consequences, Mac had thrown the last of them in the shower. She hoped she'd have the strength to do the same when the next offering arrived.

It would be nice to have the strength to kick a Dhryn where it hurt, too, but she couldn't guarantee that.

When the lights came back on, Mac took her precious bottle and wove her way to the bedroom the Dhryn had given her. The dizziness wasn't a good sign, but she was healthy. Had been healthy. She was good for hours yet.

Then . . . there were drugs in the medical kit—enough for perhaps another day's grace. *After that?* Mac rubbed her arm over the spot where Nik had implanted the bioamplifier.

They'd find whatever was left of her—eventually.

There was a comforting thought.

Mac eyed the stack of mattresses and settled on the floor rather than climb up. She pulled out her imp, intending to make another recording. What she'd say she didn't know, but it was something to do. The workscreen brightened in all its cheerful, Human colors over her knees, showing her the list of what she'd left to read.

Emily's personal logs.

Wrong imp. Her brain must be addled. But instead of switching to the other, Mac watched her fingers lift and slide through the 'screen, keying the logs to open.

Password required.

A puzzle. Mac grew more alert. She keyed in Emily's code from Base.

Denied.

She tried a variety of old passwords Emily had used for other equipment.

All *Denied.*

On a whim, she keyed in, "there's no sex in this book."

Denied.

Then, for no reason beyond hope, Mac entered her own Base code.

Accepted.

So Emily had expected her to get these logs, if anything happened. *She'd wanted Mac to access them.*

"What's going on, Em?" Mac whispered, fighting back the tears her body couldn't spare. She stared at the new display forming on her 'screen, at first making no sense of it.

These weren't personal logs. They were sub-teach data sets. Labeled "Dhryn."

Mac surveyed her preparations, one hand on the wall for stability. Her head tended to spin if she challenged it with quick movement. She'd blocked the bedroom door of her quarters on the *Pasunah* as best she could, using the mattresses and some crooked metal poles that had been standing in a corner. She'd found what she needed in the medical kit: *Subrecor*. Its tiny blue and white capsules were familiar to students of every age, allowing access to the subconscious learning centers. Those in the kit were larger than any Mac had seen before. *Perhaps spies had to learn more quickly.*

In this instance, she agreed, uneasy about making herself helpless while on the Dhryn ship. Even if it might be her only chance to be understood.

Mac took her imp, feeling for the dimples that said it was hers, and switched the 'screen to teachmode. In that setting, the display went from two dimensions to three, hovering over the mattress like a featureless, pink egg. She'd already queued Emily's data sets—all of them. She might not have this opportunity again.

For more reasons than the obvious, Mac assured herself.

One sip of water left in the bottle. One capsule. Mac swallowed both without hesitation, then lay down on the floor with her head within the "egg" of the display. She closed her eyelids, still seeing pink. The input would be delivered as EM wave fronts stimulating the optic nerves, shunted to the portions of the brain responsible for memory as well as those of language and comprehension.

All she had to do was relax and let the drug turn off cognition and will until the data sets had been dumped into her brain.

. . . *not unconscious, but at peace* . . . *not paralyzed, but detached* . . . Mac had never enjoyed being sub-taught, though many she knew did. Her father had told her teachers that she'd never liked taking a nap either.

The kaleidoscope began, flashes of light and color representing the data being transmitted. Normal . . . *familiar* . . .

. . . *Wrong* . . .

. . . *Pain!* . . . *Whips of fire* . . .

Mac writhed without movement; screamed without sound.

. . . Knives of ice . . .

Numbness spread from their tips, as though whole sections of her mind were being sliced and rebuilt.

As Mac plunged helplessly into an inner darkness, a cry built up until it finally burst, sending her into oblivion.

Emily!

How perverse, to be drowning when dying of thirst.

"Mac! Mac!"

She gasped and found air through the liquid spilling over her cheeks and neck. Her eyelids were too heavy to lift; Mac rolled her head toward her name. ". . . argle . . ." she said intelligently.

More liquid splashed against her face, filling her nose and mouth at the same time. Some landed on her eyes, making them easier to open as Mac sputtered, caught between swallowing and breathing. *Water?*

A gold-rimmed darkness filled her view, easing back at her startled cry to reveal a face that cleared to familiar when she blinked her eyes. *Brymn?*

"Ah, Mackenzie Winifred Elizabeth Wright Connor. You had me worried. You are such fragile beings."

"Brymn?" she managed to croak. Mac blinked again and focused beyond the anxious and silk-bedecked Dhryn. Same room. The door looked like it was in the wrong place.

He noticed her attention and gave a low hoot. *Amusement?* "You'd blocked the entrance, so I had to push a little harder. The *Pasunah* is a flimsy ship."

"Flimsy . . . not good word . . . about our transport," she managed to reply, starting to sit up. Four strong hands made it easier. "Thank you," Mac said, resting her shoulders against the mattress stack. She licked her lips.

"Do you require more?" Brymn lifted a bucket with one of his free hands, water sloshing over the top.

Famine or feast, Mac told herself, finding herself thoroughly damp from head to toe. Sure enough, a second, empty bucket stood nearby. He must have poured it over her. The tissues of her mouth were absorbing the moisture as gratefully as cracked soil soaked up rain. Mac licked her lips. "That's enough for the moment. Much better. Thank you. How did you know?"

Brymn sat, his mouth downturned. "I gave those in authority a list of Human requirements, Mac. They didn't understand these were essential for your survival. Instead, they regarded them as mere preferences, an imposition at a time when all aboard worry that your presence attracts the Ro. There was talk of leaving you behind."

Mac studied his face. "You don't mean at the way station, do you?"

"No, Mac."

Somehow, she found a smile. "If it wasn't for you, Brymn, I might have been dead soon anyway." Mac winced.

"Are you damaged?"

She shook her head, once and gently, then rubbed her temples. "No. Well, a few bruises. I seem to have a whale of a headache, though."

"I deactivated it for you." He held up her still dripping imp. "I trust it isn't damaged by water."

"Not and survive my line of work," she said absently, busy looking for the duplicate device. *Good, it was out of sight in the luggage— one less thing to explain.* Mac wondered when she'd become quite this paranoid.

She also wondered what could have been in that capsule instead of, or with, the Subrecor. Sub-teach might be boring and restrictive; it certainly wasn't painful. Her head felt swollen as well as sore. With all the flexibility and speed of someone five times her age, Mac rose to her feet, tugging her soaking wet clothes into some order. Her hair, as always, was hopeless. "How long until we reach the transect?"

Brymn blinked, one two. "Tomorrow. And may I compliment you on your word use? It is unexpectedly sophisticated this soon."

It was Mac's turn to blink. "It is?" She repeated the two words without sound, holding her fingers to her lips. Her mouth wasn't moving as it should be. "I'm speaking another language—I'm speaking Dhryn?" Then, the words "this soon" penetrated and her eyes shot to him. "You knew I would be. How?"

"You were using the subliminal teacher," he said matter-of-factly. "For what other purpose could it be than to accept Emily Mamani Sarmiento's gift?"

For a moment, Mac believed she was hallucinating under the drug, that she still lay on the floor, dehydrated and dying, only dreaming Brymn had stormed through the door to her rescue with buckets of odd-tasting water marked . . . she stared at them, reading "sanitation room" with no problem at all.

The words weren't in Instella or English. They were in some convoluted, narrow script that made perfect sense to her.

"Where did this water come from?" she heard someone ask.

Brymn waved four of his arms, two more helping him sit and the seventh, as always, tucked away. "Don't worry. No one will miss it. It is a regular product of our bodies. Most Dhryn don't care to know how it is removed from the ship."

She was drinking Dhryn urine. And was covered in it.

Somehow, that wasn't the shock it might have been.

"You knew Emily left me a sub-teach of the Dhryn language." *Possibly explaining the headache,* Mac told herself, given her brain had been forcibly retooled to think in—whatever this was. She couldn't tell if she was thinking in English, Instella, or blue marshmallow bits. Her temper started rising. "How did you know?"

"I helped her build it." Brymn paused. "It's the *oomling* tongue, so you do not have to worry about your disability with sound. All who hear you speak will adjust. It will be useful everywhere you find Dhryn. We thought you'd be pleased." He seemed a trifle offended. There was the hint of a pout to his mouth, which was almost cute in a giant seven-armed alien wearing sequined eyeliner.

Who had probably just saved her life, Mac reminded herself, although why was a question for later.

"You—" Mac found herself wanting to say "lied," but failed to find a word to utter that conveyed her meaning. Closest was "delayed information." She tried another tack. "Emily visited Dhryn colony worlds. Was she visiting you?"

"Yes, yes. Although my research keeps me moving about." His

brow ridges lowered. "Why, Mac, do you ask what you already know?"

"Because I didn't. Not until now. Not about Emily. Not about you knowing her. Not about the sub-teach."

A silence that could only be described as stunned. Mac used her elbows to support herself against the mattresses, feeling a certain sympathy for the big alien. "You didn't?" Brymn echoed finally.

Mac thought back to their conversations as a threesome. She'd been the one leading the conversations with Brymn; Emily had volunteered very little. Why would Brymn have thought to mention what he supposed she knew? As for any Human-like show of familiarity, for all Mac knew it wasn't polite for a Dhryn to rush up and greet an old "friend" in front of others.

Emily had only needed to keep quiet while Mac blundered on, never guessing, never suspecting.

Lies scabbed over lies.

She'd blamed herself for drawing Emily into danger. *Had it been the other way around?*

Emily had asked for forgiveness. Why became clearer every day.

"My humble apologies for any misunderstanding—"

"Don't worry, Brymn," Mac heard a new edge to her voice. "There are many things about my friend I'm learning as I go."

"I'll answer any questions, of course, Mackenzie Winifred Elizabeth Wright Connor, but if you will excuse a personal comment, you are beginning to sway from side to side in a most alarming manner."

He had a point. Mac steadied herself with an effort. "Pass me that piece of luggage, please." When the Dhryn put the larger case on the mattress within her reach, Mac opened it and pulled out the medical kit.

He crowded close, eyes dilated. "This is how you correct damage to the body?"

Mac tried to find better language equivalents for illness and injury, but failed. "There are some—chemicals with specific effects on the body. I'm looking for a . . . here it is." She ran her fingers over what she'd intended to use as a last recourse, then made her decision. Having Brymn here, and cooperative, was not a chance to waste by passing out. "This is what the students call Fastfix: a high concentration of nutrients and electrolytes—whatever's necessary to bring a depleted Human body chemistry closer to normal—plus a powerful stimulant of some sort. I should feel more energetic." *As opposed to about to fall on her face.* She held up the loaded syringe. "The needle is a way to deposit the chemicals under my skin, where they will do their work."

"Isn't that causing more damage?"

"Skin—Human skin closes after the needle is removed." It was hard enough steeling herself to shove the thing in her arm, without Brymn looming overhead, hands twitching as if he longed to dig into the medical kit for himself. Mac gritted her teeth and pressed the point into herself as hard as she could. The syringe was intended for novices, set to puncture only as deeply as required by the type of medicine loaded in its tube, and sterilizing on insertion and withdrawal, so she could use it again if necessary.

"Ow!" *Practice must help*, Mac thought ruefully, rubbing her arm. Mandy's boosters didn't hurt like this. Of course, the syringe in a field kit need not be as patient-friendly as those in a clinic. "See? Easy as can be." She put the syringe away, counting the number she had left. Two.

Everyone knew Fastfix was addictive with repeated use, the body adjusting its base level requirements upward and upward until a user became essentially nonfunctional without a fresh dose. Mac assumed the kit contained a safe number, then wondered why she'd believe that.

As she waited for the drug to work its magic, she noticed Brymn's nostrils had constricted to slits while he continued to examine the medical kit. *Well*, Mac thought, *she was soaked in Dhryn urine, or its equivalent.* "Why don't you take that in the other room while I change out of these clothes?" she offered.

"May I?"

"Sure. Just don't sample anything. I've no idea what the effect on your physiology would be." *Not to mention her supplies were finite.*

He picked up the kit as tenderly as if lifting an infant—*assuming the Dhryn had that type of parent/offspring interaction*, Mac reminded herself. "Are you sure you will not require my assistance?" he asked, looking torn between his fascination and a desire to help.

Mac smiled and touched his near arm. "I'll be fine, my friend. Thanks to you."

With Brymn safely preoccupied, Mac worked as quickly as she could. Although warm, the air in the *Pasunah* was so dry the dampness of her clothes evaporated rapidly, chilling her skin. She stripped, keeping only the waist pouch into which she put her imp, Kammie's note, and the Ministry envelope. She felt warmer immediately, though she couldn't be sure how much of that was an effect of the 'fix.

Mac tried not to think of the chemicals circulating in her blood. There was nothing she could do but hope she'd done the right thing. Abused by the spuds, dehydration, and Subrecor, her body systems were doubtless plotting their revenge. The 'fix was only postponing the inevitable crash.

Until then, Mac reminded herself, *she had things to learn and do.*

First. Despite its origin, and now perceptibly musty smell, Mac went to the bucket of mostly water and, cupping her hands, made herself drink slowly. *She'd had worse from a stream*, she judged, although part of her mind was already busy thinking of how best to distill any future contributions. As a precaution, she filled her water bottles and put them aside. Finally, she soaked her shirt and used it to scrub herself clean as best she could.

Better than the 'fix, Mac decided, feeling herself becoming more alert by the moment. She didn't bother trying to bring order to her hair, beyond wringing out the braid and tying it up again as tightly as she could. Dressing was quick, the luggage again providing a yellow shirt and pants. Mac began to wonder if the color had significance to the Dhryn.

Or, her hands paused on a fastener, *was it much simpler?* To Human eyes, the color would stand out, making her easier to find.

A concerned boom. "Are you all right, Mac?"

"Yes. I'm almost finished." Fearing the Dhryn's active curiosity,

Mac grabbed the other imp from the small case and crouched on the far side of the mattress stack from the now permanently open door.

Just as she was about to record what had happened, Mac closed her mouth and stared at the 'screen. She presumed she was thinking in English, because she could conceptualize terms for which there were no Dhryn equivalents. But, unlike her experience in switching from English to Instella, for all she knew, she was speaking English as well. Only the novel movements of her lips and tongue proved Dhryn, not English, was coming from her mouth.

How didn't matter—though the question was fascinating—what mattered was the consequence. What would Nik—or any Human—think of her voice suddenly switching to fluent Dhryn? Mac swallowed, feeling her pulse race. *Could they even understand her?* She had to believe so. The Dhryn had been members of the Interspecies Union long enough for actual translators to exist, although given how it had rewired her language center, Mac didn't recommend Dhryn for sub-teaching.

Brymn had told her they'd enter the Naralax Transect tomorrow. Mac checked the chronometer. Ship's night was only two hours away. Was tomorrow at midnight? How long did she have?

Mac started recording:

"This is Mackenzie Connor. I've been taught—" *how was that for skirting the issue?* "—to speak Dhryn, specifically what I'm told is the '*oomling*' language. I—can't speak anything else at the moment.

"We'll enter the transect tomorrow. I don't have an exact time. I've met Brymn at last. He brought me water, possibly saving my life."

Mac paused, then described, in clinical detail, her experiment with the cylinder food. She couldn't call it spuds, not in Dhryn.

"In case I am unable to add to this recording before it is sent," she went on, keeping her voice calm and even, "please tell my father I'm all right. Please tell Nik, if he—" *lives* stuck in Mac's throat, "—if he is available, that he was right. It wasn't just one." She hoped he'd understand she meant lies. *And Emily.*

Voices, low and angry, erupted from the other room. Mac

ended the recording and secured the imp in her waist pouch under her clothes, on the principle that while the aliens would be unlikely to note a new lump around her middle, they could very well separate her from her luggage, or confiscate it altogether. She glanced longingly at the handle with the beacon, but had no way to remove it.

Mac walked into a dispute. "What's going on?" she asked, eyeing three new Dhryn, dressed in the woven blue she'd come to associate with crew of the *Pasunah*, and Brymn, resplendent in his red and gold silks. They were gathered around the table, on which Brymn had placed her medical kit. Two of Brymn's right arms were protectively covering the flat box, his left set gesticulating wildly.

"There you are, Mackenzie Winifred Elizabeth Wright Connor," her ally/*lamisah* exclaimed. "Tell these Ones of No Useful Function they have no right to search your quarters!"

The "Ones of No Useful Function" didn't look at all pleased by this announcement. They were armed, as the Dhryn on the way station had been. One was missing a lower hand and he—she really did need to check on the appropriate pronoun—was the one who spoke. "Our apologies, Esteemed Passenger, but Dyn Rymn Nasai Ne has ordered that we confirm before transect to Dhryn space that you have brought nothing forbidden on board."

Mac guessed they'd already tried to check her belongings, only to find her luggage locked. "What is forbidden?" she asked.

He looked pointedly at her medical kit. Before Mac could even form a protest, Brymn hooted loudly and said: "Have you no education? These are Human cosmetics."

"Cosmetics," the other Dhryn repeated, eyes on Mac.

Cosmetics? Mac tried to keep a straight face. True, all the Dhryn were wearing some sort of artificial coloring on their faces, although compared to Brymn's bold use of adhesive sequins and chartreuse to outline his ridges, the crew's subtle mauves were next to invisible. Mac, on the other hand, was wearing healing scratches, a bruise or two, and that lovely pink of healing skin.

Still, this was the group who hadn't grasped that another species might have differing dietary requirements. "Don't all civilized beings take care of their appearance?" Mac demanded, swooping up the kit and closing the lid. She tucked it under one arm, gearing herself to defend it.

"Our mistake, Esteemed Passenger."

Something in Brymn's posture suggested the other was somehow insulting her. *By not using her name?* "What is your name?" Mac asked, making her voice as low and stern as she could.

"Tisle Ne is all of my name."

"Adequate," she sniffed. "I take the name Tisle Ne into my keeping. You have, I believe, mine? Mackenzie Winifred Elizabeth Wright Connor is all my name." Mac couldn't help emphasizing the *all*.

A rising bow, tall and seemingly sincere, from all three. "A prodigious name. I am most honored," said Tisle Ne. "I take the name Mackenzie Winifred Elizabeth Wright Connor into my keeping."

"Would you care to examine the rest of my belongings, Tisle Ne?" Mac asked, waving expansively at her bedroom. "Please. Be my guest."

Their noses constricted and the other two crew Dhryn wrapped their arms around their torsos. *A better-than-Human olfactory sense*, Mac decided, grinning inwardly. The mattress on the bedroom floor had soaked up most of the first bucket.

"If you would vouch that there is no forbidden technology in your luggage, Mackenzie Winifred Elizabeth Wright Connor, these Ones of No Useful Function can trouble someone else."

Mac had a feeling Brymn was pushing his luck with Tisle Ne, and hoped "her" Dhryn knew what he was doing. It seemed he did. "That would suffice," Tisle Ne said, his tiny lips pressed together after the words.

"You are most kind," Mac told him, doing her best to imitate their bow without tipping over backward. Then she considered the possibility of months with these beings and took what seemed the safest possible course. "Remind me what is forbidden, please. Then I can truthfully vouch I don't have such things."

"That which is not Dhryn." Flatly, and in every way a challenge.

Brymn bristled, arms rising and hands opening and closing. He put himself slightly in front of Mac, torso lowered so she could see right over his head. *Physical threat*, she judged it, clear and simple. *An unlikely knight.* "Then there can be nothing forbidden here,"

Brymn rumbled, "for the Progenitors have declared Mackenzie Winifred Elizabeth Wright Connor welcome."

Tisle Ne's body tipped forward to the same angle. "You overstep yourself, Academic."

The crystals of a lamp tinkled. Infrasound, Mac realized, feeling the rumble through the floor as well. Presumably they were growling at each other. It seemed she was to be inflicted with territorial posturing even here.

However, in this instance, Mac felt no desire to interfere. Instead, she took a discrete step back, then another, wishing her huge protector luck.

Chime!

Mac took a discreet step back, then another, wishing— She stopped dead, bewildered. She'd done this before.

What had just happened?

The Dhryn knew. Tisle Ne straightened. "It is too late for arguments now, Academic. We are home." With that, he turned and left the room, the other two Dhryn following behind.

Brymn clapped his hands together joyfully. "We are safe from the Ro, Mac!"

"That was—was—" Mac tried again. "The transect?"

"Yes, yes. From Human space, to no-space, to Dhryn space. It always amazes me. Does it not you?"

"You can get used to anything." *He didn't need to know it was her first time.* Mac headed for the viewport. "Which Dhryn space is this?" she threw over her shoulder. Nik had implied she was being taken to a world of only Dhryn. Her guidebook to the Naralax Transect had listed the Dhryn as having one home system, unnamed and closed to aliens. That might be it. But there was also a relatively modest colonization of forty-eight others whose exits were open to traffic from members of the Union. Some of those might also be only Dhryn. None had been identified in the guide as the Dhryn birthplace; Seung's text had emphasized that not every species shared such information willingly.

She couldn't tell from here. The view was disappointing. If Mac hadn't experienced that odd déjà vu, she would have assumed that fingernail-sized spot of yellow was the sun she'd always known.

Just as well. A different view might have taken what her mind knew and transferred it to a gut certainty. Light from that sun wouldn't reach Earth for millions of years—an impossible, unfathomable distance. There was only one way home—the Naralax Transect.

Of course, if the transects ever failed, her problem would be trivial on the grand scale. That failure would end the Interspecies Union. Every species would be separated by an impassable gulf; each isolated and alone, as they'd been before the Sinzi had made their discovery and shared it.

Mac had no doubt Earth would continue, as it had before the transects. She was equally sure every species would work to rebuild the system and eventually succeed—but would reach out to their own lost colonies first.

So, if the transects failed, Mackenzie Winifred Elizabeth Wright Connor would be trapped on the wrong side of this one until the end of her days, an alien curiosity for the Dhryn. Their token Human.

When she died, would they have her stuffed for a museum?

Mac's stomach, though empty, expressed sincere interest in emptying further.

Brymn came up beside her. "This system is called—" A vibration.

"A little deaf," she reminded him.

"Ah. My apologies." He paused, then his eyes brightened. "You may call the system: Haven. Any Dhryn would agree."

Haven? Mac shifted the medical kit from under her arm to in front of her chest and wrapped both arms around it. When she noticed, she shook her head at her own defensive reaction. It was only a name, like "Earth."

"What's it like, Haven?"

"There is one world—our destination. You may call it Haven as well."

She might not find her way around a star chart the way she could a salmon scale, but Mac knew enough to feel a shiver. "No other planets? Asteroids? Moons?"

"There were, but they were unsuitable for Dhryn," Brymn told her, his tone implying surprise at her question. "Such are hiding places for the Ro. The Progenitors do not tolerate them in our home system. We must protect our *oomlings*."

The home system. *Well, now she knew where she was*, Mac told herself. *Not in the guidebook*. But . . . *one sun, one world*. Feeling somewhat faint, a not surprising reaction to technology capable of sweeping an entire system clear of unwanted rock—and a species that would use it—Mac put the kit on the table and sank into a chair. "The Progenitors. Tell me about them."

Brymn sat as well, after checking the floor for debris. *She really should tidy the place*. "They are the future," he said.

Cryptic. *Or was it?* How much of what the Dhryn said should she take literally? "The Progenitors produce new generations of Dhryn?" Mac hazarded, too curious to worry about offense. "*Oomlings?*"

Brymn clapped his hands and smiled at her. "You see, Mackenzie Winifred Elizabeth Wright Connor? This is why I value your insights into living things. You understand us already."

"I wouldn't go that far," she said under her breath. Louder: "Are they your leaders as well?"

"Of course. The Progenitors are the future. Who else could guide us there?"

There had been an entire unit on alien reproduction in the xeno text, sure to titillate the most jaded students. All Mac recalled was having the familiar reaction that nature found the most ridiculous ways to propagate. Adding intelligence and culture to biology seemed only to compound the issue, not simplify it. "I don't know anything about Dhryn biology," Mac reminded him. Before he could be too helpful, she continued: "And now isn't the time, Brymn. It's Human biology—mine—that concerns me at this moment. I need a constant supply of water. Here, on the *Pasunah*, and on . . . Haven. Can you provide it?"

A debonair wave of three hands. "Water I can guarantee."

"Wonderful. How about distillation equipment?" At his puzzled frown, Mac shrugged. *Archaeologists*. "I'll manage that myself. Let me talk to a chemist. But food's another matter." She went to the table and picked up one of the remaining spuds. "Is this all you have available?"

Brymn took it from her. Bringing the cylinder almost to his lips, he deftly plucked the contents from the cylinder by the hairs, then sucked them into his mouth before they could ooze free with a slurp that could only be described as gleeful. "Ah. They listened to me about this one thing. I remembered your delight in the soufflé and thought you'd enjoy another sweet."

Dessert? Mac didn't know whether to laugh or pull her hair. "So there are other types of—wait." *That damned soufflé.* She had to know. "Did you put a message—anything—in the bag with the soufflé? Something for me?" Mac hesitated, then went on: "Or for Emily?"

Brymn startled her by tilting his head on its side; combined with his golden eyes, it gave him a striking resemblance to a perplexed owl, albeit a giant blue one. She had no idea that thick neck was so flexible. "Was I supposed to?" he asked.

"No. No, you weren't." She couldn't help a sigh of relief. *So much for Nik's suspicion.* Mac wasn't sure how real investigators went about their business, but her own research typically involved eliminating the obvious before the truth began to appear. *As now.*

More and more, she was coming to believe the truth was that Brymn had been used, by the Ministry, by Nik, and by Emily. He'd traveled far from his kind, alone, in search of answers—and been betrayed by those who were supposed to help him.

For two aliens, they had a remarkable amount in common.

"Are you sure, Mac?"

"Forget the soufflé. It isn't important. Brymn," she said, choosing her words with care, despite an urgency to *know* that had her hands clenched into fists. "What were you told happened on the way station?"

"Only that you were found without difficulty and brought to the *Pasunah* ahead of schedule." He pursed his lips and looked troubled. "Was there a problem? I admit to having felt some concern. There was unusual urgency about our departure and I wasn't to visit you until permission came from the Progenitors."

"Before I could leave with your people, the Ro found me," Mac told him. "I—" She stopped to let the big alien compose himself. The word "Ro" had started his limbs shaking.

"I—I—" Mucus trembled at the corners of Brymn's nostrils. "We wanted to keep you safe from them, Mac, as we would our *oomlings*. Were you—damaged?"

"No," Mac assured him. "I ran. Your people found me and brought me to safety. But . . ." She hesitated a heartbeat, unable to control her own trembling. *Great pair of brave adventurers they were.* Mac struggled to remain calm and detached. "Emily was there, Brymn."

"What? You saved her? You found her? Is she here?" He looked around wildly, as though Mac might have tucked Emily into a corner.

"Em didn't need saving. She wasn't a captive. On the way station, the Ro chased me to her. She asked me to come with her, with *them*. Nik—Nikolai Trojanowski, he was there. He tried to stop me. Then she—then Emily—shot him."

Her voice failed her. Vision went next, blurred behind tears. Mac waved her hands helplessly.

Then she was almost smothered in a six-armed hug. His uppermost shoulder was almost nonexistent, his skin was the wrong temperature and felt like rubber, and his ear ridge dug painfully into her head. None of this mattered.

She wasn't alone.

Mac let go and sobbed until she would have sunk to the floor without those arms for support.

- Portent -

THE DROP WIGGLED and slipped its way down the shaft, leaving a faint green stain behind, its reflection in the gleaming metal leading the way. New, the shaft, as was all the equipment collected here.

Another drop. Another. They drummed and chimed against every surface, mirrored as they struck and stuck.

As they wiggled and slipped downward.

Until there was no surface without its trails of green.

The drops met each other in antenna couplings and on access covers, at joints and along ductwork. They grew together in pools and spread until they tumbled over new edges. Wiggling and slipping downward again.

Seals began to bubble and ooze.

More drops fell, tracing the paths of the first.

A hatch cracked. The drops poured through, a hungry flood.

Giving those inside no time to scream.

17

APPROACH AND ANTICIPATION

"WHAT ARE YOU doing, Mackenzie Winifred Elizabeth Wright Connor?" boomed the voice from the doorway.

Mac, her nose touching her left knee, thought this should be obvious even to a Dhryn, but as she uncurled, she wheezed: "Exercising."

Brymn walked around her as she continued to lift her head and shoulders from the floor and lower them again. He leaned up and down with her, as if keeping her face in focus, arms carefully folded. "Is this pleasant?"

Surprised into a laugh, Mac gave up. She tucked her chest to her bent knees and wrapped her arms tightly around her legs, feeling the stretch in her lower back as she squeezed. "It's better than the alternative," she informed the alien. "Don't your muscles atrophy without regular use?"

"Muscles?"

Ah. "Don't you feel stiff if you remain still for prolonged amounts of time?"

A one/two blink. "Stiff? No. Bored, yes."

This was a hint, Mac knew. Now that Brymn was allowed to visit her on the *Pasunah*, he preferred to stay with her. She'd had to insist on privacy while she slept—or rather crashed—yesterday, a blissful oblivion that lasted about three and a half hours before he'd walked in to find out how much sleep a Human required and was she finished?

Not that she'd minded the company, but she'd been groggy enough to keep the conversation to safe, neutral topics like the difference between Coho and King salmon, Brymn countering with an enthused lecture on ways to detect technological remains, such as electronics, under layers of soil and rock.

At least he'd left once the lights went out.

With the perversity of an exhausted body granted peace, Mac hadn't been able to fall asleep right away. The 'fix had raced along her nerves for restless hours. Then, when she had dozed off . . .

She flushed, remembering she'd dreamed hazel eyes and a kiss . . . dreamed warm breath along her neck . . . dreamed more and more until the heat of her body had awakened her to lie gasping and alone. Staring at the ceiling, bright with the *Pasunah*'s version of morning instead of any hope of home, Mac had judged herself a pathetic fool. It hadn't been passion. It had been a release of tension between virtual strangers, perhaps attracted to one another, nothing more.

She'd known herself vulnerable at the same time. She hadn't been caught in such intense fantasy about anyone since Sam. *What did it say about a woman whose fantasy lovers died after a kiss?*

Not that she knew Nik was dead. *And he'd kissed her three times, all told.*

Which had occasioned more thoughts, waking ones, about a fantasy lover.

Which had led to exercise. Given the lack of cold showers.

Mac focused on Brymn. *Exercise surprised him?* She'd assumed the Dhryn had evolved under heavier gravity, but that in the *Pasunah* was set to what felt Earth normal. Through that thick skin, it was impossible to tell which was a lump of muscle and which of fat. "How often do you need to eat?" she asked, getting to her feet while ignoring the immediate growling of her stomach. She'd manage on nutrient bars until Haven. The *Pasunah*'s crew was unwilling or unable to understand her request for analytical equipment. After their dessert, Mac had no intention of further personal experimentation.

"As often as I am served food." Brymn had sat, looking content. *Semantics or biology?* "Don't you get hungry?"

"Adults do not become hungry until food is within reach. To feel otherwise would be impractical. *Oomlings* are preoccupied with the seeking of food—but they have little else to do."

Mac chuckled. "Reminds me of students." Which reminded her of less happy things, wiping the smile from her lips. *What was happening back home?*

Today, before they reached Haven—*who knew what access she'd have to Brymn there?*—it was time to discuss what they hadn't yesterday. Things less safe and definitely not neutral. "Did you get an answer about the com packet?" Mac asked, dropping into a chair. Intersystem communications traveled the transects as packets, signals collected at an entry, then cued to a particular exit. Regular and reliable. *If you had access to the result.*

"There have been several since we entered Haven," he told her, but his expression turned sober. *Not a good sign.* "I'm told they go directly to Haven for distribution and only those affecting the operation of this ship within the system would be shunted to us." Some of her disappointment must have shown, for he offered: "I can ask again."

Mac took a long drink of water—imagining it tasted better after being filtered through several layers of fabric—and shook her head. "Getting them faster won't change what's happened. And there's no guarantee a packet to Haven would carry news from Earth anyway."

No guarantee, although Mac couldn't help but hope. Maybe Nik or the Ministry would find a way to send her a message. Maybe they'd plant something in the news for her benefit, something broadcast so widely it offered no clues to the Ro, but might reassure her.

The more pragmatic part of her, the part that relied on Mac first and the universe second, disagreed. *Maybe they wouldn't bother.* After all, she was here now, where they'd wanted her to be. Mac wasn't naïve enough to imagine her peace of mind was important in the larger scheme of things, although being informed about other attacks by the Ro could be useful.

Or terrifying.

"Where is Haven in relation to the attacks?" she asked Brymn, very aware of the Ministry envelope in the waist pouch she now wore waking or sleeping. Then Mac realized her mistake and blushed. Distance was irrelevant, given the attacks were along the same transect.

But the Dhryn, perhaps as little attuned to the rigors of space travel as she, didn't think it a foolish question. "The reports coming from the Consulate were of locations farther and farther from here. More importantly, Mac, the Progenitors of Haven have recorded no attempt against Dhryn for several years. Here you are as safe as any *oomling*. It is why we came to this place, over all others. For you."

Farther from the recent attacks meant closer to the Chasm. Mac took another, more deliberate swallow. In a way, it helped that the invisible Ro were more frightening than any imagined ghouls could be. Nik—perhaps others at the Ministry—saw a connection. She didn't attempt to make one, not yet, not on so little evidence. Finding the Ro homeworld, learning how the Dhryn successfully resisted them, those were her goals. Fortunately, she had Brymn for help. "What's Haven like?"

"I have no idea." Her sequined, brightly garbed archaeologist actually beamed. "I haven't been to the Dhryn home as an adult, Mac. I was sent to a colony shortly after Freshening."

" 'Freshening?' " Mac echoed, her heart sinking. *Fine time to learn her local guide wasn't local.*

"My attempt at the real word." He boomed something that went lower and lower, then became silent. "Freshening is like your Human passage from child to functioning adult. Emily Mamani was kind enough to explain how this affects Human behavior. If you forgive me, it's quite bizarre, *Lamisah*. What is your word?"

"Puberty," Mac supplied. She fought back a rush of questions about Emily to focus on the more pressing issue. "Are you familiar at all with Haven or its Progenitors?"

"I've seen images, but I'm sure they fail to reveal the true beauty of the place. This is as much an adventure for me as for you, Mac! We will be tourists together and explore this magnificent world."

Had Brymn's distinctiveness misled her? To a Human, individual style was a mark of self-confidence. Was it to a Dhryn? To a

Human, being the first Dhryn to set foot on Earth imbued Brymn with importance. Did it to other Dhryn?

He published in non-Dhryn academic journals. He associated with Humans.

Was he even sane, by Dhryn standards?

Mac sank back in her chair. At least Brymn hadn't coauthored "Chasm Ghouls—They Exist and Speak to Me." *As far as she knew.*

He might be an alien crackpot, but he'd learned to read Human expressions. "Something's wrong, Mac. What did I say?"

There was no way to be tactful about it—and lives, including his, might be at stake. Mac straightened and looked Brymn in the eyes. "I don't mean to insult you, Brymn, and I'm grateful—more than I can say—for the help you've given me. But I need to know. What's your status among other Dhryn?"

He didn't appear offended, answering mildly: "I have not yet served in *grathnu*, Mac. But this is obvious."

Mac heard "*grathnu*" as a Dhryn word, as she did "*oomling*," implying her mind held no equivalents for it in English or Instella. "Let's not assume anything between us is obvious," she cautioned. "What's *grathnu*?"

Two pairs of hands danced in the air, making a convoluted pattern ending in a paired clap. "The creation of life. One must earn the honor. I have not yet accomplished enough in my life so 'Brymn' is all my name. But you. Surely you have served in *grathnu* abundantly, to become Mackenzie Winifred Elizabeth Wright Connor."

In Dhryn terms, she'd been listing her sexual exploits? Mac didn't simply blush. Her face burned. *Who else knew about this?*

Beyond doubt, Emily. Given five minutes alone with a new species, she'd ferret out such a thing and more.

Nik? He'd known about the importance of naming, back at the Field Station.

"Oh, dear," Mac said aloud.

"Is there a misunderstanding?" Before Mac could possibly form a reply to that, Brymn went on anxiously: "I hope not. Your accomplishments require other Dhryn to treat you with respect and do their best to accommodate your needs. Our time on Haven will be much less comfortable and productive if I have been mistaken."

"I'm not Dhryn—" Mac started, then paused, unsure what to say next that wouldn't land her in more trouble.

"Of course you are," Brymn said, eyes wide. *Surprise?* "Otherwise, you would not be here. Only that which is Dhryn may enter the home system."

Mac had prided herself on avoiding any major pitfalls during her conversations with Brymn. In fact, she'd begun to think herself rather talented at this interspecies' communication stuff.

She changed her mind.

"Define," Mac said carefully, "if you would, 'that which is Dhryn.' "

Brymn's eyeridges scowled exceedingly well. "Everyone knows that."

"Humor me, *Lamisah.*"

He looked uneasy, but obliged. "When it is necessary for the survival of *oomlings* to think about the Ro, it is clear that all which opposes the Ro is Dhryn. I reported your deeds and your bravery—which were far beyond my own. I gave them all of your names. The Progenitors named you *lamisah*, ally, to all Dhryn. You, Mackenzie Winifred Elizabeth Wright Connor, are Dhryn!" He became passionate throughout this little speech, rising to his feet, his eyes almost flashing with enthusiasm. Then, a little doubt crept into Brymn's expression. "Did I misunderstand?"

Mac crossed her fingers, a childhood habit. "No, no," she said briskly. "You were quite right. I was only checking that the Dhryn properly appreciated my—accomplishments. Thank you. You've set my mind at ease."

"I am most gratified." Brymn settled himself, then went on in a very matter-of-fact voice: "Of course, being Dhryn, you must adhere to Dhryn ways while on Haven." He shrugged all his shoulders as if admitting an impossibility, adding: "Or appear to do so. It's fortunate you learned to speak fluently before our arrival. Home system Dhryn would find it alarming to meet anyone who could not communicate properly." His little mouth assumed a grim line. "We don't want to alarm them."

Mac folded her hands on her lap and studied how the fingers laced together. Ten fingers, not six, twelve, or twenty-one. *How wide a gulf in comprehension did those numbers represent?* "You told Emily this, didn't you." It wasn't a question. It couldn't be, not when it answered too many. Why the sub-teach disguised as personal logs . . . why logs cued to Mac's password . . . why Emily Mamani chose to work with her and salmon instead of studying manatees . . .

Why they'd become friends.

Mac watched her knuckles turn white.

Promise to forgive me, Mac.

As much as the Ministry and Nikolai Trojanowski had taken advantage of events to get Mac here, where no Human had been, Emily Mamani and her "allies" had wanted her here even more, and planned for years to achieve it.

Why?

"It's time you told me everything, Brymn," Mac said in a tone that expected complete and total compliance. "Starting with where you met Emily. And how."

It had been a classic Emily pickup: transit station, spots a likely guy waiting and looking bored, asks directions to somewhere very close by, a place that turns out to be a cozy bar with Emily's favorite music filling the dance floor. A playful night ensues. Mac found it eerie, hearing about something—someone—so familiar through the interpretation of a stranger.

Oh, there was a modification or two. Brymn had already been in a cozy bar, waiting for a skim ride out to an archaeological dig on Renold 20. He'd been pleasantly surprised to be approached by a Human of culture and education, even more surprised when she'd asked directions to the same dig. Another scholar, he'd thought. A common interest.

Interest? With a sour taste in her mouth, Mac thought of Emily falling asleep in her office. Exhaustion? More likely the boredom of hours pretending to read what she'd already read.

Their first meeting had taken place two years *before* Emily applied to Norcoast.

Brymn, used to being alone, had been easy to charm. He'd seen it as a mutual regard and growing friendship. Mac, hearing the steps Emily took to win his confidence, gain access to his work, saw it as something else.

Premeditation.

Emily had chosen Brymn as her target—a Dhryn crazy enough to work on his own, far from his kind. Mac wondered if any Dhryn would have done, but it didn't matter. Here was one ripe for the taking.

Not that Mac let her thoughts interrupt Brymn's recital. She let him keep talking, taking sips from her water bottle, eventually pulling up her knees so she could watch him over the top of that barrier. He needed no encouragement to continue; a natural story-teller who must rarely have an audience. Emily's rapt attention must have been intoxicating.

Brymn and Emily made plans to meet in a few months and work together. She would help Brymn with his work and teach him English so he could directly access the material of those Human researchers who didn't publish in Instella. Meanwhile she was building a dictionary of Dhryn and wished to test terms and grammar on him.

His work. Mac knew it from her readings, but it was clearer described this way, filled with the fervor academic writing leached away. The Dhryn was hunting through the past of space-faring species, looking for evidence of the so-called Moment—the date of the destruction of the worlds within the Chasm. His hypothesis? That there had been transects connecting these worlds, and these had failed during the same catastrophe, stranding species where they hadn't evolved.

No one doubted there had been transects—or the technology to develop them—before. The discovery by the Sinzi proved at least the beginnings had been around for over three thousand standard years. But had such a network existed within the Chasm and beyond? Could all of those transects have failed at a single point in time? If so, was that the cause of the disaster that had befallen all of those worlds?

Even "Chasm Ghouls—They Exist and Speak to Me" devoted

less than a footnote to the idea. Despite his years of searching, Brymn had yet to find a single shred of evidence.

That didn't mean he was wrong, Mac thought.

Her project. Emily had been coy, but eventually Brymn had convinced her—*hah!*—to admit they shared a related goal. She hoped to prove the existence of the Survivors, an entire species rumored to have escaped the Chasm. Legend painted the Survivors with everything from advanced technology to a godlike beauty no matter your physical preference. Emily's expectations were simpler. If such existed, they might be able to explain the mystery of the Chasm once and for all.

Were the Survivors the Ro? Had Emily found them, or they her? Regardless, Mac had a question of her own. *Had they escaped the annihilation of life on those hundreds of worlds—or been its cause?*

Were they starting again?

Perhaps Emily would have chosen to work with manatees and travel to the Dhryn home system herself—*they might never have met*—but for a single consequence of teaching Brymn English. Among the obscure publications in that language, he discovered a series by that curiosity to Dhryn, a biologist. Not any biologist, but one working on how species survived catastrophic events. He expressed the desire to meet this scientist.

It took Mac a moment to realize he was talking about her work. *About her.*

She could only imagine what had gone through Emily's mind then. Why was the Dhryn interested in an obscure salmon researcher's work? Was this a problem, or an opportunity?

Brymn went on, blithely unaware of the impact of his retelling of events on his audience, liberally adding mentions of the weather at each dig and other nonessentials. Mac lowered her chin to one knee, her arms wrapped again around her legs, but this time to hold herself in, not to stretch.

Not surprisingly to anyone who knew her, Emily had chosen to consider Brymn's interest an opportunity. She confessed to being a biologist and more. She claimed to be already working with the esteemed Dr. Connor. What a happy coincidence! Brymn had been delighted, especially when Emily promised to forward any new work from Dr. Connor directly to him, so he could keep up with her—their—findings.

Mac's head lifted, nostrils widening like those of a startled doe searching for a hidden predator. She couldn't help but remember her joy at finding Dr. Mamani's application on her 'screen, how she'd rushed to complete the year's budget in order to clear funds to bring the highly reputed scientist to Norcoast, even how they'd all pitched in to give the place a quick cleaning, in case appearances would make a difference.

It's never one lie.

Forgive me.

Brymn remained oblivious, words flooding out of him now to tell her how anxiously he'd waited to receive each transmission, how honored he'd been to hold raw data and see her analysis taking shape, how enthralled by each leap to a new experiment . . . then, finally, the opportunity of a lifetime. The Interspecies Union had quietly alerted the authorities of member species along the Naralax Transect to what it called "a mysterious threat," asking for investigators with knowledge of the Chasm to cooperate. When the Progenitors searched for such a Dhryn, there was only one choice: Brymn.

And Brymn chose to work with Humans, so he could finally meet . . .

"You, Mackenzie Winifred Elizabeth Wright Connor!" he finished, holding four arms toward her. "Despite all that has happened, meeting you has been the most joyous and significant moment in my life. For this reason, I had the name of Emily Mamani Sarmiento recorded within the vault of my Progenitors, in gratitude for having made our meeting possible." When Mac didn't immediately reply, the Dhryn wrapped his arms around his middle and looked worried. "Are you not pleased we met?"

"I could wish for better circumstances," she said honestly. "But not a better companion," this with a depth of emotion that surprised her. *She was,* Mac scolded herself, *anthropomorphizing.*

Still, his sudden smile implied the Dhryn could understand and reciprocate what was, to Mac, a Human feeling. "We are *lamisah,* Mac, and friends. As is Emily. Do not let yourself worry. I am sure she will be able to explain what happened on the way station. She will be well—we will find her."

Perilous thing, friendship. Mac rubbed her chin on her knee, debating which of Brymn's illusions to shatter first. "I don't believe Emily needs our help, Brymn."

"What? How can you, her friend, say this?" Outrage, in a Dhryn, appeared to involve standing, lowering the torso angle, and arm waving. Brymn did all three before blurting out: "She was taken by violence from her sleep! I saw the reports, the images. There was fluid over the walls—her fluid! The Ro—" His limbs trembled. "The Ro—"

"Oh, I believe they took her," Mac agreed miserably, hugging her legs. "But the signs of a struggle can be faked. Humans can lose a fair amount of fluid—blood—without permanent damage. Broken furniture?" She nodded at the pile in one corner, where she'd collected the remnants of her assault on the door. "Nothing easier."

"But why make it look—? I don't understand."

"I don't have answers, Brymn. For what good a guess will do? Emily knew I'd never willingly leave Earth. For some reason, she—and others—wanted me to do just that. Badly enough to fake her own kidnapping. Badly enough that the dictionary she built with your help was to make a sub-teach of your language—for me. Badly enough that they made it seem impossible for me to be safe anywhere but here. In the Dhryn home system."

"A Human working with the Ro? Impossible!"

Mac raised a brow. "I'm working with a Dhryn."

"Even if it could be—why? With apologies, Mac, you make no sense. Why would they do all this to force you here, the one place you're safe from them?"

"That's the question, isn't it?" Mac tucked her chin back on her knee.

Brymn sat in front of her, one three-fingered hand covering hers. "What if you're wrong about Emily?"

"Then I'll owe her a beer. More likely ten," Mac promised. "But there's too much at stake, Brymn, for us to ignore the evidence. Emily wasn't working with me before you told her of your interest in my research. She lied to you. Emily knew you—she'd prepared the sub-teach in your language before arriving at Base this year, before the Union knew there was an emergency. She lied to me."

"She must have had good reason."

The alien's staunch defense of Emily—*so like her own, to Nik and to herself*—wasn't making this any easier. "At this point," Mac decided, "I don't care about her reasons. We need to be careful. Why am I here? Why does it suit Emily, and perhaps the Ro, to have me on Haven? Something's going on, Brymn."

He took his hand away. "We must not trouble the Progenitors with this—supposition, Mac. They would not react well. Not well at all."

Mac studied Brymn's face, seeing the fear there. Reluctantly, she nodded. "When it comes to Dhryn, I must rely on your judgment."

As he nodded, seeming more relaxed, Mac caught her reflection wavering within figure eight pupils, surrounded by gold. What did he see, when he looked at her? What did he think, feel? How could she begin to fathom what had no connection to her flesh?

How could she know if he lied?

18

REGULATIONS AND ROUTINE

M AC HAD HAD her preconceptions of other worlds. They'd all be Earths, of a sort, perhaps with different shapes to their treetops or unusual birds in their skies. She'd even imagined some sort of alien marketplace, filled with otherworldly scents and sounds. But there would be treetops, birds, and skies.

Until she was brought to Haven, home of the Dhryn, enclave of Progenitors, and home to only three forms of life: cultured fungi, the Dhryn . . .

And one *Homo sapiens.*

As for a sky?

She'd never complain about the rain at Base again, Mac vowed, staring out her window. It hadn't stopped pouring since their arrival. Four days without variation, without thunder, lightning, or wind, just this heavy, monsoonlike drenching. Handy for distilling, but she'd filled every container Brymn had obtained for her by the end of day one.

Be grateful, she reminded herself.

Water and food. On her second day, Mac had received a portable analytical scanner to rival any at Base. In fact, it had been exactly the same model Kammie had ordered last year for her lab. Mac couldn't recall the species of manufacture, just the price tag. Seemed the Dhryn, like many Humans, obtained technology "off the shelf." They'd even adopted the habit of having tiny vidbots along their streets and hallways, in such numbers that they seemed more like swarms of small round insects than machines. Useless against the Ro, but perhaps it reassured the average Dhryn to know there were watchers on their streets. Mac did her best to ignore them.

After testing various Dhryn offerings other than spuds, while arguing with her stomach that it could exist empty a while longer, Mac had succeeded in finding several preparations that contained nutrients her body needed, without toxins to cause less happy results. Although the food ranged from bland to eye-watering heat in taste, and lack of texture was definitely a Dhryn issue, she had the start of a diet to live by.

For which she was also grateful, Mac thought, watching rain wall the world. *For however long it took.*

Day, night, weeks. Like most sentient species in the IU, the Dhryn divided and tracked time. Mac had entertained herself by working out Earth equivalents. A twenty-seven hour rotation, with eight of that being night—summer, perhaps? A more northern latitude?

What did it matter on a one-species' world?

Not that the Dhryn allowed the dark outside their rooms. From what Mac could see from her window and terrace, the city was illuminated throughout the night, buildings and concourses aglow to extend the dull light of Haven's day. A city that extended from pole-to-pole, she'd been told. *Perhaps the light did as well.*

Brymn had professed himself in awe of this place. While Mac had tested tray after tray of sculptured, vividly colored fungal concoctions—most with hair—he'd explained how the rain was deliberate, part of an ongoing program to remove an ocean from the other hemisphere by filling artificial underground reservoirs here. The lighting? A convenience for a species that needed very little sleep and prided itself on productivity. He'd assured her Dhryn colonies were also highly developed and civilized, with full weather control, of course. Then he'd looked wistful. Very few colonies could approach the population and energy of the home system. All had to rely on the home system for *oomlings*.

None had Progenitors of their own.

Because of the Ro.

She might be safe from them here. At the thought, Mac closed the shutter, a process that took two hands and force. Doors were hinged as well, as if Dhryn didn't waste power on what could be slammed by six strong arms. Quaint, until the second day of struggling with what could have been controlled by civilized wall plates.

Where was Brymn? He'd come faithfully the first three days, though his visits were shorter each time. Mac presumed his duties elsewhere were increasing. But he hadn't come or sent word since. All she knew was that he'd warned her not to leave her apartment, that she had to wait for the Progenitors' permission.

Mac adjusted a lamp, then fussed the bright gold and red tablecloth into a straighter alignment, wondering why she bothered. Her hosts had provided generous accommodations for her, but the furnishings from the *Pasunah* looked lost and out of place in rooms designed for Dhryn, the perpendicular angles of chairs and tables at war with walls that tilted in—or out—and asymmetrical window frames placed at differing heights. Lining up the tablecloth only fueled the discord.

The furniture was fine, Mac told herself. *She was fine.*

There wasn't much choice in attitude for either.

The Dhryn, at least in this area, lived in apartments which appeared to be built on top of preexisting ones. Mac's was the highest on an elongated pyramid, with access to one of a spiral of round private terraces that stuck out like so many tongues. She'd braved the rain out there more than once to try and make out the details of her surroundings. At best, she'd gained a vague impression of rounded rooftops and irregular shapes, punctuated by straight towers. A great deal of traffic flew overhead, at all hours; not skims, but vehicles at once longer and sleeker. Silent and grouped, they were like so many schools of fish passing through the gray ocean of cloud.

Entertaining as it was to stare at the undersides of rapidly moving fliers, Mac wasn't on the terrace often. Constant and straight down, Haven's rain was—different—from the one she'd grumble happily about back home. This rain was sharper, harder, as if falling from a greater height. Drops stung any exposed Human skin, though they probably felt fine to a Dhryn.

Not that Dhryn liked being wet, but they appeared capable of cheerful endurance when necessary. On the way from the space-port, Mac had glimpsed walkways filled with pedestrians, each clutching two, four, or six brilliantly colored umbrellas. The effect, despite the dim light, was as if giant blue-stemmed bouquets with rain-bent petals paraded between every building. *Not that there were living flowers here.*

Mac tugged the tablecloth askew again, knowing exactly what was the matter with her. She was so far beyond homesick, so of-fended by this place, it amazed her she still bothered to breathe.

The rain. *It didn't matter.* There was no soil to turn to fragrant mud, no vegetation to grow lush and wild, no overflowing rivers to tempt fish into flooded meadows. Here, the rain bounced against stone, metal, umbrellas, and other lifeless things, collecting in downspouts and gutterways to be carried underground before it could disturb the tidy Dhryn.

She couldn't bear to think of the ocean about to disappear, being literally flushed away. *It didn't matter.*

There was no struggle here, no change, no surging, inconven-ient mess of living things competing for a future. Everything Mac knew, everything she loved. *Didn't matter.*

Mac refused to judge, knowing other species lived on worlds like this, where technology took the place of ecosystem. Even within Sol System, Humans had colonized sterile moons, many professing to prefer such a life.

She didn't judge. But, as each waking hour passed, she felt a lit-tle of herself slip away.

Did it matter?

"Maudlin Mac. Melancholy Mac. Oh, hell, let's go straight to the Mighty Melodramatic Mac, why don't we?" In sudden fury, Mac swept up the tablecloth and draped it over her head. She spun around and around, the fabric a maelstrom of red and gold, her hands slapping furniture to keep herself upright. "The Famous Dr. Mac—" *slap,* "—taking full advantage of her unprecedented access to a unique species and culture—" *slap, slap,* "—discovers her true calling! Self-pity!" The final *slap* sent a chair tumbling backward and Mac lost her balance, falling after it. The tablecloth drifted to the floor.

"Is this typical Human behavior, or are you mad?"

Mac scrambled to her feet. "You aren't Brymn," she blurted at the Dhryn standing in front of her.

"Are Humans incapable of recognizing individuals?" the being asked reasonably.

"Sorry." Mac blinked, belatedly taking in details. This Dhryn was smaller than others she'd met, intact, and had adorned his face with chubby lime and pink curlicues that matched the bands of cloth wrapped around his middle. His hands were burdened with several boxes and his expression was frankly curious. "Are those for me?" she ventured.

"Do Humans make assumptions?"

For some reason, Mac found herself grinning. "All the time. We can recognize individuals. And yes, all Humans probably spin at some point. Mackenzie Winifred Elizabeth Wright Connor is all my name."

"Oh! Truly magnificent!" A bow that faltered as the Dhryn realized he couldn't clap with his hands full. He settled for tapping four of his boxes together. Mac hoped there was nothing fragile inside. "I take the name Mackenzie Winifred Elizabeth Wright Connor into my keeping. Ceth is all my name."

"I take the name Ceth into my keeping. A privilege," Mac said, tipping back her head and offering her own clap. "May I ask why you are in my apartment, if those aren't my packages?"

"You invited me. These are for the esteemed Academic."

"Brymn?"

Ceth shuffled impatiently from foot to foot. "He is waiting."

Mac opened her mouth to say she hadn't seen Brymn for over a day, when a clatter announced her kitchen was occupied. Wordlessly, she pointed in that direction, then followed the small Dhryn.

Her apartment had four rooms, designated in Dhryn-fashion by function. The one with a desk, other furnishings, and a door to the terrace, her place of work. *Where she spun with tablecloths.* The one with luggage, bed, and shower—which had thoughtfully been re-

placed with a sonic variety safe for Human skin—her place of recu-
peration. *Where she longed for water and dreams that didn't include
fantasies about a man who was probably dead.* An entranceway, with
display screens she'd yet to figure out. Her place of greetings. *Obviously not locked.*

And a kitchen, as well as, oddly to a Human, the biological accommodation, called the place of refreshment. *Where she practiced
her chemistry.*

It seemed she wasn't the only one. "You aren't Brymn either," Mac
informed the Dhryn busy emptying the storage unit where she kept
her Human-suited foods. This one wore bands of white and gold, not
silk but something woven. He looked up as they entered, a packet
Mac recognized in one hand. His gold-irised eyes blinked one/two
beneath ridges painted silver. "And that," Mac said, "is my supper."

"Ah!" Looking at the packet as if it was now more interesting,
the new Dhryn punctured it with a sharp, hooklike object carried
in a left hand. "And why is this your supper?" he demanded as he
read some type of display on the object. A scanner, she presumed.
"Why not—" and he rattled off a list of food names that meant
nothing to Mac.

"Because— What are you doing in my kitchen?"

"Have you found anything peculiar yet?" A third Dhryn, also in
gold and white, squeezed into the narrow space—just missing
Mac's toes. "I made a wager with Inemyn Te."

"I have the items you requested, Esteemed Academics," Ceth
announced, adding to the confusion as he put his boxes on top of
Mac's precious analyzer.

"STOP!"

The three Dhryn paused to look at Mac. She coughed and said
more politely. "Who are you and why are you here?"

"I am Ceth—"

"I know who you are. These others?"

Despite the facial dissimilarities, all three gave her a look of thoroughly offended dignity as plain as any Mac had seen displayed by
Charles Mudge III. She drew herself as tall as possible—unwilling
to risk leaning forward in threat display to beings three times her
mass and of unknown motive—and glared. "I am Mackenzie

Winifred Elizabeth Wright Connor and these are the quarters I was provided by your Progenitors. I demand an explanation for this—this intrusion!"

"But you invited us, Mackenzie Winifred Elizabeth Wright Connor," the one with her supper dangling from a hook said quizzically. "We are researchers interested in developing new presentations of—" he lifted the hook, "—food. You requested equipment and samples from us."

"And I brought more," Ceth volunteered.

The other Dhryn spoke up, shaking the room before uttering what Mac could hear. "—curiosity is not welcome? If so, your entry misled us."

It seemed she had an interspecies' incident brewing in her own kitchen. Had to be some kind of record—not that Mac was happy about it. "I am honored by your presence," she said cautiously, on the assumption it was a safe enough phrase.

"Ah! You have met the Esteemed Academics!" This voice she knew. Mac turned with relief to see Brymn's smiling face. He couldn't fit into the kitchen unless she climbed on the lid of the accommodation, something Mac didn't want to attempt in a room filled with so many swinging arms. Mind you, both Academics were missing at least one hand. *Grathnu*, she reminded herself. *Great. Rank.* Even more like dealing with an Oversight Committee.

"These are the individuals who made sure you had what you requested, Mackenzie Winifred Elizabeth Wright Connor," Brymn continued glibly. "Did I not tell you they would want to examine the results of your investigation?"

Mac scowled at Brymn to let him know he most certainly hadn't, then smiled at the scientists stuffed into her kitchen. "A moment of confusion," she said graciously. "How may I assist your esteemed selves?"

She only hoped they didn't want to examine her as well as her diet.

Much later, Mac dropped into the most comfortable of her chairs and looked at Brymn. "Well, that was fun."

"Sarcasm or truth?"

She put her feet up on another chair and grinned. "A bit of both." The two scientists had been charmingly fascinated by her food requirements, if a little inclined to doubt her analyses until they'd repeated each and every one for themselves. *Some things*, Mac had concluded with satisfaction, *crossed species' barriers with no trouble at all*. They'd left intrigued with the challenge of finding more fungal preparations she would prefer.

The notion of Mac having a functionally distinct digestive system was carefully avoided by all parties.

"I am gratified. You look more as you did, *Lamisah*. If you don't mind a personal observation."

Mac eyed the Dhryn. She did feel unexpectedly at peace. "And you, my dear Brymn, are becoming much too good at reading Humans."

He didn't look worried. "It is not as difficult as I once thought."

"I could say the same."

Two more Dhryn wandered into the room, exchanged the briefest of bows with Brymn, then wandered out again. Mac watched them leave and sighed. "I guess this is going to happen all the time."

"Of course not. You keep inviting them."

"I—I do not."

"You do, you know." Brymn hooted.

Mac narrowed her eyes. "I'll bite. What aren't you telling me?"

He seemed overcome with laughter, rocking back and forth, hooting softly to himself all the while.

She pretended to throw something at him. "What's going on?"

"Ah. I see there remains a gap in your excellent knowledge of Dhryn." Another hoot. "Come with me, *Lamisah*."

Brymn wouldn't explain until they stood in her place of greetings, nothing more than an almost square room forming the entrance to her apartment. It was marked by a door to the large common hallway that faced an inner wall decorated with a painting; the remaining walls opened into arches that led into her place of work and her kitchen. Mac waited, more or less patiently, for the big alien to get to the point.

"This is your problem." Brymn lifted his three left arms to the display in her hall, a rendering of a selection of fungal food items.

"It's a painting," Mac said dubiously. "I found the display controls yesterday." She didn't bother mentioning that she'd gone through about fifty choices before finally settling on what looked recognizable and hopefully harmless.

"Of course it's a painting. It is also an invitation. By exhibiting food in your entry, you elicit the reaction of hunger and the expectation of a social gathering. There is a pronounced subtext of professional discourse which doubtless excited the Esteemed Academics beyond restraint. Let us hope your dispute with them over the analysis did not leave a bad taste." He hooted at his own joke.

Mac looked at the painting, then at Brymn, then back at the painting. "You're saying that this is why I have strange Dhryn roaming through my apartment? Because I changed the display?"

He smiled. "Insightful as always, my *lamisah*."

"Then why didn't any walk in before today?"

"Ah." Brymn tapped the wall below the painting and a tiny door opened to reveal a now-familiar control. "This is the catalog that controls your greeting display," he explained, holding up the silver oval to activate a shimmering screen on the wall, similar to that displayed on a Dhryn reading tablet. "There. This is what I left when I was here." Now a plain green cube slowly rotated in the air before the wall. As it spun, one side flashed blue.

Mac made a face. "I know. That's why I changed it."

"Leading to your visitors. This is a request for privacy. No Dhryn would enter. The Human equivalent—" Brymn gave it thought, then looked smug. "An agenda posted on a door. Home system Dhryn expect you to display a meaningful work of art."

"Then you'd better leave me an all-purpose 'ignorant Human' piece," Mac said. "I don't know anything about art beyond my own reaction to it. And that goes for Human as well as Dhryn."

A quieter but no less amused *hoot*. "Neither do most Dhryn. Don't worry, Mac. The catalog is organized by conversational topic. Once I show you how to search it, you will have no trouble conveying your meaning to potential visitors." Brymn paused, then made another selection. "However, knowing you are deaf, I'm switching off the audio art option just in case."

Brymn had brought his company—and put an end to the invasion of Mac's apartment—but no real news. The situation remained unchanged. The Progenitors had granted Mac sanctuary; they had yet to decide if they'd grant her access to anything outside of it. The Dhryn delivered this with a wary look, as if Mac was likely to explode. Another day, she might have. Today, she simply nodded and questioned her *lamisah* on protocol and manners, in case any more home system Dhryn came to visit.

Whether her earlier mood had been caused by coming off the Fastfix, the change in food, or real homesickness—or all three—Mac found herself finally jolted back into the mind-set that kept her happily busy at the most inhospitable field stations. *The work.* She made Brymn promise to bring more information the next day.

Not that she needed to wait, Mac thought triumphantly. *Had the Dhryn realized what a tool they'd left her?*

She almost pushed Brymn out the door. The moment he was gone, she dragged a chair into the place of greetings and pulled out her imp. *The one that would transmit her data.*

Focus, Mac, she told herself. The choice of art was determined by the topic about to be discussed between host and visitor, or visitors. Brymn claimed it inspired and focused the conversation, something Mac thought could be very useful at Norcoast before funding meetings. Here, Mac deemed it a stratagem to cope with a very dense population. Brymn had told her that his kind liked being close together. "A Dhryn is with other Dhryn or he is not," had been the phrase of the moment. But even if they enjoyed close proximity, Mac thought, it must help to have a mutually understood protocol.

Brymn had shown her how to use the catalog. Many pieces were abstract, listed by mood as well as topic. *Perfect.* She didn't have to know what a Dhryn thought of what he saw for her purpose.

Mac began flipping through the cataloged pieces at random,

recording her emotional response to each on her imp. After a while, the place of greetings filled with semiconscious whistling as she became more and more absorbed. The chair was abandoned for the floor, then the floor for the chair.

Biological necessity interrupted, so while Mac was in the kitchen she grabbed a packet and water bottle. Back to work. Supper was a blue stick that reminded Mac of chalk, washed down with tepid water. The Dhryn didn't refrigerate.

Globes, bubbles, spheres of all sorts. Lines and shadow plays. Harsh geometrics. Mac gave each equal consideration, sometimes wincing at the colors, sometimes struck by beauty that perhaps crossed species' lines. Or her pleasure misunderstood the artist.

That was the point.

She stopped when her eyes could no longer focus. After rinsing her head with water, Mac returned. This time, she recorded the expected Dhryn response to each abstract as claimed by the catalog. The entries were filled with florid and extravagant language—*what was it about describing the impact of art?*—so Mac was careful to only use those that referred specifically to reactions. There were colors listed by the catalog for which her mind had no English equivalents, implying the Dhryn saw into the ultraviolet end of the spectrum. Mac avoided those works of art as well.

Mac carried her results to her workplace, noting absently that it was night. Leaning her elbows on the desk, she watched the flickering display as her imp took her responses and compared them to the Dhryn's.

Ah. Reasonable congruence over which shapes, colors, and tones induced feelings of peace, contentment, or harmony in both Dhryn and herself.

Mac's fingers drew through the display, bringing up a troubling divergence when the emotions involved alarm, discomfort, or rage.

Turquoise, for instance, was the dominant shade in images the catalog listed as eliciting anxiety and anger. Black was not an option before civil conversation, sure to incite violence. And yellow?

"Well, well." Mac tilted her chair back, shaking her head in disbelief. Apparently, the brighter hues were guaranteed to set one's limbs trembling with fear. The catalog recommended its use only for hazardous material storage.

So naturally, her entire wardrobe was yellow.

No wonder the poor Dhryn tended to be agitated around her. Mac couldn't begin to guess what *Pasunah*'s captain and crew must have thought.

"Another great first impression, Em." Mac's chuckle came out tired, but real. "Drenching myself and my quarters in their urine couldn't have helped."

A fine way to introduce humanity to the home system.

Mac took the time to make a recording for the folks back home, viewing this as the least she could do for Haven's future Human visitors.

Mind you, she'd love to see the faces of those who'd done her shopping.

The next day, Mac enlisted the aid of the Esteemed Academics to make her wardrobe more suitable, envisioned panicked crowds should she walk about clad in yellow. They'd accepted the challenge with alacrity, fascinated by the various fabrics of her clothes.

She then spent two long and anxious days wrapped in a tablecloth, reading reports and hoping for the best. Eventually, Mac found herself nursing the increasingly faint hope the Dhryn had understood she expected her clothing back.

She needn't have feared. The Dhryn managed the improbable. Even her raincoat, a thoughtful inclusion in her luggage, was returned a different, more Dhryn-friendly color.

Colors.

Mac had put on the quietest of her improved wardrobe and been unsure whether to laugh or tear at her hair. Bold stripes of purple, red, blue, white, and lime-green had raced around her middle, lined both arms, and plunged to her feet. *She'd just needed a pair of oversized shoes and a red nose.*

"*Lamisah.* You look wonderful." Brymn had applauded her new look, but Mac held dire suspicions that her Dhryn's taste didn't match that of anyone else on this world. She tried not to believe the Esteemed Academics had done their best to turn her into either a laughingstock or a target.

Clothing issues aside, over the following week, Mac discovered that Brymn hadn't exaggerated the importance of her greeting hall. Her *lamisah* might be exceedingly casual in his approach to such matters, as Dhryn went, but home system individuals were only truly comfortable with her after the ritual exchange of names. Better still were greetings that included a lengthy admiration of whatever art was on display—a decided inconvenience, since Mac hardly knew what to admire. Fortunately the same works were available to all Dhryn, so her visitors came equipped with compliments no matter what she'd picked.

Mac wasn't at all surprised when her increasing grasp of things Dhryn was matched by a decrease in the number of her visitors. The novelty factor she provided by simply existing must have worn off. Even the Esteemed Academics had realized she had no startling Human insights into their subject. Food, tablets, and other supplies were delivered without requiring a formal greeting. Of course, Mac, not realizing this for the first while, had done her utmost to prove she knew the protocol and insisted on bringing the delivery beings into her place of greetings to admire art. As a result, those bringing deliveries now left them outside her door, preferring to knock, then run.

Brymn found it amusing, though he still didn't bother with any ceremony with her. As the days passed, however, her constant companion had become less so. Soon, he was coming only once each morning to deliver more reading material. Not even offers to discuss his own research would tempt the Dhryn into delay. He claimed to be busy "making arrangements" and "consulting with colleagues." Mac, in response, busied herself as well. She was here, after all, to learn about the Dhryn.

Who knew she'd miss the company of a big blue alien?

19

ADVENTURE AND ANXIETY

MAC CHECKED the time display on her desk. *He should be here in a few minutes.* She'd breakfasted and dressed in record time, anticipating a welcome change in routine. Brymn had promised her a tour of the city today. *Maybe*, Mac thought, *the rain would actually let up a bit.*

Eleven days. She was ready for a break. *To be honest, she was ready for anything that took her out of this apartment.* Already her desk was cluttered with the digital tablets the Dhryn used in place of mem-paper. More lay on chairs around the room. The Progenitors had allowed a Human on their world—they hadn't, until today, been ready to let her walk around on it. It was being deliberated, Brymn had promised day after day, asking her for patience.

In return, Mac had asked for information.

Her collection had grown rapidly: Brymn's work, abstracts from other fields, the Dhryn version of local news reports, and even samples of fiction, though these were presented in verse and difficult to follow, since the rhyming conventions were based on tones below her hearing. It didn't help that fiction presupposed the reader was at least familiar with the author's culture.

Mac was doing her best to learn the Dhryn's. She'd reached the point of being able to tell which public announcements were from the Progenitors, on topics ranging from finance to the proper education of *oomlings*. There was a distinctive formality, almost an aloofness—as though they considered themselves removed from the rest of Dhryn society, yet at its core.

Although she dutifully and unsuccessfully hunted references to the Ro, Mac found the Dhryn themselves becoming something of an obsession. The air of respect and mystery surrounding the Progenitors tantalized her. There were no images in any of the materials she'd assembled with Brymn's help. He'd expressed belief such didn't exist. So Mac had asked to meet one.

Apparently that request was being deliberated as well.

Their persecution by the Ro was another reason she'd begun to focus more of her attention on the Dhryn themselves. Apparently no adult Dhryn had ever been harmed by the Ro. The invisible beings stole or abused *oomlings* whenever they could; the heinous crimes stretching back almost two hundred standard years.

No wonder Brymn trembled at the name.

No wonder the Progenitors guarded the home system. Under the circumstances, Mac was amazed any Dhryn dared leave that protection, let alone continuing the practice of sending almost mature *oomlings* to the colonies. It was a stiff price to pay for interstellar travel, since the transects were obviously how the Ro were able to come and go. But the Dhryn had come to a sort of peace, having developed technology to keep the Ro at bay, at least here, and chose to exist that way, always on guard.

The average Dhryn didn't think about it.

They appeared to lack interest in other things as well. Selective ignorance was a blindness Mac was beginning to deplore in herself, let alone in an entire species. She ran into it again when trying to determine if the Dhryn had evolved here or elsewhere. There were no living clues left, no animals strutting about with bilateral symmetry and three pairs of arms. A fossil record would have been helpful, but Brymn had confessed such a thing would not have been valued or saved, if found. The study of life, he reminded her regularly, was forbidden. If she was to live here, she would have to be careful no one suspected her of such interests.

Mac shuddered. Over time, a place like this, ideas like this, would kill her. She knew it. Brymn was keeping her sane as well as safe, a combination of amusingly eccentric uncle, friend, and comrade-in-arms, bundled in a package surely unusual even for Dhryn.

And rarely on time, Mac thought fondly, gazing at the clock. She pulled on her raincoat, but left it open. The Dhryn had turned down the heat in her apartment after numerous requests, although Mac still found it too warm. In their way, they were good hosts. Not xenophobic in any way she could detect—though there was that issue of her being deaf, as Brymn called it. Careful that she not be bored or neglected. Curious, where her interests crossed theirs.

Speaking their language had proved essential, as well as safer. Brymn had checked and found that only a few official translators on Haven spoke Instella. That skill was reserved for the colonies, where one might reasonably expect to need it.

Not on Haven, where Mac was the only alien—other than attacking Ro—to ever set foot.

Some mornings, that was inspiring. In a "just don't look down" kind of way.

Where was *he*?

Mac went to her place of greeting and began flipping through the art catalog to keep herself occupied.

Where was he? Before Mac could do more than form the question again, a knock on the door answered it. *Finally.*

Brymn didn't wait for her to open the door, bursting through with a cheerful: "Ah, Mackenzie Winifred Elizabeth Wright Connor! Good morning!"

Mac stepped out of the way. As she closed the door, he paused in front of her art display, which her random shuffling had left at an abstract of silver reflections of globes within globes, gave an inexplicable *hoot hoot*!, then kept marching into her workroom. "I have good news!"

She hurried after him. "What?"

Brymn held out a tablet with his middle left arm, his small mouth stretched into the largest smile she'd seen him produce. "Those of No Useful Function at the communications center finally admitted I was entitled to receive non-Dhryn news reports. I have collected all those from the past two weeks for you. Here."

Mac took the tablet, her hands shaking. These would be summaries, of course. There was far too much interstellar information for every system to receive news from every other. Interests were more focused. But there could be something from the Interspecies Union. *There could be . . .* she fumbled at the display control.

"I haven't read them myself," Brymn told her. "I came straight to you. What's wrong? Isn't it working?"

"I—" Dumbfounded, Mac could only stare at the tablet. "I can't read it." The symbols were twisted and completely unfamiliar. "What language is this?"

"Instella." Brymn took the tablet and raised it to his eyes. "The display is clear enough, Mac," he said. "Are your eyes damaged?"

No, Mac realized with horror, *but her mind might be.* The subteach Emily had made for her—the pain she'd felt using it. Had the input crippled her ability to communicate in other languages?

If so, had it been accidental, or deliberate?

Mac forced herself to calm down. "Read it out loud to me, please. Instella, not Dhryn."

The floor vibrated once, as if Brymn muttered some comment about this, but he obeyed her request. " 'Bulletins from the Interspecies Union are intended for the widest possible audience. Failure to disseminate such bulletins in every applicable language will result in fines, censure, and potential restriction of transect access . . .' "

"That's enough." Mac heaved a sigh of relief. "I understood you. How about English? A few phrases."

Brymn nodded. " 'Humans consider it impolite to disgorge or otherwise release body fluids in public places. When eating in a Human restaurant, please notify your waiter if you will require a private room.' "

"That was English?" It sounded the same in Mac's ears as the Instella—and the Dhryn, for that matter.

"A quote from my 'Guide to Earth Etiquette.' A most useful resource, Mac."

Mac reached inside her shirt and dug into her waist pouch for her imp. Her original, with Emily's sub-teach, lay at the bottom of her largest water tank for safekeeping, wrapped in plastic. She carried the one from Nik, but hadn't used the device other than to record new entries in her personal log. Now that she thought about it, Mac couldn't recall paying attention to the 'screen, just hitting the right spots to control the function.

She cued the 'screen, in Instella first, then found herself staring into the incomprehensible mass that floated in front of her. A slide of her hand through the display changed it to English.

She sagged with relief. Some words looked odd, as if her mind was trying to reorganize the letters, but it was legible. Mac concentrated on one line, trying to read out loud in English. It sounded right to her, but Brymn, guessing what she'd been attempting, was already tilting his head from side to side in negation. "That was Dhryn."

Mac requested an input pad and the almost transparent keys formed under her hands. She typed carefully in English. She could read the words. But when she auto-translated to Instella, they were so much gibberish floating in air.

"It appears I have some new gaps in my education," Mac said, replacing the imp in her pouch. Her voice sounded remarkably calm under the circumstances. *Why hadn't she checked this before?*

Easy. She'd been too busy using her knowledge of Dhryn to investigate her novel surroundings, too enchanted by her new power to understand something so utterly foreign. Mac thought dourly that she'd probably never have noticed, if Brymn hadn't brought the tablet.

"In sum, I can write and read English, but not Instella. I can understand English, Instella, and Dhryn, though they sound exactly the same in my head. I speak only in Dhryn. Which also sounds the same in my head as any of the others." She sighed. "I'll lay odds there'll be some researchers itching to take apart my head when I get back."

Brymn blinked. "A figure of speech, I hope?"

Mac smiled faintly. "We both hope. Now, can the tablet translate to English?"

"No, Mac. And home system technology will not match yours. I can translate for you myself, but it will take some time." He brightened. "Or I can read to you—our tour will include several hours of traveling the tubes."

The tablet was still in his hand. Mac looked at it hungrily. If there was any message or information for her from Earth, it would be there. Whether she trusted Brymn to read it accurately or not, she had no other choice. She nodded.

"Let the tour begin."

A world without vegetation, yet with individual works of art given their own plazas and viewing stands. A city wrapped around the equator that shot itself upward in magnificent towers and rooted it-self with a labyrinth of spacious tunnels. Buildings whose design could be breathtakingly strange—the Dhryn no fonder of the per-pendicular outside their rooms. An endless rain gathered into wa-terfalls and used to animate statues before plunging below the surface. And a people as varied in dress and manner as any gather-ing of Humans Mac had seen.

"It's not what I thought," Mac confessed to Brymn as they walked toward the tube entrance along a concourse shielded from the rain. She suspected Dhryn kidneys worked hard enough to re-move excess water from their bodies, so it wasn't surprising they'd avoid unnecessary exposure to more. Not slavishly. Some ventured out under umbrellas but she'd witnessed several at work in the downpour, bodies protected only by the decorative bands around their torsos. Their waxy skin was probably better protection than her raincoat.

Not evolved under such conditions, Mac pondered.

"In what way, Mackenzie Winifred Elizabeth Wright Connor?" In public, where they might be overheard, Brymn was careful to use her full name. Under the circumstances, Mac wasn't about to argue.

"It seemed—bleak from my apartment," she explained, gazing about in wonder. Here, the tiles of the walkway extended up the slope of a neighboring wall, their colors forming a mosaic. The mo-

saic in turn formed an illusion of other walkways and other buildings, stretching into the distance. Mac imagined at least some
Dhryn walked right into it. They had a pronounced sense of
humor, much of it able to tickle Mac's funny bone as well.

There were a great number of Dhryn walking everywhere she
looked. As they passed one another, they'd briefly and seemingly
automatically raise up their bodies and heads, then dip again, turning any dense crowd into a blue sea with waves that passed along
in remarkable synchrony.

Unlike the media madhouse that had ambushed Brymn at Base—
or the rapt curiosity of Base's own inhabitants—Mac found herself
treated like any other Dhryn. Those passing her only bowed, as
they did to Brymn. She couldn't copy the full movement without
losing her step, but Mac lifted her chin each time in acknowledgment. For her neck's sake, she hoped there'd be less bowing in the
portion of their tour through the tube system.

Brymn excitedly brandished a map of the system at every opportunity, as if they didn't look sufficiently like tourists. *Another behavior that apparently crossed species' boundaries.* Mac
had taken a peek at it before they'd started, trying for a sense of
how long they'd be traveling, but Brymn had refused to spoil
what he referred to as her anticipation by providing a destination. Given she'd no idea what Brymn would consider a reasonable amount of time for a "tour," and knowing her hosts by
now, Mac had hurriedly stuffed a bag with her three sealable
water bottles and some of what she'd christened "cereal bars."
They weren't bars or cereal, being more like flat, wrapped sticks
of purple gelatin with thicker lumps of white along one side.
But they were the most completely nutritious, to a Human,
food item she'd discovered on the Dhryn menu thus far, and,
well, pleasantly peppery.

On the principle that her life had become highly unpredictable,
Mac had also retrieved her original imp from its bath, tucking it
into the waist pouch with the envelope, the imp from Nik, and the
letter from Kammie. *No one could say she didn't know how to travel
light.*

The tube system, according to the map, dove under the planet's surface in a maze of crisscrossing angles. If the scale was accurate, some penetrated the crust to a depth of 50 kilometers, while others skimmed barely beneath the footings of the buildings above. Mac hoped the Dhryn grasp of seismology was on a par with their chemistry, because the overall effect was that Haven consisted of more tunnel than rock.

Not to mention souterrains of every size, from small artificial chambers budding from tube junctions to what appeared to be cavities extensive enough to hold a midsized Human city. Altogether, the interior of Haven could well offer the Dhryn more living space than its surface.

Space for how many Dhryn? Mac ignored the temptation to guess. Salmon were amazingly prolific, but only if you knew where—and when—to do your counting.

"There it is!" Brymn's exclamation was hardly necessary. As they turned the corner at the end of the plaza, the entrance itself loomed in front of them, easily five stories high and wide enough to accommodate several walkways. The clusters of vidbots kept to the sides as aerial traffic zipped in and out without changing speed, implying either reckless abandon or a great deal of space inside.

It made even Brymn seem small.

"Is there a fee?" Mac asked, endeavoring to be the practical one of their twosome. She hadn't seen any evidence of money or credit among Dhryn; her deliveries and supplies were apparently the responsibility of the Progenitors. That didn't mean there wasn't commerce at the service level.

"Fee? For something required by Dhryn?" Brymn was almost light on his feet. "What a Human notion, *Lamisah*."

"Only kind I have, Brymn."

He hooted, the volume attracting the first overt attention Mac had noticed. "Shhhh," she urged, waving her hands at him.

"There is nothing impolite about expressing pleasure in a companion's wit," he countered, but his voice dropped to something closer to a whisper. Brymn saw her look at the nearest hovering 'bot. "They watch for signs of trouble, not humor, Mac. Visual only."

Mac slipped her arm around the arm nearest her, his lower right, and chuckled. "Just don't get us arrested—or whatever the Dhryn version is."

The tube Brymn had selected for the start of their tour was immense. Mac could feel the pulses of warm, humid air climbing upward before they reached the station complex itself and she took off her raincoat, tucking it into her shoulder bag. Ahead, pedestrians boarded disappointingly normal, Human-looking trains, albeit with doors twice as wide. Fliers zoomed by overhead, disappearing beyond the first great downward dip in the distance. Mac presumed they navigated the tube under their own power and resolutely ignored the potential for disaster, in light of the nonchalant way every other being was moving toward their trains.

Mac was standing beside Brymn on one of the long, tiled platforms, waiting their turn to board, when a movement along the wall caught her eye. As the Dhryn ahead in line were now sitting where they'd been standing, she judged there was time to indulge her curiosity before the train left.

There couldn't, in Mac's estimation, *be an entire world without its version of a rat.*

She turned to ask Brymn, but he was deep in conversation with their next-in-line neighbor, again waving his map and generally making sure everyone in earshot knew he was from a colony. The vibrations of what they were saying came up through her feet.

A step to the side gave Mac line of sight. There was a slice of shadow, beginning where the end of a pushcart full of packages waited against the wall.

Mac let her gaze rest on the edge of the darkness, as patiently as she'd ever waited for a fin to reappear by a rock, keeping herself peaceful and still.

There!

But what slipped across the line of darkness and back again wasn't a fin. It was a three-fingered hand, wizened and strange.

No one else appeared to have noticed. Mac eased closer. One step . . . then another . . . keeping her eyes on the boundary of shadow rather than challenge the privacy of the one hiding within.

An odor, thick and foul on the humid air. The breeze of beings passing, distant trains, the breathing of the tube itself carried it to her, then past. Again. Mac wrinkled her nose, knowing that smell.

Rotting flesh.

"Are you all right?" For some reason, she whispered, as if only the being in the shadows and herself should hear. Reaching the limit of light, she slowed, then crouched lower, trying not to seem a threat. "Do you need help?"

The darkness roared at her, followed by a nightmare form that fell against her, knocking her flat. Panic-stricken, Mac fought to free herself, only to realize the weight pressing on her was completely limp, as if lifeless.

Hands tugged at her arms, shoulders, and bag, plucking her from underneath . . . *what?*

Even as Brymn half carried her to the train, Mac looked back at the form collapsed on the platform, trying to glimpse what she could of it between the Dhryn walking by; the only attention they paid to the unconscious form being to avoid stepping on it.

It? Suddenly, Mac had a clear look. A Dhryn lay there, facedown, all its limbs splayed on the pavement. The body—something about it wasn't right. Mac gasped as she saw it was shriveled, the blue skin split everywhere along thin, irregular lines, those lines dark as if oozing some fluid. The arms were no better, mere sticks with the twisted remnants of hands at each end.

One of the hands *moved*, turning so the fingers grasped at empty air.

"Brymn." Mac resisted, a futile effort against the determined alien. "We have to help him."

"Hush. You must not see—there is nothing there." He heaved her in front of him and through the door. Other Dhryn were coming in behind them, blocking Mac's view.

There were windows, if no seats. Mac hurried to the nearest, muttering apologies as she bumped into already seated Dhryn.

But when she looked out to the shadow, the pathetic form was gone.

"We do not think of it."

"What kind of answer is that?" Mac braced one foot on the luggage rack, the closest thing to a seat on the Dhryn train, and glared at Brymn. Despite the number waiting on the platform, it seemed there was more than enough room. The crowd had spread itself through the various cars. Theirs was almost deserted, shared by the usual handful of 'bots near the ceiling and a group of three Dhryn busy in their own conversation at the far end. They wore the woven blue that reminded Mac of the *Pasunah* crew.

The privacy should have made Brymn more communicative, but so far, he'd refused to admit there'd been a 'damaged' Dhryn on the platform at all.

"I'm a trained observer, Brymn," she said, not for the first time. "I know what I saw. What I don't understand is why you won't tell me what was wrong with that Dhryn."

"A Dhryn is robust—"

Mac held up her hand to stop him. "I know the rest. Are you trying to tell me damaged Dhryn are left to die in the streets? I don't accept that. You may not have—" *even a* word *for medical care*, she realized with frustration, "—but you have sanitation. That being was rotting away!"

Brymn looked as miserable as she'd ever seen him, arms tightly folded, brow ridges lowered, mouth downturned. After meeting her eyes for a long moment, he said very quietly: "It is the Wasting."

" 'Wasting,' " Mac repeated, leaning forward. "What is it?"

"We do not think of it." He shivered, looking around as if to see who might overhear.

She had an answer for that. "Speak in English."

"English?" The Dhryn pulled out the tablet, an almost pathetic eagerness on his face. "Then shall I read the news reports, Mackenzie Winifred Eliza—"

As the Ro had been the other Dhryn reality they preferred "not to think about," Mac had no intention letting Brymn slide past this without an answer. She pushed aside the tablet, though gently, and shook her head. "Later. Tell me about the Wasting. Please."

"Why do you want to know?"

"Asking questions is what I do." For some reason, she thought of Nik, of how aggrieved he'd looked whenever puzzled. "I don't like mysteries—or secrets."

"What if the answer is something you do not like?"

Mac's lips twisted. "I seek the truth. It has nothing to do with likes or dislikes."

"Ah." A sigh, barely audible over the soft whoosh of the train through the tube. They were moving at a pace that made Mac queasy each time she glanced at the lights flashing by the windows. "The Wasting is a truth, Mac, which we Dhryn do not like. This is why we do not think of it." Mac held her breath as he paused, willing him to continue. After a moment, he did.

"I do not know how it is for other species, Mac, but we Dhryn have stages in our lives—moments of great change. The Freshening is the one that turns us from *oomling* to adult." For some reason, Brymn stroked his eye ridge with one hand. "After the Freshening, next comes the—the nearest word in English is 'Flowering.' Its timing is less predictable. We can Flower at almost any age and, for most Dhryn, Flowering is a peaceful, almost unnoticed event that marks maturation." His expression turned suddenly wistful. "A privileged few are transformed and set on the path to becoming Progenitors."

When he stopped, Mac could almost hear the word he didn't want to add. "But—" she offered.

"But if the Flowering goes wrong, instead of change, there is—degradation. It is the Wasting. The body loses its flesh and proper shape. The mind goes mad. Some—linger. In the colonies, they may wander into the wild areas. Here, it seems they haunt the tunnels." Brymn's nostrils oozed yellow. Distress. *At the topic, or a memory?* Mac wondered. "None live more than a week or two."

"And you don't do anything? Aren't there—" Mac bit her lip,

then said carefully: "You could ask other species. Some must have knowledge that could help."

Brymn gave another, deeper sigh. "It is not something one helps, Mac. The Wasted are just that—Dhryn who have failed to be Dhryn. We give them the grace of ignoring their fate."

"That's not good enough," Mac objected. "Any such metamorphosis has a biochemical basis. You have chemists—surely some could find ways to monitor the change, control it, help those who are in difficulty—"

Brymn looked horrified. "You'd ask us to tamper with the very process that defines our future, that determines the rightful Progenitors of our species! Are you mad?"

A rebuttal trembling on her lips, Mac made herself stop and think. *Who was the alien here?* she asked herself. *How dare she impose her values on their biology, their culture?* Chastened, she subsided, settling farther back on the luggage rack. An arm around the upright support kept her from slipping, but the rack itself was making serious efforts to reshape her posterior. "I withdraw the suggestion, Brymn," she said quietly. "I never meant to offend you. It's my nature, part of being Human, to be affected by such suffering. I feel a need to act . . . to help."

He held out an empty hand and she willingly put hers into it. "I could never be offended by you, Mackenzie Winifred Elizabeth Wright Connor. Confused, yes," this with the tiniest of smiles. "But that is the beauty of our differences, that you see possibilities I do not. Perhaps I shall surprise you, one day."

"Oh, you've already done that, Brymn." Mac gave his hand a squeeze, then let go, along with her questions. *She'd find the answers herself.* "Do we still have time for the tablet?"

A broad smile now. "But of course! I have taken the liberty of reorganizing the reports by system of origin. Excuse me," he said, while he relocated himself with a bustle of moving limbs and shuffling bags—he'd slung two around his torso. Eventually he sat so his right side was against the rack and she could look over his shoulder—thoughtful, even if the words on the tablet in his hand were no more legible now than they'd been in her apartment. "There. I shall start with reports from Sol."

As he began to read aloud, something about sports scores, Mac stretched out on her side as best she could, finding it more comfortable if she laid one arm over his warm, rubbery shoulders.

Even as she listened to his deep bass rumble, she couldn't help but wonder.

How close was Brymn to "Flowering?"

- Portent -

IN HER DREAMS, the world was hinged and could swing open like a door. She struggled with bar and latch, with lock and bolt, until only her hands held the world closed. Held the world safe.

In her dreams, green liquid, like pus from a wound, seeped under the door that was the world, leaked along its sides, dripped from its top until it burned her from toe to hand to face, until it ate from her skin and flesh and bone.

In her dreams, she had the choice. To turn away and run, letting the world take care of itself . . .

Or to hold the door against death as long as she had life . . .

". . . We're losing her."

"There's nothing left to lose—"

"Tell that to her family! Forget the legs—get more gel on her midsection. Damn it—I said more . . ."

"No use. It's over."

In her dreams, the world was hinged and could close softly, like the lid of night, shutting out pain and fear, letting her rest.

"Next."

20

CAVERNS AND CURIOSITIES

MAC PRESSED her nose against the window. Another stop identical to the five before. "You could at least tell me where we're going," she complained, pulling back.

"No, no. I know Humans enjoy surprises."

Mac nudged Brymn with her toe. "Some Humans. Others are happier knowing where they are going."

"That is coaxing. I am able to resist."

She grinned. "I'm impressed."

Of course. He'd had Emily to teach him about humanity.

Mac pushed aside the thought, shunting it deep inside with the bitter disappointment of no message from Earth. *Or none she could find.* The reports from Sol System had consisted of racing results from Neptune's rings and the announcement of discounts to species who brought their own ship engineers when accessing Earth's repair and refit facilities. Brymn had reread them until they'd both memorized every word. Nothing sounded like code. Nothing hinted at a hidden meaning.

So there was nothing she could do, about Emily or Nik or Base. Mac had decided she owed herself—and Brymn—a few hours without the troubles of the universe.

Brymn seemed to have less difficulty immersing himself in the moment. "It is the very next stop," he proclaimed cheerfully, waving four arms about. One clutched the ever-present map; the other three, assorted bags. She assumed he'd brought snacks as well.

Mac had saved her cereal bars, but gave herself a carefully small drink of water. Given the rainfall, she hadn't expected a shortage. Then again, she hadn't expected Brymn would be taking her what felt like halfway across—or, more accurately, through—the planet. *Rationing seemed prudent.*

"Next stop, is it?" Mac tried to snatch the map, but his arm bent at an impossible angle to keep it out of her reach.

"You will see, *Lamisah.* Soon enough."

"Soon enough" translated into the longest distance between two stops yet on their journey through the tube. Mac loosened and re-braided her hair uncounted times. Brymn's bright blue eyelids closed and he let out tiny, quiet hoots, as though dreaming something amusing. Eventually, Mac found a way to scrunch herself into the luggage rack so she could almost nod off, if not quite. The train was making too many turns for her to trust any one position.

They were alone in the car. Fellow travelers—in three instances—had chosen to move elsewhere at their first opportunity. *Nothing to do with her,* Mac decided, though the presence of a Human must seem bizarre to home system Dhryn. It was Brymn the Tourist, who missed no opportunity to praise Haven and explain he was from the colonies, making his first trip back since Freshening and wasn't the tube system a magnificent achievement involving a full century of effort and did they appreciate how many . . .

Mac could recite the spiel verbatim—in fact, it was hard to get the facts and figures to stop dancing around in her head hours later. She gave up and twisted upright again. *Time for another walk.*

On straightaways, like this, the train might have been standing at a station. There was no vibration underfoot she could detect. *To avoid interfering with infrasound conversation?* Intriguing concept. As Mac paced down the middle of the empty car, her fingers automatically tugged her braid from its knot and undid it, combing through the hip-length stuff.

Seung was always looking for quieter tech, quieter in terms of whale acoustics. She should arrange for a Dhryn engineer to work with the Preds at Base next season. *You never knew where you'd get a breakthrough,* Mac hummed to herself, splitting her hair into three and rebraiding as she paced. *Or from whom.*

Take the Dhryn technology to defend against the Ro. Judging from the tube system and the removal—Mac still found that incredible—of whatever else had orbited Haven's sun, part of that defense relied on physical barriers. *For a reason?* Was the attack on the pods typical Ro behavior, when stealth failed them?

An idea—no, less than that—*a combination of possibilities* paused Mac's busy hands, slowed her feet to a standstill. She adjusted to the slight tilt of the flooring without thinking, accustomed to more unstable surfaces than a polite train.

The Ro hadn't made a single mistake in their attack on Base.

Minimum action for maximum result. The anatomy of a salmon modeled the concept. Power applied where the least amount of effort would push the streamlined body through the water—or air—with the greatest force.

No mistakes, minimal action implied advance planning. Advance planning meant a source of knowledge.

Mac tied her braid in a tight knot and shoved it inside the back of her shirt. *Base wasn't that sophisticated,* she argued with herself, *not to beings who could knock out power and evade sensors.* The Ro didn't need any help.

But she'd told Brymn: *"I seek the truth. It has nothing to do with what I want."*

She'd better damn well mean it. Mac stared ahead and saw nothing but a face with its trademark smile, a touch lopsided for perfection, which made it so perfectly friendly.

Emily could have given the Ro the plans to Base. She could have told them how best to knock out the power. She could have . . .

. . . *been responsible for the injury and death of how many innocents?*

Forgive me.

Mac ground the heels of her fists into her eyes.

"*Lamisah?* Is something wrong?"

She dropped her hands to meet Brymn's anxious gaze. "Too much thinking, my friend. That's all."

"Ah. Soon you will have new things to think about. Are you ready?"

Feeling the train slowing beneath her feet, Mac knew what he meant. "I don't suppose you'll tell me now where we're going?" she asked one final time, going to the rack to pick up her bag.

"Where we will stand between one beginning and another."

"Riddles, now?" She made the effort to smile as she turned to face him. No need to spoil Brymn's pleasure.

He wasn't smiling. She noticed the map was no longer in sight. His body was canted down, not as far as threat, but certainly lower than it had been for the role of Brymn the casual tourist.

This was Brymn with a mission.

Mac nodded to herself; somehow, she'd known. "This isn't a tour, is it?"

"I wish it could be, *Lamisah*," the Dhryn said. "But I have something to tell you, something I couldn't mention above, where the air could have ears."

"You're so sure we're safe here?" The train slowed to a stop. All Mac could see out the windows were walls on both sides, lit only by the lights from the train. It made her feel trapped behind bars.

"If this place isn't safe, Mackenzie Winifred Elizabeth Wright Connor, then it is too late for anything we might do to save ourselves."

Not the most reassuring reason she'd heard lately.

Brymn led the way off the train. Once on the platform, Mac understood why he'd sounded so confident.

The walls were dark because they were lined with the same glistening black material as the shroud the Dhryn had tossed over her box on the way station, supposedly able to disrupt the Ro's technology. She followed it with her eyes up to the ceiling, where it became part of the shadows stretching overhead and to either side. There was more underfoot. She wanted to lift her feet from it. *Afraid of a carpet?* Mac scolded herself.

The train pulled away—backward, not ahead as she'd expected. *So this was the end of the line.*

"This way." Brymn didn't give her any choice, almost running down the platform in the opposite direction from the train. Mac swore under her breath but hurried after him.

The platform narrowed and became a ramp leading down to the tracks. There was a dim illumination in the distance. Mac squinted, trying to make out details of what looked like a large opening. She guessed the tracks continued into a cavern.

It wasn't their destination. Before they reached the tracks, Brymn halted in front of a section of wall. After studying what appeared to Mac to be more of the same glistening fabric, he spat onto one hand, then pressed it against the wall above and to the right of his head.

Smoke began to appear between his three fingers as the fabric shrank away to reveal an illuminated plate. *Finally*, Mac thought, *a civilized door control.* She wrinkled her nose at an acrid smell. *A being of unexpected resources, her Brymn.*

Her mind flashed back to Pod Three and the Ro attack. She'd only a fuzzy recollection of their actual escape—being dumped into the ocean along with the gallery and kitchen tended to overshadow fine details. Not to mention fear, horror, and utter screaming confusion. Still, Mac had no trouble remembering one very unusual aspect.

Brymn had *pushed* them through a solid window.

Seeing how he'd cleared the fabric from the control, she also remembered how. He'd *spat* at the window wall; it had shattered when he rammed it.

Not typical behavior for the transparent, strong, yet flexible material. The Preds had been caught testing the ability of the pod window walls with harpoons. Needless to say the students had suffered more than the window.

Mac eyed the smoking, ruined edge of the shroud fabric wistfully. *Never*, she told herself, *ever, travel without sample vials.*

Meanwhile, in plain view of the dozen or more tiny vidbots stationed along the ceiling, Brymn was tapping what had to be an access code into the plate. "This is going to get us in trouble, isn't it?" Mac asked with what she considered remarkable aplomb, considering she stood in the bowels of an alien world, a world she was visiting on the sufferance of its leaders.

With an individual whose sanity hadn't been confirmed.

"Ah." The fabric split along two lines that met overhead, the triangle thus formed moving away from them and to the side so Mac stared into a very unappealing and dark cavity. A cavity out of which rushed cooler, damper air.

She covered her nose with one hand. "What's that smell?"

Brymn was already half inside, his stooped body posture fitting perfectly within the available space, although he had no room to spread out his arms. "Hurry, Mac."

Couldn't a Dhryn smell that? Mac swallowed hard and obeyed, breathing as little as possible through her fingers. It wasn't so much sulfur, she decided, as rancid cream. With sulfur. And maybe the stomach contents of a five-days dead seal.

Whatever it was, it diminished to a background misery after her first few steps. Either her sense of smell had overloaded and quit, or opening the door had released a pocket of collected fumes, rapidly diffusing into the tunnel.

Mac only hoped to avoid finding the source.

The cavity proved to be part of some kind of accessway, with a maze of branches to the left and right. They were free of 'bots, at least. There were lights, but they were little more than glows on the walls. Brymn moved confidently enough, so perhaps the lights were brighter in the nonvisible, to a Human, part of the spectrum.

Mac let her mind worry at Dhryn senses and experiments to test their differences. It was better than letting her mind think about the mass of planet mere centimeters above her head, or the way her imagination raced back to all the old horror films she'd watched with Emily, in which the heroes were inevitably lured into a dark, deadly basement.

She'd complained how unrealistic the scenario was. *Who would do such a thing?* Emily had argued that each basement was a test of courage. Until the heroes faced such a test, the audience couldn't believe in their ability to ultimately defeat the monster.

Mac didn't feel courageous. She felt trapped. And she didn't feel capable of arguing with one exasperating Dhryn, let alone defeating a monster.

If this was a trap, and she never left here again, what was the range of the bioamplifiers accumulating in her liver and bones? Even if the rock overhead didn't matter, what of the shroud lining every cavity down here? Was she as hidden from Human sensors as the Dhryn's *oomlings* were from the Ro?

If so, she'd become a mystery that should annoy Nikolai Trojanowski for some time.

Thinking of another Human was the last straw. Mac stopped, hands carefully away from the walls leaning together over her head. "Brymn! Wait!"

If anything, her shouts spurred him to move faster. His voice trailed back to her, low and anxious. "No, no. This is no place for us, *Lamisah*. The Wasted could come to die here. Hurry."

"Wonderful." At the thought of rotting, mad Dhryn waiting to grab her from the more-than-abundant shadows—yet another horror staple Mac could do without—she scampered after the Dhryn, almost running into him from behind. "I hope you know the way out of here."

"As do I."

Luckily for Human-Dhryn relations, Mac had no time to formulate a suitable response. The very next bend in the accessway brought them to where it almost doubled in width and height. A welcoming brightness streamed across the floor from an entrance larger than those they'd been passing. As her eyes adjusted, Mac sniffed cautiously. The breeze lifting the wisps from her forehead was warm and sweet. She took a step toward that beckoning light.

"We aren't going that way," Brymn said. "Come, Mac."

She paused. "Why? What's there?"

"A crèche. Come. It's only a bit farther." He pointed down another of the dark, forbidding accessways.

"*Oomlings?*"

Mac was already moving, Brymn's plaintive, "we've no time!" echoing in her ears.

The sight greeting her eyes made her forget the Ro, forget Emily, forget herself.

She wasn't standing in an entrance. This must be the opening of a ventilation shaft of some kind, for beneath her feet the wall dropped at least thirty meters to the floor of the cavern in front of her.

Cavern? As well call Castle Inlet a rock cut, missing the glorious play of light, water, and life. This hidden place was nowhere as large, but it gave the same feeling of wonder. The far end of the crèche was so distant Mac couldn't make out its shape, but its tiled, colorful side walls swung out and open like the arms of a mother. Golden rays of light from suspended clusters on the ceiling bathed the floor below, crisscrossing so even the shadows were faint and welcoming.

The light was only the beginning.

The floor, which rose and fell in wide steps, was covered with what Mac could only think of as immense playpens, each carpeted in some kind of soft green and bounded by woven silk panels in rainbow shades. Each held one or more adult Dhryn surrounded by a mass of miniature ones. Her first impression was of ceaseless movement and Mac eagerly searched for patterns. Sure enough, within a 'pen directly below her, the *oomlings*—for the tiny copies of Brymn could be nothing else—were sitting carefully on their rears, heads oriented toward an adult who was gesturing with four arms, the way Brymn would do whenever enthused about a topic. In the adjacent 'pens, *oomlings* were milling around their adults, every so often hopping into the air with a random exuberance that brought a smile to Mac's lips.

And the sounds. Low booming voices almost disappeared under what could only be called cooing. *The oomlings?* The hairs on her arms and neck reacted to something—more infrasound. *From the adults*, oomlings, *or both?* Mac wondered. In such a large space, the lower frequencies could be heard by all. Perhaps something being taught to all at once? Or was it as simple as a communal lullaby, for many of the 'pens held jumbles of smaller *oomlings*, arms and bodies wrapped around one another in peaceful confusion as they slept.

As if all this wasn't enough, Mac thought, thoroughly enchanted, *the* oomlings *weren't blue or rubbery.* From the tiniest to the ones almost the size of adults, they were white from head to footpad, and either wearing clothing like feathers, or their torsos were covered in down.

They might have six arms—she couldn't see any with a seventh—but they called forth parental instincts even from a distance and even from an alien.

Brymn had come to sit beside her, his arms folded. "Our future," he said warmly.

"Are those the Progenitors?" Mac nodded into the crèche to indicate the adult Dhryn.

"Of course not." A subdued hoot. "Why would you think such a thing?"

Mac was tempted to retort: *because you Dhryn keep your biology as secret from others as you to do from yourselves,* but settled for: "If these were Humans, the parents—Progenitors—would be responsible for caring for their offspring—*oomlings.*" She couldn't help but think of her dad.

And hope she'd be able to describe all this to him in person.

"Ah. Our Progenitors are responsible for the Dhryn. What you see below are—" he paused as if searching for the right word. "These are caregivers. They remain with the *oomlings* at all times. Just as the *oomlings* must remain here until they Freshen."

"To keep them safe from the—" Brymn touched her mouth to stop what she would have said.

"Please do not speak that name here, *Lamisah,*" he said as he took his hand away.

Mac nodded, seeing the crèche from a new perspective—that of a vault protecting a living treasure. She tried to estimate how many such vaults would be required to house the new generations of an entire planet, the organization to feed and care for them, and gave up. But her imagination could encompass the desperation of a species that had to bury its helpless young to protect them.

The Ro had a great deal more to answer for than the destruction of Base.

"A sight to warm the hearts," Brymn said softly, "but we haven't time to waste, Mac. Come. It's not far."

Mac turned to follow her guide, resisting the temptation to look back.

"It is here. The answer to everything."

Given the conviction in Brymn's voice, Mac sat on the nearest cratelike tube, pulled out a water bottle, and studiously broke off a piece of cereal bar to chew. They were, barring any more secret doors and chambers the Dhryn hadn't revealed, sitting in a storeroom.

A storeroom packed to its ceiling with tubes marked: Textile Archives. Some were dusty enough to have been down here since the Dhryn began burrowing.

She watched Brymn dump his bags, then rush to one particular stack, running his hands greedily along the outside of the bottommost tubes as if they were treasure. "Help me, *Lamisah*," he ordered, busy peering at labels. "We must find the oldest specimen. It will be marked the 'year of beginning' or some such thing." He gave a dismissive gesture to the packed corridor they'd walked through to come here. "Anything outside this area is too recent. The curator was adamant."

"Why?" But she was already packing away her snack and coming to join him. "What are you looking for, Brymn?"

"Proof. I know it's here."

That was all the explanation he'd give her, perhaps assuming, correctly, that Mac was ready to desert him if she had the slightest idea how to get herself back to civilization. The labyrinth they'd traversed to reach the crèche had been nothing compared to what Brymn had taken her through to reach this . . . this . . . storeroom. Twists, turns, another small access door to break through . . .

Implying, Mac suddenly realized, looking at the large storage tubes, *that there must be another, more normal way in—something she could find and use herself.*

She set to work with greater will, part of her attention on the labels, and the rest looking for any sign of a door. It wasn't going to be obvious, of course. Who'd worry about the inside of a storeroom, for one, plus shroud fabric lined these walls as well as those of all the accessways. The time and labor to shield nonessential areas had to have been staggering, a convincing display of the belief of the Dhryn in its effectiveness.

Mac hoped they were right.

The labels were straightforward enough, date of preservation—Mac thought it likely the tubes contained a controlled climate—and a code number that she came to realize was the order of preservation. The process had begun not that long ago, hence the relatively uniform nature of the tubes, and it appeared the curators had elected to preserve the older specimens first. Perhaps they valued the antiquities most.

Or they'd been deteriorating fastest in the nearly constant rain on the surface. Mac chided herself as she climbed over a low stack to see what was behind it. She was growing too familiar with them, with Brymn, with the Dhryn as a whole. Drawing conclusions as if they were Earth-born and she understood what drove them, as if they were Human and foreign, not alien.

"I've found it! Mac! Mac!"

Obeying the summons and her own curiosity, Mac climbed back into the main area in time to see Brymn staggering into the middle of the open space, a tube taller than he was clutched in all three pairs of arms. Before he teetered forward again and dropped it, she added her arms to his and helped him put the heavy thing down.

Mac read the label and blinked in awe. Without doing the conversion to standard union years, she didn't know how long ago it had been preserved. But the code was a single digit. *Dhryn for one.* She had no idea how old the specimens inside might be, but they were doubtless the irreplaceable gems of the archives. Mac couldn't believe Brymn, an archaeologist, had almost dropped the tube.

"Quickly, quickly! We must open it. No. Wait!" Almost panting, Brymn bounced away to get one of his bags, then bounced back, ripping the bag open. "I must be ready to take the readings. Now open it."

"What? You can't open it—there have to be preservatives inside. You know better than I do what could happen to the contents if they contact the air." *She was guarding the cultural heritage of a species from a mad being.* "What readings? Brymn, what's going on?"

For a wonder, he stopped waving his arms and gave her his full attention, his expression both sad and solemn. "We both seek the truth, Mackenzie Winifred Elizabeth Wright Connor. Trust me. Help me. I know what I'm doing."

"Then will we go home? Up there? Out of here?"

"I promise, *Lamisah.*"

Mac threw up her hands in surrender. "Fine. What do you want me to do?"

Her job, it turned out, was to crack the seal of the tube while Brymn stood ready. The hooklike device in his hand resembled that used by the Esteemed Academic on Mac's food supplies. It didn't look like any scanning tech Mac knew, but then these storage tubes were odd enough themselves. He had to show her how to unlock them first, a matter of sliding four sections of metal past one another in a specific order. Not a lock, but protection against doing accidentally what they were doing deliberately.

Mac held her breath as she slid the final section and broke the seal.

A cool mist formed along the edge within seconds, condensing along the tube itself. Brymn avoided it as he pushed his device inside the tube, the hook slipping in as if designed for that purpose.

He read the display in silence. *Not quite,* Mac thought, feeling vibrations along the tube.

"What is it?"

His eyes didn't leave the device. "Pull the lid wide open, Mac."

In for a penny . . . Mac didn't bother with the rest of her dad's saying, too busy struggling with hinges meant for Dhryn musculature. The lid lifted, then toppled over so she had to dodge smartly out of its way or risk her toes. It fell to the floor with a clang.

As the metallic echoes died away, Mac came around to Brymn, peering over his shoulder. Three of his hands were busy inside the tube, pulling free pieces of fabric so fragile they crumpled in his fingers as he brought them close to his device, their bright dust sparkling as it drifted back into the tube.

"Brymn." Mac tugged one arm. "Stop it. You're ruining the specimens!"

He stopped, but not, Mac decided, at her urging. The Dhryn sank to a sitting position of his own accord, staring into the tiny display of his device as if trying to burn the image into his brain.

"So it's true," he boomed slowly. "I believed. Yet at the same time, I couldn't. But here is the proof."

"Of what?" Mac did her best to sound patient.

"That what is Dhryn, on this world, in our history, began no more than three thousand standard years ago. We began, when so much else ended forever."

She sank down herself, using the end of the tube as a bench, despite its damp chill. "The Moment. This is why you've been trying to fix a date," Mac said wonderingly. "You believe the Dhryn survived the devastation of the Chasm and came here, before the transects failed." Mac paused, feeling the irony. "So Emily was working with one of the mythical 'Survivors' all along and didn't realize it." She frowned at Brymn. "Why didn't you tell her?"

A halfhearted hoot. "I'm thought crazy enough by my own kind—do you think I'd spread that to other species?"

Mac patted the tube. "But you weren't. You were right. But why? Why was this a secret?"

"The Progenitors must have decided it was for our own good."

"Why? Surely it was a great triumph for your kind?"

"Or so great a fear, so intense a trauma, that our ancestors chose not to think of it, in case thinking made it stay real. Without that fear, the Dhryn could rebuild, move outward, accept the gift of the transects when it was offered us."

"For the second time," Mac mused.

"What do you mean?"

"You must have had the ability to travel between systems to arrive here, Brymn. The question becomes, did your species develop the transect technology in the first place, only to somehow lose it?"

The Dhryn was embarrassed. *She could read that by now.* There was a shifting of his eyes from hers, a rising slant to his posture. "We Dhryn do not value innovation or change—the Progenitors prefer we adapt the technology we have, or use that of others, wherever possible. Having been to the worlds of other species, to Human worlds, I can say without any doubt, Mac, the Dhryn are fundamentally incapable of such a thing."

"Well, we didn't invent it either," she soothed. "So your entire species, as far as you know, abandoned its past when it fled here, to this world. Quite a feat."

"And one we must keep to ourselves, Mac," with a worried look at her, "until I can prepare a full argument to present to the Progenitors. It is not our place to release such inflammatory information. Others, wiser than we, will know what to do with it."

"I won't say that's been my experience," Mac warned him, but she nodded. "I promise, of course."

Brymn stood, scanner in hand. "Thank you, *Lamisah*. When the time is right, we'll tell everyone. You do realize, this is more than confirmation the Dhryn came from the Chasm—it also provides the first clear dating of the Moment. It was at least three thousand five hundred and seven years ago, using the system of the Interspecies Union."

Since life was stripped from hundreds of worlds, leaving only ghosts, ghouls, and ruin. Mac didn't need the shiver running down her spine to remind her. "I don't care about the dating, Brymn. Do you realize this world might contain the truth about the Chasm? We could find out what happened—what's starting to happen again!"

"The Ro." He wrapped his arms around his middle, tightly enough to crush the blue silks wrapping his torso. His nostrils oozed yellow mucus. *Distress or anxiety?* "Ah, Mac. I may be a fool, but you're a dreamer. My ancestors must have decreed that everything from before our arrival here be destroyed. I've questioned other historians and archaeologists. They have no interest in anything earlier—because nothing earlier exists."

"There's a way," Mac pressed. "We need to find your place of origin. The world within the Chasm where the Dhryn began."

He looked puzzled. "Dhryn have always been."

Archaeologist, not biologist, Mac reminded herself. *Fine.* "Where the Dhryn lived before they came to Haven. That place could tell us what we need to know."

"Ah! Yes, I concur." Then his little mouth formed an unhappy pout. "Even if we could find it, Mac, how would we get there?"

"You're asking me?" Mac snorted. " I don't know how to get to my apartment from here."

A definite hoot. "That I can do," Brymn reassured her. "Through the main entrance will be a commuter tube. It will take us almost into your place of greeting!"

Thinking of the past hours spent tunnel-skulking, Mac felt entitled to some exasperation: "We couldn't have come that way?"

Brymn spread six arms. "If we had, you would not have seen the *oomlings*."

And you would have been seen breaking in here, Mac added to herself, but didn't question the Dhryn. She was all in favor of a more direct route home. Perhaps his culture was one in which you could be stopped from committing a crime, but weren't punished once it was a *fait accompli*.

Home. Wondering at how comfortably the word wrapped itself around a cockeyed apartment on an alien planet, Mac helped Brymn close the tube, hopefully protecting what he hadn't irreparably damaged, then push it behind some others. *Did she feel at home here?* Or was this more evidence of the adaptability of the Human psyche, that she could satisfy her need for shelter and territory using whatever was offered?

Even her? The self-proclaimed "Earth is quite enough" Mackenzie Connor?

As she pondered, Brymn went to a section of seemingly ordinary wall, spreading his arms so all six hands could touch certain points at once. As it obediently revealed itself as a wide, slanted door, Mac realized why she hadn't found the exit. *Damn Dhryn don't know how to make anything convenient for humanoids*, she told herself, rather fondly.

They did know how to intimidate humanoids.

The door flashed open to reveal a bristling fence of weapons aimed in their direction. Mac lost count after thirty-six, implying more than half a dozen guards waited behind those ominous bores.

To make matters worse, the floor began vibrating underfoot. Brymn wrapped himself into a silent knot, responding to what Mac couldn't hear.

Swallowing hard, and doing her best to imagine a staff meeting, Mac stamped her foot. "I am Mackenzie Winifred Elizabeth Wright Connor," she informed the host of round black muzzle tips, attempting to stretch a little taller.

"We know."

21

VISIT AND VIOLATION

"THIS IS so exciting, *Lamisah!*"

Mac, busy trying to maintain some dignity while walking quickly enough to keep her heels from being trampled by their escort, rolled her eyes at Brymn. He was beaming, insofar as his small mouth allowed. Those hands nearest her—the Dhryn was on her left—kept patting her shoulder or arm at random intervals. It was as if he had to reassure himself she was with him, a friend to witness this "so exciting" moment.

They weren't being arrested, or the Dhryn equivalent. Mac had figured that much out when none of the twenty-two Dhryn waiting in the wide corridor had bothered entering the Textile Archives nor waited to close the door. Instead, she and Brymn had been informed they were late.

They were expected below.

Below, Brymn had whispered to her, were the Progenitors.

Their escort had ended further conversation by raising their weapons again. It hadn't quelled Brymn, who'd almost danced beside her. She'd only hoped the big alien didn't burst into ecstatic song and land them both in deeper trouble.

"Below" was accurate enough. Within their cluster of armed Dhryn, each wearing individual colors but similar in that all had lost one or more limbs and so were of higher accomplishment than Brymn, they'd been taken into the heart of Haven. First had been a series of sloping ramps, each barred by a massive door better suited to being an air lock under the ocean in Mac's estimation. Following the ramps had been a lift, which had carried all of them, in very tight proximity, down for a remarkably long time. Mac had leaned on Brymn after a while, grateful she'd never suffered from claustrophobia.

Yet.

Now they walked very quickly down another, much wider ramp. The soft-soled Dhryn feet were almost silent on any surface, but here lush carpeting underfoot muffled Mac's boots as well. Without voices, they walked to their breathing alone, Brymn's the loudest and most rapid.

Well aware hers were the first Human eyes to see the Dhryn's inner sanctum, Mac did her best to memorize everything she saw. The shroud material was everywhere, of course, but here spirals of silver began to overlay the black, illuminated so they appeared to be in motion. There were words picked out in silver as well, as if the spirals were the breath carrying the sound. Between the bodies of her escort, and Brymn, Mac couldn't make out more than snatches of what was written. It seemed a combination of historical record, exhortations to enjoy life, and the occasional complaint about building standards.

Then Mac remembered. Brymn had told her he'd recorded Emily's name in the hall of his Progenitors. At the time, she'd taken it as metaphor. Obviously, she'd been wrong.

Was her *name here?* If so, what did the other Dhryn think of it?

Not that she'd have a chance to find out on this trip. Mac didn't understand the urgency of their escort, but there was no slowing the pace. When she'd attempted to do so, they'd grabbed her as if to carry her along. Only a loud protest—and a well-aimed kick— had put her back on her feet.

The spirals and their utterances grew denser and denser until the silver was almost blinding. The air grew as fresh as a summer's day, though the scent of growing things was replaced by an unknown but pleasant spice. Mac belatedly thought to look for more mundane aspects such as lighting fixtures, ventilation grates, and doorways, but unsurprisingly the Dhryn technology eluded her. *Well, security wasn't hidden.* Since leaving the archive, tiny round vidbots had hovered in every corner. Several had followed overhead, as if accompanying them. Mac had expected no less on the route leading to the Progenitors.

She would have liked to ask questions, prime among them: why was she, an alien, being brought here? *On the other hand, this way she couldn't get into trouble by saying the wrong thing—until she stood in front of the leaders of the Dhryn.*

There, Mac would let Brymn do the talking.

As if their escort had heard her thoughts, one came close to her on the opposite side from Brymn. "Mackenzie Winifred Elizabeth Wright Connor. I am Parymn Ne Sa."

Two hands missing, two extra names. *Hopefully coincidence*, Mac thought. "Accomplished," she said politely, doing her utmost not to pant. They hadn't slowed during this consultation. "I take the name Parymn Ne Sa into my keeping."

"Gratified." Parymn seemed older than the rest, grimmer somehow, although, like Brymn, he favored lime-green eye ridge paint with paired sequins. He was frowning. *Not at her*, Mac guessed, but as if worried by some task she represented. Sure enough, "There is a strict protocol which must be followed when intruding on the space of a Progenitor. Failure to do so will have—extreme consequences."

Given their entire escort carried weapons in all six hands, Mac had little doubt about the nature of such consequences. "I trust your guidance," she said, determined to put the onus on her escort instead of Brymn. That worthy was still bouncing along, seeming oblivious to the importance of the occasion, or the armament surrounding them. *Great.* Mac thought. *Stuck with a famished student sniffing pizza.*

Parymn sheathed the weapons in four of his six hands, using those in a gesture Mac recognized from Brymn's fits of anxiety. "Your ability to speak is remarkable, Mackenzie Winifred Elizabeth Wright Connor, and there is no doubt you are Dhryn, but—but— you lack the physical equipment required to—" Words seemed to fail him, then: "I fear you will offend simply by being what you are."

At some point, the ridiculousness of the universe rendered all other things moot. Smiling, Mac shook her head and patted Parymn on one arm, as familiarly as she would Brymn. "Don't worry. You said the Progenitors invited me—they must know what I am."

"Knowing isn't the same as believing."

A philosopher? Mac raised a brow, impressed. "Should I wait outside, then? I have no wish to offend them."

"It is too late. Your presence is expected."

Brymn, who'd seemed oblivious, suddenly jumped into the conversation. "Gloom and doom," he challenged. "That's all you *erumisah* ever say. If I'd listened to you, I'd never have studied the past, never have traveled, never learned—" Somehow, Mac managed to transform an artful stumble into a firm kick at what would have been an ankle on a Human leg. Brymn gave her a look, then closed his mouth.

Parymn didn't appear to notice. "It is our role to consider the consequences, Academic, and guide the growing generations of Dhryn along the safest path. In this case—ah. We have arrived."

Mac's eyes widened. The shroud-and-silver walls and ceiling continued through the entranceway ahead, but the passage itself was blocked by a mammoth vaultlike door of gleaming metal. Curiously, it was arched by gaps wide enough for Mac to squeeze through on either side and at the top. As she puzzled at the point of a door surrounded by holes, an inset within the door opened, nicely Dhryn-sized and shaped.

"Follow me," Parymn said, moving to the head of what now became a single file column of two Dhryn guards, Brymn, Mac herself, then two more guards. The rest of their escort took up stations on either side, apparently remaining behind. The 'bots rose to the ceiling as if ordered to wait as well.

They walked through the door, itself fifteen of Mac's steps deep, which opened into a passage both metal-scented and cold. She tried to see past Brymn, but could only make out a brightening ahead. Their escort moved too slowly now, as if there was some barrier ahead to be passed. Mac would remember the rhythmic movement of warm air past her face and neck, then back again, for the rest of her life.

Between one footfall and the next, she left what she understood or imagined, to enter a place nothing could have prepared her to meet.

Her eyes lied, frantic to make sense of what they saw. Mac was several paces into the Chamber of the Progenitors before she appreciated that what she thought was the ceiling was a shoulder, that what she thought a floor was a *hand*.

Believing and knowing weren't the same at all.

You've swum with whales, Mac reminded herself, even as the hand drew them away from the door, as steady and level as any machine. *At least they weren't underwater.*

Though they might have been. She wrenched her eyes from a vista of hills and valleys cloaked in dark blue skin, mottled with ponds of shining black liquid, and stared at what else lived here.

Her first impression was of rather silly-looking pufferfish, her mind fighting for equivalents. Her second was that the creatures looked nothing like fish at all. They were similar in size to herself, a relief after the shock of the Progenitor, but their oblong bodies were inflated, as if filled with gas. Indeed, many were drifting overhead like lumpy balloons. Fins lining the back and sides stroked at the air, guiding them in all three directions. Boneless arms hung below those drifting, as if they'd lost their function.

Most were crowded around the ponds, their bodies flaccid and low to the "ground," arms in the liquid. Mac couldn't tell if they were somehow taking it up or replenishing the Progenitor's supply. They had heads, but smoothed, so only the mouth and nostril openings remained. They varied in color, but all were pastel, like so many faded flower petals strewn about by the wind.

Air moved through Mac's hair, and back again. Over and over. The Progenitor's *breathing*.

These, too, were Dhryn?

From a world of only technology, she'd been transported to a wonderland of only biology. Mac crouched to brush her fingertips over the palm of the hand supporting them. Warm, rubbery, muscular. Like Brymn's.

"That is not permitted!" This urgent whisper from Parymn.

Mac looked up from her crouch. *He had to be kidding.* However, she stood. "My apologies, Parymn Ne Sa," she said absently, looking around.

Two pufferfish Dhryn intercepted them and hovered, close enough for Mac to touch, their arms—no, they were more like tentacles—groping the air toward her as if hunting for something lost. Disconcerted by the eyeless, silent beings, Mac eased back as much as she could. Parymn made a shooing motion with his upper arms and the two veered away with unexpected speed.

"Who are they?" she whispered to Brymn.

He blinked. "Who are who?"

Mac pointed to the flying forms now on all sides. "Them! Who are they? Those two seemed interested in me."

Brymn gave a low hoot. "Not who, what. Those are the Hands and Mouths of the Progenitor. They cannot be 'interested' in you, Mackenzie Winifred Elizabeth Wright Connor, or in anything else. They no longer think for themselves."

"Then they weren't always like this," she said, fighting back horror.

"It is an honor to become one of those who tends Her," Parymn broke in, his stern look at Mac intended to quell more questions.

Her. They were passing over what had to be the torso, as if the Progenitor brought them up and along her body. Mac moved as close to the edge of the palm as she dared, in order to see over the edge.

The blue skin below was smudged with white, as though every ripple was frosted with sugar. Mac fought the imagery to understand what was below. Not sugar crystals. *Oomlings!* They were erupting through the Progenitor's skin—thousands upon thousands upon thousands. As they appeared, they were being swept up in the arms of the pufferfish Dhryn, to be taken away into the distance. *To the nurseries?*

But their own destination almost shattered Mac's trained observer's calm. She glanced up and saw it coming. All she could do was grip Brymn for comfort and try to breathe without screaming.

Beneath nostrils the size of train tunnels whose breath filled this chamber, the Dhryn-who-had-been smiled at Mac with its normal mouth, blinked its normal eyes one/two below their sequined ridges, and said in its quiet, normal voice: "Welcome, Mackenzie Winifred Elizabeth Wright Connor."

The remnants of the face were embedded in a wall of blue flesh. The hand came to rest with its fingertips pressed against that wall, a platform as solid beneath Mac's feet as the deck of the *Pasunah*, and as much a lie. She spared an instant to long for a piece of honest granite, then deliberately let go of both Brymn and her fear. "Thank you—" She glanced at Parymn for the right honorific, but it was Brymn who answered.

"Progenitor! It is I, Brymn."

As Brymn was bouncing up and down, much as he'd done on the walkway to the shore, Mac waited to see the reaction. Their escort, predictably, looked highly aggrieved, bodies lowering in threat. The Progenitor, however, hooted. "Yes, I can see that. Welcome, Brymn," she/it said in a soft voice, higher-pitched and with a slower cadence than that of other Dhryn Mac had heard. "You have done well."

"I—have?" Brymn turned to Mac and picked her up with three arms. The rest were busy flailing about. "Did you hear that, *Lamisah*?" he bellowed in her face, squeezing tightly enough to threaten her ribs again. "I've done well!"

Mac fought for air and considered a timely kick. Fortunately, Brymn put her down before either became an issue. "Congratulations," she gasped, keeping an eye on the weapons all too nearby.

"Does this mean . . ." Brymn's voice faded into a whisper, ". . . dare I hope?" Mucus trailed from his nostrils and one hand groped blindly for Mac. Not understanding, but assuming it was an improvement over being grabbed, she took and held it. Then, in a heart-wrenching tone, he asked: "*Grathnu?*"

The Progenitor's eyes were identical to Brymn's. As they moved to pin Mac in their gaze, she was struck by the warmth that could be conveyed by yellow and black. "*Grathnu*," she agreed, then shocked them all. "To be served by Mackenzie Winifred Elizabeth Wright Connor."

Brymn's hand left hers.

Mac coughed into the ensuing silence. "If I may, Progenitor, Brymn is much more deserving of such an honor," she said cautiously, making every effort to focus on that disembodied face and ignore the city-sized body that supported it.

A whine of weapons being activated. "You mustn't argue with the Progenitor!" Parymn shouted furiously.

"I'll argue with anyone I please!" Mac shouted back, then closed her mouth.

With a minor shake, the floor space doubled. Another hand rested beside this one. "Leave us, Parymn Ne Sa."

The older Dhryn bowed without a word, then glared at Mac as he and the remaining guards obeyed, climbing on the Progenitor's other hand. They were whisked away, *hopefully*, Mac thought, *to the door.*

She had to smile.

"What amuses you, Mackenzie Winifred Elizabeth Wright Connor?"

Something about the Progenitor's gentle tone made Mac grin even more broadly and admit: "I was wondering if you ever clap your hands, Progenitor."

The laugh was only on the face—likely wise, given that otherwise it would shake the world of all those Dhryn below and startle the *oomlings* during their first breath of life. Mac imagined there must be a small respiratory shunt formed, to allow the mouth to form sound so the Progenitor could continue to communicate with other Dhryn. *Quite the metamorphosis.*

"A habit I left behind," the Progenitor assured her with a smile of her own.

Along with mobility, independence, and the sky, Mac thought, feeling the weight of that choice—or was it a choice? Brymn had said they only knew the next Progenitors when those individuals Flowered into their final state.

As if following Mac's line of thought, the Progenitor continued: "As you can see, I have gained far more than I left, Mackenzie Winifred Elizabeth Wright Connor."

"How long does it take to grow this big?" Mac asked, leaning her head back as she estimated the bulk of shoulders and what had been head looming over them. Brymn made a strangled noise; Mac ignored him.

"Five hundred or so of your years," the Progenitor answered. "I am the most recent to begin producing *oomlings*. My name—no longer matters. Few endure the change; fewer still the growth." A tinge of pride. "Those who do, are the Dhryn. What else would you like to know?"

At this, Mac looked straight into the face in front of her. "As Brymn can testify, Progenitor, I have a great many questions."

"Once *grathnu* has been served, you may ask until I tire."

Mac had no idea what *grathnu* involved, but she was sure she wanted it to happen to someone else no matter how curious she was about the Dhryn. But as Mac opened her mouth, the Progenitor smiled. "Yes, Brymn may serve first."

Brymn stammered his thanks until the Progenitor frowned slightly. Then he gave a bow so deep he almost tipped over backward, which would have sent him over the palm and tumbling onto the torso far below. Mac breathed a sigh of relief when he straightened again. "My life's work has been for the Dhryn," he announced, coming to stand before the face. "I am Dhryn." He spread his six arms outward, fingers outstretched.

The seventh arm burst into the open, its edged fingers stretched as well. As if it had eyes, it swayed and turned, boneless as the hanging arms of the pufferfish Dhryn. Mac took a step closer, fascinated. The fingers stopped and oriented toward her.

"Not so close," warned the Progenitor quietly. Mac backed a step. The fingers turned to Brymn.

"I return to my Progenitor that which I am." He brought his lower left arm to his chest. Like a striking snake, the fingers of the seventh lunged forward to seize the limb at the wrist. Before Mac's horrified eyes, the sharp fingers sliced through the arm.

Brymn's left lowermost hand dropped to the palm of the Progenitor, followed by a few splashes of blue-black. *The wound must be self-sealing*, Mac realized numbly. The Dhryn's face bore an expression of rapture and his seventh arm, task complete, hung limp down his chest.

"I am Brymn Las," he said with so much joy in his voice Mac hurriedly reassembled her face into something less horrified.

She hoped.

"I take the name Brymn Las into my keeping," the Progenitor acknowledged. "And his gift of self, which shall enrich that which is Dhryn through my flesh."

Mac flinched to one side as a pufferfish Dhryn swooped down, battling its way through the streams of air leaving the gigantic nostrils above to hover beside her. This close, it looked even less like a Dhryn. Instead of thick blue skin, it appeared made of membrane and air, its organs tantalizingly visible. Before she could study it further, the pufferfish Dhryn collected Brymn's hand in its tentacles and lifted away again.

If she hadn't known, Mac wouldn't have believed.

Brymn was looking at her expectantly. *How could he be thrilled to have been maimed?* Mac, feeling more Human than she had for days, licked her lips and said, "I take the name Brymn Las into my keeping. A fine name."

"Now it is your turn, Mackenzie Winifred Elizabeth Wright Connor."

Mac's pants had pockets. She rammed both hands into their protection, as if that could possibly help. "I'm not worthy," she said weakly.

"You saved Brymn Las, you forced our ancestral enemy into flight, you left your home and risked yourself in order to protect what is Dhryn. You are Dhryn. You are more than worthy. Come," the Progenitor insisted gently. "Serve."

Of the predicaments Mac had ever imagined for herself, or dreamed in her worst nightmares, being trapped on the hand of a giant alien who expected her to cut off her own hand wasn't remotely one of them. It likely would be from now on.

They don't know biology.

Mac stiffened her shoulders and tried to remember Brymn's phrasing. *Ah, yes.* "My work has been for the Dhryn." She tugged her braid from the back of her shirt, letting it fall down her chest. "I am Dhryn." She stretched out her arms, then brought both to her chest. "I give to the Progenitor that which I am." She'd palmed the small knife from her pocket in her right hand. Now, she grasped the braid in her left hand and sliced it off with her right.

The hair twisted as it fell to the palm of the Progenitor. What remained on Mac's head tumbled asymmetrically over her cheeks and down her neck, a lock dropping into her eyes. Without brushing it aside, Mac said firmly: "I am Mackenzie Winifred Elizabeth Wright Connor Sol." It hadn't been as hard as she'd feared to find one syllable to add to her name, something she could stand to hear repeated every time a Dhryn spoke to her. The name of Earth's Sun would be a promise to herself.

She would get home.

"I take the name Mackenzie Winifred Elizabeth Wright Connor Sol into my keeping," the Progenitor said gravely, "and her gift of self, which shall enrich that which is Dhryn through my flesh."

The pufferfish Dhryn who arrived to pick up Mac's braid appeared slightly confused, dipping up and down several times before finally grasping its find and heading away with it.

Brymn wasn't the least confused. He swept Mac into a hug, thoughtfully not using the arm still dripping fluid. "I knew you would serve *grathnu* with us as well as your own Progenitors, Mackenzie Winifred Elizabeth Wright Connor Sol!"

Mac's hand strayed to the jagged remains of her hair, a fair amount just past shoulder length and nodded, unable to smile. She'd broken her promise to Sam. *He wasn't coming back.*

How odd that letting him go had taken this.

The Progenitor was as good as her word, willingly answering Mac's questions. Unfortunately, despite Mac's care to avoid forbidden topics such as biology, every one of those answers was the standard Dhryn "we do not think of it," complete with a warm smile. After a dozen such responses, having learned nothing useful about the Ro or the Dhryn, Mac decided she'd tire before the Progenitor.

Now, she sat cross-legged beside Brymn on the palm of a giant. Amazing how easily the mind could put aside considerations like incredible size and inconceivable power when it came to a war of wills. Mac eyed the face on the blue wall of flesh and knew there were real answers behind it. *Good thing*, she told herself, *she herself was stubborn to a fault.*

"What should I ask you, Progenitor, that I haven't?" she inquired innocently.

The eyes blinked, one/two, as if she'd surprised the other. "I—"

Mac took advantage of the Progenitor's slight hesitation. "You must have expected me to ask you something in particular, or you wouldn't have invited my questions." She kept her voice set to sweetly courteous when it tried to slip into sarcasm. "I'd hate to disappoint you."

Brymn gave her a look that, from a Human companion, would have been asking, "What the hell do you think you're doing?" Mac ignored it, on the basis that from a Dhryn, for all she knew, it meant approval.

"I admit, Mackenzie Winifred Elizabeth Wright Connor Sol, that I have waited for you to ask why the Progenitors who preceded me chose to destroy our past, why we allow our system to remain at risk through the transects, and why I permitted you to be the first alien to meet a Dhryn Progenitor face-to-face."

"Good questions." So good, Mac hadn't dared ask them. "Would you answer them?"

They stared at one another, Brymn shifting unhappily as if he wished to say something but didn't dare. In this instance, Mac realized, she had an advantage over her friend. He was too used to revering the Progenitors, handicapping his ability to challenge different viewpoints.

Mac, on the other hand, was well past caring about protocol, and her only feeling about the Progenitor was a familiar awe for the way biology managed to work around civilization.

"Very well." The Progenitor pursed her small lips. "Our past has not been destroyed, although it has been made inaccessible to most Dhryn, including curious academics such as Brymn Las. Progenitors live a very long time. The three who survived the attacks of the Ro to settle this world lived long enough to share their knowledge with the next generation of successful Progenitors. That knowledge has been passed to those of my generation. Thus, we know what has been, what is, and what may be the consequence. Other Dhryn do not need to think of it."

"So the Ro are responsible for the destruction in the Chasm?"

"We barely escaped them," the Progenitor acknowledged, her eyes closing. "Had we not discovered technology to defend against theirs, we would have been destroyed again."

"Then why the transects?"

Her eyes opened in a flash of yellow-gold. "Before the Ro found us again, we had reached a point at which our *oomlings* must have new homes or suffer the consequences of overcrowding this one. We cannot change what it is to be Dhryn, Mackenzie Winifred Elizabeth Wright Connor Sol. Our colonies are essential to our survival."

Population pressure. Mac had to give the Dhryn credit—from what she'd seen, they'd made thorough use of this planet before venturing outward to others. If the Progenitors were physically incapable of slowing the birth rate—and culturally unwilling to find a biological way out—new worlds were the only answer.

The last of the three. Mac tilted her head as she asked: "Why did you permit me, a Human, to meet you?"

The Progenitor's eyes, though embedded forever in this mountain of flesh, could still sparkle. "Young Brymn Las is not the only curious Dhryn, Mackenzie Winifred Elizabeth Wright Connor Sol. I wished to see an alien with my own eyes, not through sensors and vids. At the same time, only one who is deemed Dhryn may be allowed in this chamber. You are both."

Mac pressed her hand against the palm supporting them. She doubted its thickened surface could feel something so small, but the Progenitor could see and hopefully understand the gesture. "I hope I haven't been a disappointment, Progenitor."

"In no sense, Mackenzie Winifred Elizabeth Wright Connor Sol, though I fear I must now disappoint you. One final question, if you please. I tire easily."

One? Mac almost panicked. *What if she asked a question that received only the stock answer? What if she missed the most important one?*

For no reason, Mac thought of the envelope in the pouch around her waist. She settled herself, abruptly sure what Nik would want her to ask. "If the Ro are beginning to attack other species as they did yours in the Chasm, what can we do to protect ourselves? Will the Dhryn share their effective defense?"

Two questions, but they would be one if the only answer was the
Dhryn technology. Mac chewed her lower lip as the Progenitor deliberated. At least, Mac thought, the delay meant it wasn't going to
be another "we don't think of it."

It wasn't. The palm shifted beneath them, sending both Mac
and Brymn to their feet, staggering to keep their balance. "We remember!" the Progenitor cried out in a pain-filled voice, eyes wild.
Mac heard cries from below as the torso landscape shook with
emotion, churning the pools, spilling *oomlings.* "There is no protection! No safety! There is only emptiness and regret!" The wall
in front of them became stained with yellow as mucus boiled from
the huge nostrils above. Quieter, but no less intense: "The gates
between worlds will close again and the only hope is to run before
they do. Tell your species to run, Human! Run while you still can!"

The hand swept them away from the grief-stricken face before
Mac could open her mouth to reply.

Mac had worried the distraught Progenitor would mean equally
upset guards. But the Dhryn escort waiting at the doorway might
not have noticed, Parymn nodding a greeting and beckoning them
forward. *Perhaps,* Mac thought, eyeing their impassive faces, *the
emotional turmoil of a buried Progenitor was another aspect of Dhryn
life they chose not to think about.*

She could think of little else, silent and self-contained throughout their journey back to the tube trains, offering no more than a
nod of farewell to Parymn and his guards at the station, curling up
in a luggage rack without a word to Brymn.

The Progenitor knew what life had been like for the first of her
kind on this world. The three survivors must have arrived on ships,
but then? Mac tried to imagine such huge, fragile creatures lying
out in the open, desperate to repopulate their species, utterly vulnerable until they had established themselves. The fear of the Ro
following and finding them, despite the closed transect, must have
been horrific.

No wonder they had spared their children that nightmare. *No wonder*, Mac thought as they passed from the area protected by shroud and rock, *they had reacted as they had to the Ro's return.* Hiding here, sending only the newly adult outside the system. The Progenitors must have been nearly hysterical at the news that the Ro had begun attacking other species again—that the nightmare from their past was coming to life, exactly as they'd been told.

No wonder they'd sent Brymn to Earth. *They must be trying everything.*

"Mac. Are you in pain? Should we hurry? Do you need your case of special supplies?" The concerned whisper from a being cradling a mutilated arm shook Mac from her preoccupation.

"I'm fine, Brymn. How about you?" The wound itself was covered in a pale blue membrane, but Mac couldn't imagine the underlying damage had already healed.

Brymn looked tired but found a smile. "A Dhryn is robust or a Dhryn is not. I have been honored beyond my dreams, Mac. What we gave the Progenitor will inspire the coming generation of *oomlings*." At her puzzled look, he explained. "*Grathnu* is required for a Progenitor to perform her function. Only adult Dhryn such as ourselves can provide what is needed."

Mac studied Brymn's chubby three-fingered hands with new interest. Sexual reproduction in many Earth species involved the female receiving a packet of sperm contained in a male body part. It offered the convenience of allowing the sperm to be stored for later use, not to mention dispensed with several potentially unsuccessful methods of exchange. "Will it grow back? Your hand, I mean."

He looked shocked and tucked all his hands under the silk banding his torso. "Certainly not!"

"Sorry. Just curious." Mac combed her fingers through the remains of her hair and hoped the pufferfish Dhryn could detect that her gift didn't have quite the same potential. "Was that your Progenitor?"

"Of course. All Progenitors are mine—as they are for all Dhryn."

She'd definitely disturb him if she pursued this, Mac realized, longing for a good DNA scanner. She changed the subject. "We need to take another look at all the reports, *Lamisah*, now that we've

confirmed your theory about the Chasm and the survival of the
Dhryn. I don't understand why the Ro have suddenly stepped up
their attacks—against others as well as your people. Perhaps there's
a clue we've missed."

"We shouldn't talk of private matters here, Mackenzie Winifred
Elizabeth Wright Connor Sol." Brymn freed one of his hands to
wave at the lone 'bot still hovering at the other end of the train car.
"This one has come with us from the Chamber. It could have more
capabilities than the others."

Startled, Mac stared up at the thing. It looked like all the rest, a
featureless globe, but then again, she'd stopped noticing them.
*Parymn probably set it to follow them after he and his guards put
them on this car.* She restrained the impulse to stick out her tongue.

"When we get home, I'm going to trim this," Mac said instead,
flipping back the hair that seemed intent on falling into her left eye.

She was as good as her word. A pair of Dhryn scissors—which took
two hands to use—and an underlying anger at a universe out of
control had proved a potent combination. Mac dug her fingers into
her scalp and ruffled its minimal covering, unexpectedly pleased.
Who knew there was still curl? The stuff was out of control, of
course, twisting in any direction it chose, but it couldn't get into
her eyes now. She pulled a few pieces down over her forehead, unsurprised to find some were gray.

Mac studied her reflection, comforted by a stronger resemblance
to her Mom than ever. There had been a lady who could cope with
the strange and alien.

She sighed. *Coping.* That was a word to live by. Mac pulled out
Nik's imp and entered as complete a description of the past few
hours as she could. She had to believe such things mattered, that
what she was learning would make its way to others.

Done, she headed for the "place of refreshment." Mac tossed
the last of her shorn locks into the biological accommodation and
watched them flash into nothing, thinking of Emily's story about
the Sythian living with Humans, who'd cremated her mandible

trimmings every night. Sitting in a tent on her own world, Mac had judged the behavior amusing and more than a little pathetic. Now the shoe was firmly on the other foot. Mac didn't want any Dhryn to find samples of what she'd given in *grathnu*. Although she hadn't really served, as Brymn, she appreciated the significance of the Progenitor's request. It seemed—impolite—to leave extras lying around.

Mac discovered Brymn had been busy while she'd tamed her hair. Having learned which foods suited her, he'd prepared a meal for them both. As usual, however, while waiting, he'd nibbled his way through most of his portion. Mac imagined the stress he'd endured was taking some toll, even if he'd never admit it.

"Ah!" he exclaimed, staring at her. "A healing process?"

The hair? "Of a sort," Mac answered, her stomach growling. Her head felt strangely light, something she chose to attribute more to hunger than haircut. "Let's get started."

Shoving a piece of what she'd come to call "bread" into her mouth, Mac made room on the table—Human and thus not slanted—for an assortment of items. Prime among them was the shimmering envelope that had drawn her into all of this. Brymn added the tablet of news reports. "I don't hold much hope for more information from these sources, Mac," he rumbled. "We've gone over them all."

Mac chewed and swallowed, managing not to make a face at the bitter aftertaste. "Interpretation is affected by other knowledge," she reminded him. "I analyzed these without knowing the connection between the Chasm, the Ro, and the Dhryn—or the time frame involved. Information about your biology might also influence what we find in here."

"How?"

She gulped something yellow and lunged for water, having forgotten the heat the innocent jellylike substance contained. Eyes watering, Mac gasped: "If I knew how, I wouldn't need to look through this again."

"You are not savoring your meal, *Lamisah*. These can wait until you are done."

Mac shook her head, then tried to explain the driving anxiety she'd felt since leaving the Progenitor. *Had it been the utter vulnerability of the creature and her offspring?* "We can't assume we have time to spare. We don't know for sure what's happening outside this system. I—" She stopped, staring at the water in her glass.

Ripples stirred its surface.

Within the same heartbeat, Brymn surged to his feet, turning toward the window.

"What is it?" Mac asked quietly, standing as well.

"I'm not sure." He headed for the door to her terrace. Mac started to follow, then, muttering a curse at her own paranoia, changed her mind. She grabbed what she'd brought to the table, returning the imp and envelope to the waist pouch, tucking Brymn's tablet into her shirt. She even took a bottle of water with her, feeling like a fool.

Better a fool now than sorry later, she told herself.

Mac caught up to Brymn at the door. It was raining outside, of course, and he hesitated to step out in it. She patted his shoulder as she went by, starting to offer: "I'll take a look—" Suddenly, the vibration intensified, shaking loose objects inside the apartment, making Mac clutch at the doorframe for safety.

"Quake?" she shouted.

Brymn was holding on to the door with all five hands. "Alarm!"

The shaking stopped and Mac stared at Brymn. "That," she said in the eerie silence, "was an alarm? For what?"

The flash and concussion swept away his answer—*was the answer,* Mac knew with despair as she whirled to look out.

A fireball had plunged into the midst of the Dhryn city, sending gouts of flame and debris—whole buildings—into the air. No—not a fireball—the tip of an unseen torch that continued to burn its way down, down, as if seeking the core of the world.

Not the core of the world. Mac *knew* the area under assault. They'd come out of the tube tunnel right there. *The core of the Dhryn!*

"The Progenitors!" Mac gasped. "The Ro are attacking the chamber." She found herself at the railing of the terrace, staring out at a violence all the more terrifying because she knew its target.

"How could they?" Brymn was beside her, his entire body vibrating with distress. "How could they know where to dig?"

It was as if horror had heightened Mac's senses. She spotted the gleam from the shadow of the leaning wall. "Brymn. Brymn!" He answered to her tug on his arm, followed her pointing finger to the vidbot hovering harmlessly above.

"What—? Those are Dhryn."

"Not that one! We have to get it," Mac said desperately. She threw her water bottle at the thing, but it only dipped aside. "Brymn!"

Whether the Dhryn's outrage at the attack helped or if he was always this accurate, Mac couldn't guess, but he *spat* at the 'bot, striking it dead center. Metal hissing to vapor, the device plummeted from the air, landed on the terrace, and rolled to Mac's feet.

Wincing at the sounds of destruction from behind her, guided by a red, glowing light that wasn't from the sun, Mac bent to study the half-melted device and saw what she'd feared. She tried to speak, to tell Brymn, but her voice trapped itself in a sob. She tried again.

"I led them!" She had to scream to be heard over the rain of bricks and girders, tile and rock. The words tore from her throat like vomit, scalding as they came. "It's one of Emily's Tracers! She used it to track me into the chamber. I led them there, Brymn!"

Emily and the Ro had wanted Mac on the Dhryn home world for only one reason. To get them past the Dhryn shrouds and protections. To guide them to their helpless quarry.

To help them kill the Progenitors as they'd failed to do three thousand years ago.

Another vibration, deep enough to shudder through Mac's heart.

"Mac! Mac! Hurry. We must get below."

Still crouched, Mac blinked through the ash now filling the air. The torch tip had sunk below the surface now, the sky darkening. The world hissed in pain as the true rain fought the fires clawing toward them. "Below?" she echoed. "What can we do? We can't fight—that—" a wave at the crater growing before their eyes.

"The alarm has been given. The Progenitors want all from the surface below. There isn't much time."

When she simply stared in confusion, he gave a deep thrum and picked her up. "Below, Mac!"

Another shake—sharper, shorter.

It meant they were already too late. Mac knew by the way Brymn's movements abruptly stopped. He put her down again, steadying her with his hands. "I am sorry, *Lamisah*."

Mac looked outward, expecting—what? What did you see when attacked by an invisible foe?

You saw death, she told herself numbly, holding onto her friend.

- Portent -

"OVER HERE! Quick! We have a survivor!"
    The sounds had no meaning. *The world had ended; how could there be a survivor?*

"Take it easy. Help's here."
    The words had no truth. *There could be no ease, no help. All was over; all was lost.*

"There's the transport. Careful. Don't hurt him."
    The voice had no future. *Had they thought it was safe? Had they thought the mouths gone?*

The wordless screams made more sense.

22

RESCUE AND REDEMPTION

L IKE HER aunt's terrier, the Ro were single-minded in their vi-olence, expending all their force against a hole in the ground. Mac and Brymn huddled together on the terrace, feeling that force through the ground beneath their building. Mac tried not to imag-ine the carnage and destruction deeper still, in the tunnel system, but her breath caught in her throat at the thought of the helpless *oomlings* and their caregivers, the Progenitors and their pufferfish, even the Wasted hiding in their tunnels.

She wasn't proud to hope she might not die, too.

Brymn had his own opinion, expressed in a doleful bass. "The end is near, Mackenzie Winifred Elizabeth Wright Connor Sol. I am grateful to spend my last moments with you."

Mac used the hand not trapped against the Dhryn to thump him gently. "I won't admit to last moments just yet, Brymn Las. They seem to be confining their attack to one area. We may be safe here—"

"It is not the Ro which will end our lives, but the Progenitors."

"The Progenitors? How?" Mac rubbed soot from her eyes, al-ready stinging from the acrid Haven rain, and tried to see anything through the low clouds of smoke. At least the constant downpour was washing the lighter particulates from the air, making it possi-ble to keep breathing and watch for falling objects. She'd dared to relax, very slightly—until now. "What do you mean?"

"It will be a spectacle, *Lamisah*, worth dying to see."

"I prefer living, thank you."

His arms tightened. "As do I. But I see no—ah. It begins."

It? Mac didn't see anything happening, beyond the Ro's assault. Brymn's more sensitive hearing must have given him advance warning, for the terrace abruptly began to tremble in earnest, the vibrations continuing until portions of the rail began to spring loose and drop away, landing with a clatter on the terrace below.

Brymn might have sounded fatalistic, but he moved as quickly as Mac could wish to pull them both close to the shelter of the wall.

The trembling went on and on, enough to put Mac's teeth on edge and drive her heart to pounding so hard she thought it could be heard outside her chest. Except that Haven was making noise of its own.

The planet was screaming.

Mac covered her ears, but the sound drove past flesh and bone, threatening her sanity. Just when she started screaming herself, it changed to a dull grinding from every direction at once. She closed her mouth and dropped her hands, looking out on the unbelievable.

Lines drew themselves in the city below, some crossing the angry sore that was the Ro attack. The lines deepened as Mac watched, ripping wider and wider. All of them at once.

The destruction caused by the Ro was nothing to this. Buildings toppled into newly formed valleys, roadways were torn apart, and still the lines widened as far as Mac could see.

"What's happening?"

Brymn didn't hear, or he didn't know.

Then, Mac no longer needed to be told. She could see for herself. The planet was breaking apart. Her mind's eye flashed to the tunnels, the massive doors she'd compared to air locks. *What if they had been exactly that?* What if the Progenitors had rebuilt this world so it couldn't be a trap for them?

Being on the surface was a very bad idea, Mac decided.

"We have to get below," Mac shouted at Brymn. "Maybe there's a door still open!" Standing was like riding a skim through a gale. Mac braced herself and pulled at the Dhryn. "We have to try!"

"We do not matter. That which is Dhryn will survive," he said, lowering his big head. "The Progenitors have always been ready."

"To run again?" Mac found herself trying to shake him, as if her muscles could shift Dhryn immobility when the entire planet couldn't. "The Ro will follow. We can't let—"

The universe *winked*.

"The Ro will follow. We can't—" Mac stopped. "I've said that before . . . I just said that—"

"Mac. Mac. Look!" She turned as Brymn stared past her, two arms pointing.

The fire-rimmed hole caused by the Ro was no longer empty. Now, it contained a towering splinter of bronze and light, shaped like no ship or machine Mac had ever seen before. More splinters, smaller yet identical, hung in the air above it. More, smaller still, above those.

And breaking through the clouds were ships Mac did recognize. "Those are Human!" she yelled at Brymn, jumping up and down. "Human!"

The Human ships headed straight for the Ro, weapons firing. Mac was no expert, but the combination of percussions and light-ninglike arcs looked deadly as they landed among the motionless Ro. She waited for the splinter-ships to fall from the sky, or blow up, or . . . do anything but what they did do . . .

. . . which was to rise into the sky, large and small combining into one blinding mass, then disappear.

"The Ro—in retreat?" Brymn sounded astonished.

Mac was almost tossed to her knees by another, more powerful tremor. The Human ships hunting the Ro were flying over a landscape being torn apart along multiple fault lines. "Is there any way for the Progenitors to stop splitting the planet?" she demanded. "Is this reversible?"

"I do not know such things, Mac."

"Next time—" she staggered and grabbed Brymn for support, "—next time I'm stuck on a dying alien world, remind me to make sure it's with an engineer, not a damn archaeologist!"

A faint but courageous hoot. "I'll do my best, Mac."

Settling down together, side by side, Mac and Brymn looked out over the end of a world. In the distance, entire portions of the planet were already lifting free, shedding their thin cover of civilization to reveal the thickened forms of the ships beneath before vanishing into the clouds. Wind was howling around the remains. Mac wondered what the Humans thought of it all. They'd come to vanquish the Ro and, instead of triumph, were watching the planet they'd successfully defended destroy itself, its inhabitants so many refugees fleeing what should have been victory.

"Someone's coming for us, Mac. There."

Had too many hopes failed? Mac wondered when she could feel nothing but numb at this news. She glanced up anyway. Brymn wasn't wrong. One of the Human ships had released a handful of skims, now heading in their direction through the rain.

Self-preservation took over from hope. Mac rose to her feet on the cracking terrace, pulling Brymn with her. She started to wave, then dropped her arm. *They'd never see her.*

It didn't seem to matter. The skims continued straight on course toward them. How? *The bioamplifier!* "Nik?" she whispered, tasting the rain and soot on her lips, feeling life surging through her entire being. "Nik!"

Mac drew in a deeper breath, when from behind and above she heard:

Scurry . . . spit! Pop!

23

DESTINATION AND DISCLOSURE

TIME SAT on a shelf.
Rolled off.
Landed at her feet.
Turned into a shiny salmon and wriggled its way *into* the floor.
"Okay, now I know I'm crazy."
She heard the words but stretched so thin she could *see* eternity between each syllable.
When was she?

Breathing. That was the sound. Deep breathing, so deep it was more a moan than exhalation. A moan so full of pain she hurt to listen.
It wasn't her.
Who was she?

"Don't open your eyes."
Mac opened her eyes on light, fractured and moving, filled with shapes formed in impossible dimensions. She promptly threw up.
"I warned you." A pressure on her now closed eyes, hot then cold, wet then dry. Hot/wet, cold/dry. Mac rolled her head, trying to be rid of the confusion.

"Give it time, Mac. You've got sensory overload on top of the sub-teach."

Mac? The voice thinned and thickened, deepened and raised, but the name caught her attention. *She* was Mac. If she was Mac, where was . . . "Brymn?"

"He's here. Don't ask me why."

Mac grappled with consciousness, feeling it slipping away again, knowing herself close to an answer.

Where was she?

Brymn. The moaning had to be Brymn. Mac groped in the dark, fingers catching on cloth—a blanket?—then on a hard coldness—rock? Her eyes fought the dark even as she remembered legs, feet, and a body, even as she somehow contorted all of those to rise to her . . . knees. Hands and knees.

Good enough.

The moaning had direction, if no consistency of volume or tone. Mac stayed as she was to follow it, moving her left hand forward on the hard, rough coldness, then the right, bringing forward her left knee, then her right, all motions small and cautious. *Just because she was blind, didn't mean others were.*

Time remained slippery and unpredictable. Mac couldn't tell if she'd crawled for seconds or hours before her outstretched fingers touched *something.* Warm, rubbery. She sagged with relief. "Brymn," she whispered. A moan answered. She sat, freeing both hands to explore what she'd found.

One touched flame!

With a cry, Mac fell back, but her hand stayed in the fire. No matter how hard she pulled, it wouldn't come free. The flesh was searing off—the bone would be next—it would take her arm—

"I should have known you wouldn't stay in bed, Mac."

Light blinded her as the fire went out in her hand. Whimpering, Mac cradled her injured fingers to her chest, only to find they were no longer burning. She touched them with her other hand, amazed to find them whole, as if nothing had happened.

The light was more normal this time. Mac blinked over and over again, trying to make sense of the images moving in her field of view.

"You'll see soon enough. Go back to bed and stay there." The voice was as distorted as the images; as distorted as time itself. Mac let herself be guided to an area of rock that felt the same as the rest, then lay down while the blanket was replaced.

Under it all, the moaning.

Time found its teeth at last, ripping apart illusion.

"Emily!" Mac shouted, sitting bolt upright as she *knew* the voice.

"Here."

Here . . . ? Mac squinted against what still seemed too bright a light. She brought her legs underneath, but didn't try to stand. "I can't see you."

"How's this?" The light dimmed, cut by a piece of familiar fabric held as an umbrella. A Dhryn shroud.

Mac focused first on the figure blocking the light. The stylish black jumpsuit was coated in pale dust and cut down the left sleeve, the edges of the cut ragged and frayed as if the damage had occurred weeks ago. The face was older, worn to the bone.

But the raised eyebrow and challenging look was pure Emily Mamani.

Mac had her priorities. "Where's Brymn?"

"Behind you."

They were outside, in some rough sort of camp on bare rock. That much Mac gathered as she looked around for Brymn. When she saw him, she scrambled to her feet with outrage. "Take those off! Take those off now!"

The Dhryn had been wrapped, once more, in the painful threads of the Ro. Mac curled the fingers of her hand, reliving the burning pain. No wonder Brymn moaned with every breath.

"Not my call, Mac."

Mac took a step closer to Emily, moving so the sunlight wasn't in her eyes. "Then whose is it?"

"The Survivors." Emily tossed the shroud material to one side. "The Dhryn are your damned Survivors!"

That challenging look. "Are they?"

It was so—*normal*—of Emily to force Mac to rethink her position on a subject that she actually paused. Then Mac shook her head in disgust. "If you have something to say, say it. Otherwise, either give me what you used to free my hand from that stuff, or get out of my way while I look for it."

Not that there were very many hiding places. The camp, such as it was, consisted of two large dirty-white bags, some sheets of shroud material—one of which had been Mac's blanket—and a fist-sized portable heating unit. Their surroundings were even less hospitable: an overbright sun, dry air with a bite of morning chill to it, and dull gray rock that formed a cuplike shelter around three sides.

Except it wasn't rock, not all of it. Mac's eyes narrowed as they traced what might be the line of a wall, the remains of a doorway, perhaps a window. Farther away, what appeared to be the ruins of other buildings rose in the distance, giving the horizon a jagged edge. *She'd seen that lack of perpendicular before.*

"I take it this is somewhere in the Chasm," Mac said, refusing to be impressed—or terrified. A lower moan than the rest brought her attention back to Brymn. "I'll ask why here later. Right now?" She made her hands into fists. "Help him."

"And have this two against one? Do you take me for a fool?"

"I took you for a friend."

The word hung between them until Emily's lips tightened. Without grace, she reached into a pouch on her belt and drew out a tiny vial she tossed to Mac. "Use this on the nodes—where the threads cross." She brought out a weapon. "If he makes one move I don't like, he dies."

Vial in hand, Mac paused to look back at Emily. "Like Nik?"

"The bureaucrat?" Emily frowned. "He's dead?"

"You should know!" Mac snapped. "You were the one who shot him!" She believed she'd seen every expression possible on that face. Now she watched puzzlement flash across it, followed by stunned comprehension.

"I remember now. You'd think you'd never forget something

like that," Emily said in a strange voice. "But the trans-ships mess with the brain—the humanoid brain, at any rate. I'm sure you noticed. Takes days, sometimes, to sort it all out. Some stuff is just . . . gone. Takes getting used to, Mac, believe me." A pause. Emily opened her mouth, inhaled a sharp, deep breath then let it out slowly. "I do remember. Shooting our Nikolai, that is. Didn't know who he was at first, but it didn't matter. I was making the wrong move, Mac. I knew it even as I called out to you. I thought I should get you out of it—I couldn't handle it anymore. But everything was in motion, the players onstage. It was too late to stop. Wrong. I shouldn't have tried."

"You aren't making any sense!" Mac cried.

"The idea was to make everyone believe you were in danger, convince everyone you were important to the Dhryn. That way, they'd offer you their very best protection. The protection they only give their own. But you've figured that out."

Mac pushed the words aside with an angry gesture. "You killed him, Emily."

Emily raised her eyebrows, something closer to sanity in her eyes. "Didn't. He wasn't dead—not from that, anyway. Sore, maybe. Mad as hell, likely. Not that you'd care, right?"

Emily knew her face, too. Before it could betray her, Mac turned back to Brymn, blinking fiercely in order to see what she was doing. Bad enough her relief was making the ground as unsteady as the death throes of the Dhryn world. *All this, including shooting Nik, so she could blithely lead the way to the hiding place of the Progenitors?*

Forgive me, Mac . . .

Mac had never experienced anger like this, anger that waited deep inside her like a mountain lion ready to leap from ambush, nerves aquiver and muscles locked.

The vial had a closed slit along its length. Mac took a guess and aimed the slit at the nearest "node," squeezing the vial from both ends. It didn't spray out a substance, as she'd anticipated, but instead released a narrow beam of greenish light. The thread reacted to this as it had to Nik's weapon, shriveling away from that contact in both directions. It was the work of seconds to free Brymn.

He stopped moaning, but remained still, eyes closed. "How long was he bound?" Mac asked, running her hands over his skin and relieved to find no areas of oozing or obvious damage.

"Two hours," Emily answered. "Maybe three. We came straight here, but you didn't take the trip well."

Straight here? What did that imply about the Ro? Mac shook her head to dismiss what didn't matter at the moment. She eased the positions of two of the Dhryn's arms, then sat beside him on the rock. Or rather dust. The dullness of their surroundings was due to it, a fine powder that filled in crevices and pillowed corners. She glanced down at herself. Her brilliant Dhryn colors had picked up a layer already, especially on the knees. "Why did you bring us here?" she asked coldly, finally looking at Emily. "Wasn't my work for you done?"

Emily did contrite better than anyone. She tried it only as long as it took for Mac to stare her down. "Two reasons," she said then, sitting on the bags and stretching out her long legs. Despite this show of relaxation, Mac noticed her dark eyes flicked constantly to Brymn and her hand rested on the weapon she'd put back in her belt. "We need to—share—certain facts with you. And I'd made them promise you wouldn't be harmed. I told you I'd help you."

Mac ignored the wistful look on Emily's face. "You're helping the Ro," she accused.

Emily shook her head. "The Myrokynay," she corrected. " 'Ro' is a Dhryn corruption of the name."

Myrokynay? Mac dug her fingers into the dust. "The transects—"

"Were their invention, yes. Their—gift." Emily's mouth twisted over the word. "The Myrokynay are masters of no-space. Their entire technology is based on it. You've experienced some of it. Their ships create their own temporary transects. They wear suits that allow an individual to be here and not here, at the same time. It would drive most other sentients quite mad. Sometimes I wonder if it's why communicating with them is so difficult."

"But you can."

"To a point. The effort to understand us originated with them; first contact, if you can call it that, was made by their choice. Me. Others. I don't know who or how many, so don't bother asking."

"Why?" Mac breathed. "Emily, what could they possibly want that's worth any of this?"

Her friend's face had never looked this old and tired. "What *we* wanted, Mac, was to stop this—" her toe kicked the dust, "—from ever happening again. But we've failed." Emily lifted the corner of a piece of shroud fabric with one finger. "Did you give this to Nik and his misguided cronies?" At Mac's puzzled frown, she shrugged and let the fabric fall. "Irrelevant. We're a clever species, Mac. Too clever for our own good, sometimes. Show a monkey a new approach to a problem and *caramba!* A new problem."

"What do you mean?"

"You were there, Mac. On the Dhryn world. Where we so-clever Humans took the Dhryn's method of nullifying the Ro's devices and adapted it into something that could yank their ships right out of no-space. Quite a shock, believe me. I thought the Ro were going to abandon us there and then."

Mac held up her hands. "Whoa, Em. Yes, I was there. And the Ro weren't helping anyone—they were attempting genocide. For the second time!"

Another flick of the eyes to Brymn, then a somber gaze at Mac. "Yes."

- Portent -

THE RAIN continued to fall, obedient to gravity and dew point. It cratered dust and puddles, it slipped through abyssal cracks to become steam and rise again.

It tracked like tears over the great ships as they pulled free of the earth below, froze as they passed beyond cloud into the fierce glow of the sun, outgassed to randomly drifting molecules as those ships left air and world behind.

The great ships, silent and swifter now, ran for the Naralax Transect. The Others, witness to grief and flight, gave way. Well wishes followed the survivors of a world as they fled its system forever.

Back on that world, the rain continued to fall, driven by new winds, controlled and remarked by no life at all.

24

EDUCATION AND ENDINGS

"'Y ES?' THAT'S all you have to say?" Mac kept her hand on Brymn.

Emily leaned forward. "No. That's not all." Her eyes flashed with fury. "We had a chance to end it for good. You gave us that chance, Mac. You and my Tracer, with some modifications. The Dhryn had learned to shield themselves from the Myrokynay's scanners, to keep out their scouts. We couldn't sample the population anymore. All we could do was wait for the signs—"

Mac cut in, her own voice hoarse with passion. "Signs? Of what? Did traveling with them scramble what's between your ears, Emily? Or have you somehow failed to notice it's your damn Ro killing people—not the Dhryn!"

"Some casualties—"

"You helped them sink Pod Six. It was midday, Emily. You know how many students were in it. You know who they were." They both rose to their feet, but Mac didn't let Emily speak. She flung her hand toward Brymn. "I lived with them, Em. Thanks to you and your 'friends,' I know the Dhryn better than most of my own relatives. They're alien, I'll grant you, but they're a lot closer to us than your murderers."

"Don't you think I wanted them to be wrong?" Just as hot; just as sure. "Don't you think I went over the data—searched for another answer—did everything I could *not* to believe them? Gods, Mac, you should trust me by now!"

Dry-eyed and utterly still, Mac let the words drop between them, listening to the sigh of air over the ruins and the slither of dust that followed.

Emily spat out a string of Quechua epithets and went to the bags, digging through them with a violence that promised to leave little intact. She pulled out a too-familiar waist pouch. "Here." The pouch landed at Mac's feet, stirring a knee-high cloud. "My personal logs are in there, too. The real ones."

Mac bent down and picked up the pouch. She opened it and looked inside. Both links and the envelope. "So you aren't a thief," she said coldly. "Yet." The words were to give her time to think. *The imp from Nik—had it sent its record? Could it tell them where to find her? Could a Human ship reach this system at all?*

"I know what's in there, Mac. I know you respected my privacy enough to keep what you thought were my logs in your own imp, away from our Nikolai and his cronies."

The logs? ". . . sensory overload on top of the sub-teach." *Had she dreamed hearing that?* Mac worked her mouth around the words without speaking them, finding the movement of her lips and tongue suddenly unfamiliar. "What language—?" she fumbled.

Emily's expression was grim. "Some of the Myrokynay defense systems are cued to the sound of Dhryn. You were muttering it. For all our sakes, I retaught you English and Instella. I don't know what Dhryn you'll recall, but I advise you not to use it."

"No 'is this okay with you, Mac?' Or 'do you mind if I meddle with your brain again, Mac?' " Mac growled. "Why am I not surprised?"

"Hey, I left your imps alone—with the exception of adding my logs to both."

"Both?" Mac tried to look puzzled.

Emily's laugh was forced. "Don't bother. We knew all along, between the tech we have and knowing the Ministry's standard operating procedure. Which included that beacon they stuck in you. Boosted the gain for our needs nicely. Don't worry," she said, misinterpreting Mac's look of dismay. "I've sent your location. We want you found."

"So you can kill Nik when he comes for us?" Mac accused. "That is your next move, isn't it? To kill anyone and everyone who knows about the Ro and their tech?"

"Mackenzie Connor!"

"What?" Mac countered icily. "Can you be shocked at any level? Is that still possible, Dr. Mamani?"

Emily ducked her head then looked up, the ghost of the old smile on her lips. "Well, the hair was a surprise. What did you use? A filleting knife? And those clothes . . ."

They were enemies. *How could they still feel like friends?*

"Damn you, Em," Mac said, feeling the rage draining from her, leaving something harder to name behind.

"That's what my dear mama always said."

"Wise woman."

"Stubborn, too."

"And you aren't?"

"I've known worse. A certain salmon researcher comes to mind."

"Salmon." Mac squeezed her eyes shut, then opened them again. "I don't begin to understand how we got here," she waved one hand at the desolation, "from Field Station Six. I don't want to know, to be honest. But wanting—it's not something you and I can put first, is it?"

Emily shook her head, once, her dark eyes suspiciously bright.

"Where do we go from here, Em?" Mac asked wearily.

"You? You go over that hill." Emily's long fingers traced the low rise before the next cluster of ruins. "You'll find some people there, including Humans. They'll take care of you until the cavalry charges into orbit. Archaeologists, treasure seekers, ghoul hunters. I doubt they know what this place is. He will." She nodded at Brymn, still unconscious on the dusty rock. "You do," with a challenging look.

"The Chasm—and the Dhryn Homeworld."

"The start of it all, Mac. You'll find some of the answers here. Don't take too long. Time isn't on your side."

"And you?"

Emily drew herself up, her face assuming an expression Mac hadn't seen before. Regal, determined, and unutterably grim. "The

Interspecies Union picked the wrong enemy, Mac, and won. Now you'll face the real one and lose—unless I can convince the My-rokynay not to abandon our sector of space."

"You're going with them."

"It's the only way."

Mac took a step closer, held out her hands. "It isn't. If there's something dangerous about the Dhryn, you can warn us. If there's something about the Ro—the Myrokynay—we need to know, you can help us communicate with them. You don't have to leave."

Emily took Mac's hands in hers. "It's not that easy, Mac," she said, turning their clasped hands so the tear in her left sleeve was uppermost.

Mac gasped. The cast that should have been there was gone. *It had only been a disguise.*

The skin that should have been there was gone, too—replaced by what looked like a slice of space, dark as pitch and dusted with stars. Mac gripped the fingers within hers as tightly as she could, as if Emily might drift away at any moment. "What is that?" she breathed.

"It's what it appears to be," Emily said gently. "The Myrokynay use space and no-space the way we use electronics or sound. This—diversion—of my body is part of what allows me to communicate with them, helps me endure travel on the trans-ships. It—I think the closest description is that it enfolds me as required."

"Can it be removed?" Mac released Emily's right hand, so hers could ease open the tear. The slice of space continued up the other woman's arm, but didn't encompass it. Tanned, olive-toned skin edged the depths. *Life guarded the emptiness.*

"Some changes are for the better," Emily said evasively, using her free hand to ruffle Mac's new curls.

"Em—" Before Mac could finish, Emily let go and took a step back.

"As I said, time's not a friend. My ride's waiting and they've been unusually patient while you recovered."

Mac sent a despairing look at Brymn. "Brymn has saved my life. He's as dear to me as—as you are. At least tell me why I'm sup-posed to fear his kind."

"I—" Emily shook her head. "Mac, I don't know all the details.

I've put everything I could beg or steal from the Myrokynay in the imps. I hope you can work it out. I do know one thing. It involves the metamorphosis. That's why the Myrokynay wanted to check the Dhryn offspring before they became adults. They were watching for a particular change in the species. Something that's happened before."

"Before—before when?"

"Before this." It was Emily's turn to wave at their surroundings. "Before the Myrokynay understood that not every species should be given the ability to leave their systems. Before the Dhryn—" She winced, drawing her left arm to her side. "They're calling me. Mac, I have to go—now."

"Be sure you're back before the next field season, okay?" Mac warned, her voice unsteady. "And don't be late. We've work—work to do."

"I will. I'll try." With each word, Emily backed a step, as if it was important to put space between them. "Look after the old rock for me."

Mac lifted a hand in acknowledgment, no longer trusting her voice. Dust began to whirl between them. *A Ro version of a skim*, she assumed. Yet she could see Emily through it, see the tears scoring the dust on her face.

"Mac!" The urgent words sounded oddly distant. "The Ro never took adult Dhryn because of the risk. Injury can trigger the next metamorphosis. Be careful!"

This from the woman leaving in an invisible ship? Mac found herself smiling through her own tears. "You, too!"

The dust grew to a column taller than Mac and she moved away, covering her mouth and nose with one hand.

The dust blew past her in a single, violent gust, then the air grew still again.

Emily was gone.

Mac smeared away dust and tears with the back of her hand. "A camp over the hill—possibly with real food," she reminded herself in a thick voice. "Human ships on their way—possibly containing someone I—well, someone. Life could be worse." She glanced at the very still, very large Dhryn decorating the rock. "Okay, so maybe there's still a problem."

But it was a Mac-sized problem, as opposed to an end-of-life-as-we-know-it-sized problem. She busied herself at the bags, presuming Emily had left them for her use.

The first contained more strips of the shroud fabric. Toxic-to-Ro waste being dumped on her? Discards from Ro experiments? Trophies? It didn't matter. The stuff was soft and strong, so Mac stretched out each strip, organizing them by size. None were quite as large as Brymn, but together she had enough for either a shelter or a sled.

The second bag proved more interesting. That was the one where Emily had stashed Mac's waist pouch. Sure enough, Mac pulled out several long boxes. Two contained stiff brushes of varying sizes, an assortment of drills, sieves, and hand scanners—all well-used. The tools of an archaeologist. Emily's own, perhaps.

Well, Mac thought, putting them aside, *they were probably of more use on this planet than those of a biologist.*

The next box contained a tent, sleeping bag, and other outdoor equipment, definitely not new. Mac hoped not to be out here long enough to need them, especially after she opened the last box.

No food or water. No signaling device. The box was full of bright scarves and baskets, dresses and shoes. A folded jewelry case. Emily's notion of traveling equipped, back when she traveled with Humans.

Mac closed the lid carefully, her hands shaking.

"No clouds. It's going to be cold at night." The dryness of the air didn't promise much in the way of condensation, but Mac knew, in principle, how to make a dew-catcher. Dhryn physiology gave her another source of water, but she'd have to be very thirsty before she'd go that route again.

However, her priority was Brymn himself, so she went to sit beside the big alien. "We've three—make that four—choices," she told him, stroking the handless arm. "I find a way to wake you up and we walk to the camp. I drag you to the camp. I go to the camp and bring back help. Or we both wait here for the ships Emily said will be coming."

Mac sighed. "I agree. There's only one choice," she said, as if the unconscious Brymn had expressed an opinion. "Who knows how far the permanent transect is from this planet? They could take days getting here from there. I don't want to leave you—and I doubt I could roll you onto a sled, let alone pull it. We'll try the waking up."

She'd been thinking about this. The composition of the ruins, here at least, appeared mostly ceramic, with some natural rock beneath. Perhaps the original building had been tucked against a cliff. Brymn was lying on what might have been a floor. Or a collapsed roof.

It took Mac a few moments to find the implement she wanted, a rounded, solid piece of stone. She pushed Brymn's head so one ear was against the floor, then took a few steps away. Lifting the rock over her head, Mac let it fall.

Definitely a vibration beneath her feet, as well as the sound of the rock smacking into the ground. The Dhryn didn't so much as twitch.

She retrieved the rock, lifted, and dropped it again.

And again.

And again. *Had an eyelid moved?*

Her arms began shaking as she lifted the stone yet again. "C'mon, Brymn," Mac urged, keeping her voice as low-pitched as possible. Down went the rock.

His eyes shot open. Mac rubbed her sore arms as she hurried to his side, falling to her knees. "Brymn. Brymn!" She hesitated, belatedly remembering the violence of his last awakening, and prepared to scramble away if it was repeated. "Brymn?"

Fortunately, this time all the Dhryn did was open his eyes and turn his big head in the direction of her voice. "Mac," he said weakly, his mouth working as though struggling to find words. "What—? Where—?"

"What was Emily. She'd arranged for us to be scooped up from Haven during the Ro attack. Where?" Mac found a smile. "Where you've wanted to go since you first believed it existed, *Lamisah*. Home."

"I really think we should find that camp before nightfall," Mac observed, not for the first time. She had to grant Brymn was enthusiastic about his subject. Once he'd fully comprehended where they were, he had to explore everything, consumed by the wonder of Dhryn artifacts older than any he'd seen before. Mac had made the mistake of mentioning Emily's toolboxes, so now he was waist-deep, in Human reckoning, in a hole whose location Mac suspected was pretty much a matter of chance, humming to himself. She had to admit, multiple arms made for quick digging.

However, the sun was closing in on the far horizon, stretching long fingerlike shadows in the direction they should be heading. *Now.*

"Brymn. We can come back tomorrow. For all you know, there's a better site over the hill."

"I'm almost through to the next level. The floors collapsed on one another, Mac. It's quite fascinating."

Mac stood up and brushed futilely at the dust coating her arms and legs. "What's going to be fascinating is seeing if you can keep up with me."

Two giant yellow-irised eyes appeared at the top of the hole. "You wouldn't leave me, Mac?" He'd turned from blue to gray with dust. "I don't feel safe without you."

The Dhryn outmassed her two to one, not to mention his extra appendages. He was also a touch superstitious. Mac sighed and assured him again: "There are no such things as Chasm Ghouls, Brymn."

"How do we know for sure?"

She shook her head. *Archaeologists.* "Nothing could live here." Mac had used one of the hand scanners to test the dust and air. No organics. Almost no water.

"Something did," Brymn pronounced, as if this was proof.

"Yes, something did." Mac looked into the distance. The shadows teased images of the original buildings from the ruins, their odd angles joining into a growing darkness.

The Dhryn used his upper arms to pull himself from the hole, like a sea lion climbing on shore. "You don't believe what Emily said, do you?" he asked in a low rumble after standing. "About the Dhryn and the Ro—the Myrokynay? You don't believe we could harm other species, that we caused this ourselves?" He didn't bother to indicate the ruins.

"I—I know that we don't know," Mac said with frustration. "All we have is finger-pointing, like two kids standing beside a broken skim, each blaming the other. Who to believe? Your Progenitors? The one who spoke to us admitted to hiding your past. The Ro? I'm hardly sympathetic to a culture that either hides or kills, but that could be Human prejudice. I'm a salmon researcher, Brymn, not a diplomat." Mac controlled herself. "What matters is that people are dying and this place . . . this place could hold some answers. That's what Emily said."

"So I should keep digging," Brymn offered hopefully.

"So we should walk over that hill and learn what's already been found."

"Are all Humans this stubborn?" he asked.

Mac began piling the boxes under the shroud fabric, using stones to hold the material in place. "There's worse things to be," she said.

There wasn't a roadway or tracks to guide them, but Mac had memorized the most distinctively shaped ruins as landmarks. She was hoping those at their destination would have lights up and running. Despite finally budging Brymn from his hole, they'd be lucky not to be walking in full darkness before reaching Emily's promised camp.

The one thing Mac didn't doubt was that the camp existed. Emily would have left her rations and water if there had been any doubt she could find those on her own. While Mac was unhappily sure Emily could commit murder if she had to, it wouldn't be like this, by marooning her friend on a desert planet.

She and Brymn carried only what they wore. As for weapons— or proof of identity? Mac was counting on the envelope in the pouch, now safely under her clothes and around her waist.

The terrain rose in low upward swells, but the footing was better than Mac had expected. The dust had been blown into firm curls and dunes, often exposing the tiles of what might have been courtyards and walkways. Her boots created echoes. They rarely had to walk around the remains of walls, although there were tall piles of debris. Mac was uncomfortably aware that this meant the buildings had been destroyed, not left to time and the elements. She was even more uneasy about the lack of life. It was one thing to read about the Chasm and its stripped worlds—quite another to be the only living things on one.

Brymn, on the other hand, was thrilled to his core, keeping up an unceasing commentary on their surroundings. "Do you see that . . ." indicating a partial archway that looked like all the rest. "Could we stop and measure . . ." this, concerning a raised basin, filled with dust. "This could be a good place to stop and rest . . ." at almost every new ruin they passed.

Finally, her feet starting to hurt and far too thirsty for patience, Mac snapped at him: "Must you talk the entire way?"

Brymn was silent for several more footfalls, then said in a small voice: "Dhryn worlds are never this quiet."

"Oh." Mac ran the fingers of one hand through her hair. "I could hum."

He tilted his head to look down at her. "You mock me?"

Mac kept any hint of a smile from her face. "Never. Humming makes it easier to hike."

"Ah. Then we shall hum together."

And they did.

"Who's out there?"

The faceless challenge in Instella was reassuring. Mac put her hand on Brymn's nearest arm to hold him beside her. They'd just crested the top of the hill and, as Emily'd promised, there was a collection of tents and a solar array below, all the markings of a field camp. Mac felt a certain sense of homecoming. The tents were illuminated from within—everyone settling in for the night.

They likely hadn't expected humming from the darkness. Discordant humming at that.

"Drs. Mackenzie Connor and Brymn Las," she called down. "We're looking for shelter."

The subsequent rush of bodies from the tents was even more familiar. *Grad students*, Mac thought fondly.

A very short while later, she and Brymn were seated in the largest tent, surrounded by curious faces. Well, she assumed the look on the faces of the four Cey was curiosity and not indigestion, and it was anyone's guess what was under the writhing mass of tentacles that served the five Sthlynii for mouths, but the Humans, in the majority here, were unabashedly bright eyed and intrigued.

Mac smiled at them all before taking another sip from the glass of juice they'd provided, her taste buds sparking with joy.

"Yes. We have Ministry ships insystem, Dr. Connor, and on approach. They're about two days from here. Yours?" Lyle Kanaci was the group's spokesperson—a short, chubby Human with pigmentless hair and skin. Mac found this living evidence of diversity within her own species fascinating and had to remind herself not to stare.

"My ships? Unless you were expecting visitors, they should be," Mac said.

"Weeee dooon't aaaallooow viiisiiitooors." The Sthlynii who hissed this leaned over the table, saliva dripping from its tentacles.

Mac felt Brymn's annoyed rumble and nudged him. "Good, good. That's essential to our work, isn't it, Dr. Brymn Las?"

Either his new name or her nudge conveyed the desired message. "Essential. As is the availability of . . ." Brymn began to rattle off technical questions about the camp's equipment, excavations, findings, and other minutiae understood only by archaeologists. Mac settled into her chair, trying to decide between cookies and soup.

It hadn't hurt their reputations one bit that the text of choice in the camp was Brymn's collected works, a discovery that meant Mac didn't have to produce her envelope, nor explain her clothing.

Much better to be accepted as one of the group.

Mac nibbled and watched, finding herself less comforted by the Human faces than she'd expected. *Probably instinct*, she told herself. Several should have had "crackpot" stenciled on their foreheads before being allowed out, just to save time. She knew the type. They probably slept with "Chasm Ghouls—They Exist and Speak to Me" and hoped desperately for an encounter with the undead.

They should meet the Ro.

On the way here, she and Brymn had discussed whether or not to reveal that this world had been home to the Dhryn. In the end, it was a moot point. Despite the presence of several nonscientists, the rest were doing significant work here. They'd already determined the former inhabitants had been Dhryn. In fact, they'd sent their findings to the Progenitors but had received no acknowledgment. *No surprise*, Mac thought. They'd been worrying about the protocols involved in releasing such information elsewhere without permission.

Yet another reason they were overjoyed to see Brymn.

Mac's first opportunity to ask her own questions came when the majority of the camp researchers headed off to rearrange the sleeping quarters to accommodate the new arrivals. *First things first.* "Brymn," she whispered. "Can you eat any of this?"

"It is not permitted to eat that which is not made by Dhryn."

Great. "Preference or physiology?"

"Are they not the same?"

Mac snorted. "One you can bend; the other bites back."

"Ah." He considered. "My preference, then, would be to wait until the ships arrive with your fine medical supplies, in case of bites."

She grinned. "Converted you, have I?"

He looked smug. "I have always been open to new ideas, Mac."

"I'll remind you of that," she warned, then spotted Lyle deep in conversation with someone who'd just entered the tent. From the way those nearby stopped talking and turned to listen, the news was either very good or very bad. Mac stood. "Excuse me a moment."

Lyle saw her coming and waved her over. "Dr. Connor. This is Nicli, our meteorologist."

Another Human, female, in a coat buttoned against the growing chill outside. She gave the newcomer a distracted glance before turning her attention back to Lyle. "We have to lock everything down. It's the biggest event we've had yet."

Of course it would be bad *news.* Mac was learning to expect it. "Dust storm?" At Lyle's nod, she asked: "Where do you want us?"

"Here," Lyle told her, looking grateful. Perhaps he'd expected a list of demands; Mac, having lived through her share of storms, planned nothing of the kind. "We get pretty wild ones—kick up out of nowhere and can last days. This tent is the sturdiest. We'll set up the kitchen here as well."

"We'll stay put and out of the way," Mac assured him.

After the violence of the Ro assault on Haven, and the dismantling of the planet right under their feet, Mac had been confident a simple dust storm would seem an anticlimax. She'd been through pounding surf and rain, floods and landslides, lightning and hail. This was only a bit of wind and a bit of dust. She'd planned to curl up with a blanket and snooze.

She should have known better.

"Remind me again why I let you and Trojanowski talk me into this!" she shouted into Brymn's ear at the top of her lungs.

Snoozing in a blanket? After the rousing excitement of losing the tent and most of what was inside it, they were now huddled under the only remaining structure, a massive transport vehicle that rocked with every new gust of wind. The Cey on her left side had talked about some taking shelter in the excavation itself. Mac hoped so. She'd lost count of the others with her almost immediately. She thought there were six of them here, out of nineteen, but Brymn's extra arms made it tricky to tally by feel.

The dust made it hard to breathe, as well. Mac had wrapped her head in the filter hood they'd provided. They'd had a bag large enough for Brymn, though Mac presumed the Dhryn would close his blue inner lids to protect his eyes. The mask helped her, but she had to keep her eyes closed and continually spat dust from her mouth.

Meanwhile, why had Mac thought this a lifeless world? Surely the dust storm argued with itself. A low roar shook the ground and a shrill voice shrieked and gibbered. Competing with both was the dust hammering into whatever it could hit.

The noise must be worse for Brymn, Mac thought, with his sensitivity to the lower ranges. She held one of his hands. Or he held hers. She was sure he worried as much about her reaction to all this as she did his.

Emily had warned her about the Dhryn, about Brymn himself.

The Myrokynay, so advanced and powerful, had tried to extinguish the entire species.

Did Brymn know about the storm raging inside *her head?*

Mac squeezed the three thick fingers holding hers. Of course he did. This was more his nightmare than hers. Either his species was being persecuted to extinction or his species threatened all others.

She couldn't imagine living with that choice.

"Dr. Connor. Dr. Connor."

"Mmphfle." Mac spat out what tasted like half a dune's worth of dust in order to answer that anxious call. "Here."

"Storm's over, Dr. Connor. You can take off the filter." Someone began helping her. *Two someones*, Mac decided, feeling herself being pulled bodily from a pile of dust and the filter coming unwrapped. The first thing she saw was a bottle of water. "Here. Rinse and spit. Then drink."

Mac took the bottle from the nameless Human and obeyed, making her mouthfuls as small as possible. There couldn't be a limitless supply here, especially in the wake of the storm. "Everyone all right?" she managed, handing back the bottle and peering around.

The storm had aged the camp into another ruin, broken walls and sticks jutting through smooth mounds of gray dust, an overturned table now one side of a small dune. Figures of dust moved through the setting, salvaging what they could find to add to the growing heap in the middle: a jumble of broken equipment and still intact boxes. A few more were winching the transport upright. It must have flipped sometime in the night. Mac hadn't noticed.

Then again, she wouldn't have noticed an attack by the Ro at the height of the storm.

Had she fallen asleep or unconscious?

"We haven't found Nicli," her caretaker said, enunciating each word with the exaggerated care of someone running on nerves alone. "She went to clear the com tower. But she knows the digs. We'll find her yet."

"Go." Mac passed the bottle back to him. "I'll get my partner and we'll help look."

"Your partner?" Human faces were too transparent. Mac felt the blood draining from her own face.

"Where?"

The man pointed to where some rescued tent material had been used to form a makeshift shelter.

Mac broke into a run.

25

CATASTROPHE AND CRISIS

THEY FOUND Nicli, suffocated at the base of the tower she'd gone to check.

Mac found Brymn, being cared for as best the camp medic knew how. The Dhryn's shoulder and three left arms had been pinned under the transport when it was lifted and dropped by the storm. He was conscious and smiled at her. She took one look at the dark blue seeping through the bandages and smiled back.

"That bad?" Brymn gave a weak hoot.

The medic shrugged, safely out of Brymn's line of sight. Mac nodded as imperceptibly as she could. "*Nie rugorath sa nie a nai,*" she reminded Brymn. "A Dhryn is robust, or a Dhryn is not."

"Your accent remains impeccable, *Lamisah.* If only we could do something about your squeaky voice."

Mac fussed with the blanket covering his torso. They'd put two others in here, both seriously injured from the look of the transfusion gear. Sedated and free of pain. *Naturally.* Both were Human. Male and female. She should ask their names.

Brymn first. "Is there anything I can do to make you more comfortable?"

"It will be all right, Mac. My body knows what to do." Brymn's eyes were unusually bright. *Fever?*

Emily had known. *Injury can trigger the next metamorphosis.* "You're changing," Mac guessed uneasily. "Is it the 'Flowering'?"

Brymn nodded. "I can feel it, as I did when I was but an *oom-*

ling, waiting to become adult. The damage I've sustained will be repaired. I enter the next, more worthy stage of my life." A pause and the corners of his mouth turned down. "You must stay with me, Mac, in case something goes wrong. Promise."

She glanced around. There was no one within earshot—no one awake, at least. She remembered the terrible figure at the train station and said: "The 'Wasting.'"

"I—" a tremor racked his body and the blue stain spread. "It would not be a kindness to let me live through that."

Mac took one of Brymn's good hands in her own, then nodded. *She'd decide if and when the time came.* "You'll have to tell me how."

His smile was a beautiful thing, lighting his eyes. "Spoken like a biologist. I will, *Lamisah*, and trust me, you will know if it is necessary. But—" his smile disappeared. The Dhryn seemed to struggle for breath, then recover. "But there is something worse I fear."

Worse than failing to change and having his only friend on this world kill him out of mercy? Mac stared at Brymn and thought she knew. "You could change into a Progenitor, couldn't you? Is there something I have to do then? The Dhryn ships should be in contact with the Union."

Brymn rolled his heavy head from side to side, leaving impressions in the bag they'd made into a pillow for him. "An honor, but so rare as to be most unlikely, Mac."

Finally, she understood and shook her head vehemently. "No, Brymn. No. Emily was wrong."

"We don't know for sure. You said so yourself."

"Guesses. Assumptions. Incomplete data. The Ro can't be trusted—"

"Mac. What if she's right? What if I change into something uncontrollable, something dangerous. I might hurt these people—I might hurt you. You must promise me you won't hesitate if that happens. A Dhryn is vulnerable to a puncture or projectile here." He threw off the blanket and stabbed his torso along the midline, just below the bulge marking where his seventh arm began. "If that fails, insert a sharp object here or here." Throat. Eyes. "Do not bother with blunt force. A Dhryn is robust, after all."

"Or a Dhryn is not," Mac finished for him, sick at heart.

She made herself comfortable beside Brymn and began to wait. *Not that she knew what she was waiting for*, Mac told herself.

Obviously, the Dhryn didn't wrap themselves in cocoons for this act of self-reconstruction. She would see the transformation. Mac's curiosity warred with her concern for Brymn. He was weak—surely a factor. He was away from his kind, not that they provided care. *Survival of the survivors.*

And he was afraid. For himself, for his species. She could see it in how he lay, arms wrapped as if to hold himself together, eyes rarely closed. "Mac," he said during a period of restlessness. "I have studied the Chasm. I know how much was lost—the life, the culture, the potential. I can't believe my kind were responsible."

"I know."

"We aren't violent—we couldn't even hunt the Ro, despite what they did to us. We didn't fight back. We'd rather laugh than be serious. How could we be something so terrible?"

She understood he would accept nothing but honesty. "If it's true," Mac said slowly, "then there's an answer, a way to understand how it could be. I'll find it. I promise."

"If it is true, what will become of the Dhryn? Must we be destroyed, for the safety of all?"

"I can't—" Mac stopped, unsure if she meant she couldn't answer the question, or she couldn't bear the answer. "Please, Brymn. Rest. The Ministry ships will here tomorrow. That's all you have to do. Rest until tomorrow."

"They're here!"

Mac rubbed her eyes, still half asleep, and blinked at the flapping curtain. Whoever had brought the news was already gone, but she could hear excited voices outside in the dark. From the snores closer at hand, the other two patients hadn't noticed.

"Go."

She glanced down at Brymn. "Are you—?" What she saw took the words from her lips. "How do you feel?" Mac asked instead, pleased her voice was steady.

The lanterns hanging in the shelter were enough for her to see that the metamorphosis had begun while she'd dozed. His eyes were *smaller*, though no less warm; the bony ridges that had surrounded them and defined his ears were now smoothed back into the skull. The intense blue of his skin seemed to have washed away, leaving it light and almost translucent. His arms lay flaccid on the blanket, thinner, so that their bandages, soaked in drying blue, had come loose and slipped around. She couldn't be sure without moving the blanket, but she had the impression his torso was wider, flatter.

His voice had changed, too. No longer a bass, with that hint of infrasound, it came out sounding almost Human. "Feel? Glorious, Mackenzie Winifred Elizabeth Wright Connor Sol. I feel glorious." A pause. "And hungry."

She reached out her hand but drew it back, fearing the consequences of touching a body in the midst of re-forming itself so quickly. "The ships arriving will have synthesizers, Brymn Las. I know the makeup of your food. Hold on a little longer, okay."

"I do not know this self. What am I to be, *Lamisah?*" Brymn asked her, giving a one/two blink. He lifted an arm and stared at it. So did Mac, fascinated. The bone was distinctly pliable between joints that had shrunk to one third their former size. The musculature was less rounded beneath the skin, as if what had been distinct bundles were lengthening and connecting. Brymn tried to open his hand but couldn't. The fingers were fusing together at their base, forming a hollow where there had been a palm.

"Not one of the Wasted," Mac assured him, for lack of a better answer. He nodded as if satisfied, then used a free hand to poke at the coverings on his shoulder. "Do you want the bandages off?"

"Please. They—itch."

Mac looked around. There wasn't much in the shelter besides the three cots, the other two still occupied by slumbering Humans, and the ration boxes she'd arranged as a seat. "I'll have to get scissors. Will you be all right?"

Another blink/blink, and a smile. "In your care, Mackenzie Winifred Elizabeth Wright Connor Sol, how could I be otherwise? But you should greet the arrivals."

Mac brushed her fingertips over the blanket. "They'll find us," she assured him. "I'll be as fast as I can." She stood to leave.

"Mac."

"Yes, Brymn Las?"

"We've come a long way together, you and I."

Mac smiled down at the Dhryn. "There's an understatement. I don't even know where this planet is."

"I meant—"

"I know what you meant." *There were no words.* Instead, Mac put her fingers to her lips and blew Brymn a kiss. "I'll be right back with those scissors."

The camp was alive with lights, bobbing in hands, hung from poles. And people, dozens more than Mac remembered, busy transferring gear to and from a bank of skims parked in the dust. She kept to the shadows, not deliberately, but from a sudden shyness. She wanted to see him first.

No, she wanted scissors.

Mac spotted the medic standing with two others and walked over to him. "Excuse me," she said brightly, having to look up. "I need a pair of scissors. For bandages."

The other two were in uniform, beneath sensible coats. Seeing those, Mac felt the bite of the night air for the first time and wrapped her arms around her middle.

The medic, presumably in the midst of arranging transport for his patients, spared her hardly a glance as he produced a microscalpel from a pocket. "This do?"

"Yes, thanks."

They resumed their discussion. As Mac headed back to the shelter, she flipped on the 'scalpel to check its power supply. The tiny blade formed in the air with a reassuring gleam.

"Mac!"

The shout gave her barely time to turn the 'scalpel off again before she was being crushed while a voice said desperate, incoherent things into her hair.

Rather nice things.

The universe could stop right here, Mac decided, putting her arms as far around Nikolai Trojanowski as their length, and his gear, permitted.

It didn't, of course. A shaky breath later and they were apart, Nik doing his best to look official and not flustered; Mac grinning like a fool. After a second, he relaxed and smiled down at her, his hazel eyes taking green sparks from the lights.

"You're alive," she said, finding it necessary to say the words.

"So are you. And it's over, Mac. We did it," he told her. "Drove away the Ro."

The name sent a shock through her body. Mac managed to ask: "What about the Dhryn?"

"Don't worry. The IU made sure all of their colonies received the equipment to disrupt the no-space fields. The Ro's advantage is gone. It should be a case of alerting Union members what to look for—what's wrong?"

"Maybe nothing." Mac looked up at Nik, drinking in the sight of him, wanting to believe in safety, then had to say it. "Maybe everything. Emily told me—"

The first scream hit the air.

- Portent -

THE FIRST drop fell.

It was the purpose for being.

Green and glistening, it landed on the blanket, etching through the woven fibers as fire would consume kindling.

Another followed. Another.

That which is Dhryn must survive.

Another, reaching the bandages beneath, eating through those to find flesh.

Another. Another.

The flesh responded, instinct fighting drug. The scream should have had meaning.

That which is Dhryn must find the path for the future.

More drops, until they began to collect in the dust.

And the mouths could drink.

26

REVELATION AND REGRET

BECAUSE she didn't need to understand, grab weapons, or bark orders, Mac was first to the shelter. She tore back the flap that protected the occupants from the dust and staggered inside.

The screaming had stopped.

The lights were gone.

"Brymn?"

Air stirred wisps of her hair. "Goooooo," it said. "Gooooo."

Gooseflesh rose along Mac's skin. She felt the flap open behind her and reached to stop Nik, knowing beyond doubt it would be him.

"Brymn. It's Mac."

"Goooo—ooo."

That voice alone could give nightmares. *No wonder they'd inherited legends of ghouls and monsters from the Chasm.* Mac wrinkled her nose, smelling rot. "There are two people here," she whispered to the man waiting by her shoulder. "We need light to find them." When Nik hesitated, she pushed. "He won't hurt me."

He won't want to hurt me, Mac told herself, trying to keep very still. She heard Nik ordering people away, calling for a light. Closer, she heard rain and pictured Brymn curled in agony, bleeding from his wounds. She could picture it, but something kept her at the entry.

A hand touched her arm, followed it down to put a light in her hand. Mac aimed it at the dust, then switched it on.

On Brymn. *What had been Brymn*. He—it—was lying on the floor, arms ending in a pool of bright green, a pool disturbed by drips from . . . Mac let the light trace the drips upward . . .

. . . from what had been a woman. Now, ribs dissolved as she stared, the mass turning into droplets as Mac tried to breathe, the droplets collecting in the pool, the pool where Brymn—*drank*.

The light had followed her gaze. The metamorphosis was complete. His hands had become mouths. His shoulders and sides had grown membranes that shimmered. His organs shone through his skin, including the stomach where green gathered with each sucking sound. *A pufferfish Dhryn*, Mac thought inanely, too terrified to move, unable to believe she'd seen this form before without screaming.

She had to help Nik. He'd yanked the other casualty from his bed, and was now dragging him to the door flap without care for anything but speed.

But Mac couldn't move. She watched as yellow mucus trailed from Brymn's nostrils. *Grief?* His eyes, lidless, their orbs sinking below the skin as she watched, looked at her. *Knew her*—even as the light of intelligence flickered and died. Still, his real mouth trembled around a word: "*Promisssse*."

"I know, *Lamisah*," Mac said, activating the 'scalpel even as she threw it into one sinking eye.

What had been Brymn filled its body with a single breath and launched itself toward the ceiling, green drops spraying outward from the mouths. One hit Mac's hand as she covered her face. She screamed. Another. Somehow she remained conscious as Nik grabbed her around the waist to carry her outside.

Behind them, she could hear weapons fire and closed her eyes, sobbing with more than pain.

27

REUNION AND RENEWAL

THE LAST salmon run was over, the harvesting fleets were docked, the students had gone home. Mac leaned her shoulders against the damp outer wall of Pod Three and took in the unusual neatness of cleared walkways and laundry-free terraces. "Looks like the start of winter," she told Kammie.

"That it does. Same old thing, every year."

Mac glanced at the chemist. "You don't have to do that."

"Do what?" A look of innocence in the almond-shaped eyes.

"Treat me like I'll break."

Kammie tried to look outraged and failed. "That obvious?" she relented, then smiled. "Must be the hair. Not used to it yet."

"Or this?" Mac held up her left hand and wriggled the fingers. The prosthesis was excellent work. *The Ministry looked after its own*, Nik had told her. Mind you, she'd upset the warship's surgeon by insisting on a ceramic finish rather than regrown skin. The resulting pseudo-flesh tone had a faintly blue tint in sunlight.

She could stir acid with the fingers.

"The new hand?" Kammie shook her head. She stared out at the ocean for a long moment, then said softly: "If you must know, it's your eyes, Mac. Since you got back, you always seem to be looking somewhere else."

The Ministry had maintained the fiction that she'd been staying at the Interspecies Union Consulate, learning Dhryn, hunting for Emily. The loss of her hand and wrist? A skim accident on the way home, adding to the delay. Mac was reasonably sure Kammie and some of the others—not to mention Charles Mudge III—suspected this wasn't the whole story. She hoped they'd never need to know it.

She almost wished she didn't. *Almost.*

"Elsewhere?" Mac managed to keep it light. "Let's say I've discovered an interest in extraterrestrial biology. I may do a sabbatical offworld, one of these years."

That earned a laugh from Kammie. "You? This I have to see. Seung—" She faltered, then went on: "He'd have liked to hear you say that."

Mac nodded. The casualty list had been hard reading. Nik had given it to her while she was receiving her new hand, since everyone at home believed she knew and had grieved. Five dead, including Dr. Seung and the irascible Denise Pillsworthy. Her grieving had only begun. Still, the alarm had saved far more than she'd dared hope, even in Pod Six.

Mac tossed her head. "Let's go over the reconstruction estimates. I want to be sure you didn't grow an extra lab while I was gone."

"Well, I didn't. But that's not a bad idea. You do realize this is the optimal time in which to rethink some of the space allocations within the pods . . ."

Mac let Kammie's peaceful voice wash over her, the way the waves were washing over the bleached logs and stone of the shore. She drew in the rich, moist air and held it inside her lungs, filling her eyes with ocean, forest, cloud, and mountain.

The Dhryn had vanished as effectively as the Ro, their colonies as empty as the rocky remnant of their former home world, a mystery on every level. How had they reached the planets they'd attacked without being seen? Why? The Ministry had Emily's logs, experts presumably going over every entry. She might have a turn—but only if they ran into messages that could make better sense to a friend. *Need-to-know*, they'd told her, before sending her home. They did reveal that the IU had sent urgent messages to all its members about the Dhryn "feeder form," as they now called the pufferfish transformation.

And that the foremost archaeologists from fifty species had been rushed to the Chasm. *Brymn would have been pleased*, she thought, cautious around what felt like an open wound.

Nik? Mac could close her eyes here and now and see his face. He'd been there, when she'd awakened to find her arm gone; he'd stayed until ordered away. Had looked at her in a way that still warmed her, before going where he had to go.

It might have been respect and sympathy. It might have been something more. She'd have to ask Emily's advice.

When, not if, she found her again.

"Forgiven," Mac whispered.

"Pardon? Mac, you haven't heard a word I said. Are you sure you're all right?"

Mac focused on Kammie's concerned face and smiled. "Fine. I'm fine. You go ahead and I'll meet you in your office."

"And where will you be?"

Where? Everything and everyone Mackenzie Connor cared about, on Earth and off, was at terrible risk, including the Dhryn. But, abruptly, Mac could let it all go for now, leave the worry to others. *For now.*

Salt spray kissed her lips. A gull complained overhead, then tipped its wings to slip straight down to the water, snapping level above the waves at the last possible instant with what could only be called a laugh. In the distance, a whale breached, conquering the boundary of ocean and air with a casual toss of its mammoth head.

She was home.

"I think I'll call my dad."